W9-CFG-489

The Naked Warrior

A Novel

Nelson O. Ottenhausen

The Naked Warrior

First Edition 2012
Copyright © 2012 by Nelson O. Ottenhausen
All rights reserved.

ISBN-13: 978-0-9846638-8-0

Senior Editor: Doris Littlefield
Cover Illustration by Dari Bradley
Cover Photo by Jennifer Ralston
Cover Model: Eric Ralston

This is a fictional story. Use or mention of historical events, places, names of anyone or any similarity of the story line to actual persons, places or events is purely coincidental.

Published by
Patriot Media, Incorporated
Publishing America's Patriots
P.O. Box 5414
Niceville, FL 32578
United States of America
www.patriotmediainc.com

'... and in righteousness, he doth judge and make war.'
The Holy Bible - Revelation 19:11

The Naked Warrior

Chapter 1

Washington, D.C.

At eleven o'clock on a crisp November morning, President of the United States, James Alan Walker, began his usual daily jog with an entourage of seven U.S. Secret Service agents in a secluded area at Arlington Cemetery, Virginia. As the small group passed a stand of trees, multiple bursts of gunfire erupted from three men concealed in the underbrush, breaking the cool, morning silence.

The President's chest exploded with thumping sounds as a half dozen or more bullets blasted holes through his body. All seven Secret Service agents received wounds also. Ambulances rushed the fallen men to a nearby hospital where the on-duty ER doctor pronounced President Walker and three agents dead on arrival. The President died instantly at the assassination scene while the three agents succumbed to their wounds on the way to the hospital. The other four agents would survive their wounds.

Because the ambush happened so fast, the bodyguards had no chance to return fire, and the unknown assassins escaped unseen. Later, when questioned, none of the surviving agents could provide any information as to who attacked them or why the attack occurred.

A short time after the assassinations, an anonymous person made a call on a Washington, D.C. pay phone to a number in New York City and when the party answered, the caller said, "We missed three of 'em on the list."

"How the hell did that happen?"

"They're not in DC," answered the caller.

"Which ones?"

After reading off three names from a small piece of paper, the caller paused for a response.

On the other end, an agitated voice snapped, "They can't be left alive. You find 'em and take care of it or make arrangements for outside contracts. In any case, you better be damn quick about it."

Then the New York party hung up the phone.

President Walker's brutal assassination came just two days after his inauguration to a second term in office by a record landslide vote. His opponent, an older man, never had a chance to unseat the popular, young incumbent President, and when polled, over eighty percent of the American people said they thought he did an excellent job during his first term. Unemployment fell to an almost negligible level, the trade deficit favored the United States and the economy as a whole had continued to improve.

The slain President had the honor of being the youngest man to ever hold the presidential office when elected to his first term, just six months younger than John F. Kennedy when he took office, and like Kennedy, Walker distinguished himself at Harvard Business College, graduating with honors. Being a handsome and popular United States Senator helped Walker get the party's nomination for his first term in office. All this, combined with a beautiful wife, had many people saying the young President and his family reminded them of the Kennedy years back in the early 1960s. Many times during his first term, political pundits compared President Walker's governing style to the Kennedy administration.

Although he won by a very large margin of the popular vote for his second term, a lot of influential people did not agree with Walker being reelected, and just as with the Kennedy family, some of them held a strong and intemperate hatred for the young President. Most of the dissension happened when President Walker chose a black man for a running mate for his second term because the incumbent Vice President became too ill to accept the re-nomination.

Members within the President Walker's own party opposed the choice of a black candidate as a running mate and resisted by running another candidate against him in the primaries. The bitter fought campaign exposed negative undertones of racism from both the primary opponents and the opposition party, which became irrelevant with the election's final results—a Walker win.

The day of the assassination, the former Vice President lay in a Washington hospital bed gravely ill and slowly dying. He too, like so many within the party, vetoed the choice of a black man as a replacement, but not because of any racial prejudice. He felt the consequences of the choice would be politically detrimental to the young President and his party, especially when dealing with the opposition who controlled both houses of Congress. However, the stricken Vice President did support the choice of the individual and thought him the best qualified candidate for the position.

The black candidate, an honorable man, distinguished himself while serving two terms as a United States Senator from Illinois and then as Chief Justice of the Seventh Circuit Appellate Court. While serving his fifth year on the bench, President Walker asked him to be his running mate.

At the same time as the attack on the President, three masked men armed with automatic weapons broke into the home of the President's National Security Adviser, Admiral Edward L. Emerson United States Navy, killing both him and his wife as they sat in their kitchen eating an early lunch. They died as did President Walker, in a hail of automatic gunfire.

Assassins also killed two other important people at the same time as the others, the Attorney General of the United States and the President's personal secretary, both important members of the President's staff. He relied heavily on their expert advice during his administration, and did so quite often.

The first name on the list of people that escaped assassination, Earl Emmett Williams, the recently elected Vice President of the United States, and by legal succession after the death of President Walker, became the first black President of the United States.

During the same time as the other murderous attacks, three armed men broke into the Washington residence of the new Vice President to kill him, but he had left town the night before on an unannounced trip back to his home state of Illinois where he owned a large farm in Jo Daviess County, just east of Galena. He felt he needed a well deserved rest from the long ordeal of the campaign and the inauguration hoopla.

The second name on the list, also a black man, Benjamin A. Hawkins, and he too left town the night before to visit his family for a few days before returning to the business as usual in Washington. When Walker began his brilliant political career some twenty years ago, he hired Ben Hawkins as a close and trusted personal advisor.

United States Army Major General Lance N. Stalwardt, the third man to escape being brutally murdered, sat on a plane flying from San Francisco to Chicago, and in another hour or so the plane would be landing at O'Hare International Airport on time. Everyone on board the flight had finished their cocktails, a hot meal and after dinner drinks. More than two hundred passengers either slept or dosed, including General Stalwardt who avoided assassination by not being at home in Washington.

Like the other passengers, he began drifting into a kaleidoscope of thoughts and half dreams, half asleep, half awake, but still aware of his surroundings and what went on around him.

He traveled in civilian clothes so no one on the plane knew who he was or what he did, and only three people in the whole world knew what his duties were—the President of the United States, the National Security Adviser Admiral Emerson, and a black man he knew only as Hawkins. Although officially assigned as a military aide and courier to the White House, the general unofficially commanded a highly secret covert action group, reporting directly to the President.

At age forty-nine, General Stalwardt stood six feet two inches, weighed near one hundred and eighty-five pounds and could run a marathon in acceptable time. He kept his body well tuned for the rigorous physical tasks required for his highly specialized job, a job he did extremely well.

He had just concluded a speaking engagement at the Presidio Naval Station of San Francisco, accepting a last minute invitation as a replacement for another speaker who had taken ill. Although unaware of it at the time, his acceptance of doing the forty-five minute lecture about American intelligence gathering capabilities on known world anti-terrorist groups, actually saved his life.

When arranging for the California trip, he scheduled two weeks annual leave after the lecture because he felt it an opportune time to visit family in Illinois where his mother lived, especially since he had no direct assignments for a while. He hadn't been there since his father passed away three years before and hadn't seen much of his family because he only stayed one day to attend the funeral.

During this trip, he planned to spend more time with his mother and to also visit with some of his old high school friends. However, his first stop would be to see his daughter Lynn and her husband Gordon, and to see Meredith, his one and only grandchild he had never seen. He felt excited about seeing his first grandchild, born a little over a year ago after his own birthday in February.

While half asleep and still in a dreamy state of mind, he began to drift back in time during his elementary childhood days, back to his hometown of Cedarville, Illinois. This small, sleepy, rural village is located about one hundred miles northwest of Chicago and five miles north from a town called Freeport on highway 26. It's the birthplace of Jane Addams, the internationally famous social worker and founder of Hull House in Chicago.

He remembered the townspeople as nice country folks, warm, friendly and especially proud of their famous lady, now interred in the local cemetery. Her stately home became a historical site being preserved and maintained as a live-in residence. The house Lance grew up in as a child sat on the original Addams property only a few doors south of the Addams's home. His mother and one sister still lived there in the same house.

As a youngster, Lance had visited the famous home many times, calling on a school friend whose family rented the Addams estate, and it was his relationship with the family that ultimately got him started toward a military career. His friend's father, a U.S. Army officer in World War II, and eventually a full colonel in Korea, encouraged Lance to explore the possibilities of attending the U.S. Army Military Academy at West Point in New York. Through this man's efforts, a local politician appointed Lance to the school after he decided to go into the military service.

Although four years at West Point seemed hectic and stressful, he thrived on the tension and pressure. In his senior year the school commandant appointed him Commander of Cadets. Lance finished second in his graduating class, the only time he would finish second in any of the military schools he attended over the length of his Army career. After the academy, he always finished as the top graduate in his class.

An above average student in elementary and high school, Lance had no mental challenge. He seldom studied and his high IQ easily got him through classes. Only when he attended the academy did he come close to taxing his mental capacity. His excellent memory helped to solve military tactical situations with rapid precision.

With his well built frame and muscled body he had no trouble participating in any of the rigorous sports required at West Point. He excelled in basketball, baseball, football, and soccer as well as most other physical sports, and during his senior year, he became captain or co-captain in four of the varsity teams competing in collegiate play. While playing football and soccer in his last year, he received national recognition for his efforts, receiving a special trophy awarded for being chosen by a national sportswriter's poll as a member of the all around U.S. college soccer team.

Lance also excelled with the opposite sex. Not so much as a womanizer, but they pursued him. Being popular during his high school years, he had no trouble getting dates. In the middle of his junior year he settled on one girl that seemed to be more intelligent and mature than the rest. She appeared as a person who knew what she wanted, and as he remembered later, she eventually went on to college and became an accountant.

He met Marilyn in his junior year and remembered her as the prettiest girl in school with dark hair and green eyes. Eventually they started going steady and at the end of the school year in May, she and her family moved away to the east coast because her father was transferred by the electronics company where he worked. They occasionally wrote to each other during the following summer, but when school started in the fall, the letter writing stopped.

Three days after Lance returned to high school as a senior, a girl named Alice caught his attention. He became almost dumbstruck when a friend introduced her to him. She had blond hair, a good figure and the prettiest blue eyes he had ever seen.

Two months later they started dating steady and did so until they married. During the time Lance attended the military academy, Alice remained faithful to him and didn't date anyone else because she loved Lance, and he loved her. So much so, they planned for and married the day after he graduated from West Point.

For the next few years they spent as much time together as his military assignments would allow. He attended the Infantry Branch Qualification Course, Ranger training and the Airborne School at Fort Benning, Georgia then took the Jungle Warfare and Pathfinder training in Panama and rarely saw his wife during that time.

After a year and a half of special warfare schools, he received an assignment at Ft. Polk, Louisiana as a company officer responsible for training newly drafted recruits. Within a year his daughter Lynn was born and three days after her birth, his beloved wife Alice died.

The loss of his wife devastated Lance and he almost resigned his commission. He felt that being in the Army and away from Alice for so long had something to do with her death, and believed if he had spent more time with her then perhaps she would have lived.

He thought, *How am I going to care for the baby while I'm in the military?* He figured it would be best to get a civilian job so he could better care for the child. However, his commanding officer finally convinced him to stay in the military. Lance knew in his heart that staying was his best choice, and felt he would eventually come to regret it if he resigned.

There were plenty of volunteers to take the child and raise her, but Lance wanted to have her brought up by a family member and finally decided to let her Aunt Norma, Alice's only sister, raise the little girl. The woman had no children of her own and had recently lost her husband to a fatal heart disease. Of all the volunteers, Lance felt this woman would be the best one to bring up his daughter, and as it turned out, Lance felt he made the right decision.

A month before Alice died, Lance received a promotion to first lieutenant, and shortly after her death he volunteered for the first of three tours in Vietnam. President Lyndon B. Johnson at that time had just started to increase the in-country military strength to put pressure on the Viet Cong and the North Vietnamese, cranking up the war a notch. Lance learned a few valuable lessons during his tours that helped him later in his career, especially during the covert operations he conducted in South America, Africa and the Middle East with his special ultra-top secret unit.

He received many combat service awards and became one of the most highly decorated heroes during the Vietnam conflict. Among his combat ribbons, the Bronze Star with three oak leaf clusters and V device, the Silver Star, the Distinguished Service Cross and the Medal of Honor, the nation's highest combat award. Along with the Combat Infantryman's badge, he received four Purple Hearts for wounds received in combat on four separate occasions.

Lance adapted well to combat conditions. A shrewd tactician in the field, he always managed to accomplish his assigned missions. He would study and analyze his enemy so thoroughly that he could anticipate their operations, and many times he would catch them totally unprepared. After several successful missions, his superiors began to think he had his own network of spies in the Viet Cong camps. Also, units under his command had the lowest casualty rates during the entire war because of his ability to understand the enemy war doctrine, and to apply this knowledge to his own combat tactics.

As the steady hum of the plane's jet engines lulled him deeper into sleep, thoughts of his impending visit home began to wane and flashbacks that sometimes came to him in his sleep became more vivid. They did not come often, but when they did, they always appeared in the same sequence.

First, he would flashback to the time he arrived in Vietnam as a young lieutenant. Next, he would dream about being wounded the first time then relive the attack on the battalion mess hall where his battalion commander received serious wounds. Often he would flashback to the harrowing operation where his actions earned him the Medal of Honor. Occasionally, he would recall one of the highly secret missions he conducted after the war, but not as often as his Vietnam experiences.

Fifteen Years Earlier
Vietnam, First Tour

"Lieutenant Stalwardt … welcome to Vietnam. I'm Captain Tom Nichols, CO of Bravo Company."

Lance felt the tall officer who just greeted him might be a Texan because of his slight accent. He did indeed come from Texas and commanded Company B, 1st Battalion, 2nd Brigade of the famous 101st Airborne Infantry Division.

"You'll be the platoon leader for the first rifle platoon. This here's your platoon sergeant, Staff Sergeant Diehl," said the captain as he turned slightly and pointed with his hitched thumb over his shoulder to the NCO (Non Commissioned Officer) standing behind him. "Have a beer 'cause it'll probably be a while before you get to see the next one."

Lance shook hands with Sergeant Diehl then took the can of beer offered to him by Captain Nichols and said, "Thank you, sir."

The captain continued, "Better drink fast, and since this is your first combat, I suggest that you get real acquainted with Sergeant Diehl. He's on his second tour here and knows his shit pretty good so be a listener for a while until you get to know how we function out here. He knows what he's talkin' about, and it just might save your ass someday."

"Yes, sir," said Lance.

"He's already got one Silver Star and up for another and he's a damn good soldier to boot. You play straight arrow with him and he'll back your ass to the hilt."

The captain picked up a folder lying on a nearby table, opened it and read from it for a moment then said, "I see by your two-oh-one you graduated second in your class at the Point and first in your Branch Qualification course at Benning." The captain closed the folder, tucked it under his arm, then stepped closer to Lance and said almost in his face, "Looks like you got a good head on your shoulders, Lieutenant. You listen to Sergeant Diehl here and maybe you just might keep it there."

Lance became aware of a helicopter coming closer and thought, *Sounds like it's gonna land just outside of the Quonset hut.*

As the sound of the engine and thumping of the whirring blades grew louder, Captain Nichols said, "We're due in battalion HQ in about thirty mikes (minutes) so we don't have a lotta time here for idle chitchat. Sounds like our transportation's here so let's go. Sergeant Diehl … grab the lieutenant's duffel."

Lance didn't get a chance to respond to his new commander because as the captain finished speaking, he turned abruptly, left the hut and boarded the left front seat of the UH-1D Iroquois Bell helicopter, affectionately called Hueys by the troops. Already on board, the pilot and two gunners, each gunner manning an M60 machine gun mounted on both of the ship's side doors.

As Lance boarded the aircraft behind Captain Nichols, he saw several small holes in the fuselage near the open rear door.

The gunner noticed him looking at the holes and shouted above the increasing noise of the aircraft engine with a grin on his young freckled face, "Just a few reminders that we're not wanted here, sir. Took those rounds on the way in about ten klicks (kilometers) out. They'll most likely try again on the way back."

Lance looked at the young specialist, then without a word he sat in the seat next to Sergeant Diehl, snapped on his seatbelts and pulled them tight as the helicopter lifted off and headed north. The thought of the enemy shooting at him and the fact that he could die when he had only arrived in country less than an hour ago became somewhat frightening.

The thought of dying didn't initiate Lance's fear; after all he believed in the old adage concerning his work—to do or die—and soldiers died every day during a war. What scared him most of all—not being able to prove himself a good soldier.

Lance didn't know it then, but soon he would more than prove his mettle.

Chapter 2

Vietnam

For the next six months Lance planned and laid out patrol routes, set up field defenses, and learned how to beat the south Asian heat the way Sergeant Diehl had shown him. Every three or four days he conducted simple reconnaissance patrols, with a combat patrol now and then. Somehow, amidst all the patrolling and other company tasks assigned to him, he always managed to complete his jobs to the company commander's satisfaction. With Sergeant Diehl's help, he fast became a good combat soldier, and under Lance's leadership the platoon did very well for themselves during occasional firefights with enemy troops.

One morning around 0800, at the beginning of his sixth month in country, Lance had just finished his breakfast and looked out across the valley toward a low ridgeline north of the compound. In some heavy thicket, about 900 to 1000 meters away, he noticed a small puff of bluish-white smoke slightly off to one side and wondered what it was.

Without warning, everything went black.

Lance woke up flat on his back with a severe headache and a bandage around his head. Opening his eyes, he saw a female nurse in an olive drab uniform standing over him, a stainless steel water pitcher in one hand and a towel in the other.

He asked, "What the hell happened?"

"You've been hit in the head by a bullet."

"I'm wounded?"

"It's only a superficial wound, but I think you're going to have a terrible headache for awhile."

To Lance it felt like the top of his head would blow off at any second, and he moaned as he tried to get up.

"You shouldn't move. It'll only make it feel worse."

"I just wanna clear my head," said Lance. "I feel so groggy."

"The doctor gave you a shot with a strong sedative to make you sleep for a while," said the nurse. "Soon you'll sleep like a baby."

Lying back down, he asked, "Where the hell am I?"

"A Marine field hospital," the nurse replied.

"Marines … how the hell did I get into a Marine hospital? Does my unit know I'm here?"

"Yes, Lieutenant, they do. It was someone from your unit that brought you in here."

"Why here?"

"I guess we're closer than your brigade hospital so they brought you here instead of hauling you there."

"Where's my stuff?"

"All they brought with you is your helmet, web gear and your pistol." The nurse reached down, picked up the helmet and while showing it to Lance she said, "See? Thank God you had it on otherwise it might've been a direct hit. It looks like the bullet was deflected by your helmet just enough to crease the side of your head and then went out the back. The doctor said the bullet just bounced off your skull a bit because of the angle of entry."

Lance looked at the helmet trying to focus his eyes on it as best he could. About two inches up from the front rim and at a slight angle, he saw a small entry hole about the diameter of a ballpoint pen. In the back of the helmet and to one side, he saw the exit hole about the size of a golf ball.

"Guess this is my lucky day," said Lance.

The nurse put the helmet back on the floor then said, "Why don't you try to sleep now? By this afternoon you'll be up and around and ready to go back to your unit."

"Where's my weapon and web gear?"

"Under the bed."

During the time with his unit, not once had Lance ever come close to being hit, even though his company engaged in some heavy fighting a few times. So far he had always managed to come out unscathed. But now he lay flat on his back, ears ringing like hell and the worst headache he'd ever had. Soon the medication took effect and he drifted into a deep and peaceful sleep.

BAAROOM.

Lance awoke to a tremendous roar and shouted, "INCOMING!"

The Viet Cong had initiated a mortar and rocket attack on the hospital, creating total confusion and chaos inside the tent. Lance took only an instant to clear his mind then reacted by training instinct. First he lifted the Marine next to him off the bed and put him under it, then covered the helpless patient with a mattress. At the same time he began yelling instructions for the nurses to do the same for the other patients that couldn't be moved to the protective bunkers outside.

A moment after they lowered the last patient to the floor and covered him, a mortar shell dropped through the open doorway of the large tent and exploded when it hit the ground, sending its deadly shards of hot steel in every direction. By some miracle the blast caused injury to only one person, a nurse whose exposed right leg extended from underneath the protection of a mattress. The wound seemed to be only a scratch and not serious.

At the moment of the explosion, the canvas structure filled with a caustic smelling smoke. Lance could feel it burn his nostrils as he breathed in the fouled air, making him and everyone else inside the tent choke and cough. He looked around, trying to assess the damage, but his eyes burned and his vision became momentarily blurred because of the smoke.

As the air cleared, Lance couldn't quite believe what he saw. For some unknown reason the big tent still remained intact and still standing. The blast hadn't knocked it down.

Lance threw aside his mattress and made a quick verbal and visual check to find out if everyone was okay, then put on his web belt and ran outside, coming face to face with a Marine captain who shouted above the explosions still going on around them, "Anybody hurt in there?"

"No sir," replied Lance. "They're under mattresses."

The Marine looked inside the tent and exclaimed, "Damn! I can't believe this thing's still standin'."

"Probably because the side flaps were up, sir."

"Unbelievable," said the Marine officer as he shook his head. "I'd have never believed it if I hadn't seen it with my own eyes."

As the captain turned around, Lance asked, "Sir, what the hell's goin' on out here?"

"Charlie's gotta crew of small mortars up on a hill about twenty-five hundred meters to the north of here," said the Marine officer as he walked by Lance, heading toward his men. "We're on our way to get the bastards. Wanna come along?"

"Hell yeah … I mean, yes, sir, I'll go."

"How's your head?"

"It's just a scratch," said Lance as he followed the captain.

"You sure you're all right?"

"Yes, sir. It's just a slight headache now," Lance said as he lightly touched his right hand up to the bandage above his ear.

After approaching the other Marines, the captain stopped and said, "Just a minute, Lieutenant, you're gonna need a helmet for this operation. We've got an air strike comin' in on those bastards and sometimes these fly boys drop their stuff pretty close in so you'll need some head protection. You're gonna need a rifle and some ammo too. That forty-five you're carryin' ain't gonna do the trick. Not where we're goin'."

Almost as if by magic a corporal came up and handed Lance an M16 rifle and a helmet, along with four magazines of ammunition.

He turned to the young Marine and said, "Thanks."

When Lance finished putting the magazines in his web belt and placing the helmet on his head, the captain said to him, "I'd like you to take charge of my second platoon. I lost the platoon leader this morning and I haven't gotten his replacement yet."

"All right, sir."

"Lieutenant Kelly was a damn good combat officer and a damn fine soldier. You got any combat experience?"

"Six months in country."

"You'll do. I hope you don't mind?"

"No, sir, not at all," replied Lance.

"Good, because I can surely use the help."

"No problem, sir. Just so I get back to my unit soon."

The captain continued. "We're supposed to join up and conduct a passage of lines with elements of the hundred and first tomorrow mornin'. I'll be glad to drop you off then."

Lance yelled over the blasts of more incoming fire, "That'll be fine with me, sir."

"Okay, Lieutenant, wait here and I'll have a Private Grayson meet you. He's the second platoon's radioman. They should be along in a few minutes." The captain turned to his radioman and said, "RT, tell Grayson to pick up the lieutenant on his way by. He'll be in front of the field hospital tent in the north bunker. By the way, Lieutenant … what's your name?"

"Lance Stalwardt, sir, Bravo Company, First Battalion, Second Brigade of the Hundred and First Airborne."

Turning to the radioman again, the captain said, "RT, relay the lieutenant's info to battalion HQ so they know he's on board and they can tell his unit where he's at." Then he turned and looked toward the ridge where he believed the shelling came from, saying, "Okay, RT … let's go."

The captain gave an arm signal to the first platoon and they moved out while incoming rounds exploded intermittently in and around the area. The lead squad formed into a loose skirmish line and headed toward the ridge with a three-man point team on the main trail leading out of the compound. The remaining two squads followed in single file on either side of the trail, parallel to each other with the squad members spaced about five meters apart.

The captain positioned himself between the two trailing squads about seventy-five meters directly behind the point team, with the radioman following just a few paces behind. Lance watched from the bunker as the formation moved out.

When the first platoon reached a spot about three or four hundred meters out, a tremendous force lifted the captain from the ground and threw him backward into the radioman, knocking them both to the ground, blown down by a shell that landed directly in front of him. Lance couldn't see the actual explosion, but he heard it and saw the rising debris cloud afterward. To him it seemed as if some unseen giant hand picked up the captain and threw him backward to the ground in what appeared as a slow motion effect.

Lance ran to where the two Marines lay. The captain's body covered the radioman and Lance knew when he saw the officer's face that he was dead. The radioman moaned and tried to move.

Rolling the dead captain off the young Marine, Lance quickly looked over the radioman for wounds then asked him, "You okay?"

Hesitating a bit, the young Marine replied, "I think so, sir. At least I don't feel like I've been hit, but my ears are ringin' like hell."

After checking over the young Marine again, Lance determined he had no wounds, just shaken up a bit then pulled him to his feet. Blood and bits of body tissue from his captain's wounds covered the front of his uniform in places. The dead company commander had shielded the radioman from seeing the blast and getting hit by shrapnel. The RT didn't actually know what happened because it happened so fast.

Over the noise of exploding shells, Lance yelled, "Private! Check the radio. Does it work?"

After a second the radio operator replied, "Yes, sir. It's okay."

"Good. We've got to get in touch with the rest of the company and tell them what's happened. Better radio for a medic to see to your captain, but I don't think it's gonna do any good."

"Yes, sir."

"Where's the platoon leader of the first platoon?"

"They don't have one, sir."

"Who's in charge?"

"I don't know, sir."

"Where's the squad leader of the first squad?"

"He's behind and to the right of the point man about ten meters off the trail. Can you see the horizontal white tape on the back of his helmet?"

"Okay, I see him." Then Lance asked, "Has he got a radio?"

"Yes, sir, but I think it's out. I haven't been able to raise him for a while."

"Then we'll have to go to him, let's go."

"Yes, sir."

As they started a slow run toward the lead squad the mortar shelling continued. Two rounds hit nearby and Lance felt the hot blast of the explosions and heard pieces of metal shrapnel fly by his head. When the next round hit closer to him than the other two, he dove into a small depression with the radioman right behind him.

Another shell landed even nearer and the blast would have killed or seriously wounded them both had they been standing.

While lying on the ground, Lance said, "Tell the rest of the company that I'm assuming command until your people can get somebody up here to replace me. Also tell them we're still goin' after that mortar emplacement up on the ridge. Give that info to your battalion HQ, and while you're on the horn with them, ask about that air strike. I need to know when they're scheduled to come in. You got all that?"

"Yes, sir."

Lance shouted, "Let's go," as he got off the ground and began running to the lead squad leader who lay prone on the ground because of the intense shelling.

When Lance reached the sergeant, he knelt down beside him and said, "Sergeant, I'm Lieutenant Stalwardt, Hundred and First Airborne. Your captain is dead so I'm assuming command of this operation until we get those mortars … have you any objections?"

Rolling to one side the sergeant looked up at Lance and replied, "No, sir." Then he asked, "Whatcha got in mind, Lieutenant?"

"First, we gotta get the hell outta here as fast as we can. We'll continue up to the base of the ridge and wait for the air strike. Maybe they'll do a good enough job we won't have to work so hard once we get to the top. You ready?"

"Yes, sir."

"Okay … let's go."

No sooner had Lance quit speaking when four Marine ground support aircraft came roaring overhead in battle formation, firing their rockets into the suspected enemy positions. Immediately the mortar shelling stopped.

The radio operator came up to Lance and asked, "Lieutenant, the fly boys wanna know if you want them to stick around or should they go on home?"

"Tell them they did a good job, and ask if they'll stay for awhile. We don't know what's up there and we can use the support if we happen to run into something we can't handle."

Lance moved the company to the base of the ridge in quick time then sent the first squad up the rise. Automatic weapons and rifle fire opened up, coming from about 800 meters up the side of the hill. Everyone reached cover without suffering any fatal injuries.

Lance thought, *The commander of that bunch must have a case of the jitters or he's just inexperienced.* Lance knew the enemy had opened fire too soon and at that distance their inaccurate fire would not cause many serious casualties among the advancing Marines.

The first squad leader moved to a better vantage point near Lance and found a spot with a good view of the enemy position, plus excellent cover.

Lance said, "It must be the mortar crew's security force."

"Yes, sir, I think so too," said the NCO. "I make maybe ten or fifteen of 'em, along with four or five automatic weapons. I think there's a small rocket tube up there too."

Turning to the radioman behind him, Lance yelled, "Air strike the bastards!"

Three minutes later the four Marine aircraft began strafing and blowing away enemy real estate with their remaining ordnance. After the second pass, the enemy position fell silent for a moment then started again with sporadic fire on Lance and the Marines.

Lance shouted to the radioman, "Have the second platoon get up here and form a skirmish line on the right side of the trail."

Within minutes after the radioman made the call, the four squads of the second platoon assembled in place, each laying down a withering field of fire as they came on line and into position. While the second platoon provided the base of fire, the first platoon began a left flanking movement using the tactic of shoot and maneuver. When they closed to about 50 meters from the enemy position, the platoon formed a skirmish line and began to lay down a covering fire so the second platoon could move up the right flank.

As soon as the second platoon came on line with the first platoon, they both rose up and formed into a single line, sweeping over the enemy position without any resistance. After the sweep, the Marines set up a temporary security perimeter to protect against any counterattacks while they took stock of their situation. The Marines suffered no fatal casualties, only some minor flesh wounds, but found only dead enemy soldiers at the site.

Lance walked through to the center of the enemy defensive position and looked around. From where he stood, he could see the mortar emplacements just a few dozen meters up the hill. No one appeared to be alive in either position.

Lance turned to the radioman and said, "Tell the fly boys they can go back to the barn."

"Yes, sir."

As Lance walked toward a squad leader of the second platoon he asked, "Where's the platoon sergeant?"

The NCO answered, "He was killed this morning along with Lieutenant Kelly. Sniper fire, sir."

Lance thought, *Probably the same bastard that shot me.* Then he asked, "Who's the ranking NCO here?"

"I am, sir," replied the sergeant who led the first squad in the assault on the ridge.

"Good, you're now both platoon sergeant and platoon leader. I want you to set up a defense on the other side of the ridge with your second and third squads linked up with the first platoon. Use the first squad to clean up the mess around here. We'll stay here on position until your people at battalion decide what they wanna do. When the third and headquarters' platoons show up, I want a perimeter defense around this entire area … and set up the radio over by that rise. Any questions, Sergeant?"

"No, sir."

"Good, I'll see if we can get some hot chow flown up here for the evening meal. You boys did a fine job here today and you sure as hell deserve it."

"Damn straight, sir."

"Do we need a DUSTOFF?"

"No, sir … the only serious casualty we took this afternoon was the CO, and somebody already took him back to the field hospital. Everybody else made it."

"Good. I'm gonna look around for a bit and see what we've got here then we'll contact your battalion."

Lance moved throughout the enemy stronghold and found four destroyed mortar tubes, ten dead Viet Cong in the mortar position and twelve dead enemy troops in the security force position. He reasoned either the Viet Cong had all been killed or that some of them may have escaped after the air attack. Then he found some evidence that made him believe that some of the enemy survived and had indeed pulled out leaving their dead behind.

Within fifteen minutes the rest of the company arrived on the position and Lance found only one other officer in the company, a Second Lieutenant Roger Hill, acting as the unit's executive officer as well as the third platoon leader. Lance briefed Lieutenant Hill on what happened earlier and the plan for the night. Lieutenant Hill then left to supervise the defense setup and to find out what the company needed for resupply in ammunition and provisions.

As Lance thought over the day's events the radioman came up to him and said, "Lieutenant, the battalion CO is comin' up in the resupply chopper along with the hot chow for the men. He said he wants to talk to you when he gets here."

"Thanks, RT."

"He's also bringin' some reinforcements and takin' the wounded back with him."

Within an hour the Marine battalion commander arrived with the hot meal. Lance met the two incoming helicopters and saluted the senior ranking officer as he came out of the first aircraft.

"Sir, I'm Lieutenant Stalwardt."

The Marine officer returned the salute then offered his hand for a handshake while saying, "I'm Lieutenant Colonel Frank Kohl. How are you, Lieutenant?"

"Fine, sir, just fine," replied Lance as he shook the battalion commander's hand.

While walking back toward the center of the company area, the Marine officer asked, "What's the story here?"

"Sir, we ran into two enemy positions. The one further up the trail had four mortar tubes and ten bodies. This position had twelve bodies and a couple of automatic weapons."

"Is that it, Lieutenant?"

"I suspect there were more here to start with, but I believe the survivors bugged out."

"What makes you believe that?"

"Well, sir, when we first came up to the base of the ridge we were about eight hundred meters out when they opened fire. I counted at least four automatic weapons, but we found only two. We know they had a rocket launcher up here also, but it wasn't here when we took the position. Somebody must have taken it out."

"I see," said the Marine commander as he looked around. "Well, it appears like you've got things pretty well in hand here so I'll just have a quick look around and then leave you alone. I'll come back in the morning with your replacement. I hope you don't mind staying until then."

"No, sir," replied Lance, "no problem."

"Good, I'll contact your battalion CO and let him know what's happening so he doesn't get too concerned about you. I'll fly you back to your unit in the morning."

"That'll be fine, sir."

"By the way, Lieutenant, damn fine job ... wish I had more company commanders like you."

"Thank you, sir," said Lance, "I appreciate the comments."

"How's your head? I see you still have a bandage on."

"It's a minor wound, sir."

The two officers continued to talk until they finished the meal then the battalion commander said goodbye and left with the cooks. Afterward, Lance began to mull over the day's events and discovered he had lapses in his memory. He couldn't remember all of the details concerning the operation or what he did and said. He wondered why. *That's strange*, he thought, *I must have functioned on pure instinct.*

That night, one third of the company stayed awake and on guard at all times, staying on alert throughout the night and into the morning hours. All remained quiet and calm, but occasionally a parachute flare would light up the night sky in the distance and a jet aircraft would fly high overhead.

Early the next morning, Lance met his replacement, Captain Bill Jackson, a Marine career officer from Chicago, Illinois. They talked about their home state for a while then Lance said goodbye and left on the outgoing helicopter.

Within ten minutes after landing, Lance reported to his battalion headquarters ready for duty.

As he left the administration bunker, the battalion commander, Lieutenant Colonel Evans, approached him and said, "Lieutenant Stalwardt, I'd like to see you for a moment."

"Yes, sir," Lance answered then saluted his commander.

The colonel returned the salute and said, "Lieutenant, you're the first man I've ever sent to the hospital that literally fought his way back to his unit." Smiling, the colonel said, "Good job, Lieutenant."

"Thank you, sir."

"I gotta call this morning from the brigade commander. He's recommending you for a bronze star with V device because of the actions you took after assuming command of that Marine rifle company and eliminating that enemy position yesterday."

"I was just doing my job," said Lance. "There's nothing heroic about doing what I was trained to do."

"Nonetheless, Lieutenant, you're still getting a medal. I guess the Marine regimental commander called the brigade CO and wants you decorated. Anyway, that's what we're gonna do." The colonel paused as if thinking about something then added, "I want you to come to work at battalion for a while."

Lance looked surprised and said, "Me, sir?"

"Yes, Lieutenant, I want you to help out the new S-three, Major Reynolds. He needs a field-wise sidekick and I'm bettin' you're the guy. Besides, you can learn a lot up here."

"Anything you say, sir. When do you want me aboard?"

"How about now? Say by eleven hundred this morning. Is that gonna give you enough time to get everything in order?"

"Yes, sir."

"Good. You can take my jeep and driver to pick up your duffel. Anything else you need?"

"No, sir. Not at the moment."

"Good, then I'll see you back here by eleven hundred."

Lance saluted the colonel and left the compound in the battalion commander's jeep. He arrived in his company area a few minutes later and reported to Captain Nichols.

The captain rose from his chair and came to Lance, extending his hand. "Glad to see ya back, Lieutenant," said the captain then asked, "How's your head?"

Taking the captain's hand, Lance shook it with a firm grip and replied, "Not too bad, at least my ears have stopped ringing."

Captain Nichols grinned slightly as he said, "I hear you taught the Marines how to fight."

"I wouldn't go so far as to say that, sir."

"Well, maybe not, but good show, Lance, damn good show."

"Thank you, sir."

"I hear tell you're goin' up for a bronze star."

"Colonel Evans told me the same thing, sir."

"I know ... I was just talkin' with him on the landline. He tells me he wants you up in the Three-shop. When you leavin'?"

"He said he wants me there by eleven hundred hours today, sir."

Just as the captain began to say something, a company clerk rushed into the tent and blurted out, "Capt'n, Lieutenant Parker's patrol just ran into a mess a Charlies and they're gettin' pretty well shot up. He's callin' the rest of the world for support and all the medevacs he can get."

"Crank up the third platoon. I want them on the choppers in ten ... GO!" The captain turned back to Lance and said, "Lieutenant, I'd love to sit here and jaw some more with ya, but I've got a serious problem to take care of. Good luck, Lance, I'll see ya around."

The captain picked up his combat gear and rushed out of the doorway to his waiting helicopter already warmed up and waiting to go. Within ten minutes the third platoon boarded their aircraft and departed the field. Five empty helicopters and four medevacs left with the combat troops to help pick up the now besieged troops of Lieutenant Parker's platoon.

Lance went to his quarters, cleaned out his footlocker and packed his few belongings into a canvas duffel bag.

While packing his things, he looked at the helmet setting on the bed and mumbled, "I'm probably the only guy in all of the United States Army wearing a gyrene helmet."

He picked up the helmet and saw something written in ballpoint ink on the sweat band—Lt. Andrew Kelly, USMC, Semper Fi.

Chapter 3

Vietnam

Lance arrived at battalion headquarters shortly before 1100 hours, processed in with the S1 Personnel Section then went to the assigned bunker he would share with another first lieutenant.

Lance asked the clerk, "What's my roomy's name, Specialist?"

The clerk turned around, glanced at a manning chart on the wall and as he turned back to Lance, he said, "First Lieutenant Michael Polaski, sir. He's the S-Two."

"How do I get to my hooch?"

"It's the dugout across from the entrance to the S-three shop. You can't miss it, sir."

"Thanks."

"You're welcome, sir."

Lance left the S1 area and began walking toward the bunker for spending his off-duty time and sleeping. As he approached the bunker he heard an artillery gun open fire a short way down the slope from him.

He thought, *105 Howitzer*.

Looking in the direction where the sound of the gunfire came from, he noticed the tube pointing toward the northwest, the area where Lieutenant Parker and his platoon ran into a large element of Viet Cong. He continued to walk toward the bunker with his duffel slung over his shoulder.

Then from behind and to his left, four artillery guns began firing at a rapid and sustained rate.

Whatever they're shooting at, it has to be big, thought Lance. He had never heard that many artillery pieces shoot a combat fire mission before, and the sound deafened him.

When he found his bunker, he went inside and started to unpack amid the tremendous noise of the artillery gunfire outside.

As he put away his gear in the empty locker, he heard someone from behind him shout, "Lieutenant Stalwardt?"

Lance yelled in return, "Yeah, that's me," as he turned and saw a young corporal standing in the doorway. "Come in closer so I can hear you better."

The young corporal stepped inside the doorway and said, "Sir, I gotta message from the old man and the S-three. They said yer supposed to wait for them in the Three-shop till they get back."

"Where're they at now?"

"Sir, they're up lookin' around the area where that Bravo Company patrol ran into some Charlies. I guess it got pretty bad out there for those guys."

"Have you heard any news?"

"Only that the Bravo CO's chopper went down along with a few medevacs. I ain't heard about any Bravo Company casualties."

Astonished, Lance asked, "Did Captain Nichols make it?"

"Yes, sir, I think so," said the corporal, "but one of the medevac crews didn't."

"Do you know what happened?"

"No, sir, but maybe the guys in the Three-shop across the way can tell ya. They're monitorin' the radios and they pretty much know what's goin' on."

Lance dropped the gear he had in his hand onto the sleeping cot and hurried out of the bunker to the operations center and asked the first soldier he saw, "Who's in charge here?"

A young private said, "Sergeant First Class Washington, sir."

From behind him, he heard, "You must be the new Assistant S-three, sir. We've been expectin' you."

Lance turned and saw a tall well built black sergeant standing in front of the S2-S3 situation boards just as a radio operator yelled out, "HEY SARGE, IT LOOKS LIKE CHARLIE'S HAD IT. THEY'RE BUGGIN' OUT."

Within a few moments the artillery guns outside became silent.

The sergeant glanced toward the radio operator then back to Lance, waiting for a response to his earlier comments.

Lance took a quick look around and said, "That's right, Sergeant, I'm the new assistant S-three, First Lieutenant Lance Stalwardt."

Sergeant Washington smiled, extended his hand and introduced himself, saying, "Welcome aboard, Lieutenant, I'm Sergeant First Class Corry Washington, senior NCO."

Lance shook the sergeant's hand. The sergeant then introduced Lance to the other soldiers inside the bunker.

When finished with the introductions, Sergeant Washington said, "As you can see, sir, the S-two and S-three sections are set up in a combined work area. This unified concept is very efficient and effective, especially when combat situations get hot and heavy, like that little skirmish Lieutenant Parker's platoon got caught up in. It saves us a lotta time and duplicated effort. We can keep on top of things much better this way."

Sergeant Washington brought Lance up-to-date on the current operation with a short briefing. As he finished, a helicopter flew in, returning to the encampment area with the battalion commander and the staff members with him.

The colonel went to his command bunker while the two staff officers came to the operations center. Once inside, they introduced themselves to Lance, giving him an after action briefing about what had just happened.

The S3, Major Reynolds began. "Here on the situation map you can see the division is set up in a perimeter defense because we're out here by ourselves. The only other friendlies in the area are the Marines on our left flank where they're tryin' to join up at Charlie Company, but right now they're really too far away to be of any effective protection on that flank." The major paused then said, "That's why you ended up in a Marine field hospital yesterday instead of the brigade hospital. The Marines had one closer."

The major then went to the large map board and continued, "That firefight you were involved with late yesterday afternoon ended up to be a bigger operation than any of us first thought. It appears now that Charlie had a small force up on that ridge to shell the Marine compound, trying to soften them up a bit for a larger force waiting on the other side, ready to attack when the shelling was done. Evidently your little excursion up to the ridge forced them to rethink their plans. Then Lieutenant Parker stumbles in on them late this morning before they had a chance to mount any kind of a major attack."

Lance asked, "I wonder why they didn't attack us last night?"

"My guess is, they were stalling because they didn't know how many Marines were up on the ridge, and I think they didn't wanna hit the main compound without support from the ridge. They knew it would've been suicide to try without their mortar support."

The major walked to the situation map and looked at the area where Lance had spent the night then said, "Looks like you were almost on top of Charlie last night."

Lance stood next to the major looking at the map and asked, "Where was Parker ambushed?"

"He wasn't exactly ambushed," said the major as he pointed to the spot on the map where the action had taken place. "He just ran into a whole mess of Charlies. Anyway, the artillery blew the hell out of them this morning and a Marine battalion moved in there afterwards and mopped up. Parker can thank the Marines for savin' what's left of his platoon."

Lance asked, "Sir, how bad was Parker hit?"

"Real bad I'm afraid. He lost twenty-five dead out of forty-five men and everyone else was wounded at least once, most of them with multiple wounds."

"What about Lieutenant Allen's platoon?"

"When Bravo's third platoon went in to extract Parker, they lost six of their own men dead and ten wounded."

"And Captain Nichols, sir?"

"His chopper went down, but everyone in the aircraft survived the crash and got out okay. However, one of the medevacs took a direct rocket hit. Nobody survived that one."

Lance didn't reply to the major's comments, but stood looking at the map.

The major stepped closer and with an apathetic tone in his voice said, "Look, Lieutenant, even with the losses, the old man believes the best thing that coulda happened to us was Parker runnin' into those people this mornin'. Hard tellin' how bad we might've gotten hit if they'd have come up on us undetected. You can thank your lucky stars this bunch is history."

The major's remark about the Viet Cong being history wasn't quite accurate. For the rest of his tour Lance worked with Major Reynolds at the never ending process of trying to clear the area of the enemy. No more would the battalion clear one area and the enemy would reappear in another, one already thought to be cleared.

One day Lance remarked, "It's almost like fighting ghosts."

A few months after his transfer to battalion HQ, Lance woke up one morning, looked at his calendar and saw that he had only thirty-one more days left in country then he would rotate home. He got up, shaved, showered, put on a clean uniform and went to the mess hall where he met his bunker buddy, Lieutenant Polaski, who had already finished eating and sat at a table waiting for him. Lance and Mike had become fast friends and worked well together.

Lieutenant Michael Polaski, an ROTC (Reserve Officer Training Corps) officer from Buffalo, New York, graduated in the top ten percent of his college class and the Army offered him an RA (Regular Army) commission. Although branch qualified in armor, he cross-trained in intelligence and became assigned as the battalion S2. Single, he planned to marry a girl back home after completing his tour and rotating to the states about two weeks after Lance.

Like Lance, Mike Polaski loved the action and challenge of trying to outguess the enemy. The working combination of Lance and Mike together increased the battalion's combat efficiency, making it the best operated infantry battalion in the division. Partly because of their efforts, the battalion received a Presidential Unit Citation, and Lance received his second bronze star.

One week before Lance's scheduled rotation to stateside, he joined Mike for breakfast at a table in the front of the mess hall. Only a half dozen cooks, the battalion commander and two members of his staff sat at a table in the rear of the dining area.

Lieutenant Colonel Evans sat at the head of the table with his back to the north wall. Major Reynolds sat on his left, and on his right, facing Major Reynolds, sat the headquarters commandant, First Lieutenant Riley. Two DRO's (Dining Room Orderlies) stood nearby, ready to pour coffee and serve breakfast to the three officers.

A sudden explosion filled the room with flying debris, dust and heavy black smoke, sending everyone at the commander's table flying. An enemy charge had blown a huge hole in the earthen and mud brick wall just behind and to the right of the colonel, a hole big enough to allow a man to run through in a crouched position.

Immediately after the blast, Major Reynolds jumped to his feet and began to drag the unconscious orderly who had been standing nearest to him. The others lay on the floor, blood splattered and motionless. Both Lance and Mike reacted instantly to the blast by grabbing their M16's, jumping up from their table and running to the major, trying to help him with the wounded man. Through the smoke and dust, Lance saw someone in a black uniform with an AK-47 entering the gaping hole in the wall.

Lance pointed his rifle toward the hole and shouted, "VIET CONG ... CHARLIE'S IN THE COMPOUND!"

He leveled the M16 and fired off a short burst of rifle fire at the enemy while Mike grabbed the wounded private and helped the major drag the wounded man outside. Lance knew his intermittent covering fire wouldn't stop the Viet Cong from coming into the building, but it did cause them to hesitate for a moment, making them seek cover rather than shooting at the others. This allowed the four men enough time to get out of the building without injury.

They all made it through the door and into a trench about 25 meters from the south side of the mess hall. As soon as they reached safety in the trench an automatic weapon started firing at them through one of the mess hall windows, kicking up dirt and gravel, knocking it down on top of them.

Both men returned rifle fire in quick bursts over the top of the trench, but didn't know if it was effective or not because they didn't have ample time to aim. As Lance and Mike engaged the enemy and kept them busy, Major Reynolds crawled to the nearest intersection in the trench about ten meters away and looked in both directions. To his left he saw nothing, but to his right saw six or seven mess hall personnel huddled together.

"You men ... get up here ... NOW," ordered the major.

Instantly the men obeyed and came to Major Reynolds, crawling on their hands and knees.

Major Reynolds looked down the empty trench and said as he pointed, "You people go down that trench, go out the other side, get yourself a weapon and get your ass back here A-SAP. One of you see if you can find an M-seventy-nine ... and try to get an M-sixty. Two of you grab hold of this guy and take him to the aid station. Now move it."

The men left and four of them came back within minutes with M16's, one M60 machine gun and two bandoleers of ammunition. Heavy fire came from the mess hall windows indicating a squad size or larger force had gotten into the compound and inside the building. Lance figured about a dozen enemy armed with automatic AK47 rifles and at least two machine guns.

Mike asked no one in particular, "How the hell did they get into the compound?"

"They must have been part of the civilian construction crew," said Lance. "It's the only way."

The two men kept firing as best they could at the windows and within minutes of the blast, the rest of the compound reacted and began pouring heavy fire into the mess hall, eventually suppressing the enemy fire.

Lance heard a sudden shout. "CEASE FIRE ... CEASE FIRE!" The shooting stopped. Again someone yelled out. "LOOK, THE COLONEL'S BODY ... STOP FIRING AT THE WINDOW!"

The enemy took advantage of the lull and again began heavy fire out the mess hall windows, pinning down the forces gathered in the trenches around the building on two sides. The men in the trenches returned fire, but no one shot at the window where the body of the battalion commander lay draped over the sill. The enemy used him as a shield, placing an automatic weapon on his body and firing out into the compound. The maneuver became an effective deterrent. Soon the Viet Cong placed two other bodies over window sills.

As the morning wore on, the firefight became a standoff. The Viet Cong couldn't come out of the building and the soldiers couldn't get in. About a half hour into the battle, Lance signaled Mike to meet him at the other end of the trench. The trench ran in front of the mess hall and turned to the side where the enemy blew the hole through the wall. Just beyond the end of the building where the trench ended, Lance found a place to observe the hole.

Lance and Mike huddled in the trench looking where the blast occurred. They saw no one guarding the hole outside and they suspected that only one Viet Cong would be just inside the hole.

No one fired into the building on the north side because the wall had no windows or doors in it. All the shooting concentrated on the other side of the mess hall where all the windows were. The north side of the building faced the outside perimeter so the engineers didn't put in windows or doors when building the mess hall.

"Maybe we can rush the hole and get inside," said Lance. "Let's work our way down the side of the building, and then go through."

"Stalwardt, your nuts," said Mike, "but let's go before I think about it and change my mind."

Jumping up from out of the trench, Mike ran to the wall with Lance right behind him. They reached the hole without being detected. Both men checked their M16 rifles and put in fully loaded magazines then checked their 1911 Colt .45 automatics to ensure they too had a full ammo load.

Mike asked in a low voice, "How we gonna do this?"

Lance replied, "Successfully, I hope."

Whispering, Mike said, "That means we don't have a plan."

"Roger that, ole buddy," said Lance with a broad grin.

After a quick look around, Mike stooped down and picked up a handful of pebbles and underhanded threw one that landed about two feet on the other side of the gaping hole. No response.

They moved closer.

Mike threw another pebble and again nothing. They moved within two feet of the large opening. Mike dropped another pebble and a head popped out looking in the direction where the pebble landed then turned and looked straight up at Mike—the last thing the Asian ever saw. Mike crushed his skull with the butt of his rifle then yanked the body outside.

Without hesitating, Mike crouched and went through the hole and dove for cover behind an overturned table with Lance right behind him. They hadn't been seen. In the next few seconds, the two men shot and killed all eleven Viet Cong inside the building. Only one returned fire, but Mike shot him dead as the Viet Cong fired off a burst of about a half a dozen rounds in Lance's direction.

Lance looked around and heard the firing from outside so he yelled out, "CEASE FIRE, EVERYONE ... CEASE FIRE! WE'RE INSIDE AND THE CONG ARE ALL DOWN!"

Lance heard someone outside repeat the cease fire order and almost immediately the firing stopped. Lance moved to the window where Lieutenant Riley lay draped over the sill.

He checked for a pulse and found the Lieutenant still alive just as he heard Mike shout to the outside, "THE COLONEL'S ALIVE! GET A MEDIC IN HERE ... NOW!"

Lance ran to the double doors, removed two benches jammed against them which prevented them from being opened from the outside. He flung open the doors. Major Reynolds and four medics rushed in and attended to the wounded men, lying unconscious from the initial blast, but all three still alive.

As Lance stood looking at the medics working on the three men, another medic came up beside him and said, "Sir, please sit down on the bench and I'll take a look at your arm."

"What? What're you talking about?"

"Your arm, sir ... you've been hit."

Lance looked down where the medic touched his arm and noticed a hole in the front and back of his left sleeve. He took off his fatigue shirt and saw the bloody hole through his upper left arm. He couldn't remember being hit. In fact he could barely remember what had just happened.

Lance thought, *I wonder if I'm beginning to lose it.*

For their heroic efforts and rescue of their battalion commander and the other two men, Lance and Mike received the Distinguished Service Cross. Lance also received his second Purple Heart. The major received the Bronze Star for commanding the forces outside and for saving the young private he carried out of the mess hall.

During the war in Vietnam, battalion and company level units often fell short of officers, and the First Battalion was no exception. It had no executive officer to take command of the battalion after Lieutenant Colonel Evans went to the hospital so the brigade commander cut orders giving Major Reynolds the job as CO. Lance then became the S3 for his remaining one week left in country.

Chapter 4

Cedarville, Illinois

Less than forty-eight hours after leaving Vietnam, Lance arrived in his hometown to stay with his mother and father. He had thirty days leave and would spend the time with his family, especially his daughter who could walk and had just recently started talking. The first day he visited with the shy child, she wouldn't come to him, but as the day wore on the little girl toddled over to him and stretched out her tiny arms to be picked up. For the next four weeks the two became almost inseparable.

During the first few days of his leave, Lance hadn't noticed the restrained mood of the townfolks, but soon after, he began to hear such comments as, "The United States ain't got no business in Vietnam." One of the towns people called it, "A politicians' war and the boys are being sent over to be killed for nothin'."

He mentioned this to his father one day and his father told him, "Son, the war in Asia is fast becoming unpopular. People don't like our boys fightin' in another country, especially one we don't know anything about."

A week after arriving home, Lance received orders to attend the Army Infantry Career Course for officers at the Infantry School, Ft. Benning, Georgia. He also received a letter promoting him to the rank of captain and granting him an extra week's leave because the school didn't start until a week after his original leave time expired.

With the leave extended, Lance could attend Mike Polaski's wedding in Buffalo. Before leaving Vietnam, he knew Mike's schedule to rotate back to the states and that Mike had planned to get married as soon as he got home. Mike's arrival originally coincided with the last Saturday of Lance's leave so Lance felt he would not be able to attend the wedding, but now with his extended leave, he had the time to go.

Before Lance left Vietnam, Mike gave him a telephone number to contact him, so on the Saturday morning of Mike's in-country date, Lance called.

A woman's voice answered the telephone, "Polaski residence."

"Mrs. Polaski, this is Lance Stalwardt. Is Mike there?"

"Yes, he is. He just got in early this morning and told me to expect your call. If you'll hang on a moment, I'll get him for you."

After a few seconds Lance heard the familiar voice over the telephone say, "Lance, how the hell are ya?"

"I'm fine, Mike. I just called to see if you made it in today."

"Yeah, I got in about two this mornin'. What's up?"

"Good news, my leave's been extended so it looks like I'll be able to get to Buffalo this week after all. When's the wedding?"

"Ain't gonna be one, ole buddy. She married somebody else a month ago. I didn't find out about it until this mornin' when I talked to her mother. She told me."

"Jesus, Mike, I'm sure sorry to hear that. Kind of a kick in the ass for you, ain't it?"

"Nah ... not really."

"Got any plans?"

"I guess I'll just hang around home for a while," replied Mike.

"Tell you what, maybe we can get together somewhere out east and have ourselves a good time." Lance had thought of the idea to go to the east coast because he figured Mike could probably use the support of a close friend. "Whadda ya say?"

"Sure, I'm game," said Mike sounding rather halfhearted about the idea. "Anywhere particular?"

"How about the city? We can stay at Ft. Hamilton and from there we can go see the sights. Maybe take in a few shows."

"Okay by me. When ya wanna meet?"

"If I get there by Tuesday evening, that'll give us three days, but I gotta leave Saturday morning to get to Benning by Sunday night."

"Sounds good to me," said Mike. "I'll make the Q reservations at Hamilton and see ya there on Tuesday."

They spent a few more minutes on the telephone with idle talk, but Lance sensed that Mike wasn't in the mood for conversation, so he said his goodbyes and hung up the receiver.

Lance had only two more full days at home so he spent as much time as he could with his daughter. On Monday morning he said goodbye to his family and left for New York.

While in Vietnam, Lance had his car stored in a shed his father built into a machine shop behind the house. Before arriving home, his brother-in-law serviced the car and Lance drove it to New York. He would keep it with him during his stateside assignments.

Arriving at Ft. Hamilton early Tuesday evening, Lance met Mike at the BOQ (Bachelor Officers' Quarters). Mike didn't seem like his old self, but he did appear glad to see his good friend and bunker buddy once again. Like Lance, Mike too had received orders for his next duty assignment along with a promotion to the rank of captain, and just as Lance had, he too had orders to attend a school, the Army's Intelligence School at Ft. Holabird, Maryland.

The two men tried to have a good time while in New York City, but as Lance expected, Mike felt bitter that his fiancée had married another man and it put a damper on the fun activities. It would take time, and Lance knew all too well the feeling of losing a loved one.

Saturday morning came too soon for Lance. He said goodbye to his best friend and left for Ft. Benning while Mike returned home to his parents in Buffalo.

For the next six months Lance immersed himself in his training and became the number one graduate of his class. After finishing at the infantry school, DA assigned him as a troop commander to a newly activated air assault division at Ft. Benning. Four months later he began his second tour in Vietnam. His entire unit, the First Air Cavalry "Black Horse" Division, joined the Asian war effort.

Lance became serious in his job as a commander. He had over two hundred men in his unit, and he knew if he didn't concentrate on his duties one hundred percent, he could cost someone their life. He also demanded the same total dedication to duty from his platoon leaders and noncommissioned officers.

He ordered a standing policy that the enlisted men came first and would be treated with respect at all times. Anyone mistreating a subordinate in the unit, Lance dealt with them severely, regardless of rank. It quickly became clear to his line officers and senior NCO's alike that Lance would reprimand and or transfer anyone who thought otherwise. His leadership reputation became quickly known among the men in his command and they greatly respected him for his efforts to look out for their welfare. By the time the unit landed in Vietnam, Lance had a well dedicated and trained fighting force. One that he felt he could count on down to the last man.

Vietnam

Three months after they arrived in country, Lance received a combat mission involving the entire troop. The squadron's S3 chose to air drop his unit onto a hilltop and secure an area around it for forward spotters while they plotted artillery concentrations in a nearby valley. Up until this point, his troop had seen only limited combat, usually in smaller platoon and squad size patrols, but for this mission they would conduct it as a unit. On this operation, Lance received the Silver Star and his third Purple Heart.

Two days before the mission, Lance received an operations warning order and orders to attend a meeting in the S3 operations center to receive his mission and battle plan. The S3 conducted the mission briefing.

The major said, "Captain Stalwardt, your mission is to act as a security force for artillery spotters laying out concentration fires in a valley just west of here. We think this area may be part of a main supply route to the Viet Cong because of the heavy night traffic along the trails out there. Infrared photos from air recon flights have been showing a lot of activity there recently so we think Charlie is up to something big."

Turning, the major pointed to the bright red circle on the map that encompassed the terrain coordinates in the briefing and said, "You are to be in the vicinity of the objective no later than oh-six-hundred hours tomorrow morning and secure this hill by oh-nine-hundred. You will hold this position for two days and will be extracted starting oh-eight-hundred hours on the third day. Because you'll be out there by yourselves, you'll have additional resources."

"What kind of resources?"

"For starters, we'll give you four additional weapon squads, two machine gun squads and two one-oh-six recoilless. You will have four artillery tubes totally dedicated to you while you're on the objective. Also, we're gonna send two squads of combat engineers with you. They'll have some extra defense items such as anti-personnel mines, claymores and wire. We don't expect a lot of enemy activity up there, but if there is any trouble, we want you to be prepared and be able to take care of yourself. Have you got any questions on anything I've covered so far?"

Lance paused then said, "Yes, sir. Forget the recoilless. Can I have more M-sixties instead?"

"No problem, if that's what you want. Anything else?"

"Yes, sir. Will the LZ be hot?"

"We think not, but I've been wrong before. If it were me going in there, I'd damn sure as hell act like it was. My opinion is there's no sense in taking casualties before you need to."

"Yes, sir, I was planning on it anyway," said Lance.

"Good, anything else?"

"What if the LZ is a real hornet's nest? We still go in or do I get discretionary judgment on this one?"

"I think the colonel can answer you better than I can."

The colonel said, "No problem, Captain. This is not a crash and burn situation. If you land on a superior force, abort the mission and hightail it outta there. Just let us know and we'll turn on the big guns. That hill has plenty of heavy stuff aimed at it and if we have to unload on it, I don't want any of my guys on the ground."

"Yes, sir, I understand," said Lance.

The major added, "Captain, be here by fourteen-hundred this afternoon with no more than two of your people for a flyby recon. I'll be takin' up the artillery spotters and FOs so they know exactly what we want and the area we want spotted. You can take a good look over the area where you're going in and check out your LZs."

"All right, sir. Where do we meet?"

"Might as well come to the Three shop since the artillery people are coming here. No sense in setting up two meets."

"Yes, sir, fourteen-hundred here with two of my people."

After the briefing ended, the participants rose, saluted the commander and left to return to their respective units. As Lance arrived back at his command post, he could see things being done to prepare for the upcoming operation.

Although the unit didn't know exactly what the mission required when they received the warning order, it didn't matter because they always prepared for a combat operation in the same way. Lance felt that for a fighting force to be effective then certain preparations must be SOP, no matter what the operation was and the less change in preparing for any combat situation the better.

Lance called an immediate meeting of his platoon leaders and gave them the essentials of the mission as he received earlier. He told them a detailed briefing of his battle plan would be held after the reconnaissance flight. Although it wasn't normal policy to include the platoon sergeants in the upcoming operations briefing, Lance requested they be there. Because of committing the entire unit into combat for the first time, he wanted to make sure that every one of his senior NCOs knew the battle plan.

Another reason for having them there, all four of the platoon senior NCOs were return combat veterans to Vietnam and Lance knew he would need their experience in order to have a successful mission. In fact, he counted on it because all the platoon leaders were, as the first sergeant called them, *combat virgins*.

The battle plan would be brief and simple. Lance believed that complicated plans always failed when the action started. He also believed that SOP and consistent training led to success and had proven it many times while a platoon leader with the 101st Airborne Division. Although he had a larger scope of responsibility, and at a higher level, he still felt it more important than ever to keep the operation's execution plan a simple one.

At 1400 hours, Lance and two platoon leaders met with the recon party and fifteen minutes later they overflew the objective.

When Lance saw his objective hill, he became a little concerned. Defending the hill in three of the four directions, west, north and east would not be a problem. The hill sloped down from the top at a gentle grade into an open grassy field for several thousand meters on all three of those sides, but the southern slope bothered him.

He saw a steeper grade and just one hundred meters down from the crest of the hill ran a stream. Thick woods on both banks of the stream ran for miles and would give the enemy ample cover and concealment if they decided to attack his assigned position—a perfect primary avenue of approach.

As the helicopter circled the area, he thought, *I must make sure to reinforce the southern defense with the extra weapons.* After a ten minute flyover the group returned to the battalion compound.

Early the next morning, Lance and his men loaded onto their aircraft. As the helicopters began to take off, they momentarily obscured the area by dust kicked up from the downdraft of the rotor blades. Then, like the mythical Phoenix, they rose above the thick dust clouds into the clear morning air, shining like golden birds in the bright early sunlight, heading north in battle formation.

Arriving at the objective, the first two platoons put down onto the ground at their primary LZs without any difficulty. However, just as the third platoon came in to unload, the Viet Cong opened up with mortar and automatic rifle fire from the tree line south of the hill and from the western slope. The third platoon couldn't land on their primary LZ so they aborted the drop and headed toward an alternate landing site.

At this point, hostile fire pinned down the troops on the ground while the airborne troops couldn't land. The Viet Cong pulled off a superb tactical ambush, but Lance had anticipated trouble and preplanned an air strike on the tree line where most of the enemy firepower seemed to be concentrated.

Circling the hill, Lance could clearly see the enemy positions and directed a napalm attack on them within minutes from the time the enemy opened fire. The first two Air Force fast movers hit the southern slope targets with pinpoint accuracy, suppressing most of the enemy's firepower coming from inside the tree line. Lance then realized he faced an enemy force much larger than first anticipated, but he thought if the Air Force stuck around and gave him a few more minutes of close ground support, he might come out of it okay.

While the Air Force attacked the tree line again, Lance and the remaining airborne aircraft went immediately to an alternate LZ, a short distance northwest of the objective hilltop. With the enemy out of action on the southern slope, the two platoons on the ground began concentrating their defense efforts on the western slope.

Lance and his remaining forces landed on the enemy's northern flank catching the Viet Cong out in the open in a vicious cross fire between the two separated elements. Once the enemy troops went to ground, Lance called in the artillery. The heavy artillery attack of HE (High Explosive) air bursts and WP (White Phosphorous) shells took only ten minutes to decimate the enemy force.

The whole firefight lasted a total of twenty minutes, and a quick check by Lance found no one killed, but several soldiers received serious wounds. He had the injured evacuated immediately by air, and within minutes after being wounded they arrived back at the base camp to receive medical aid.

Once on the ground, Lance felt better about the mission. The platoons joined up, got to their assigned positions on the hill and began setting up defenses. Lance figured Charlie had enough for one day and wouldn't be back that night, but he knew tomorrow night would be another story.

For the remainder of the day, all that night and all the next day, the men and engineers prepared defensive positions, concentrating on the southern slope. They set up a series of obstacles consisting of trenches with punji sticks implanted in the bottom, strung out concertina wire along high points and in likely avenues of approach, along with preplaced claymore mines. They also booby-trapped the slope with anti-personnel mines and noise making devices, making the southern sector almost impenetrable.

Lance knew this would not stop the Viet Cong totally if they wanted to get into his position badly enough. He knew they had sappers extremely good at their work and they could breach his defenses in a matter of minutes if he didn't make other preparations.

Early the next morning, he called a meeting of his platoon leaders. "I want five volunteers to act as sapper listening posts in the obstacle field on the southern perimeter. I want only veteran listeners, if we've got them. Otherwise take any volunteer, and make sure they're ones who can keep awake at night."

By noon Lance had five NCO's, a corporal and four sergeants. All of them at one time or another served in obstacle field listening posts with other units and had experienced silent killings. Lance saw one sergeant's pistol equipped with a silencer, though against the international rules of warfare; Lance said nothing.

The second night the enemy came just as Lance had expected they would. First came the sappers who tried to breach the southern defenses, but the men in the listening posts did their jobs well, and none of the dozen or so enemy entering the obstacle field did much damage. However, one of the sergeants received a serious wound when he had to go hand to hand combat with his last sapper. The Viet Cong soldier wounded the young sergeant in the side with a knife just before the sergeant got a headlock on the Asian and broke his neck. The sergeant would live, but the serious wound needed medical attention by the next day or the man could die.

All through the night the enemy tried to breach the defenses all around the perimeter, but on the southern slope they tried a major breakthrough. Around 0300, the enemy initiated a mass frontal assault up the southern slope. For over half an hour a fierce battle raged on, but the obstacles held the enemy in check and the reinforced rifle platoon positioned in the southern sector had too much firepower for the Viet Cong to overcome. Just as he had done the day before, Lance called in artillery concentrations laid in when he first arrived on the hill.

The artillery salvos demoralized the enemy and they broke off the attack, but they still continued throughout the night to harass the outlying perimeters. The defenses held, and just before daybreak the enemy gave up entirely and broke off all contact. After the sun came up, Lance felt the enemy would retreat across the river and regroup during the daylight hours.

He called a meeting of his platoon leaders and told them, "Feed and rest your men in four-hour shifts. Leave at least two thirds of your personnel on the line at all times, and get some rest yourselves. You'll need it because tonight's gonna be awfully busy. They sure as hell won't let us sleep tonight."

A young lieutenant asked, "Are ya sure, Captain? Didn't we just kick the hell out of 'em?"

"Lieutenant … that was just a preliminary bout. The main event comes tonight. And, to answer your question, I'm not only sure, but I'm damn sure."

After giving the junior officers the rest of their instructions for the day, Lance dismissed them and went to the area set up for the makeshift chow hall and got a hot breakfast that had arrived with the resupply helicopters. When he finished eating, he walked over to the east section of the hill and looked out toward the far tree line about 2000 meters away.

As he stood looking over the terrain, he heard a voice behind him say, "My guess is that's where most of them will come from, probably sometime before first light."

Lance turned and saw the first sergeant standing behind him then asked, "Why do you say that, Top?"

"Capt'n, you know damn well I'm right," replied the sergeant.

"I know, but I just wanted to hear why you thought this would be their main attack."

"Same reasons you know, Capt'n," replied the sergeant. "I've been here before, same as you."

The first sergeant handed Lance the morning report and he took a quick look at the counts then signed it and handed it back. The sergeant took the report and without a word, he left.

Lance knew what his first sergeant meant and felt all along that tonight the enemy would hit the unit on at least three sides, feigning the main attack all night long, then strike hard from out of the east right at or just before dawn. He also knew the enemy would not try breaching the southern defenses again because of the high number of casualties they would suffer, and he knew it would be too high a price for them to pay. They would not come up the western slope because they had already lost a sizable force there to heavy artillery concentrations the day before.

Lance figured their most likely and viable choice of approach for the main attack would be the eastern slope only because the enemy's troops would be exposed too long to go around and come in from the north, especially if the attack failed and they had to retreat.

Yes, thought Lance, *they'll surely come in from the east because they need the trees close by. We'll just have to prepare a good old-fashioned welcome for them.* He also thought about the extraction the next day at 0800. *It could be a major problem.*

When Lance awoke from a long nap just after sundown, he knew it wouldn't be long before the harassing enemy fire would begin. First came a few rounds of mortar fire every ten or fifteen minutes. This kept up until after midnight, then for about an hour things quieted down. After a quiet period, the enemy began firing a rocket into the perimeter about every half hour or so. Lance cautioned the listening posts to be especially watchful.

At approximately 0330 the Viet Cong began to probe the south slope defensive positions, but within fifteen minutes they withdrew. The platoon on the southern perimeter had been instructed not to fire unless the enemy breached the obstacle field. A few men in each fire team would fire into the fortified defenses, but only if targets of opportunity presented themselves.

Again Lance's predictions came true. The Viet Cong faked their main attack on the southern slope, trying to get Lance to move the bulk of his forces to defend it and to expend his ammunition. Only the designated riflemen responded to enemy fire, and only when a target presented itself. The others held their fire.

Just before first light, the enemy began attacking out of the east with a large battalion-size force, but they didn't know that Lance had already guessed their tactics and his troops waited for them, ready to do battle. Under the cover of darkness the night before, he set up an ambush site along the enemy's suspected avenue of attack, putting two reinforced rifle squads on a slight rise just north of the eastern slope and out front of the hill's perimeter about 300 meters. He assigned extra weapons to the group—six M60 machine guns and eight M79 grenade launchers.

The 52 man detail dug in and formed a skirmish line parallel to the enemy's avenue of advance, facing south on the enemy's right flank. The enemy force never suspected the trap and when they had advanced well into the killing zone, Lance gave the order to fire the mortars and preplanned artillery concentrations.

Executed letter perfect, the plan confused the enemy and they froze in position, stopping their advance. First, the mortars fired rounds aimed at the middle of the attacking force to cut it in two. Then artillery fired air bursts of HE and WP over the enemy's rear area to demoralize their reserve troops and to keep them from moving up to support the main attacking force. Next, a preplanned air strike came in and hit the cutoff front section of the enemy's main force with napalm and cluster bombs. After the air strike, both the artillery and mortars shifted fires to the main body of the attack, firing their rounds as fast as they could load.

Up until this point no one at the ambush site or on the hill fired their weapons. They merely watched as the artillery and Air Force put on a fireworks display. However, the time soon came when the infantry had to defend their turf.

Confused, frightened and completely demoralized, the enemy ran in every direction with abandon. The ambush site and the hill's eastern defense line erupted simultaneously into a deadly cross fire catching the unsuspecting enemy along the front line and right flank by surprise. The firefight that resulted from the enemy's confusion took about ten minutes then the remnants of the attacking force retreated. Lance shifted artillery and mortar fire to bear on the enemy troops as they tried to reach the safety of the trees.

In a period of about thirty minutes, Lance's troops annihilated seventy percent of the attacking enemy force. Lance knew that no matter how large the force was that had just confronted him; the enemy had a larger force ready and waiting somewhere to reinforce the battle at any moment. A force of around five hundred Viet Cong as he later found out.

At daybreak, Lance believed the larger enemy force, waiting for a chance to attack, would come soon. He also knew they would probably attack the moment they discovered helicopters extracting his troops in just a few short hours, and he knew he couldn't stop them. He couldn't use the artillery because of the risk of hitting his own aircraft as they came in and went out. He couldn't depend on air cover because the Air Force had other priorities and if the weather turned bad they wouldn't be able to help. He had to figure something else, but that would have to wait. He needed to take stock of his situation and to see to the casualties among his troops.

To his surprise, his unit only suffered one fatality, but eight men received wounds, two seriously. After Lance got the figures, he thanked God with a silent prayer and asked for guidance in the upcoming hours. He also said a silent prayer for the dead soldier who had been his jeep driver for the last four months. At a company party two weeks before, the young soldier did the presentation of a gift to him from the men in his command—an engraved wristwatch.

Lance felt a deep sense of loss and sadness.

At 0800 sharp the helicopters arrived to pick up Lance and his men. Most of the troops boarded and evacuated the area safely. However, rocket fire shot down the last four inbound aircraft designated to pick up the remaining troops on the ground. Everyone survived the crashes because the helicopters hovered only a few feet off the ground and the rockets either hit in the engine compartment or the rotor blades. Several soldiers on the ground received severe injuries as well as helicopter crew members.

Lance had his aircraft circle above the area waiting for the last of the troops to come out when he saw from his vantage point, all four aircraft being hit and the men scatter out away from the wreckage. He called for immediate close air support from helicopter gunships and Air Force ground support aircraft, knowing the men on the ground had no chance to survive without it.

Over the intercom, Lance demanded, "Put me on the ground near the last wreck."

The pilot responded, "Captain, are you nuts? There's a helluva lot of Cong down there."

Lance shouted, "NOW … DAMN IT!"

"Okay, but it's your funeral," said the pilot as he banked the helicopter around and headed into the wind for the approach.

"While I'm down there, you stay in the area and help give me some support."

"With what, rocks?"

"You gotta door gun, use it."

"Okay, okay, I'll stick around."

When the helicopter neared the ground, Lance jumped the last few feet and ran to a group of about eight men now facing toward the southern slope. Some of the enemy had breached the obstacles and began to come over the crest of the hill. Lance instructed the men to form a skirmish line and begin firing at the enemy. Next he ran to each of the other three groups in the area and told them to form up in a defensive position near the men on line.

He took two men and pulled two M60 machine guns and ammunition from the nearest wrecked helicopter and told the men to set them up. He then went to a second helicopter, removed a third M60 and rushed to where a small group came together into a platoon-size unit and established a formidable defensive position. The small group stalled the enemy's advance on their position by fighting together and concentrating their firepower where it did the most good, on the southern slope.

One man on the ground had a working radio. Lance called for artillery. It seemed like hours before the first round came in, but the words "SHOT OUT" actually came back over the radio in less than two minutes. After the round hit, Lance adjusted fire to within fifty meters out front of his position. He knew the rounds landed close, but he felt he had no choice. He had to keep the enemy from making an all-out attack and overrunning his small force.

For fifteen minutes the firefight raged on. The artillery rounds hit in front of Lance's position so close he could feel the heat as well as the shock wave from the blasts. He could smell the acrid odor of the explosive residue mixed in with the smell of fresh earth. A few rounds landed so close they would have killed anyone in Lance's group had they been standing. Fortunately, the group managed to dig in a little and protect themselves.

The deafening battle noise drowned out Lance's commands, but none were needed. The men shot at anything that moved and did it as fast as they could aim and fire. They didn't need anyone to give them target direction. The enemy kept coming in front of them. Being somewhat cautious the Viet Cong didn't rush headlong in because of the artillery barrage out front of Lance's small ad hoc platoon, but made advances in small, slow moving groups, causing casualties among Lance's defenders.

As the defenders began to run out of ammunition, a large force of helicopter gunships came out of the north, firing on the enemy troops with rockets and machine guns. Within minutes the enemy withdrew back down the slope to the safety and cover of the tree line along the stream. Four Air Force fighter bombers came in dropping napalm and heavy bombs into the trees where the enemy had just retreated. A few minutes later, five helicopters came out of the north, landed near the small group, loaded them all on board and removed them safely back to the their base camp.

Of the forty-eight men on the ground with Lance, thirty were wounded, ten seriously, but all still alive. When Lance boarded the helicopter, he discovered he had a wound in his thigh and during the ride back to base camp, it became painful. He couldn't remember when it happened. *It's strange,* he thought, *to get these memory lapses during a firefight and can't remember anything afterwards, especially when I'm wounded.*

Lance rotated stateside because of the severity of his wounds. He had been in Vietnam for only four months, but during that time he had distinguished himself as an outstanding leader and received his third Purple Heart for his wound and the Silver Star for his gallant efforts and bravery in returning to his men on the ground.

The higher command later determined that without Lance's leadership, the men on the ground would have most likely perished because they had been separated into small scattered groups without leadership, creating an ineffective fighting force that would have surely lost to a superior force.

Two junior officers with the group received severe wounds at the outset of the attack and could not provide any leadership. As it turned out, after Lance appeared on the scene and personally rallied the small force, they fought a determined battle, accounting for over two hundred Viet Cong killed in the short time they engaged with the enemy. During the entire time Lance and his men occupied the hill, HQ estimated the enemy had lost well over a thousand troops.

Lance lost only one.

Chapter 5

Stateside

During his stay in a military hospital in San Francisco, Lance received a telephone call from his old friend, Mike Polaski. Mike would be in California in a few weeks and called to see if they could get together for a short reunion. Mike had volunteered for another combat tour in Vietnam and would be passing through the area before going overseas. After being bedridden for most of three weeks, Lance welcomed the opportunity and the two made plans to meet on the weekend before Lance left San Francisco to go home on convalescent leave.

Although Lance's hip wound didn't threaten to end his life, it did have some damage to the bone and it needed major surgery to repair it. Small pieces of bone splinter had to be removed from the surrounding muscles in the leg and a bone graft done to ensure the wound would heal properly. It would take several months before he healed completely and until then, Lance would have to keep the leg somewhat immobile.

He needed to walk with a crutch for a short time, but one of the doctors told him, "It won't be for very long. You'll spend a few weeks in the hospital after the surgery then you'll be sent home to convalesce for about six months."

After renting a car at the airport, Mike drove to the hospital and met Lance early Friday afternoon. As Lance explained on the telephone, it would be difficult for him to meet Mike's flight so Mike got the rental car. The hospital scheduled Lance for release on the following Wednesday, the day Mike was to leave the country for Vietnam, so they had the rest of Friday and four whole days to have a good time. However, their night life would be somewhat limited because Lance, not yet officially released from hospital care, had to return to his room by eleven o'clock each night.

When Mike arrived at the hospital, Lance sensed a change in his old friend. He no longer seemed to be the happy go lucky character that Lance knew in Vietnam where they first met. Mike seemed reserved and somewhat guarded. Lance didn't know what disturbed Mike, but he knew it had to be something serious. Mike acted as if he didn't want anyone close to him, not physically, but emotionally.

Mike asked, "Well ole buddy, you got anything in mind?"

"Not really," replied Lance, "I thought we'd just play tourist and see some of the sights."

"You mean take some of those guided tours?"

"Why not?"

"Well, I guess it's as good as anything."

"Good, let's start by going for a ride on a cable car. I've always wanted to do that."

"Yeah, that sounds good."

The two old friends enjoyed themselves by seeing the sights of San Francisco, attending a couple of ball games, visiting Chinatown, having a seafood dinner on Fisherman's Wharf and patronizing some of the better known watering holes in the city. One evening they sat in a bar having a few drinks when Lance learned that Mike still loved the girl who jilted him.

"I'd still marry her in a heartbeat if she'd divorce the moron she's married to," said Mike.

Mike closed himself off again. Being quite drunk, he let it slip about his old fiancée, but then realized what he said and quickly changed the subject.

Lance also found out on the same night that Mike's parents had been killed a few months before in an auto accident when their car failed to negotiate a curve and hit a tree. The last surviving member of his family, Mike had no living relatives left.

After that night, Lance never mentioned Mike's fiancée or his parents again. He reasoned that Mike had to deal with his own demons, and Mike made it very clear that Lance should mind his own business. Lance knew if he didn't heed Mike's demands, they would no longer be friends.

On Wednesday morning, after the four days of good times, both men went to the airport to fly out of San Francisco, Lance to Chicago and Mike to Hawaii. Both men appeared awkward for a moment and Lance thought he sensed that Mike would rather leave without any further conversation. During their brief time together, Lance thought at one time that Mike may even have a death wish, especially after one particular morbid conversation, but Lance dismissed the idea afterward.

Soon Mike's flight called for boarding and the two friends said goodbye with a handshake and a bear hug with a few slaps on the back. As the plane pulled away from the tarmac, Lance felt a sudden twinge of sadness for his old friend.

"God speed, soldier," said Lance as he took one last look at the aircraft then left and went to his own boarding gate to catch his flight to Chicago.

Four hours later his plane landed at O'Hare Airport where his mother, father, one of his sisters and his daughter met him when he came off the plane.

He heard his daughter's voice cry out, "Daddy," and ran to him with her little arms outstretched holding in her small hand three wilted flowers.

Lance scooped up the child in his arms, dropping his crutch as he bent over. He felt a sharp pain in his hip and started to fall, but his father grabbed him in time and held him up. His sister Joanne picked up his crutch and held on to it. After he hugged his mother and sister with Lynn still in his arms, he shook hands with his father and took his crutch from his sister.

"Lance," said his mother, "Lynn's picked these flowers for you and held them all the way to the airport."

"Yeah," said Joanne, "and she wouldn't let go of them. 'These are for my daddy' she kept saying."

He took the wilted flowers from his daughter's little hand and kissed her cheek.

She responded with a hug around Lance's neck then squirmed around and said, "Daddy, I want down."

Lance gave the child to his father because he knew he would not be able to bend down again without falling.

After leaving the airport, Lynn sat on her father's lap all the way home, falling asleep almost as soon as they got under way, even before the toll road. As his daughter slept in his arms, Lance thought of Alice and a strange sadness overcame him. He hadn't really thought about his dead wife lately, but the little girl on his lap had some of her mother's features that reminded him of Alice and he couldn't help thinking of her.

Lance spent the remainder of the spring, all of that summer and two months of the fall at home. He enjoyed the time with his family and spent a lot of it with his young daughter. His mother arranged for a small youth bed to be put in his room so the little girl could stay with him whenever she wanted to spend the night. Usually she stayed only one or two nights a week because she would miss her Aunt Norma and fuss until Lance took her home.

Five months later, in late October, Lance had to report to the Great Lakes Naval Hospital for an evaluation of his wound. He felt one hundred percent healed and ready to go back to active status. After X-rays and some diagnostic testing exercises with the leg, the doctor declared him fit for duty. Two weeks later an assignment came through—Fifth U.S. Army Advisory Group in Chicago with duty at the U.S. Army Reserve Center in Rockford, Illinois. It meant Lance could stay at home with his folks.

Within six months, and thoroughly bored with his assignment, Lance applied for a voluntary tour in Vietnam through the group headquarters in Chicago. He knew he didn't have much chance to ship over with a regular combat unit because of the time it would take to get a DA assignment. It would take several months, however if he requested an individual assignment to the advisory group, he could be overseas in a matter of weeks. Three weeks after applying, he received orders—75th Military Assistance Command, Vietnam.

Two weeks later he arrived in Saigon.

This tour started out completely different than his two previous tours. First, Lance had living quarters in a hotel where other U.S. Army advisors billeted, a far cry from the field accommodations he had during his other assignments. Next, he would work with a Vietnamese ranger battalion, advising and instructing the battalion commander in the fundamentals of warfare and tactics as used by the United States Army.

Lieutenant Colonel Lee Sen Yen, a Stanford University graduate and former school teacher, commanded the all Vietnamese unit. He and Lance took an instant liking to each other and became friends as well as comrades in arms. A few weeks later, after the two men had become better acquainted, Lance asked Colonel Yen about his name not sounding Vietnamese.

The colonel replied, "My father is Chinese and is a merchant in Saigon. It is my mother who is Vietnamese."

The Vietnamese battalion trained hard and learned fast under Lance's patient guidance and advice. Three months after he arrived, Lance felt the battalion ready for a combat operation. Two weeks later they received their first major assigned mission—sweep a village one hundred and fifty kilometers north of Saigon suspected of harboring Viet Cong and North Vietnamese agents.

Although they found only the natives living there, and no Viet Cong nor North Vietnamese, Lance felt the operation succeeded. He suspected the enemy had gotten word of the impending search and left before the unit arrived.

When he brought up the subject to the battalion commander as to why they had not found any enemy there, Colonel Yen said, "I suspect one of my men informed them."

Lance asked, "How is that possible, sir?"

"Because there are Viet Cong in my unit. They believe they can best serve their cause by enlisting in our units and keeping their comrades informed of what we are doing. It is a very effective method of gathering intelligence."

"Do you know who these people are?"

"Sometimes, but not always."

"Don't you take action to eliminate these people?"

"Not always, my friend. If we are sure of a particular individual, we feed him false information then do something so we can trap him. However, it is difficult sometimes because the Viet Cong is everywhere and if another unit is used to spring the trap, someone in that unit informs the enemy of our plans. So, now we have a catch twenty-two."

"Yes, sir, I see what you mean."

After the conversation, Lance became more wary of those around him. He knew he would never be able to identify a Viet Cong by looking at him or her, so he became somewhat suspicious of all Vietnamese. He also had another reason for being cautious.

About the same time he had the conversation with Colonel Yen about the infiltration problem, Lance heard rumors at the officers' billets about the North Vietnamese putting a bounty on American advisors, a rumor that held some truth to it.

The battalion continued to train, primarily in the field, often staying out for days. One day while the unit walked through a field of tall grass, Lance noticed some of the nearby Vietnamese soldiers snickering and trying to hide their laughter from him.

He turned to Colonel Yen and asked, "Is there something wrong here, Colonel?"

"Not at all, Captain. They think it amusing because you are so tall. When we walk through the high grass we are hidden, but you and your sergeant stand head and shoulders above the grass, so the enemy will shoot you first. The soldiers around you feel very safe knowing they will not be shot first."

"Thanks a lot, Colonel," said Lance as he looked around then realized what the colonel had said was true. He and the sergeant stood head high above the top of the grass. After that day, Lance made a concerted effort not to be a target.

During the next few months the battalion conducted several assault raids on suspected enemy positions, but in all except one, they found no enemy troops. The one time they did find troops, they captured the only two Viet Cong they found.

When the news of only two prisoners captured reached Colonel Yen, he said, "Captain, a South Vietnamese ranger battalion has almost seven hundred men and we have spent an enormous amount of time and energy to capture only two of the enemy. By my calculations this is not a very profitable ratio of operation."

"I couldn't agree more, Colonel. You got any ideas how we can improve the situation?"

"I might, Captain ... I just might," said the colonel, looking as if he had some particular thoughts.

One week later, Lance and Colonel Yen reported to the 75th MACV Headquarters in Saigon as requested. When they arrived at the appointed time, a guard at the information desk told them to go to the second floor. When they entered the meeting room, Lance got a mild surprise. Along with fifty other officers in the room, he saw his old friend Mike Polaski standing at the podium in front of the operations map.

Lance could hardly believe his eyes. He hadn't seen nor heard from Mike since San Francisco almost two years before.

The instant Mike spotted Lance he shouted, "Stalwardt, over here, ole buddy!"

The two old friends shook hands, grabbed each other and chatted for a few minutes, each talking over the other in their excitement of seeing one another again then Lance remembered the Vietnamese commander. "Geez, I'm sorry, Colonel."

"It is quite all right, Captain. It is obvious that you two are old friends and have not seen each other in a long time."

"Colonel, this is Mike Polaski. Mike and I go back a long time together. Mike this is Colonel Yen."

After the introductions, the two men exchanged pleasantries then Lance asked, "Mike, what the hell you doing here?"

"I'm doin' an intel briefing for your battalion and several other South Vietnamese units scheduled to replace some American units in the field. I'll tell you all about it in a few minutes. Right now grab a seat 'cause we're gonna get started now that you're here."

For the next thirty minutes Mike gave an intelligence situation briefing of suspected and known enemy positions throughout the entire country, both North and South Vietnam. As Mike continued into the briefing, Lance realized that enemy troops had invaded South Vietnam more than at any time in the past. Not only an increase of Viet Cong, but also of North Vietnamese regulars.

Mike outlined the overall operations plan that South Vietnamese battalions would replace certain key American battalions. The U.S. forces had been training the South Vietnamese units for over a year and higher command felt them ready to go into the field to fight on their own. The South Vietnamese troops would take over most, if not all, of the war effort. However, they would keep their American advisors. If they required support during the change-over period, an elaborate backup system provided American units as a reserve to the South Vietnamese.

The plan scheduled Colonel Yen's battalion to occupy an area north of Saigon and operate out of a base camp being built and fortified by American engineers. A Special Forces team and local native Vietnamese provided security for the engineers, and when completed, the colonel's battalion would be inserted by helicopter.

After the briefing, Lance and Colonel Yen agreed to go their own way until the next day because they each wanted to get together with friends of their own. They planned to meet in the officers' mess at the 75th MACV Headquarters for breakfast the next day then return to the unit.

Lance and Mike left the briefing room and went to the officers' club for lunch. They sat in one of the booths along the back wall then placed their meal order.

Lance asked, "How the hell did you ever get here in MACV?"

Mike replied, "To make a long story short, I rolled over my tour into two years. When I first came over, I was in the Mekong Delta area then when I rolled over they sent me here to MACV. I've been here for almost a year. Next month I go home and I'm never comin' back to this shit hole."

"I don't think the country's so bad," said Lance.

"I'm not talkin' about the country. It's this damn war. It's pure bullshit. It ain't the military, it's the damn politicians. They won't let us do anything. We can't cross the DMZ ... we can't use certain ordnance ... we can't bomb certain targets ... we can't go into Cambodia. Geez, Lance, we're licked before we even get started."

Lance had heard it before, about things not going well, and the blame being directed at the civilian interference within the Defense Department. The limited warfare policies enacted and established by the American politicians had an adverse effect upon the U.S. soldiers' morale, and because of the prolonged action, many officers felt it a major factor in contributing to the high casualty rates.

"I gotta gut feelin' we're gonna lose this war."

Lance looked at his friend with a puzzled look and said, "By god, Mike, I think you're really serious."

"Like a heart attack, man. You ain't been here for a while, and when you came, they stuck you down in a line unit. Me, I've been privy to all the latest hot poop at the top and believe me, I know what I'm talkin' about. The north is pilin' in more troops every day.

Hell, the damn Chinese are lined up on their border with North Vietnam ready to invade, and it'll be a bloodbath when they do."

"Jesus, Mike, should you be telling me all of this? Isn't this information classified or something?"

Mike ignored Lance's questions and continued to talk. "We've got half a million men in this country and we can't win this damn war because we're not allowed to fight the way we're supposed to. I'm tellin' ya, Lance, it's really bullshit. If the military would've been given a free hand to fight this war the way it should have been fought, it probably would've ended years ago."

Lance knew his old friend was right. As the months and years of war dragged on, Lance too felt more pessimistic about its outcome. He also knew he wasn't the only one to feel this way. He had spent enough time around civilians at home during the past year to know the war didn't sit well with many mid-western Americans, and they often expressed they wanted *our boys* out of Vietnam.

Demonstrations at home began to happen more frequently, and more young men burned their draft cards, protesting the war. The numbers of young men giving up their citizenship and going into Canada, or some other foreign country to avoid the draft increased dramatically. The people let their feelings be known publicly and openly supported the man running for president who made promises to negotiate a peaceful end to the war.

"Listen, ole buddy," said Mike, "there's one more thing I wanna tell ya. Don't be surprised if there's a big welcoming committee for you and your guys next week, and I mean real big. I tried to tell the brass that the most likely spot for an assembly area for those northern bastards was in the area just south of where you and your bunch are headed for."

"What'd they say?"

"They pooh-poohed it and said all the activity was to the west about fifty klicks. Me, I don't buy it. I think Charlie's jerkin' us around, and I'll bet even money they'll be in that valley where you're goin' in so be careful ... be damn careful."

"Are you sure about your intel?"

"Does GI Joe have a plastic crotch?"

Lance chuckled at the attempted humor, but then asked, "Which brass you talkin' about?"

"Theirs … the Vietnamese."

"I see," said Lance, pondering what his friend had just said.

Lance knew the information should not be considered too lightly because he had seen Mike work before and knew the warning had a high probability of being correct. Just to be on the safe side, Lance would inform Colonel Yen to proceed with the landing and the transfer operation as if the enemy controlled the area.

"Besides," said Mike, "now that the friendlies know where your battalion is going in, chances are that Charlie knows it too."

Lance and Mike spent the rest of the day and night together reminiscing and talking about old times. That evening, they went to the officers' club, had dinner, watched a floor show then got fairly drunk. They both knew it might be the last time they'd ever see each other and as things turned out, it almost was.

Chapter 6

On the morning after the intelligence and operations briefing, Lance met Colonel Yen for breakfast, and as they returned to the battalion compound, Lance told the colonel what Mike explained to him the day before about the possibility of a large Viet Cong force or North Vietnamese regulars being in their assigned area.

The colonel said, "The information from division headquarters does not support your friend's theory. My superiors do not believe the enemy to be in my area of influence and believes them to be further to the west. I cannot act on just your friend's hunch. I must act upon the information from my division's intelligence or I face the possibility of a military tribunal. However, you have always given true and accurate advice, and I will plan for extra support. Hopefully, my friend … that will be enough."

Five days later, Lance and the Vietnamese battalion, consisting of four elements, loaded into helicopters and flew to their assigned area. The cloudy morning skies didn't affect the flying. Fifteen to twenty aircraft flew in each element depending upon their cargo load and the number of personnel on board. Usually each helicopter carried ten men, their gear and the crew, but some carried less men and more equipment, especially with the 81mm mortar crews.

Originally, when Lance found out the designated landing zone could not be used because of the area being under construction, and heavy equipment still occupying the area, he felt it a big problem and recommended the landing be postponed. The South Vietnamese headquarters would not approve any delay and designated an alternate landing site outside the base camp a couple of thousand meters away because of the heavily laid mine field close in around the compound perimeter.

When the lead element of the battalion reached their primary landing zone, a clearing about 1500 meters east of the compound, they came under heavy attack after the troops unloaded and as soon as the helicopters all left. The second element headed to an alternate landing zone further east and landed, but they too began drawing heavy fire. Colonel Yen, landing with the second element, radioed for the third and fourth elements to land further away at a third alternate site and march in to help relieve the other two elements.

In the third element, Lance radioed to Colonel Yen and asked, "What's the situation down there, sir?"

Colonel Yen told him, "Do not come in, the area is too hot. I'm afraid we are going to be—"

The radio went dead.

Lance called the Vietnamese Air-3, riding with the battalion HQ staff in the helicopter just behind him, "Get some gunship support in here A-SAP."

Before the flight left, Lance told Colonel Yen to lay on a few preplanned air strikes just in case they ran into trouble. At first, Colonel Yen appeared reluctant to take the advice, but he relented and told Air-3 to set up the prearranged strikes. Within minutes Cobra and Huey gunships arrived on scene firing their rockets and machine guns, blasting the enemy troops hidden among the trees around both landing zones.

From the air, Lance could see the enemy troops as they overran and annihilated the entire first element. He instructed his pilot to fly back to where the second element landed in a clearing on a slight rise about a thousand meters away from where the first element had landed just moments before. He could see the troops in the middle of the small clearing, firing in three directions into the surrounding tree line. He tried to figure out where Colonel Yen might be, but he couldn't identify anyone because of being too high up.

Lance yelled into the intercom to the pilot, "Get Closer!"

"Sir, we're drawing fire now," said the pilot. "Any closer and we're sure to take a hit."

"Then drop me off by that burning helicopter."

"Captain, you don't have to go down there. You're just the advisor. There's no obligation for you to go in there."

"I said put me on the ground ... NOW, GOD DAMN IT!"

"Yes, sir. You got it."

Next, Lance contacted the battalion executive officer in the last element and told him, "I've lost contact with the colonel so I'm telling you to abort the landing of the remaining elements and to return to the battalion base camp. If you wanna save the rest of those on the ground you better get at least a brigade-size unit up here. And, get some more air support in here."

As the helicopter neared the ground Lance prepared to jump. He told the American sergeant with him, "You stay with the aircraft and get back to the base camp and tell them sons of bitches in that Vietnamese division there's at least two regiments of enemy troops in this area, and more than likely it's a whole division. Tell them they're not Cong, they're northern regulars. But first, you get this information back to Captain Polaski. You got that, Sergeant?"

"Yes, sir. Here, Captain, take my rifle. You're gonna need it."

Lance took the weapon and four magazines of ammunition from the sergeant, turned to the doorway and jumped the few remaining feet to the ground. The pilot took off and headed toward the rear.

Lance took several steps when he stumbled and fell. "Christ that was dumb. What the hell did I fall over?" As he looked down toward the ground he saw a small neat hole in his pant leg just below the knee. "Shit, I've been hit."

There seemed to be no pain so he got to his feet and ran toward an area about 50 meters away where a small group huddled on the ground. As he ran, bullets whizzed past him, kicking up small puffs of dust all around him. Somehow he made it to the small group of defenders and when he arrived, he met a Vietnamese Lieutenant Baraud that looked more black than Asian.

Much later Lance found out the lieutenant's father was a black soldier in the French Foreign Legion and his mother Vietnamese. Because of his competent military leadership, his well disciplined troops held their own in the fight. They did not stand up and try to run away as many of the others had done. Those in the first element who did try running got killed.

As Lance ran in a low crouch into the small group, he felt something tug at his right side and thought someone had grabbed his shirt trying to pull him to the ground. But then saw no one around him close enough to do it. *It must have been something else.* After he hit the ground, he felt a stinging pain in his side.

"Damn, I'm hit again," he mumbled. He rolled on his good side, pulled up his shirt and looked at the wound. *Good*, he thought, *it hardly broke the skin, but it sure smarts.*

As he lay there, a medic appeared beside him and gave him some antiseptic and a large bandage to put over the wound. After patching up his side the medic tended to the leg wound and wrapped it. Both bullets had gone completely through the flesh and had not hit anything vital, just muscle. *Funny*, thought Lance, *there's no pain, just a kind of numbness.*

While the medic attended Lance, the lieutenant asked with a heavy English accent, "Sir, are you all right?"

"Just a couple of minor scrapes … nothing serious. Whatcha got here, Lieutenant?"

"My platoon and about two other squads. Probably about sixty people alive and maybe a dozen or so dead. There's plenty of wounded, but it's been too hectic to get an accurate count."

Puzzled by the lieutenant's accent, Lance asked, "Lieutenant, where'd you learn to speak English?"

The lieutenant smiled and said, "I was educated in England, sir."

"That explains it."

"Sir, what do you think our chances are of coming out of this little fracas alive?"

"None if we stay here. We've gotta get to some cover. Where exactly is the base camp from here?"

"I think it's that way, sir," said the lieutenant as he pointed to a clearing in the tree line.

Still engaged in a serious firefight, the men in the little group fought with effective fire, keeping the enemy at bay for the moment, but Lance knew the enemy force that overran the first element would soon arrive to reinforce the troops facing them. When that happened, Lance felt the battle would be over in minutes.

Lance exclaimed, "We gotta move and move now!"

Almost as if on cue, a concentration of mortar and artillery rounds landed in the tree line on both sides of a clear corridor leading toward the base camp where the lieutenant had pointed to just moments ago.

Lance shouted at the same time as he pointed, "THERE … get your men moving through there, Lieutenant."

As the small group withdrew from their position and started for the base camp, Lance went in the other direction toward another small group of soldiers about fifty meters off to the right flank. When he arrived a medic grabbed him and told him to lie down on his face. He had taken another round in the back just above his belt and about three inches away from the backbone. Luckily, the bullet didn't penetrate very far because it ricocheted off something first and caused only a minor wound. He never felt the bullet hit.

When the medic completed dressing the wound, Lance rolled over and looked into the face of Colonel Yen, kneeling low beside him, who said, "It's good to see you again, my friend."

"Yes, sir," said Lance. "Same here. That means I'm still alive."

"But not for very long if we stay here," said the colonel.

"I know, Colonel, I saw how they finished off the first element and now that bunch is headed this way to help those bastards. Are there any more of your troops out there alive?"

"I don't think so. I haven't seen any fire from anywhere else. I believe all the others are dead because they tried to escape and were shot while running away."

"See that clearing through the trees?"

"Yes, Captain, I see it."

"That's where we gotta go through. The base camp is just on the other side of the tree line. It'll be best if we stick to the north side of the clearing and the edge of the trees. I think we've gotta better chance on that side."

"Good. We'll leave now. Do you need help?"

"If you'll help me up, I believe I can make it," said Lance.

Colonel Yen pulled Lance to his feet then turned to his troops and shouted commands in Vietnamese.

As the first small group started moving, overhead helicopters began to intensify their supporting fires which initially suppressed most of the enemy fire then kept up the attack long enough for both groups to make it to safety under cover of the tree line. They still had to cross a large expanse of open area between the trees and the base camp before being completely safe.

When the two groups met inside the tree line they joined up and started for the base camp. After clearing the trees on the other side, the camp's artillery and mortars began giving covering fire behind them. The rounds began hitting the top branches, raining death and destruction on everything below, stopping the enemy from coming through the trees and attacking the small group from the rear.

The group slowly advanced across the clearing toward the base camp and when 50 meters out, a detail from the camp came out and met them to help carry their wounded and to guide them through the mine fields. Once inside the compound, the commander of the base camp, Major Kline, a Special Forces officer, met them.

As Lance came through the fortified gate, the major said, "It looks like you've had a rough time of it."

"Yes, sir, real rough."

"How bad?"

"Out of approximately five hundred men that landed, we've got about a hundred left alive."

"Well, it ain't gonna get any better in here. There's at least two regiments of northern regulars out there, maybe more, and if they want this place bad enough they'll take it without too much trouble. We don't have enough ammunition to kill them all so it's just a matter of attrition. And they can do it before anyone reaches us."

"Sir, have you called for air support?"

"Yeah, but they say we're not a priority and we'll have to wait."

"Thanks for those words of encouragement, Major."

"Hell, Captain, what're buddies for. By the way, you better tend to your arm. It looks like its bleeding pretty bad."

"Damn, this is the fourth time I've been hit today," said Lance as he looked down at the wound in his arm. Again, he had not felt the bullet when it hit him.

"Better see a medic right away. The first aid bunker is just over there," said the major as he pointed into the compound.

Lance said, "Thank you, sir," turned and walked to the bunker about 50 meters away.

Once inside, Lance took off his shirt, turned and looked back at the major who remained in the same spot talking to a sergeant. A sudden explosion went off beside them, throwing both the major and the sergeant into the air like small dolls. Lance instinctively knew the enemy mortar round killed both men.

Turning to a medic inside the bunker, Lance said, "Medic, get a bandage on this arm and be quick about it."

The medic didn't respond. He seemed frozen with disbelief after he too had just witnessed the explosion killing the two men. Also, other rounds began hitting inside the compound and the medic felt frightened by the blasts.

Lance yelled, "NOW, DAMN IT!" The young soldier reacted as if he had been slapped in the face and within a few seconds had antiseptic and a bandage on the wound. Again, Lance had been somewhat lucky because the bullet had gone through the flesh and did not hit anything vital.

More enemy rounds began falling into the compound and men began running to defensive positions on the outside perimeter. No one had yet seen the enemy, but Lance knew they would come. For over fifteen minutes the enemy mortars pounded the inside of the camp and destroyed most of the interior structures as if each one had been plotted prior to the attack. Lance found out later, they were.

The command, communications and operations bunkers all received direct hits. Two of the four 105 howitzers and one of the two 4.2 mortar pits also received direct fire, destroying the weapons and killing the crew members.

Only the ammunition and fuel stores remained intact. Even the first aid shelter took a hit. Luckily the three medics followed Lance out of the bunker into one of the trenches on the camp's perimeter where he instructed them to tend the wounded men that came in with him and who occupied defensive positions with the rest of the base camp personnel.

As quickly as it began the shelling stopped and it became quiet, but Lance knew it wouldn't last so he cautioned everyone around him to be prepared.

When a few of the troops started to stand up, he shouted to them, "EVERYONE...GET BACK INTO THE TRENCHES! THEY'LL BE COMING SOON!"

Lance looked around and saw those on the other side of the compound starting to get up out of their positions so he turned to a sergeant and said, "Get a couple of men and go around the entire perimeter and tell everyone to get back in the trenches and stay put."

Lance suspected the enemy would stop the shelling for a while and let the troops expose themselves by thinking the shelling had quit. The enemy would then saturate the compound with another more intense shelling, hoping to catch most of the troops in the open and inflict a lot of casualties. He also knew when the next shelling began, the enemy would begin an attack with ground troops.

While the sergeant and two men carried out their task of getting the men back into the trenches, Lance hurried to the 105 howitzer artillery pit, found a second lieutenant among the troops and asked him, "What've we got here for supporting weapons?"

The young lieutenant answered with a somewhat arrogant tone in his voice, "Who wants to know?"

Lance snapped back, "I do." Agitated with the young officer he stepped closer to him. "Your major is dead and I'm the ranking officer left alive, so now I'm in command. I say again, Lieutenant, what weapons have we got left that are operational?"

With a sense of new found respect, the young officer replied, "Yes, sir, there's two howitzers, one four-deuce mortar, six eighty-one mortars, seven sixty millimeter mortars and four seven-deuce rocket launchers that are operational. There're six fifty calibers, two on each point, and about a dozen M-sixties."

"Where the hell did you get all this stuff, Lieutenant?"

"Don't ask, sir. I'd hate to lie to a superior."

"Okay, forget I asked," said Lance. "Did your major know that all these extra weapons were here?"

"No, sir."

"You got ammo for all this stuff?"

"Yes, sir."

"Look, Lieutenant, it's gonna get busy as hell around here in just a few minutes and we're gonna get more company than we want so we need to get things coordinated. Have you got a fire plan?"

"Not really, sir. Whatcha got in mind?"

"I want the one-oh-fives and the heavy mortar to support one of the triangle's three legs. Each will be supported by an eighty-one mortar. As soon as the tubes are ready I want them to fire into the areas where those enemy mortars are and keep blasting them until those mortars are knocked out or until I shift fires on my call. If anything happens to me, shift on your FOs order. I want everything air bursts. I wanna hurt these bastards big time."

"Yes, sir," said the young officer.

Lance continued, "When you begin your fire mission on the ground troops, have the primary weapon start on the right flank of their sector and the support eighty-ones on the left flank. Have each weapon fire on the same elevation after traversing every hundred meters. When the rounds meet near the middle, drop one hundred and traverse back to the starting flank, again firing every hundred meters. Then drop another hundred and start all over again."

One of the enlisted men said, "By god that'll make believers out of 'em," as he got up from the ground and hurried off to tell the crew members of the 105 gun.

Lance continued, "We haven't got much time so let's getta move on and get this show going."

"Sir, what about the other weapons?"

"Place them at your own discretion, Lieutenant," said Lance. "And don't forget to put at least two spotters on each leg. If we're overrun, blow all tubes and ammo. Have you got that, Lieutenant?"

"Yes, sir," replied the young officer. Then he turned to his men behind him and said, "All right, you heard the man. Let's get to it."

Lance went back to the perimeter and found Colonel Yen lying on a stretcher with Lieutenant Baraud kneeling alongside of his gravely wounded battalion commander. A mortar fragment struck him in the chest.

As Lance approached, he said to two enlisted men, "Put the colonel in the closest bunker. He'll be as safe in there as anywhere."

The two men responded as Lance turned to Lieutenant Baraud and said, "Lieutenant, I think you had better get back to your men now. It's gonna get real busy here pretty soon and they're gonna need you. I'm sure the colonel understands."

"Yes, sir, I'll go now," said the lieutenant.

Lance left the bunker and returned to the area where he stood during the first shelling. A second before he arrived, the shelling started again, only with more intensity than the first time.

The initial shell bursts caught some of the men on the other side of the compound out in the open, just as the enemy had hoped it would, but not many.

"This is it," said Lance to a young soldier next to him. "They're coming."

"I don't see 'em, sir," said the soldier as he peered over the top of the sandbags.

"Don't worry, Private, they'll be along soon enough."

Within minutes the enemy's lead elements came out of the tree line about 1500 meters away. It appeared to Lance as if there were thousands coming toward them in what looked like a mass frontal attack on his side. He had no way of knowing it, but at that exact moment, the same number of enemy soldiers began advancing on the other two sides of the triangle shaped camp.

As Lance watched the horde approach, a Special Forces sergeant jumped into the trench next to him carrying a bolt action rifle with a mounted scope. The sergeant took aim and fired then fired another quick shot.

Lance said, "They're pretty far out, Sergeant."

"Yes, sir, I'd say about twelve hundred meters. They never hear the gunshot until after the bullet goes thru 'em. Watch that joker with his hand in the air."

Looking down at the advancing enemy, Lance saw a small figure out in front of the others with his right arm raised. The sergeant pulled the rifle's trigger, it recoiled and a few seconds later the figure jerked backwards and fell to the ground.

"Bingo," shouted the sergeant. "Three for three."

He continued to fire and hit an enemy with every shot. As the lead comrades fell, the enemy soldiers began to falter, not sure of what to do, with their leaders being shot down by some mysterious gunfire. However, others soon took their place and the human wave started to advance again.

After the initial bursts of incoming rounds, the artillery forward observers plotted the enemy mortar emplacements and directed the ad hoc artillery fire onto the enemy positions. It only took three rounds from each tube, eighteen rounds total, and the enemy mortars fell silent, most of their crews lay dead or dying.

As soon as the enemy's supporting guns quit firing, Lance gave the command to shift fires as he estimated the first of the enemy troops at about 1000 meters out from the perimeter. The gun crews changed their elevation and traversed to their appointed flanks and began firing when the tubes came to bear. Lance marveled at how fast the gun crews could change direction of fire. He saw the air bursts of the 4.2mm and the 81mm mortar shells explode about ten feet above the large wave of enemy soldiers with intermittent smaller ground explosions of the 60's. Like a giant scythe, the deadly circular pattern cut down enemy soldiers within a thirty to forty meter radius from the larger caliber weapons and a five to ten meter radius of the smaller shells. Still they came on.

As the enemy reached about 800 meters out the .50 caliber and the M60 machine guns began to fire. More casualties among the enemy, especially the front ranks, but still they came. At 500 meters, Lance estimated the enemy about two thirds of the original attacking force. The M60 gunners began traversing the enemy's front and the advance began to slow down, but did not stop. Lance then knew the enemy meant to overrun the position or die in the attempt.

Lance asked aloud, "What the hell's so important about this patch of ground? Why do they want it so bad?"

"Beats the hell outta me, sir," said the sergeant next to Lance.

"What? What did you say, Sergeant?"

"Sir, I said it beats the hell outta me."

"What does?"

"You asked me why they wanted this patch of ground, and I said it beats the hell outta me."

"Sorry, Sergeant, I was just thinking out loud."

"That's okay, sir, I understand," said the sergeant who fired his rifle again and dropped another enemy soldier.

The battle noise began to increase. The air bursts, the machine guns firing and now the soldiers on the perimeter began firing their individual weapons on automatic and semi-automatic selections. The enemy troops soon reached the mine field and came within claymore range, their explosions adding to the pandemonium. Still the enemy advanced to within 200 meters, then 100 meters, then 50 meters, then 25 meters, then at the perimeter itself and finally started breaking through. Lance continued to run up and down the line shouting encouragement to the men, helping to shoot any enemy that managed to get through the defense line and into the compound. Occasionally he would fall to the ground hit by some unseen force.

Four times, he ran out of ammunition and had to reload the M16 with a new magazine. The pace of action became so furious he couldn't think and he didn't even try. Lance became weary and felt as if he couldn't go on. His mind clouded over and his legs felt like lead. He could see enemy soldiers coming through the defenses and turn toward him. Something hit him several times, but he didn't know what. Somebody grabbed him and threw him down. He rose to one knee and struck out viciously with the rifle clubbing an enemy soldier, then another. He could smell the acrid mixture of spent munitions and burning equipment along with a strong smell of death. He could taste the saltiness of blood, heavy in his mouth and he began to gag, almost vomiting.

Up on both knees, he could barely see the enemy soldiers near him because of the sweat and blood, his blood, running into his eyes, stinging them, burning them. His body got weaker because of the loss of blood from his many wounds, but he fought on, purely by instinct and adrenalin. More enemy soldiers approached him. He drew his pistol and through a blur fired the .45 at one figure, then another, then another. He kept firing until something slammed into him, knocking him to the ground then he slipped into a fog-like state of semiconsciousness and could no longer see.

Once, twice, three times he felt something over him. Then he heard a tremendous roar, a deafening noise to his ears. Through the terrible racket and darkness, he could vaguely hear something like his name being called. It sounded as if the voice came from far away and inside a long tunnel. He felt something lift him and he began to drift, drifting further and further from the noise.

What the hell's happening to me? Am I dying? Can't I just rest here for a moment?

No answer came, only a deep blackness as he slipped into total unconsciousness.

Chapter 7

Pacific Ocean

Somewhere in the black depths of total darkness, a subliminal flash then another then came a muffled sound, almost as if a far away voice called out to him.

What are they saying? It sounded like a name. There it is again, another flash. A light, a very faint light began to materialize like the dawn breaking out from behind a moonless night. *Again, that voice, but who are they calling?*

Then a slow and painful realization of being alive.

Lance groaned once as he came out of the anesthesia. He lay in the intensive care ward of a naval hospital ship, well out to sea and safe from the battles of war. His mouth felt dry and his throat sore, the first sensation of consciousness. Next, he recognized the smell of clean linen and the all too familiar antiseptic odors of a hospital. Lance opened his eyes. He tried to focus on a fuzzy patch of white. It soon became evident to him that a doctor stood over him with a small penlight in one hand and holding a stethoscope on his chest with the other.

He heard the doctor say with some excitement in his voice, "By god nurse, I think he's gonna make it."

Lance tried to answer, but the tubes taped in his mouth and up his nose wouldn't allow the words to form and he only managed a low grunt. He tried to roll his head but couldn't because something restrained it.

A feminine voice from behind him spoke into his right ear and said softly, "Captain Stalwardt, please be still. You wouldn't want to undo all the work this doctor has done now, would you? In case you're wondering where you are, you're on a Navy hospital ship."

Almost fully awake, Lance grunted a response and relaxed. He looked down toward his feet. Two humps.

Good, at least I've got both legs and feet, he thought. Next, he looked to see if he still had arms. *They're there ... my god, all those bandages.* He turned his eyes to the female voice. *She's a looker, not like those in the army hospitals. I wish I could talk to her.*

The nurse smiled and wiped his forehead with a cool damp cloth. It felt good. *The doctor ... where's the doctor?* A moment later the doctor reappeared back into Lance's limited vision.

The doctor leaned over him and said, "Captain Stalwardt, I want you to try not moving for a little while. You've been pretty badly wounded and you must stay very still in order to help the surgery heal. Some of it was pretty delicate and we don't want anything to tear loose. I'm giving you something to make you sleep now."

Within minutes he drifted again. His vision started to blur and his mind began to hallucinate. His body felt as if a warm rolling wave of water washed over it. A touch of sudden nausea swept over him, then back into the darkness, a deep and total darkness.

Lance slept for over twenty-four hours then awoke with a start. At first he couldn't comprehend where he was or how he got there. He started to roll his head, but a pair of hands stopped him.

His nurse bent over him from behind and whispered, "Good morning, Captain. Please don't move your head."

Then he remembered being wounded and what the nurse told him, *You're on a Navy hospital ship.*

He tried to take a deep breath, but the raw soreness in his throat caused him to stop.

The nurse leaned over him again and said, "Sir, I'm going to remove the tubes from your mouth and nose. There may be some discomfort, but please try to be as still as possible."

Lance grunted.

The nurse removed the tape holding the tubes in place, pulling small hairs from his face and causing him a little pain, but not enough for him to move his head. He stayed still throughout the whole ordeal, and when the last tube came out, he took a deep breath then heaved a sigh of relief. The nurse gave him a drink of water from a glass with a curved straw. The cool liquid felt soothing on his raw throat, easing the pain and dryness almost immediately. He tried to speak, but only a shrill raspy sound came out, like a bad case of laryngitis.

"Don't try to talk. Your throat is still too sore from the surgery."

Lance thought, *Surgery? On my throat? Why would I have surgery on my throat?* He found out why later.

Eleven separate bullet wounds and shrapnel covered his body and a bayonet wound in the left arm. In all, he had three wounds in the legs, three in the arms, two in the chest, one in the back, one in his right side just above the belt line and one through his neck where the bullet came very close to severing the vocal cords and hitting the spine. The bullet causing the neck wound had gone through another soldier's body first as did the two bullets that lodged in his chest and the three had to be removed surgically.

Hand grenade shrapnel by four different blasts struck Lance, twice in the back, once in the left side and once from the front. A large piece of steel, about the size of a dime, had to be removed from his face as did some other smaller pieces of shrapnel. Lance's surgery took seven hours and at times the doctors didn't think he would make it through.

As one doctor said during the operation, "If this guy makes it, he's gonna trip off every airport security alarm he ever walks through for the rest of his life."

Ironically, none of the wounds he received hit a vital organ or major blood vessel. He did bleed profusely, but not enough to cause death. First aid in the field and the fact the medical evacuation system got him to the Navy hospital ship's operating table within thirty minutes saved his life. However, the most important reason for his being alive—Mike Polaski came to his rescue as the North Vietnamese soldiers broke through the compound perimeter.

Not until much later did Lance put together what happened in the closing minutes of the enemy attack on the compound. He finally remembered the perimeter being breached by enemy soldiers and him running out of ammunition, both for the M16 and his .45 pistol. He vaguely remembered fighting one North Vietnamese soldier hand to hand and receiving the bayonet wound in the lower left arm—after that, nothing.

As the enemy began to overrun the compound, Mike Polaski arrived with two battalions of American soldiers and a troop of armed cavalry helicopters. With reinforcements arriving, the enemy forces broke off the attack and retreated back toward the woods. Once in the open the armed gunships practically annihilated them.

Within minutes after landing in the compound, Mike found Lance underneath the bodies of Colonel Yen, Lieutenant Baruad and a Special Forces staff sergeant named Martin, where they had been thrown into a bunker by enemy soldiers. The enemy thought all four men had been killed and piled the bodies inside the wooden bunker to burn. Mike's arrival on the scene saved the four men and many others from certain death. Of the two hundred and fifty men in the compound before the attack started, only fifty-one survived, including the two Vietnamese officers.

Medevac helicopters took the four wounded men to the rear then transferred Lance and Sergeant Martin to the Navy ship, heading back to the United States.

A month after Lance arrived at the hospital in San Francisco, he received a visit from his old friend Mike Polaski, rotating home. "Lance, ole buddy, they're giving you the Medal of Honor."

Several weeks later, Lance received a letter from the President of the United States inviting him to accept his medal before a joint session of the United States Congress in the nation's Capitol. The letter also invited him to say a few words to the governing body.

The day before the medal ceremony, Lance left the hospital and went to Washington, D.C. The next day, with his left arm still in a sling and with the aid of a cane, Lance walked slowly through the Capitol toward the speaker's podium where the President of the United States waited to award him the nation's highest combat award for heroism, the Medal of Honor.

Lance felt a powerful surge of pride and devotion well up through his body as the President placed the gold medallion on an infantry blue ribbon over his head. He had never experienced such an emotional moment before, and it took a few seconds before he could compose himself. After the sensation passed, Lance moved to the podium and looked out at the politicians and visitors now seated in the House of Representatives' chamber.

He began to speak. "Mr. President, Congressmen, distinguished guests, ladies and gentlemen. I am extremely honored and deeply humbled to be the recipient of this most prestigious award. I accept it with the understanding that this medal symbolizes the efforts and courage of those with whom I have served, and for those who have made the ultimate sacrifice. For without them, this ceremony could not have been possible."

The entire body, gathered in the legislative hall, erupted into a spontaneous round of applause. When the applause died down, Lance continued, now reading from a prepared statement he had removed from inside the sling holding his left arm.

"There are many soldiers who are more deserving of this medal than I, but most of them are not able to be here. They have paid the dearest price that anyone could possibly give. It isn't the conflict in Vietnam that caused the motivation for their sacrifice, but the belief in their country, the United States of America and the freedoms that we in America so greatly enjoy."

Again, spontaneous applause erupted lasting for about a minute.

When the acclaim died down, Lance continued. "Our freedoms are precious to all us Americans, and we in the military have taken an oath to uphold these freedoms no matter what the cost or where the cause will take us. It's extremely unfortunate that we must uphold them upon foreign soil, especially now in Vietnam. I've had three tours in that country, and I truly believe that our limited military intervention into the civil conflict of that nation is not truly justified, especially at the cost of American lives. I believe that a peaceful solution to the war should be initiated and pursued as quickly as possible so that our fighting men and women can be brought home."

More applause, but this time not everyone participated.

After the applause died down, Lance continued. "Although I feel our government has the best intentions for pressing on with the war, I believe the effort to contain the communist takeover in Vietnam is one of futility. I can only speak for myself and from my own experiences, but in conversations with my fellow servicemen and many American citizens, I feel that most of these people share the same view as I. It is a war that we cannot possibly win."

Scattered applause came again, but many of the congressmen sat motionless and appeared not to be moved by Lance's words.

"It's my personal belief that promoting and instilling a way of life on others cannot be done by invading a country and killing its citizens. This is what North Vietnam has done, but eventually their doctrine will fail because their logic is contradictory to freedom and basic human rights.

"It now appears the United States is beginning to follow the same reasoning as the North Vietnamese by escalating the war, and it too will surely fail. The intervention of our military into that civil war ... and it is just that and nothing more ... can no longer be justified to many people here in America. They now feel as I do, that the American way of life and our beliefs cannot be imposed upon a country or its people if they do not want our particular type of government. The Vietnamese have no concept of our freedoms because they have lived so long under dictatorships and totalitarian type governments. The majority of the South Vietnamese people do not want American intervention into their country's civil problems, regardless of their present government wishes. They know an American puppet government is not the answer."

Sporadic applause interrupted Lance again so he paused before continuing. "Then there is also the problem of American casualties. This is unacceptable to Americans here at home, especially the wives, mothers and fathers of those that have to fight. Losing a loved one to an unjustifiable cause is truly changing the country's attitude toward this war, and it will be these people that eventually cause the end of this travesty."

Lance paused again, and again only a little applause. He could tell his remarks caused some members in the audience a great deal of discomfort.

"I ask that each of you in this great chamber today, search your own conscience and try to honestly answer this question. Is it worth the lives of American soldiers to fight a war that cannot possibly have a winning solution?"

Lance stopped speaking, folded his notes and slowly left the podium with only a small number of the audience applauding. He didn't look back. Somewhere, deep within his conscience, Lance felt a sense of satisfaction and now that he said the words, he knew he spoke the truth. He also knew that because of his many wounds and being the recipient of the Medal of Honor he would not be sent back to combat in Vietnam.

Lance left the Capitol accompanied by an aide of Senator Earl E. Williams, the senior senator from his home state of Illinois. They returned to Lance's hotel in a limousine provided by the senator and once there he met with Mike and a few members of his family who sat in the visitors' gallery when Lance received his medal and gave his speech.

As he came through the door of the hotel room, Mike met him and said, "Jesus, Stalwardt, you really gave the ole boys hell. Think it'll do any good?"

"Probably not," said Lance, smiling at his parents and two of his sisters standing behind Mike.

"Well at least it makes you feel better now that you've got it off your chest."

"Yeah, but I'll betcha it didn't do my career any good."

Lance stepped past Mike just as his mother came to him with tears in her eyes saying, "I'm so proud of you, son."

She put her arms around his neck and gave him a gentle hug.

Next, Lance's father came to him and embraced him and said, "Glad to have you home, son."

When his two sisters joined in for a communal hug, he felt something around his leg so he pulled away from the hugging group and looked down to see his young daughter gripping his pant leg looking up at him with a big smile on her face as she said, "Hi Daddy."

Lance bent down and tried to pick up the little girl, but he was not able to and almost fell.

Mike grabbed his arm and steadied him then said, "Lance, better have a seat on the bed, I think you'll be more comfortable there."

"Good idea," said Lance as he sat down and his daughter scrambled up beside him.

He put his arm around the little girl as she hugged him and gave him a kiss on his cheek. Everyone began talking at once, but a knock at the door quieted them.

Mike said, "I'll get it," and opened the door only a few inches. He asked the two well dressed men standing in the hallway, "What can I do for you fellas?"

The taller man asked, "You Captain Stalwardt?"

"No, I'm Captain Polaski."

"We'd like to speak to Captain Stalwardt in private if we may."

"Just a sec, I'll check if he wants to see anyone right now," then Mike closed the door as the two men waited outside. "Lance, are you in the mood to see any visitors?"

"Not really. Who are they?"

"I don't know. I didn't ask."

"Find out who they are and see what they want. Tell them I'm really not up to seeing anyone right now and that I'm with my family. Ask them if tomorrow morning will be all right."

Mike returned to the door, opened it up just enough to stand in the way and said to the two men, "Sorry, fellas, Captain Stalwardt doesn't want to see anyone just now. He's with his family and they haven't seen each other for a while. You understand. Can you come back in the morning?"

The shorter of the two men stepped forward and said, "He'll see us now if he knows what's good—"

Suddenly, the taller man reached across the smaller man's chest, cutting him off in mid sentence and pushed him backward saying, "Thank you, Captain Polaski, we'll contact him in the morning. Shall we say ten o'clock?"

"And who shall I say is calling?"

Taking a card from his inside breast pocket and handing it to Mike, the taller man said, "We'll see you at ten o'clock tomorrow. Have a good day, Captain." He turned to the shorter man and said, "Let's go."

The two men left without another word. Mike closed the door and looked at the card and read aloud, "James J. Callahan, Chief of Staff to Cyrus T. Baynes, United States Senator, South Carolina."

Lance asked, "Wonder what the hell he wants?"

"I don't know, but you'll find out tomorrow," said Mike as he placed the card on the dresser. "They're coming back at ten."

Earlier, Senator Williams invited Lance and his family as guests for dinner at one of Washington's finest restaurants. The senator sent a limousine to transport them all to the restaurant, and when they arrived, the maitre d' escorted them to a private room where Senator Williams greeted them then introduced his wife along with several members of his staff.

After dinner and dessert, everyone began to section themselves off into smaller groups of twos or threes. Lance and his young daughter teamed up with the senator while the senator's wife and Lance's mother went off by themselves and sat in a corner. The chief of staff and Lance's father were off in another corner catching up on old news because they had gone to the same high school at the same time and had mutual friends and acquaintances. Lance's two sisters paired up with two female staffers and Mike corralled a young man who had been with the senator for only a few months.

Mike asked, "You must know a lot of people in this town?"

"Yes, sir, I do."

"Can you tell me about a guy named James J. Callahan?"

"He's the Chief of Staff for Senator Baynes from South Carolina and a very powerful man."

"Why's that?"

"Why's what?"

"Why's he so powerful?"

"His boss is chairman of the Senate Arms Committee along with being a ranking member of the Senate Finance Committee."

"Would you have any idea why the senator would send his Chief of Staff to see Captain Stalwardt?"

"Probably because the senator didn't like some of the things Captain Stalwardt said in his speech today."

"How'd you like the speech?"

"Hell, I thought it was great. I wish more of the military people had guts to speak up to stop the war and let those hawks like Senator Baynes know how the military really feels."

"You mean nobody will tell him?"

"He's such a cantankerous and ornery old bastard he steamrolls over anybody who opposes him about the war. He'll most likely try to get Captain Stalwardt drummed out of the service."

"Hell, they just awarded him the Medal of Honor."

"It may not happen right away, but someday this man, along with a few others in the Senate that believe the war should go on, will try to destroy Captain Stalwardt's military career."

"You positive about that?"

The aide answered, "So much so that I know that's why you're all here tonight. Senator Williams is trying to prove to Captain Stalwardt that he's one hundred percent behind him and that the Senator will do everything within his power to protect the captain from having his career ruined because of the speech he made."

"How do you feel about the war?"

"This Vietnam war is dividing the country. Demonstrations against it are happening all the time and people are getting hurt here in the states. That's not right. If the people don't support the war then we should get out."

"How does your boss feel about your position?"

"Oddly enough, Senator Williams and the whole staff feel the same way."

"And what way is that?"

"If there's gonna be a war then let the military fight it, but if a civilian political system is gonna limit the military's involvement then we should get out. It's a no win situation. It's not so much that we don't believe in the effort to stop the communist movement, it's the tactical limitations that the present administration is forcing upon the military that's creating this static no win scenario. By sticking their nose in and trying to control the military situation they're causing unnecessary casualties and sending the American people the wrong signals. Hell, they're even lying about the war and think that no one knows what's going on. People aren't that dumb and the lies are gonna catch up with them someday. We don't blame the military. They're an innocent pawn in this whole political mess."

"Young man, I believe you've got a future in politics."

"You really think so?"

"I do. What's your advice about this Baynes character?"

"Steer clear of him at any cost. If he invites your friend to a meeting, don't go. Tell the senator anything, but don't meet with him. He'll only goad your friend into an argument then try to have him cited for some reason or other. My advice for him is to go home and start his convalescence leave as soon as possible. That way nobody can bother him. Perhaps in a few months the senator will forget about the speech and leave your friend alone for a while. But, someday he'll try his best to ruin your friend's career."

That night after Lance's family went to bed, he went to the hotel bar with Mike for a few drinks.

Mike said, "I was talking to the senator's young staffer tonight and he told me we should get outta town before tomorrow morning, and by all means not to meet with this Baynes character."

"I know," said Lance. "Senator Williams pretty much told me the same thing. I guess we'll leave as early as we can."

"Before ten I hope."

"Where you gonna be?"

"I've got some leave time so I guess I'll go up to Buffalo and see some old friends."

Lance looked at Mike and immediately knew the real reason for the Buffalo trip, to find out how his old fiancée was getting along with the man she married. Lance missed Alice and wished she had lived to share the moment of getting his medal.

Early the next morning, Lance and his family left Washington, D.C. and as the year before, he would spend the next six months on convalescent leave at home. At ten o'clock the two men who came to the room the day before arrived again.

When Mike answered the knock on the door the taller man said, "We've come to pick up Captain Stalwardt."

Mike smiled as he said, "Sorry, fellas, but he and his family left early this morning for Illinois. He's had a relapse and the doctor told him to get complete rest and quiet for at least six months."

The taller man asked, "Where can we get in touch with him?"

"He's on convalescent leave now, fellas, and can't be disturbed, doctor's orders. I'm sure you understand."

The smaller man stepped forward and with an angry tone said, "Yeah, we understand all right. That coward's gonna get—"

Mike didn't hear the rest because he slammed the door in the shorter man's face.

Chapter 8

Stateside

For the next several years, Lance attended military schools, including the C&GSC (Command and General Staff College) at Fort Leavenworth, Kansas, where after graduating, he received a promotion to lieutenant colonel. He served two years with the 24th Infantry Division as a battalion commander and then DA (Department of the Army) sent him to the Army War College at Carlisle Barracks in Pennsylvania. After graduation, he transferred to the Pentagon in Washington, D.C., assigned to a desk job doing routine staff work.

After a while, Lance's job at the Pentagon became so boring, he thought of retiring when he reached his twenty years of service. He missed the fast pace of combat action and considered becoming an advisor to a foreign ally, but strict laws prevented prior U.S. military personnel from hiring out as mercenaries.

One day he said to a fellow officer, "Maybe I'll just take my pension and find some civilian job that's compatible with my experience … maybe working for the military."

The other officer asked, "But wouldn't you be in the same boat you're in now?"

Lance then realized he would gain nothing by working for the military as a civilian and said, "I'd probably end up being more bored then I am now."

A few days later a telephone call changed his life. The secretary of his supervisor, Chief of Staff of Army Personnel, Lt. General Harry G. Warren, called and told him to report to the general's office as quickly as possible. Lance put down the papers he had in his hand and went to his boss's office on the next floor, wondering, *What the hell does the old man want now?*

As soon as Lance came through the door, the secretary motioned to him and said, "Colonel Stalwardt, you may go right in, General Warren is expecting you."

Lance thanked the woman and went into the office, stopped in front of the general's desk then reported.

"Sit down, Colonel," said General Warren, leaning to one side, looking behind Lance. The general continued while gesturing with his hand, "Mr. Hawkins is here from the White House."

Lance turned around in his chair and saw a black man he guessed to be middle age, dressed in an expensive dark-gray suit, sitting on a couch along the wall behind him with his legs crossed and his arms folded across his chest.

Lance returned his attention to his boss as the general spoke again. "Mr. Hawkins here tells me that the President has asked for you personally to be assigned to his staff, effective immediately. You're to report to the Oval Office tomorrow at ten hundred hours sharp. Don't be late." The general leaned forward and looked intently at Lance then continued, "That is if you're interested."

Good God ... what just happened?

He had no time to think about an answer. The man called Hawkins got up from the couch and without saying a word left the office and closed the door behind him.

The general dismissed Lance with a curt, "That's all, Colonel."

Lance felt his boss didn't appear to be at all happy with the situation so Lance left immediately without saying anything except, "Yes, sir."

He returned to his own office, taking the stairs two at a time and feeling as if he had been given a new lease on life.

When he arrived, he summoned the secretary he shared with two other officers and told her, "Edna, I've just been reassigned to the President's office. Isn't that something?"

He tried to hide his excitement, but couldn't.

Edna did not appear to be overly impressed as she said in a sort of nonchalant tone of voice, "That's nice."

She had seen it before, and became immune to the odd comings and goings of military personnel within the halls of the Pentagon. Her only concern, reach her retirement service date within the next few years so she could retire on a nice pension. Relatively young at 53 and single, she still had plenty of time to enjoy what she called, "The real life."

The next morning, Lance made certain he arrived in plenty of time to park his car, check through the security gate and get inside the White House. At ten o'clock sharp he stood in front of the Oval Office door, accompanied by a Secret Service agent.

After the agent knocked on the door, a voice said, "Come in."

The agent opened the door and escorted Lance into the room where the President sat behind a huge desk, talking with two men standing beside him, a four star navy admiral and the man Lance had seen the day before in General Warren's office, the one the general called Mr. Hawkins.

President Walker spoke when he saw the men enter the room. "You may leave us now, John."

Stopping, the agent with Lance said, "Yes, Mr. President," then turned and left, closing the door behind him.

Lance proceeded toward the President and came to attention about four feet from his desk, saluted his commander in chief and said, "Lieutenant Colonel Stalwardt reports, sir."

As Lance stood there looking at the President of the United States, elected only six months earlier, he couldn't help thinking, *The man looks younger than his pictures show. Hell, he's only a few years older than me.*

The young President returned Lance's salute then said as he rose from his chair, "Colonel Stalwardt, let me be the first to congratulate you on your being promoted to full colonel. I realize you haven't been notified of the good news yet because I wanted to tell you myself. Also, I wanted to present you with your first pair of eagles. Hawkins will pin them on for you."

Hawkins took the small box handed to him by the President and came up beside Lance just as he said, "Thank you, sir. I really don't know what to say."

"No need to say anything, Colonel Stalwardt, just listen," said the Navy admiral. "Here are your promotion orders. You'll need these to process your pay and all the other necessary paperwork."

As Lance took the papers from the naval officer, the man called Hawkins took off the silver oak leaves on Lance's uniform and replaced them with the eagles. When Hawkins finished, he handed Lance the small box containing the insignia of his former rank.

The President said, "This is Admiral Emerson, my National Security Adviser, and Mr. Hawkins here, you already know. Now gentlemen, shall we be seated and get on with the business at hand?"

They did not sit at the big desk, but instead the group went to an oval coffee table with four wingback chairs and sat down. The President offered each man a cup of coffee except Lance.

Instead, the President gave him a cup of tea and said, "I know you prefer tea, Colonel. Plain, I believe?"

"Yes, sir, that's correct," said Lance, somewhat amazed by the fact that the President knew he drank tea. He took the saucer and cup from the President then set them on the table in front of him.

"Colonel, you may be wondering why you're here," said the President. "Admiral Emerson, will you brief Colonel Stalwardt about our plans?"

"Yes, Mr. President, I'll be happy to," said the admiral as he put down his coffee cup and looked at Lance. "Colonel, to begin with, this will be a voluntary assignment. You don't have to take the job, but it'll be one helluva disappointment to us if you don't. Also, I might add that anything you hear in this room today is strictly unofficial and will be categorically denied if anyone learns anything about what we're planning to do. If you so much as breathe a word of what you're about to hear, I will personally cut off some important parts of your anatomy. Do you understand?"

"Yes, sir, I understand perfectly," said Lance as he squirmed and shifted his body slightly at the mention of the threatened injury.

"Good, just kidding, but this is a very serious matter that we are about to reveal to you. Now, let's get down to the crux of this matter." The admiral laid a single sheet of paper on the table, an outline for a very simple and concise plan. "Colonel, we would like you to organize a group of no more than fifty or sixty highly specialized military personnel. You will command and train this group for the purpose of special covert operations, such as the apprehension of federal criminals hiding in a foreign countries to avoid prosecution, rescue of Americans being held hostage outside of the continental United States, anti-terrorist operations and any military actions that may be necessary to destroy anything that threatens the national security of this country.

"These are the things that gave the last two administrations a real pain in the ass and we're hoping to avoid some of the political bullshit they had to go through. If we can nip these problems in the bud before they become an international incident, maybe we won't suffer the public embarrassment like they did. Do you understand why we want to create such a unit?"

"Yes, sir, but don't we have specialized forces already available for these type operations, such as the SEALS, the Delta Force and some of the other highly trained units?"

"Good point. I'll explain after you decide to accept our offer. First, let me say that if you do choose to accept the assignment, your orders will come to you directly from the President and no one else. He's the only one that will command your missions and no one will be authorized to countermand his orders or to give you a mission. Do you understand what I've said so far?"

"Yes, sir," said Lance.

"Before I continue, I must now ask for your acceptance or refusal. If you accept, I will continue. If you refuse, I will stop the briefing and you may return to your office in the Pentagon."

Intrigued by what he had already heard, Lance said without hesitation, "I accept."

"Outstanding," said the admiral with a slight smile on his face as he glanced over to the President then back at Lance. "Now, I'll tell you why you were picked for this assignment. We simply felt you're qualified to do the job. Your Vietnam War record certainly speaks for itself and almost all your previous superiors have mentioned in their officer evaluation ratings that you're very capable of commanding situations that are fluid and ill-defined. It seems you have a knack for doing the right thing at the right time with the least bit of information available. I must say, it took us almost six months to find just the right person for this job and when we came across your record we felt you were the perfect candidate. There's no doubt in any of our minds that you're the man to fill the position."

"Thank you, sir," said Lance, "I'll try not to disappoint you."

"I don't think you will, Colonel," said the President. "Please continue, Admiral."

"Thank you, Mr. President," said the admiral as he again turned to Lance. "Colonel, you will be given a blank check for putting this unit together. It's to be an ultra top secret unit, modeled somewhat like the SBS in England. Have you heard of them?"

"Yes, sir, but I don't know much about them."

"Nobody outside the SBS does," said the admiral. "However, we want your unit so secret that no one outside of this office will even hear about it, let alone know of its existence. Only those ultimately assigned to the unit are to know who and what they are. Each member of the group must be absolutely loyal, totally committed to military service and must be trustworthy enough so they won't tell anyone of their true nature. In fact, they're not to know of their exact missions until you are directed by the President to conduct an operation. Is that clear?"

"Yes, sir, very clear," said Lance.

"Now then," continued the admiral, "to answer your question about the other forces you mentioned earlier. All of them are too well known by congressional committees, the press and other governmental watchdogs and are far better suited to situations where we can exploit political issues through the media. The things we have in mind for this group would probably cause the type of people I've mentioned to interfere with our operations and they could possibly cause a costly delay or even the wrong outcome.

"Although we are not being illegal about the formation of this unit, there are some people that feel this sort of force is unethical. What we want is a unit that will be available for an immediate response at the direction of the President, and believe me when I say immediate … I mean right now, not two days later."

The admiral paused as if waiting for the President to say something, but when no comments came, the admiral continued. "We envision the group to be comprised of three or four separate autonomous sections each made up of tried and true combat veterans, commanded by the rank equivalent to a lieutenant colonel, with an O-four as executive officer. Each section will have within it, six to nine enlisted men no lower than the rank of E-six. You will establish a three member command section to include yourself, an executive officer, subordinate in rank, who is capable of acting as a field commander, and an E-nine for administrative purposes. The E-nine can be substituted for a veteran warrant officer if you prefer. Any questions so far, Colonel?"

"Yes, sir, you said an exec officer to act as a field commander. Am I to command this group or to train someone to command it?"

"Colonel, you're the group commander, however you personally are not to engage in any combat situations or endanger yourself whatsoever. That is, if any situations come to that. You'll be the only link to the President and no one, and I repeat, no one in the unit, or anyone else for that matter, is to know that your orders come directly from him. If anything happens to you, we'll worry about establishing contact with the group. There is also another reason. With you being officially assigned to the White House it would raise a lot of embarrassing questions if you were seen in the field with the unit. Do you understand our concern now?"

"Yes, sir."

The admiral continued, "Before you start hiring your section personnel, there are some prerequisites. They may come from any of the four armed services as long as they have proven combat experience and are dedicated military career men. They should be single with no living relatives, airborne trained and the more combat experience the better. Officers must be college graduates and the enlisted men should have at least an associate degree. All must be bilingual and be able to speak fluently in Russian, Spanish, Arabic or French. If they are foreign born, they must be able to speak another language other than their own mother tongue and English. Each section will have a minimum of three medically trained personnel with experts in demolitions, communications and all types of foreign weapons. Cross trained personnel would of course be the ideal choice. Any questions at this point, Colonel?"

"Yes, sir, you said they shouldn't have any known relatives. What about me? I have living relatives in Illinois."

"Remember, I said you will not endanger yourself so there is no fear of capture and retaliation. You will be the only exception."

"Yes, sir," replied Lance.

The admiral continued, "You and your staff will handpick those you believe to be the men who can best serve in this unit. We would like you to bring your staff people on board as soon as possible, say within a few days. They can screen records while you and I set up an overall training program to cover a general plan of operations, much like a basic training course. As I see it, special training can be planned for and conducted as each assignment presents itself."

"Admiral, won't this unit's make up and training cause suspicion somewhere in the higher command?"

"Good question, Colonel. We'll camouflage your group under an already bona fide unit then infiltrate your people in over a six month period by transfers and reassignments. Your group will be assigned to Camp David to beef up the military security force responsible for protecting the President. We're planning to create some kind of incident that'll sanction an increase to this already established force, hopefully without raising any suspicion. Then when the unit comes together we'll set up some sort of smoke screen training program so no one will suspect what we're really up to."

"Sir, why Camp David?"

"We feel Camp David is the ideal base of operations and training ground for your unit because it's out of the normal stream of things and probably the securest training site we could possibly use. It's the only site that is under the direct control of the President."

"Sir, if we're not going to become active for another six months, why start choosing people now?"

"We can give these people some special training without them even knowing they have been chosen for the unit. For example, we'll send them to the three month anti-terrorist school in England among a group of three or four hundred other men that are already scheduled for this training. Of course we know that not all the men you choose are going to work out so I suggest you initially choose at least three people for each slot.

This school will also act as a pre-screening process. After the training, each man you've selected for the group will be thoroughly rated as to first, second and third choice with only those of the first choice being asked to participate in the unit. This will of course be strictly on a volunteer basis. If there are not enough of those from the first choice level to make up the unit, then go into the second level and so on until the unit selection is complete. The remainder will make up a selection pool if any one member doesn't work out or has to be replaced for any reason."

"What if someone starts asking too many questions or becomes too concerned about their assignment?"

"You will not consider that person any further and immediately transfer them out. Does that answer your question?"

"Yes, sir," said Lance. "Am I the only one selected so far?"

"Actually, no," said the admiral. "We've preselected about fifty officers and about one hundred and fifty NCO's that we think might fit in with our plans. You'll be given a one page profile of their records when you leave. I would hope you choose the second in command from this group and the four section commanders. The others we'll leave to your discretion."

Lance had already selected in his own mind the command group he wanted and hoped the stack of files contained their 201 personnel folders, especially one name in particular.

His thoughts changed to the subject at hand and he asked the admiral, "Sir, it appears to me this type of unit would require a certain amount of specialized logistics. Is there a support plan already in place or will we have to conceive one?"

"Some things are already being prepared for as we speak. For example, you must be able to reach anywhere in the world in the least time possible. We've already requisitioned aircraft to support you. One Starlifter and one twin jet engine staff plane large enough to carry twelve people are already being outfitted. The Starlifter is being equipped with a complete soundproof command module with an array of communications equipment along with a fully operational galley and an interior redesigned for comfort so the men will be well rested when they reach their destinations.

"Crews for these aircraft will also be under your direct command and will be selected and trained using the same guidelines I outlined earlier. You will be expected to maintain a standby readiness to move within an hour's notice and be airborne no more than the time it takes to shuttle the group from Camp David to Andrews Air Force Base. That's where the aircraft will be based."

"Sir, won't that cause a problem with the command at Andrews? Won't they wanna know what's going on?"

"Not really. The command at Andrews is already under the direct orders informing them of these aircraft. The planes will be assigned into the presidential pool as are Air Force One and Two. Andrews already knows they will only be flown by a crew assigned to the White House, they won't interfere."

"Speaking of crews, sir, does that mean we must also provide our own ground support for the aircraft, such as the maintenance, fuel and on board supplies?"

"No problem. In this case the flight crew will double as the ground crew. Major maintenance will be carried out through regular channels. These aircraft will be guarded twenty-four hours a day, seven days a week and be prepared to fly when you arrive, the same as with the other aircraft in the presidential pool. Someone in your air group will be required to be on board the aircraft at all times so make sure you choose enough people for them to rotate. There are special locks being mounted on both planes so no one will have access to them, except those with keys, and only your people will have those keys. By the way, do you know anyone in the Air Force that would be a good man for the job of air support commander?"

"Yes, sir. He was an air liaison officer with the advisory group in Vietnam, a Captain John Slaughter. I don't know what his rank is now. Anyway, I think he'd be perfect for the job."

"Any idea where he's at?"

"No, sir. The last I saw or heard of him was in Vietnam.

"Okay. We'll have Hawkins track him down and let you know where he is. We'll let you contact him and give him the news."

"Yes, sir, I'd like that. Sir, I have another question. What about transportation between Camp David and Andrews?"

"You'll use three Blackhawk helicopters in good weather or two military buses during inclement weather."

"And crews?"

"You'll have to select shuttle crews to operate the equipment from your own personnel."

"All right, sir. That shouldn't be a problem."

"Now then," said the admiral, "if you have no further questions about transportation, I'll address a recommended organization."

Lance nodded.

"As I said earlier, your group will break down into a command section, four execution sections, and an aircraft support section. The command section I've already addressed. The execution section, or the main group, will be composed of sections made up into action teams. The air section you can organize as you deem necessary."

"What about logistics, sir?"

"As for logistics support, you will be sanctioned various items and materials that are not regular issue. They are not to be traceable … therefore these items will not be obtained through normal channels. You'll understand more as I run down a list of some of the equipment you'll be expected to use, such as silencers for the 9mm pistols with fourteen round magazines, the automatic assault rifles with special ammunition and laser sights. You will have Starlight scopes and night radar devices along with similar type equipment for conducting night operations. We want this group to be able to get in, accomplish their mission and get out without being detected and we feel the night operation is our best bet. On the other hand, if you're caught in a sticky situation we want you to be able to have enough muscle to fight your way out if the need arises."

"Sir, I now understand why there's a requirement for no living relatives."

"That's right, Colonel. We only want those who will be one hundred percent on the job at hand. No other distractions. That's why we want them handpicked."

"How will I be notified when I have a mission?"

"I was just about to cover that. We have a new communication device that we call a satellite transponder. It looks like a miniature calculator, is small enough to carry in a breast pocket and can reach anywhere in the world because it's satellite relayed. It's quite a unique device in that it sends and receives both digital and hard copy messages, can act as a beeper signaling device and can easily and quickly be set on any known radio frequency. The command frequency is classified and you won't be given the exact selection, but you'll be given a number that represents this frequency which has been preset and you will be expected to monitor it at all times either by beeper or by the digital channel. You, and each of your staff, including the air force commander, will be expected to carry this device at all times. There *will* be *no* exceptions."

"When will I be issued these transponders?"

"Tomorrow when you report to my section. You'll work out of an office in the White House for the time being until we get things coordinated better, then you'll transfer to Camp David for a short time, but you'll still be expected to maintain an office here in case we need you. Any other questions, Colonel?"

"No, sir, not at the moment."

"Good, that concludes the briefing for the time being. Mr. President, do you have anything you would like to add at this time?"

The President rose from his chair followed by the other three men then looked at Lance and said, "Glad to have you aboard, Colonel Stalwardt, and good luck. Mr. Hawkins will show you the way out."

Lance came to attention, saluted the President and turned to leave with Hawkins. Going through the door, Hawkins handed him two brown manila envelopes containing the files mentioned earlier and a security pass to allow him into the building the next day. He forgot to ask when he should report, but Lance guessed they left it to his own discretion. *Anyway*, he thought, *oh seven hundred should be about right.*

When he got to his car, Lance sat for a few minutes debating whether or not to open the large manila envelope containing the officer files or wait until he got back to the office. Almost without thinking, he opened it and quickly began searching the labels for the name he hoped would be there. About halfway through the stack he found the one he wanted—Polaski, Michael A., Lieutenant Colonel, USA, Intelligence.

Chapter 9

Lance drove back to the Pentagon, parked his car in the huge lot and headed for his office. Without going into details, he told his secretary Edna about his transfer to the White House staff and to prepare the paperwork for General Warren's signature as quickly as she could. He handed her the orders directing his transfer along with those for his promotion.

While Edna typed up the necessary forms, Lance packed his few personal belongings into two small cardboard boxes, set them on the floor near Edna's desk then made the rounds to visit his friends in nearby offices to tell them he was leaving. They all congratulated him on his promotion, wished him well and told him if he ever needed anything they would be more than happy to help him out.

He returned to his office where Edna handed him the papers he needed then she threw her arms about his shoulders, gave him a hug, kissed him on the cheek and said, "Good luck, Colonel. Give 'em hell," then returned to her desk in the outer office.

Lance went upstairs to see General Warren to report his transfer. "I'll be leaving right away, sir. They want me there tomorrow."

The general did not appear pleased by the transfer and said so. "Seems whenever I get someone capable of doing an outstanding job here, they yank him out from under me and I have to train new people all over again. Sometimes, Lance, I wonder if it's all worth it." The general stood up and extended his hand saying, "Anyway, there's no need for me to rain on your parade, so good luck and if you ever need anything, give me a holler."

"Yes, sir," said Lance, "I'll keep that in mind."

Lance left General Warren's office and returned to Edna's desk for his things. She wasn't at her desk so he picked up the boxes containing his personal effects, left the building and went to his car. He drove to his Arlington apartment, changed into running clothes and went on a ten mile run, feeling as if he could run forever.

That night Lance didn't sleep well because he kept churning over the events of the day and the possibilities of once again having a command. He couldn't get used to the fact that he worked directly for the President of the United States and the excitement kept him awake for most of the night. It all felt like a dream and he feared he would wake up at any minute. Then toward morning he slept, but only for a few hours.

The next morning, Lance arrived at the White House a few minutes before seven a.m. and while going through the front gate he saw Admiral Emerson turning into the drive. He went to the admiral's office a few minutes ahead of the admiral and concluded he guessed the correct timing.

After a few minutes with the admiral, Lance went to his new office, just down the hall and next door to the admiral's own office. It adjoined a special conference room used to brief the President on foreign and domestic events concerning national security matters every Monday and Wednesday mornings.

If a major crisis happened, such as a political or military coup, a sudden escalation in an ongoing conflict or any other business that may appear as a threat to the United States, the security people briefed the President on a daily basis, usually as things developed. The admiral instructed Lance to attend these briefings while in Washington and in some cases he would provide some input.

The admiral left Lance alone in his new office after a few introductions to other staff personnel. Lance thought, *One helluva lot better than what I've ever had before.*

Approaching the desk, he noticed four small electronic devices lying in the center—the transponder communicators that Admiral Emerson spoke of the day before. They lay on a single sheet of paper, describing the device and outlining its operation. Lance put one of the units in his left breast pocket, placed the others in the center desk drawer then sat in his chair to study the instructions.

When he finished reading the paper, he put it aside and opened the large manila envelope containing the officer files, pulled out Mike's folder, looked up the telephone number of Mike's station of assignment and dialed it.

After the second ring, he heard, "Lieutenant Colonel Polaski speaking, sir."

"Mike, this is Lance Stalwardt."

"Jesus Christ, ole buddy, you're the last guy I expected to hear from. How the hell are ya, Lance?"

"Fine, Mike, just fine. And yourself?"

"Well, I guess I'm about as bored as I can get. What about yourself? Last I'd heard, you were pushin' papers at the Pentagon. You still there?"

"No, as a matter of fact, I'm not," replied Lance. "I've just been reassigned and I need someone to do a job for me. Think you might be interested in coming to DC?"

"How long's it gonna take?"

"Well, at least a few days for right now. Then if things work out we can get you permanently assigned."

"What kind of job you offerin'?"

"Can't tell you on the phone, but if you wanna check it out, I'll send a plane for you. I can have you here by tonight and brief you in the morning."

"How the hell you gonna do that?"

"Simple, I just make a phone call to your HQ, they cut TDY orders, you get on the plane and come here."

"Hey, ole buddy, it just ain't that simple. What's the reason for the trip?"

"Can't tell you. It's classified."

"Okay, I'm game. Hell, if nothin' else it'll be worth the trip just to see you. When do I go?"

"I'll have a plane pick you up at sixteen hundred hours this afternoon. You'll get here around eighteen hundred and I'll pick you up when you land at Andrews."

"Sounds good to me. I'll see ya then, ole buddy."

They said their goodbyes and Lance hung up the telephone. He opened the other manila packet and looked to see if he could find a personnel folder for the next member of his staff, Command Sergeant Major Steven Diehl.

Sergeant Major Diehl worked in FORSCOM (Forces Command Headquarters), Ft. McPhearson, Georgia, and it took several tries, but finally he came on the line and said, "Command Sergeant Major Diehl speaking, sir."

Lance told the sergeant major the same thing he had just told Mike a few moments before.

CSM Diehl replied, "Sir, this sounds interesting. However, I cannot make the trip today because I have another commitment, but I can and will be there the first thing in the morning."

"That'll be fine, Sergeant Major."

"What time you want me there, sir?"

"Try to get to Andrews by oh eight hundred. I'll arrange for transportation to pick you up no later than fifteen minutes after the hour. Any problems with the time?"

"No, sir, none at all."

"Good, I'll see you in the morning."

After the telephone calls, Lance contacted the headquarters of each man and had their TDY orders cut by verbal order of the President. Then he made their travel and pickup arrangements.

He spent the rest of the day going over the files Hawkins gave him and concluded that most of the personnel for his newly assigned unit would be comprised from these men. However, he did not have personnel folders in the packet that Hawkins gave him of some officers' names that he thought had been selected.

Lance knew one candidate for the group that he served with while assigned to the 75th MACV in Vietnam. Born in Europe, the officer could speak several languages. He could converse in French, English and in some Asian dialects, and had a natural ear for learning a language. Lance wrote his name on a sheet of paper.

He started listing more names not included in the files he already had that he wanted to check out. By the end of the day, he had twelve people listed and gave them to one of the admiral's aides, asking to have their 201 records pulled and sent to him.

At six p.m., Lance stood waiting in the operations building at Andrews Air Force Base as the twin engine command jet touched down right on schedule then taxied up to the terminal's rear door.

As Mike got off the plane, Lance went outside to meet him and when Mike saw him, he waved and yelled, "Hey, ole buddy, how the hell ... OH SHIT! You're a bird." Mike saluted Lance and said, "Congratulations ... you more than anybody deserve a promotion."

Lance returned the salute then the two old friends embraced in a bear hug with a few back slaps, but Mike sensed then and there he would never again be able to call his old friend by his first name.

"Come on," said Lance, "I've put you up at the Blair House."

"Jesus, man, you'd think you worked for the President."

"I do."

"What?" Mike stopped walking and said, "You mean to tell me you're working for the President of the United States?"

"That's right, and tomorrow you'll learn all about it. Right now let's get you settled and go somewhere for dinner, my treat."

As they started to walk again, Mike said, "I'll buy the drinks since we haven't had a chance to wet the birds yet."

"It's a deal. I'll drop you off at the room and you can get into your civvies. I'll run over to my place and change then we'll hit the town. We'll have to do it pretty soft though, we have to be ready and alert for tomorrow."

While driving back toward town, Lance gave Mike a very short briefing about the nature of what the President wanted. "Once we're out of the car, we won't be able to discuss anything pertaining to this subject," said Lance.

"I can see why. I think this might be a bit illegal."

"Not really. We'll be used entirely in foreign situations. Not at home. In fact, I don't see any situation where we'd ever be used here in the states."

"You never know," said Mike as he gazed out the passenger's side window, "you just never know."

Lance dropped Mike off at the Blair House, went to his apartment, changed clothes and returned to pick him up, all within an hour. They went to dinner at one of the fashionable spots in town and for the next few hours caught up on the missing years of old friends and acquaintances.

Around nine thirty, Mike said, "I'm ready to call it a night and go to the room. It's been a long day for me."

Lance had made arrangements to pick up both Mike and Sergeant Major Diehl the next morning, and at exactly 0900 they arrived in his office. As the two guests looked around, Lance invited them to sit at the small conference table butted to the front of his desk. A moment later, one of Admiral Emerson's aides brought in coffee, tea and a few donuts.

Lance gave the two men the same introductory briefing he'd received two days before and asked, "Do you accept or refuse the position I'm offering you?"

Both men eagerly accepted and agreed to come on board within the week. The rest of the day they spent going over the file folders of the other candidates to determine if anyone could be a definite first choice. By the time Mike and the sergeant major had to leave, they had only selected three officers and ten enlisted men to the first group. They set the rest aside for classification until a later time.

The following Monday, Mike and Sergeant Major Diehl began their new assignments, ready to go to work. First, they selected the remainder of the first choice group then selected the second choice group and by the end of the week, they had tentatively completed their task. In all, they chose and categorized twenty-four officers and one hundred forty-four enlisted men. They completed the next step, cutting the orders on the chosen group and adding another one hundred and fifty other men, assigning them to the anti-terrorist school in England. It would be required training for everyone, including Lance and his two-man staff.

Students at the English school could not wear the uniforms of their own country, but wore a black coverall jumpsuit. Also, no rank insignia could be worn by the students because the student body consisted of soldiers from many free world countries and it would be difficult to recognize the many different uniforms and rank insignias. Another and more important reason for not displaying rank benefited the students during training. Fifteen men formed a training team and each student took a turn in doing each member's job within the team, including the leadership positions. It would be difficult for a sergeant in a leadership slot to directly order a ranking superior to do a particular job if the rank were evident. Without insignia, no one gave a second thought about it and carried on their duties as assigned by the school and the student leader.

For three months the men practiced various rescue techniques, planned raids and familiarized themselves with highly specialized weapons and equipment. After graduation, they all returned to their native countries.

Before the American students returned to the United States, Lance scheduled each of the first choice members to individual meetings with himself, Mike and Sergeant Major Diehl. Lance thought this would be the best time to offer the positions to the selected men since they would all be in one place and easy to contact. Out of the forty-four first choice group, only one enlisted man chose not to volunteer for the assignment. His second choice replacement accepted without hesitation.

Next, Lance scheduled a combined meeting with all the selected finalists, where Mike gave the briefing. They decided since he would be the field commander, he should start out addressing the entire group first. Although Mike did the talking, he made it crystal clear to the group that Lance would be in overall command.

While the group trained in England, the Air Force prepared a Starlifter, however, it didn't have a crew yet. Lance decided to wait until his return to the states before filling the Air Force personnel slots. He would offer the ranking job as first choice to Lieutenant Colonel John Slaughter, and if he accepted, he would be given the responsibility for choosing and training his own people.

While in England, Lance and his two staff members formed the new unit into four sections, with each section having a commander, an executive officer and three, three-man teams. Each section would have at least three men assigned to it that spoke the same foreign language and would have personnel that spoke all of the required languages. Each three-man team would be manned with an E8, an E7 and an E6 with all the special required expertise in demolitions, communications and medical.

The staff reviewed, selected and set aside each man's file many times over before Lance and his staff felt they had workable sections within the group. The long and arduous task finally finished the four sections became an active force. If any personality conflicts, training problems or other difficulties arose that put the program in jeopardy, the people involved would be replaced without a word of explanation, simply because there was no time for any other course of action.

After the English training the selected men reported back to their respective home units then prepared to transfer within a month.

When Lance returned to the White House, he convinced Admiral Emerson to shorten the transfer time frame from six months to one month, saying it would be detrimental to the morale of the men to wait the longer period. Also, it would cut down the risk of any man revealing his true assignment.

Within a week after finishing the anti-terrorist school, eleven men, designated Alpha section, arrived at Camp David. As the men of the remaining three sections came in at one week intervals, they too received designations, Bravo, Charlie and Delta respectively. By the end of the thirty day transfer period, all of the assigned personnel had arrived.

As each section arrived at Camp David, they began a six week training period of reconditioning designed to quickly bring the men into top physical shape, using the many hills and valleys in Camp David, the perfect terrain for the training Lance wanted. After a month of daylight training, the training switched to nights. Soon, all training would be conducted at night and in all weather conditions, including rain and snow. When not conducting outside training, the sections attended weapon seminars, learning about every small arms weapon ever made, from the most sophisticated automatics to crude muzzle loaders.

While the group trained at Camp David, the Air Force personnel trained at Andrews Air Force Base in Maryland. Colonel Slaughter accepted assignment and came into the group within two days after Lance made the telephone call. Colonel Slaughter, already stationed at Andrews, needed only a paperwork transfer.

After the first meeting with Lance, Colonel Slaughter had the entire air group assembled and began training within a week. Most of the people worked in some way or other for the new chief pilot, so he simply brought who he needed along with him. Slaughter had the air group ready in three weeks to fly whatever mission Lance assigned to them. Each member of the air group trained, cross trained, checked out and certified for their primary and secondary assignments. Soon, they would be put to the test.

At Colonel Slaughter's suggestion, Lance requisitioned another C141 Starlifter. It would act as a back-up and as a second aircraft if the entire group needed to conduct a mission. The group would be split into two flying elements and could still carry on a mission in case one of the planes went down, a safety factor that Lance thought a wise move.

Three months after the group formed, Lance prepared a surprise mission. He sent the entire group to Panama, assigning each section a separate objective. The group would make a night airborne drop with each section jumping into a different area then go after several small groups of drug smugglers that had set up operations in the jungle hills at various locations. Lance told neither his staff nor the group that it was a training exercise.

With a few minor mishaps, the exercise went as planned. Lance felt satisfied by how well the group did, but he had some concerns about the control of this formidable and powerful fighting force. He realized that such a force, controlled by the wrong person, could become a major tragedy, especially if used by someone for personal and political gain. Lance vowed that as long as he commanded the group, it would never be allowed to become an internal political force within the United States.

The unit's first real bloodletting came a week later.

Chapter 10

After the unit completed the Panama exercise, they returned to Camp David while Lance remained in Washington and reported their training progress and evaluation to Admiral Emerson.

After the briefing, the admiral said, "I want you to stay in town for a while and take a few days for some R and R. Have yourself a good time and relax."

"All right, sir," replied Lance. "How long have I got?"

"Be back here on Tuesday morning."

Lance spent most of his time off by doing nothing. He did a little cleaning in his apartment, did the dishes that hadn't been done for over a week, caught up on his laundry and on Sunday went to the Redskins football game, but mostly he did nothing. Tuesday morning he went to his office at the White House.

While sitting in his chair the telephone rang. "Colonel Stalwardt speaking, sir."

A voice answered that he had never heard before. "Colonel, report to the President's office immediately."

The phone went dead with an audible click then a dial tone buzzed in his ear. Lance hung up the receiver and went directly to the Oval Office, reported to the President and waited for a response.

The President rose from his chair, returned Lance's salute and said, "Colonel, Admiral Emerson tells me your group is ready. Is that correct?"

The admiral and Hawkins stood on one side of the President.

Lance still at attention replied, "Yes, sir, I believe they're as ready as they'll ever be."

"We'll soon find out, Colonel," said the President. "Please, have a seat. Admiral Emerson will fill you in on your first mission. Admiral, if you will please."

Both the President and Lance sat down while Admiral Emerson began speaking, "Colonel, we have a little situation that developed a few days ago that might be just the thing for your group. Our intelligence people have reported that a band of rebel guerrillas are holding four or five catholic nuns and a priest as hostages in a small Nicaraguan village in the hills along the Honduras border. All of the hostages are American citizens. It'll be your mission to go in with as many men as you need, rescue the hostages and eliminate the hostiles. You're to bring the hostages out and leave them with friendly locals in Honduras. The rendezvous location is included in the packet. Any questions about what we want you to do?"

"No, sir," replied Lance.

"Hawkins, would you please give Colonel Stalwardt the map."

Without saying a word, Hawkins handed Lance two high resolution photographs and a military terrain map with a small red circle around a wooded hilly area near the border of the two countries on the Nicaraguan side.

Lance studied both the photographs and the map for a moment then said, "It appears to be pretty rugged terrain, sir. Looks like there's too much jungle to make a jump. We'll have to walk in."

"We've anticipated that," said the admiral. "Arrangements have been made for you to land in Honduras and cross the border at the point marked in blue. We've got some National Guard people in the area on an annual training mission so we know the forces on the Honduras side are friendly. Also, the active army commander in that area has been notified to expect your people to pass through."

"Has he been informed of who we are and why we're there?"

"No. He was only told that you're a friendly force and that your planes will be in his area. You're not to contact him unless you run into trouble that you can't handle on your own, and if you need some heavy support to extract yourself outta there. They've got a few Cobra gunships and a platoon of Blackhawks on the ground, but you're not to use them unless you're in absolute danger of not coming out in one piece. Is that clear?"

"Yes, sir ... absolutely clear," said Lance.

"Hawkins will give you all the intel we've got as of now. You're to wait until you get to Camp David to open the envelope. I'm afraid you won't have much time to prepare for this mission, because we want you to leave as soon as possible. Any problems with that?"

"No, sir, I see none at the moment. I do have one question though. Does the media know what's happened?"

"I'm afraid they do, but we'll handle the media from here. Hopefully there's none at the hostage site and if you do happen to run into any foreign reporters just ignore them. Besides, you won't be in US uniforms so they won't know for sure who you are. Don't, under any circumstances, use anything that even remotely resembles US military issued equipment. This could jeopardize the peace negotiations that are going on down there."

"Yes, sir, I understand."

"Good, you better get started. You've got a lot of work ahead of you. The President's helicopter is outside on the lawn waiting to take you to Camp David."

Lance rose from his chair and saluted as the President stood.

The President returned Lance's salute and said with a broad smile on his face, "Good luck, Colonel."

Lance replied, "Thank you, sir."

While leaving the Oval office, Hawkins handed Lance a large manila envelope with the information and more maps he would need to conduct the rescue operation. He would not open the package until he landed at Camp David.

As Lance left the back door of the White House that led to the waiting helicopter, he took the transponder from an inside breast pocket and punched in a prearranged code, alerting both Mike and John Slaughter of a mission being initiated. Just before he boarded, acknowledgement signals came back to him indicating both men received the alert message.

During the short ride to Camp David, Lance began to feel the excitement rise within him as he mentally went over the pre-mission checklist. Because of the checklist being written, he felt there would be no chance of missing anything being implemented by Mike and the others, but as the overall commander of the group, he still felt responsible for everything on the list. He would follow up to recheck such essentials as rations, special weapons, ammunition and the nondescript uniforms, along with the other items needed to conduct the kind of mission the group had trained for.

When the aircraft landed on the Camp David helicopter pad, a jeep waited to take Lance to the HQ building just a few hundred yards away. As he entered the building he sensed excitement in the air as he saw the men of the group preparing to leave. He went immediately to the operations room where Mike, Sergeant Major Diehl and the four section leaders waited.

After Lance entered the room, the men seated around the table became quiet and rose to attention.

He looked at the six men, walked to his place at the table and said, "Be seated gentlemen."

The men sat after Lance took his chair.

"Gentlemen, this is it. This is not a training exercise."

As Lance finished his sentence one of the officers hit the table with his closed fist and exclaimed, "All right!"

The others looked at their fellow officer and smiled, knowing they all felt the same way, an inner excitement that could only be released through an actual combat mission.

Lance opened the sealed envelope given to him by Hawkins and continued, "We have been given a mission to rescue five or six hostages in a foreign country. They are a Catholic priest and some nuns being held against their will by an armed group of rebels in Nicaragua near the Honduras border."

As he spoke, Lance could see the eagerness in the faces of the waiting men, knowing the excitement to get started. Lance began by explaining the situation as briefed to him by Admiral Emerson, but at no time did he divulge where the mission came from or where he received the order, and no one asked. Every man in the room, as well as all the other members of the group, knew that to ask would most certainly end their assignment with the elite fighting force and possibly end their military career as well. Their job, act as a combat force and serve without question.

Within an hour the group boarded the waiting Blackhawks. The group left nothing behind. No equipment, clothing or even a scrap of paper, nothing to show the group had ever been at Camp David.

It only took a short time to reach Andrews Air Force Base and the waiting Starlifters. Colonel Slaughter had both aircraft manned, warmed up and ready to go, waiting for the group to board. He would personally fly the lead plane and no one could talk him out of it. Somehow John sensed this would be the group's first bona fide combat mission and he wanted to participate in it.

When Lance came on board he called the chief pilot to the command module and briefed him on the situation as he had done earlier with his staff and the officers at Camp David. The briefing took only a few minutes then John left the module and returned to the cockpit where he took the pilot's seat and continued the pre-flight check of the aircraft with his copilot and flight engineer.

Lance prearranged he would travel in the lead plane with the Alpha and Bravo sections while Mike and Sergeant Major Diehl would follow in the other aircraft with Charlie and Delta sections.

After everyone and the equipment boarded both planes, Lance went to the cockpit and said, "We're ready, John, let's go."

With a touch of excitement in his voice, the chief pilot said "Yes, sir." John then turned to the copilot and told him, "Captain, contact the tower and tell them we're ready to roll."

The copilot radioed the tower with a special code name provided in the information packet and received immediate permission to take off. John contacted the other Starlifter and within minutes, both C141's lifted off and on the way for the long trip to Honduras.

A short time after midnight, both Starlifters landed and taxied to a predetermined point on the end of the runway, well away from the main terminal and operations area. Mike deployed a security force around the planes as the men and equipment began to off-load.

Earlier, Lance approved a relatively simple operations plan. Alpha and Bravo sections, designated as the initial strike force, would assault the objective. Charlie section would be in reserve with a secondary mission of guarding the avenue of attack so the strike force could return on the same route as they used going into the hostile compound. They would also protect the rear area while the strike force entered the village.

At the opposite side of the small village, directly across from the strike force, Delta section would act as a blocking force, preventing anyone from going into or out of the guerrilla stronghold on the only other road leading into the objective. They would be positioned far enough away so they could not receive friendly fire and yet close enough to move onto the objective if called.

Intelligence supplied by the admiral indicated the compound had no more than ten guerrillas with the hostages, and only one or two actually on guard at any one time. The guerrillas held the hostages in an abandoned mountain village that would not be a formidable obstacle for the group. An old horse stable converted to drug manufacturing, a type of building that could not be easily defended, housed the hostages.

After the group unloaded everything needed from the aircraft, they left, heading in the general direction of the border crossing point. About two hours before dawn, the group reached the border and crossed into Nicaragua. Once inside hostile territory, the group became silent and ready for battle. They locked and loaded live ammunition, applied camouflage paint if it had not already been done and rechecked equipment to ensure readiness. Every man in the group became alert to the surroundings, ready to fight.

Just after sunrise the group halted and set up a defensive position in the jungle a few kilometers from their objective. Mike, along with the Alpha and Bravo section leaders, left the group and went to reconnoiter the village and the surrounding area. They would be back sometime during the late afternoon to report their findings to the rest of the group. In the meantime, Lance and the Delta section bypassed the village, trying to get themselves into position on the other side before dark.

The assault on the hostage compound would begin an hour before dawn the next morning. Until then, most of the men rested while a few stood watch, rotating in two hour shifts.

When the appointed time came the next morning, the attack went extremely well and as planned. Within seconds, Alpha team killed all twelve guerrillas inside the compound without any resistance and freed the hostages. The hostiles, no match for the group, had been taken by surprise.

The group suffered only one casualty, a grazing flesh wound to the right buttock of an enlisted man, caused by a ricocheting bullet. The minor wound would be no problem on the return march out.

During the actual assault, the whole operation seemed like a silent movie being run in slow motion. The weapon fire made little noise because of silencers, and even the wounded soldier did not cry out when he received his injury.

Usually, in heated combat by regular troops, there is confusion, yelling or shouting, but each man of the strike force conducted the operation in absolute silence with calculated precision, speaking only to report when they completed their individual tasks. Even then some men didn't speak, but signaled using their radios by clicking the transmission button a predetermined number of times.

During the initial attack, Delta section surprised nine guerrillas coming down from a footpath paralleling the road. The section members didn't know about the path, about 150 meters away from the village, until the guerrillas came off it and approached the road. The hostiles didn't know the section members lay hidden because of their camouflage and silence discipline then a hostile tripped over one of the men and all hell broke loose.

Within thirty seconds all nine guerrillas lay dead on the ground and the section members all alive with no wounds.

Immediately after the firefight a sergeant hurried to the section chief and said, "Sir, the hostile I checked is a female so we checked the others and they're all women."

The women all wore jungle fatigues, carried AK-47 rifles, a few grenades and each had a semi-automatic pistol.

Lance guessed they came to reinforce the guards in the village and felt it would have been more difficult for the strike force if they had been there.

When the all clear signal came over the radio, Lance and Delta section left the fallen hostiles behind and moved into the village. After checking the hostages to see if they could travel, the group left the area and headed toward the border. They crossed before noon and headed to a predesignated location to drop off the hostages.

After being freed, the priest and five nuns remained separated from the main body of the group during the long march back to the drop-off point. Four men of Latin American descent escorted the hostages and spoke to them only in Spanish to create the illusion they had been rescued by Central American forces.

When the group arrived near the rendezvous point, Lance halted them and told the four escorts to take the rescued clergy to the meeting place while the rest of the group remained hidden in the jungle and out of sight from those who waited. The recipients also believed someone other than the United States conducted the rescue.

Within minutes the four escorts returned to the group and they headed back to the airfield to the waiting Starlifters. An hour away from the field, Lance sent a signal by the transponder, letting John Slaughter know they would arrive within the hour and to prepare for takeoff. Lance wanted to get the group out of Honduras as soon as they got on board, and the sooner the better. If the planes left immediately after boarding, they would arrive at Andrews during the night and the group wouldn't be as noticeable when they off-loaded as they would have been during the daylight hours.

Once airborne, Lance began to go over in his mind what had just happened during the last twenty-four hours and like his experiences in Vietnam, he couldn't remember some of the details. His mind had partially blocked out the incident and left him with time voids. One thing he did remember, the cold, calculated effectiveness of the Delta group as it went about killing the nine female guerrillas.

For the second time since the group's creation, Lance had an uneasy feeling about its existence. He felt that whoever controlled the group had a powerful tool that could conceivably be used to control political structures throughout certain countries in the world and possibly within the United States. He knew there would be no problems using the group as a reactionary force against a terrorist type threat, but feared that using them for political reasons could very well cause some serious problems.

He recalled his vow after the training mission in Panama that he would never allow the group to become involved with internal politics and he would do everything within his power to keep that vow. He thought, *This group must never become involved in any type of power struggle within the United States.*

Chapter 11

Two Starlifters touched down at Andrews Air Force Base just after eleven p.m., perfect timing for Lance. His group would leave the base under the cover of darkness and proceed to Camp David where they would conduct a hot wash debriefing, hoping to gather as many facts about the rescue operation as they could. The information coming out of the debriefing would be used to brief the President and to compile a lessons-learned list so future operations could be improved in areas with shortfalls. The last man finished being interviewed just before dawn.

After eating a hot meal, the men rested until noon then went over the entire operation again to find out if anything of importance had been missed in the first debriefing. When through, Lance held a group meeting and told the after action highlights of the operation then opened it up to discuss the lessons learned. The few minor deficiencies the debriefings uncovered would be incorporated into future training sessions, hoping to eliminate the problems before the next mission. Lance knew he had an excellent combat force and it surprised him at how little the group would need to revamp their SOP (Standard Operation Procedures) training for future missions.

Four hours after the last debriefing session, Lance stood in the Oval Office giving the President and Admiral Emerson his after action report and presenting a few suggestions on future missions. Both the President and Admiral Emerson indicated their pleasure with the rescue operation and told Lance that nothing had reached the news media so far.

The released hostages told foreign reporters in Honduras that a Spanish speaking group, presumably local anti-rebel forces, freed them and brought them into Honduras. Although the Honduran government never knew officially, they secretly suspected that American forces conducted the rescue operation, but they never once mentioned to the press what they believed.

"Colonel Stalwardt," said the President, "you have done a magnificent job, and I for one am extremely proud of what you have accomplished." The President paused then continued, "I think you and the entire group deserve some time off. Take about ten days or so. There's a small place on one of the outward Hawaiian Islands that's isolated from the rest of the population. I have used the facility myself on several occasions and I've found it to be a very pleasurable experience. Of course you understand that you'll have to do this as a group. We cannot allow separate individual R and R just yet. You must all stay together, at least for the time being."

"Yes, Mr. President," said Lance. "I understand."

"When you get back we'll discuss another project that we have in mind for you, but don't worry about that now, just take the time off and relax."

"Yes, sir … I'll be back two weeks from tomorrow. Will I need to arrange for any provisions?"

"No. It's well stocked with good food and has plenty of liquid refreshments so feel free to indulge. Since you already have a few Air Force cooks, there should be no need for outside services."

"Will I have to provide security around the site?"

"I'll arrange for Secret Service protection so you won't have to bother about that. They'll be instructed not to bother you and your personnel for any reason whatsoever."

"All right, sir."

"Any other questions, Colonel?"

"No, sir."

"Then I'll see you when you return in two weeks."

"Thank you for the vacation, Mr. President."

Lance left the White House and flew to Camp David to tell Mike and the others about the President's sponsored vacation. The group needed a short vacation to revitalize their mental energy. They surfed, swam in the ocean, went scuba diving or just relaxed in general. Lance and Mike watched over the group like fraternity parents, making sure that no one individual became *too* relaxed, just have a good time.

After the vacation, and a day to settle in at Camp David again, Lance went to the White House and reported to Admiral Emerson. The admiral arranged a meeting with the President and at two o'clock the same afternoon, the usual four men met for the briefing of a second mission—a mission that would take the group halfway around the world to Africa.

Admiral Emerson gave the briefing. "There is a crazy man, who calls himself General Mamumba, and who is trying to overthrow the elected government of Liberia. No one seems to know what the guy really stands for, and like most revolutionaries in that part of the world, his rhetoric is mostly emotional, and to us it's a lot of gibberish. However, we do know he's starting to lean toward the communist party and we think he's getting arms and ammunition from the Chinese."

"I've heard of him, sir," said Lance. "I've also heard he's not the brightest guy in the world."

"That's true," replied the admiral, "but he's got some colonel who's running the show. His name is Abdul Mohammad Salazar … a graduate from Princeton University, trained in the military at Fort Benning's Infantry School and is an expert in terrorist tactics. He's the actual brains behind the overthrow. We think he's the one that engineered the attack on the British embassy and took the people inside as hostages. Both Salazar and Mamumba claim they had nothing to do with the embassy attack, but we're pretty sure they did. We've been coordinating with MI-Five in England and they tell us that our embassy is next on the Salazar hit list."

"And you want us to go in and stop it, right sir?"

"That's right," said the admiral, "but not in a way you may be thinking. Your mission is to go in with as few men as possible and eliminate Salazar and a few selected members of his staff. Without him, we think the revolt will collapse, and Mamumba will probably have to give up the fight."

Lance said, "If we get rid of the strongman and brains, the revolution should die a natural death … is that about what you had in mind, sir?"

"Exactly, Colonel. We're not targeting Mamumba, because if we take him out, Salazar would probably martyr the guy and then we'd have a real problem on our hands."

"If Salazar is eliminated, what guarantees do we have that an uprising won't be supported by the communists anyway?"

"From what information we've been able to gather, it seems that neither the Russians nor the Chinese want Mamumba around, so chances are they won't support him if Salazar goes. It was Salazar who cut all the deals so without him the whole revolution idea will likely fall apart."

"How good is the intel, sir?"

"I can understand your concern. We think our information is as good as there is because of an infiltrator on Salazar's staff. Hawkins has all the G-two for you."

Hawkins handed Lance a large sealed envelope as the admiral said, "After the material has been studied and your operation plans have been made, destroy every scrap of paper in that packet. Leave nothing behind."

"Yes, sir," replied Lance.

"How long before your group can be ready to go?"

Lance opened the packet and while glancing at the material he said, "It looks like there may be some special training involved here so I'd have to say a minimum of two weeks. After I've studied the material, and if we can leave sooner, I'll let you know."

The President said, "Gentlemen, if there are no further questions, I believe our meeting is finished. I have a scheduled meeting with two senators and they don't like to be kept waiting. Colonel, before you go, I would ask that you not become personally involved with this operation as you did with the clergy rescue. Your job is to plan and train your group, not to execute. Remember, people know you work here in this building and if you're seen in the field with a fighting force, they'll naturally assume we're involved. It's the very thing we're trying to avoid."

"Yes, sir, I understand, Mr. President."

Admiral Emerson said, "We've prepared a fact-finding junket for some of the political people, two of them are outside now. You will be accompanying them to Liberia and that will explain your presence in that country while your people are taking out Salazar. However, you will not become involved with the operation once you've arrived on Liberian soil."

"What if something goes wrong?"

"You will intercede only if the group or members of the group are captured and as long as they remain alive. Your mission then will be to salvage as many lives as you can through diplomacy. It will actually be the state department people doing the negotiating, but you'll be there to lend military knowledge and support because you know the mission. Under no circumstances are you to divulge to anyone what you have been assigned to do, not even our people."

"I understand, sir."

"Good," said Admiral Emerson. "Now, get going and call me tomorrow morning at nine."

"Yes, sir," said Lance as he saluted the President then left.

For the next two weeks the group trained in assaulting a mock command structure that resembled the overlay sent along in the intelligence package. The mission—kill Salazar and his four staff members then destroy the command compound. Again, as they had in Nicaragua, the group would be dressed in nondescript uniforms and using weapons similar to the Liberian government troops. It must appear as if the Liberian government initiated and conducted the raid. No evidence of any kind must be left behind that involves American soldiers in the death of the revolutionaries.

Two weeks after given the mission, Lance saw the group off at Andrews AFB and told Mike to keep him posted by transponder through a secret code they had devised. One word transmissions had various meanings, such as APPLE meant the group arrived safely in country, ORANGE meant a change in plans, PEAR meant everything is okay and going according to plan and so on. If Mike ran into any real trouble, he would send the word CHERRY.

Lance arrived in Liberia the next day with the congressional fact-finding group, the day of the planned attack. He had already received two messages from Mike, APPLE and ORANGE and he wondered what the change was. He knew Mike could handle the situation, but he couldn't help worrying.

Three days later, Mike sent the word PEAR, explaining after the operation, the reason for being late. Salazar and the command group were not in the complex at the time of the assault, so he waited for the rebels to return. When the rebels did arrive at the compound, Mike's group eliminated them without a fight.

The same day the group left Liberia, Lance returned to the United States alone, leaving the congressional entourage behind. After arriving at Andrews AFB, he went to Camp David and held a hot wash debriefing, finding very little that didn't go according to plan. They encountered only one minor problem—the rebels had not been at the complex at the prescribed time. The infiltrator did not have a chance or the time to pass on the information of Salazar's last minute change in plans.

Lance briefed the President, Admiral Emerson and Hawkins about the Liberian operation the same afternoon.

With a smile on his face, the President said, "We have conducted two operations and so far only one casualty and that was a minor wound, a bullet to the butt, I believe. Isn't that right, Colonel?"

"Yes, Mr. President," replied Lance.

"How is the young man's wound?"

"He's fine, sir."

"Gentlemen, this is outstanding," said the President, slapping his hand on the desk and quickly standing up. "Can you believe how we've changed the events of history? Hard telling how many lives would have been lost if Mamumba and Salazar had been allowed to come to power."

Lance had a strange feeling as he watched the President revel in the success of the moment. The President's face appeared to have a sense of power beyond describing, and Lance felt bothered by the President's actions, like a feeling of guilt. Then the moment passed.

"Colonel, I think you should know the informant who gave us the information about Salazar has escaped and is safely out of the country," said Admiral Emerson. "He was one of MI-Five's operatives in Liberia. Also, because of the unimportance of Salazar and the others to the press, the attack wasn't even publicized, and more importantly, it probably won't be. It seems only Mamumba is upset and evidently no one has paid any attention to his accusations that Americans were involved."

The admiral spoke the truth. What Mamumba said about the Americans being involved fell on deaf ears and soon his grip on the rebels broke. Later, the government of Liberia arrested Mamumba and tried him for treason, but instead of being executed they sent him to prison for life without parole. Mamumba lost his bid for power and Liberia soon became free from what could have been a long and bloody civil war.

After Liberia, the unit conducted four more operations in the following three years—one minor hostage rescue in the Middle East, then a raid that destroyed a suspected illegal nuclear construction site, and two more missions to eliminate background strongmen who lead aggressive forces trying to overthrow elected and recognized governments in two small African nations.

During this three year period Lance received a promotion to brigadier general and both Mike and John Slaughter became full colonels. Many of the group also received promotions to a higher pay grade. President Walker announced the promotions just before assigning a mission to Columbia, South America, to apprehend and bring back to the United States an escaped convict sentenced to prison by a U.S. federal court because of cocaine trafficking. On this mission the group suffered their first real casualties.

The fugitive, a Columbian drug lord, had a well trained security force prepared to sacrifice their lives for their boss. He paid his men extremely well and took care of their every need, issuing them the best military weapons and equipment to defend his stronghold. He spared no expense to maintain their loyalty.

Both Lance and Mike knew it would be difficult to recapture their target, but they figured it could be done. They also knew it might cost lives.

The night operation began well and went according to plan until a security guard accidentally stumbled onto the group as they began entering the fugitive's stronghold. The group had circumvented the electronic security devices without any trouble and almost got into position to start the raid when a guard decided to relieve himself in the bushes. Noticing something not quite right with the security fence, the guard quickly gave a verbal alarm a moment before a group member killed him.

With the rest of the compound alerted, security guards came from everywhere. Total confusion erupted as Mike momentarily kept the group in position trying to assess the developing situation. Finally, Mike gave the word and the group went about their assigned tasks with absolute precision. Within ten minutes they captured the drug lord. The two men assigned to guard the prisoner at all times had instructions to kill him if they were wounded or interfered with by any of the opposing security guards.

As the group left the area, a security guard, hiding behind a wall, fired his rifle into the group. The bullet hit a detonator and blew up a C4 package in a pack one of the men carried, killing him along with four nearby group members and wounding six others. No one would be able to identify the soldier carrying the explosives as an American so Mike decided to leave his body parts, but the group brought out the other four bodies along with the wounded.

After returning to the United States, the reality of losing five of their buddies struck the survivors, and for over a week they mourned the loss of their fallen comrades. It also reminded each man that at any moment during a mission any one of them could be killed.

Admiral Emerson called Lance into his office for a debriefing on the Columbian raid and to describe how they left the wanted man tied up on the steps of the American embassy in the early morning hours. No one inside the embassy saw the criminal being delivered. The embassy staff took the fugitive inside, identified him as the wanted man and returned him to the United States under the guard of U.S. marshals.

As Lance spoke, he noticed the admiral seemed inattentive and asked, "Sir, what's wrong? You seem preoccupied."

The admiral appeared to snap out of his thoughtful moment and said, "There's something important I need to discuss with you."

"Yes, sir, what is it?"

"I don't know how it happened, but there may be a leak in the group. If there is, we've got to fix it ... and fix it fast."

"I don't understand, sir."

"It seems that a few senators have been hinting to the President that they suspect an American force was involved with some of the past operations we've conducted. They can't find out where any known military unit has been legally sanctioned to conduct such operations and are suspecting the President of ... as one senator put it ... 'having a secret weapon'."

Lance looked at the admiral and said, "Sir, it seems that every time something happens in the world, we get blamed. Maybe it's because the rumors that come out of these countries trigger their suspicions. I know of at least a dozen cases where rumors have indicated that we were involved in a government overthrow, when in reality we haven't even been near the country."

"I know. I've thought of that too, but in any case, we've got to be extremely careful from now on and make doubly sure of our own security. Any future missions must be well planned and coordinated to ensure that no evidence exists of US involvement."

"There might not be a leak, sir. They may be just guessing because the President is running for reelection and they're trying to force something just in case they're right. However, I will check out all of my people."

For the next six months, the group stayed in Camp David except for a training mission to Panama. Lance, Mike and Sergeant Major Diehl went over each person's record to see if any information about the unit could have possibly been leaked. They checked and double-checked relationships. Each individual went through an in-depth background examination again with an investigation more thorough than the original. They examined everyone's movements, trying to find an exposure to an outside source, especially to anyone from congress. After completing the investigation, Lance felt satisfied none of his men had been disloyal.

As it turned out, the origin of the suspicions came from another source. The congressmen, who were trying to find out if a secret group existed, tried to tip the President's hand hoping to discover if the group did in fact, actually exist. After a few months of negative results, they finally gave up their overt probing. Lance suspected that politics prompted most of their investigative activities because of the young President running for reelection.

Chapter 12

Present Day

A flight attendant snapped Lance back into the present, waking him up as she shook his shoulder slightly and said, "Sir, please place your seat into the upright position, and fasten your seat belt. "We'll be landing in Chicago shortly."

Lance set the seat up, tightened his seat belt then shook off the drowsiness and the flashback dreams. He looked at his watch and thought about the young jeep driver who presented it to him. He treasured the watch as his most prized possession, mostly because of the inscription on the back, *To Capt. Stalwardt, From the men of Bravo Troop*.

"It's one thirty, Chicago time," said the man next to him, "and we're gonna be on time for a change."

"Thank you," said Lance as he looked over at the man next to him sitting in the window seat with an empty seat between them.

The man asked, "You gettin' off here in Chicago or are you going on to New York?"

"No ... I'm getting off here."

"Business or pleasure?"

"Actually I'm going home to see my family," said Lance as he realized that he sat near the man during the whole flight and they hadn't spoken a word to each other.

"Your folks?"

"Yes," replied Lance. "I have a daughter and her family that I haven't seen for awhile. Besides, I really need a vacation. I haven't had one for quite some time."

The plane landed smoothly, taxied to the gate and parked. After a few moments of crew preparation, the passengers deplaned.

As Lance went through the waiting area and into the terminal corridor he could feel the pressure of the enormous crowd inside the building. The place seemed like a madhouse of noise and activity. People began shouting, running and hurrying everywhere at once.

He had been in O'Hare many times and each time it always seemed the same no matter what time of the day or night.

It's true, thought Lance, *this is the busiest airport in the world. It's also the noisiest.*

Lance turned into the corridor leading to the main terminal and because of his military training, he instinctively glanced around. He remembered an instructor's words from his earlier days in survival school, "Always survey the terrain before you move."

While his eyes swept the surrounding crowd, he noticed a man leaning against the far wall with one foot on a suitcase, lighting a cigarette. The man turned and their eyes met for a fraction of a second. Lance nonchalantly looked away, but a subtle reaction in the man's eyes alerted Lance's sixth sense. Then he consciously registered the man's features in his nearly photographic memory, *Five feet ten, about a hundred and seventy pounds, blond short hair, medium build, wearing a tan jacket, faded jeans, Nike running shoes and a large silver ring on his right hand.*

As Lance hurried along with the crowd to the baggage claim area, he saw the blond man pick up the suitcase against the wall and start to follow about ten meters behind. Moving along the large concourse, Lance could look into several glass fronted posters that protruded at an angle from the walls in the corridor. Each time he looked into one of the posters he saw the blond man's reflection still behind him.

The walk to the baggage claim area took about ten minutes and when Lance arrived at the carousel, he could no longer see the man with the blond hair, but he could feel his presence. As he waited for his luggage, Lance thought, *He's around somewhere, but why? Why is this man following me? Or maybe I'm just being paranoid.*

A few minutes later Lance retrieved his two bags and went to the Hertz rental service desk to pick up the keys to a car he reserved from San Francisco. He felt he shouldn't impose on his relatives for transportation, primarily because he didn't know for sure where he would be going or when. It might not always be convenient for his sisters or his brother-in-law to lend him their cars or to take him where he wanted to go.

After flirting for a few moments with the woman behind the counter, Lance started for the rental agency bus that would take him to the parking lot to pick up the rental car. Outside the terminal doors, Lance stopped for a moment and casually glanced up and down the sidewalk. Just before he started for the bus, that peculiar feeling, that sixth sense, came over him again, same as it had when he saw the man with the blond hair inside the terminal.

Lance casually glanced around behind him and noticed a man standing against the wall, just to one side of the doorway—not the blond man this time, but someone else. His gaze didn't stop, but continued to sweep the area. Lance had seen the man somewhere before, but for that split second he couldn't remember where. He judged this guy at six feet and a hundred and ninety pounds. He had balding dark hair, wore a suit and tie, beige raincoat, sun glasses and from the bulge on his left front hip he looked to be carrying a weapon. Lance thought, *Whoever you are Mister, you've got federal agent written all over you.* Then it came to him. *DC, that's where I've seen him. Yeah, that's it. He's either FBI or Secret Service.*

Boarding the bus, Lance showed no signs of recognition or concern. He put his baggage in the storage racks inside the bus and sat in the rear seat where he could get a better view of the man on the sidewalk. Looking out the bus's rear window, he saw the man hurrying across the street toward a black car parked in front of a NO PARKING sign. A passing blue van blocked his vision then as the van with two men in it cleared, he saw another man, sitting inside the black car as the first man got in on the passenger's side.

There are two of them, thought Lance. As the bus pulled out from the terminal, the black car followed a short distance behind.

When the bus arrived at the rental car parking lot, Lance didn't see the black car, but figured they had to be around somewhere. He got off the bus, went to the rental car and got in. He sat for a moment contemplating the events that just happened.

After starting the engine, he mumbled, "Why the hell are these people following me? That is if they *are* following me."

Leaving the rental car parking lot, Lance headed for the Northwest Toll Way and took the exit for Rockford. After he cleared the second toll booth on interstate I-90, he spotted the black car he'd seen at the terminal. It remained a discreet distance behind, but Lance knew it was the same vehicle.

These people are definitely following me. What is happening here? Whatever it is I'll have to wait until I get to Lynn's then make some phone calls and find out what the hell's goin' on. Why did I pack my transponder in the flight bag? Stupid thing to do.

First, he would call Mike and see if he knew anything. If that didn't turn out, he would make a call to the White House and ask Admiral Emerson or if he had to, he would call the President. He had only called the President personally on two other occasions, once when an American planeload of soldiers crashed from a bomb explosion and the other when rioters threatened a Middle Eastern American embassy.

Just calm down now, he thought. *They're staying back a ways and it doesn't seem like they want to catch up so just relax for now. There's another hour to go.*

Arriving at his daughter's house just before dinner, Lance knew she would be expecting him because he had called her from San Francisco and left a message on her answering machine at work, telling her the time he would be there.   Lynn and Gordon greeted him, a hug and a kiss from his daughter and a vigorous handshake from his son-in-law. As he came from the hallway into the kitchen, Lance saw for the first time his baby granddaughter, Meredith.

She came toddling out from the living room, stopped, looked up at the strange man before her and ran headlong to her mother with her little arms outstretched. When safely in her mother's arms she turned and gave the man a quick look then buried her face into her mother's neck when she heard a strange voice speak to her.

"Hi there, Meredith."

She raised her head and looked again at the strange man, then to her mother who smiled at her and said, "This is your grandpa, shy baby. Can't you say hi?"

The child shook her head no and buried her face against her mother's neck once more.

"Here, Gordon, take the baby and I'll show dad to the bedroom before I get dinner ready. You hungry, Dad?"

Lance heard for first time the word dad and a strange feeling came over him like a wave of remorse. She had never called him dad before, usually daddy or papa or pops, and to Lance the words were little more than names, but now the word dad had an emotional punch. He felt as if he had been left out of something and missed a very important part of his life.

Although Lance maintained contact with his daughter through letters and a few phone calls now and then, he never really felt a whole attachment to his daughter until this very instant. He sent her gifts each year for her birthday and Christmas, and attended both her high school and college graduations, but he wasn't there for her first date, her first prom, her first day of womanhood or the day she got engaged to be married. In fact, he missed the wedding, but he did make it in time for the reception. He felt a sudden sadness for having missed all of those things which are important to a young girl who is growing up.

He thought, *Now my little girl is a grown woman with a little girl of her own.*

"Yes, I sure am," he said as he followed his daughter into the bedroom off the hall across from the bathroom. "I slept a little on the plane and didn't get a chance to eat lunch."

After he set his bags on the floor, Lynn gave him another hug and with tears in her eyes she said, "It's good to have you here, Dad. We're so glad you came."

Lance held his daughter for a moment and thanked God that she was allowed to live through the ordeal that took his wife. He dearly loved his daughter and felt he made the right decision to stay one night with her.

Slowly she pulled away and wiped the tears from her face then said, "I'll go fix dinner now so you can have a little time to freshen up. We'll talk later."

She turned and hurried from the room.

As he unpacked a few things from his flight bag, Lance looked out the bedroom window and saw the same black car that followed him from the airport about half a block away parked up the street.

At the same moment he recognized the car, Gordon turned on the television and Lance heard the news report of the assassinations of the President and some of his close advisers. Stunned by what he just heard, Lance stood for an instant almost as if frozen to the spot, then his senses returned and he hurried to the living room where Gordon sat on the floor playing with Meredith.

"Gordon, what's this on TV?"

"Haven't you heard? The President and some other people in DC were killed this morning."

"My God, the President's dead? When exactly did this happen?"

"Just shortly before noon."

"Who are the others?"

"I heard one was an Admiral Emerson, the President's National Security Adviser."

"Aw god no!" interrupted Lance when he heard the name of his boss and close friend. "Who else?"

"The Attorney General, and I think the President's own personal secretary. I can't remember his name."

"Gordon!" exclaimed Lance. "I gotta use a phone. Have you got one where I can talk in private?"

"Sure thing, you can use the one in my office. It's downstairs in the basement."

Lance turned and left the living room, hurrying through the kitchen and down the stairs. When he got to the office he picked up the phone and called Mike at Camp David.

Mike answered the phone after the first ring, "Colonel Polaski."

"Mike, this is Lance. What the hell's happening?"

"Jesus Christ, General, am I ever glad you called. I've been trying to get ahold of you all day. Do you know about the President gettin' shot?"

"I just heard it on TV."

"When you never answered the transponder messages, I thought whoever killed the President might've gotten you too. It seems like it was all his close people that got it. They even went after the new Vice President."

"Did they get him?"

"No, sir, he wasn't home. I think the TV said he was on a farm in Illinois somewhere."

"How many are dead?"

"Ten that I know of for sure and four wounded."

"Ten dead?"

"Yes, sir, after we heard the President was killed we found two dead civilian guards here at the front gate shot in the head. I think they may be part of it."

"When was this?"

"Just after I got the word on the transponder that the President had been killed. We came outta the field and found them dead."

"Who sent you the message?"

"I don't know who it was, there was no signature code. At first I thought it was you, but then I remembered you were at the Presidio and it couldn't have been you."

"What about the rest of the civilian guards?"

"Can't tell, General, there's nobody around. It's like they've all disappeared. I've set up a security watch around the billets just in case whoever was here might come back."

"They were in the billets?"

"Yes, sir … it seems like they were snooping around inside while we were in the field. Good thing we take everything with us. It's spooky, General, and I've got no idea what the hell's goin' on."

"Me either, Mike. Have you heard from John?"

"Yes, sir. He called me a few hours ago and said some Air Force two star with about fifteen men tried to board the Starlifters. Of course they didn't get on board because the doors have those special locks, and John told him the officer who had the keys was over at the Dover Air Force Base and wouldn't be back until tomorrow. The general told John to have the doors opened by tomorrow noon or he'd have him arrested and court-martialed."

"Mike, there's something very strange going on here, and I think we're part of it. I want you to get ahold of John and prepare for a flight out as quietly as possible. Do it on a secure line. Meanwhile, you gather up everybody there, go to Andrews and get on board the aircraft as quick as you can. I want all of you out of there within two hours and be here in three and a half. I want the unit with me until we can get a handle on this."

"Where do you want us, General?"

"Right here in Freeport, Illinois, Albertus airport. The runway's long enough and it has a hard surface. Tell John if anybody questions him while he's landing to use some excuse of mechanical trouble. When you land, I'll be about a hundred meters north of the north south runway parked on the road. Meet me in the car."

"Yes, sir."

"I want you to tell John to park the planes on the north end of the airport. And Mike, before I forget it, give me a quick three beeps on the transponder when you're airborne."

"Yes, sir, anything else?"

"Just one more thing, I think it would be better not to tell anyone else in the unit about what's going on until you're out here. Besides, they're used to going places without being told."

"Okay, General … you gonna be okay?"

"Yes, I'm all right. I'm at my daughter's place. I'm staying here for the night. You better get going. And Mike, good luck."

"Thanks, General."

"Goodbye, Mike," said Lance.

"Goodbye, sir."

Lance had purposely not said anything about the encounters with the men at the airport in Chicago and the black car now sitting outside just up the street from his daughter's house. He also didn't tell Mike he believed it involved more than just the killing of the President. It might even mean more, an attempt to overthrow the government itself. He thought, *It may not be as impossible as it sounds, especially if there were military involved, and who better than the Air Force.*

The most important reason for getting the group to Freeport, Lance wanted to keep the unit control out of the hands of anybody who would use it for political gain, especially for exploiting its military power as an assassination group. He didn't worry about Mike getting the men and the aircraft to the airport as he requested. Mike had moved the group many times before in both practice and in actual missions without a foul up. But he did worry about the Air Force general nosing around the aircraft.

Although all operations personnel at Andrews knew the planes assigned to the President had top priority clearance for takeoffs and landings, Lance worried that with the President dead, those priorities might have been rescinded by the Andrews high command.

He turned out the light, left the office and went upstairs to the others. As he came into the dining room, Lynn and Gordon already sat at the table.

"Come on, Dad … sit down," said, Lynn motioning to the chair next to her."

Lance couldn't remember the last time he had such a good time at dinner and told his daughter so. After getting up from the table he looked at his watch. *About two hours and forty-five minutes to go before they touch down*, he thought.

Lynn asked, "Is there anything wrong, Dad? You've looked at your watch about ten times in the last half hour."

"No, not really," Lance lied. "It's just that I'm usually working and when I've got something to do, I don't notice the time as much."

"We've got a movie to watch. All that's on TV is boring stuff since the President being killed." Lynn handed him a movie cassette and asked, "Have you seen this one?"

"No, I haven't," said Lance as he looked at the label then handed the cassette back to her.

They went into the living room and for a short time, Lance became occupied by the movie. An hour later the beeper in his shirt pocket went off with three quick beeps in an almost inaudible tone. Lance thought, *So far so good.*

By the time the movie ended, Lance thought, *How the hell am I gonna shake those guys in the black car when I go to the airport? I also need to start thinking of some excuse to give Gordon and Lynn about going out.*

Before Lance could say anything, his daughter said, "Dad, I just need to run to the store for some ice cream and a few things for tomorrow. Can I borrow the rental car? My car's in the garage and I don't wanna get it out."

Lance almost couldn't believe what he heard. *This has to be a godsent opportunity.* "Here're the keys," he said as he reached in his pocket and placed them on the table in front of him.

He knew when she left in the rental car the men in the black car would follow. In the dark and from where they sat parked, they wouldn't be able to see clearly enough to determine who got into the rental car.

It happened as Lance predicted. He stood by the living room window, watching as Lynn left the driveway and drove toward the store. A pickup truck, two cars and a blue van came from other direction and as they passed by the parked black car, it swung out and followed her.

Once out of sight, Lance turned to his son-in-law and said, "Gordon, I need a favor."

"Sure thing, what is it?"

"I'd like to borrow your Jeep Wagoneer for a few hours. I just remembered something important and I have to leave right away. I don't think I can wait until Lynn gets back. Do you mind?"

"Not at all. The keys are on the wall by the back door."

Lance went to the bedroom, put on his shoulder holster and pistol then slipped on a jacket to cover the weapon.

Going out the door he said, "Good night, Gordon, I'll see you in the morning."

In less than two minutes, Lance headed for the airport. The men who followed him from Chicago didn't have a clue that he left the house. He arrived at the meeting spot, parked, turned off the lights and waited.

Should be here soon, he thought.

Ten minutes later he saw the landing lights of the two jet aircraft come on about five miles out from the end of the runway as they turned on a long final approach from the south. *Good ole Mike. He's one helluva soldier.*

Minutes later both planes touched down and taxied to the end of the runway about a hundred meters away. Lance knew Mike could see the car from the air and within minutes a dark figure came toward the car.

Mike opened the door, got in and said, "Damn, it's sure good to see you, sir."

"Same here, Mike," said Lance as he took hold of his old friend's hand and shook it. "How was the flight?"

"The flight was okay, but gettin' out of Andrews was a bitch."

"What happened?"

"When John asked for clearance, the tower wouldn't let us go. They started jackin' us around so John pretended to have radio trouble and told them he was assuming they gave approval as usual and we just took off. He headed out to sea over the Atlantic then flew north into Canada. We came down outta there on the deck, right over the middle of Lake Michigan until we got to Chicago. John figured with all the air traffic around there the military radar wouldn't know which one we were. We don't know if it worked or not, but so far there doesn't seem to be anybody chasin' us and there wasn't any radio traffic asking who we were."

"Good. Now, have you got your small radio with you?"

"Yes, sir, right here."

"Call the plane and have them send us two men. Tell them to leave their rifles and bring only their sidearms. Also, tell John to shut down and get some security out."

"Security's already out."

"Good."

Mike transmitted the message to the plane and in a few minutes, two men arrived out of the darkness and got into the back seat of the Wagoneer. Lance started the Jeep and drove back toward town, relating the incident of the two men in the black car and how they followed him from O'Hare to Freeport.

"We're on the way to find out what the hell's going on with these two," he said. Then Lance instructed the men in the back seat as to what they should do when they arrived at their destination, the black car. "I want the two of you to take the men in the car. No shooting if you can help it. I definitely want these guys alive."

Lance turned the last corner before his daughter's house and came up from behind the spot where he last saw the black car. There it was, just as he thought it would be.

As they passed the car, Lance quickly pulled the Wagoneer into a driveway, but not all the way, just enough to block the front of the other vehicle. As soon as he braked to a stop the soldiers in back quickly got out and pulled the two men out of the black car. Half asleep and taken completely by surprise, they didn't resist.

Walking up to where the four men stood, Lance collected the weapons and wallets of the two prisoners. He told one soldier to take his prisoner to the Wagoneer, the other soldier to get in the front seat of the black car and have his prisoner drive.

Lance said to Mike as he started to get in the back seat of the black car, "Mike, you drive the Wagoneer and go back to the plane. We'll follow."

"Yes, sir," said Mike.

On the way, no one said a word, but when they arrived at the airport and turned out the car lights, the man Lance had seen in Chicago outside the terminal asked, "What're you guys gonna do with us?"

Lance said nothing. *Let the bastard sweat,* he thought.

The six men got out of the two vehicles, went to the lead plane and boarded. The guards put the two prisoners in the command module while Lance and Mike went forward to the cockpit to see John Slaughter.

The Air Force colonel said, "Good to see you again, General, especially after what's been happenin'."

"Same here, John. I hear you had a little trouble."

"Nothin' that we couldn't handle, sir. Looks like you got some of your own."

"I don't know yet. Come on back to the command module with me and let's see what these two guys have to say."

The chief pilot asked, "Who are they?"

"Their IDs say they're White House Secret Service."

Mike asked, "What the hell they after you for?"

"I don't know," said Lance, "but I'm sure gonna find out."

The three men went into the soundproof command module, closed the door and sat down. Mike and John sat in the booth type seats blocking in the two agents.

Lance sat on the end chair, looked at the two men and asked, "Gentlemen, what's going on here?"

The agents looked at each other and then the older of the two spoke. "Well, General, as you already know, we're Secret Service. We're assigned to the White House."

"I know every agent in the White House. How come I don't know you two?"

"We've been assigned to retired US Presidents and just recently to Vice President Mitchell in the hospital."

"So, how come you aren't in DC?"

"When the President was killed, we were sent to Chicago and told to wait for you."

"What for?"

"We're supposed to just keep an eye on you, that's all."

After a long pause Lance said, "That's it? You were only to keep me under surveillance?"

"Yes, sir, that's all we were told."

"Who gave you these orders?"

"Our supervisor, Walter Bradley."

"Did he tell you why?"

"No, sir. We just thought they wanted you protected because so many of the President's people were killed when he got shot."

"What other instructions did he give you?"

"Just to call in and let him know where you are. Honest, General, that's all."

"This is Saturday. When's your next call due?"

"We don't have a schedule, but I think it's probably expected sometime tomorrow morning."

Lance felt the man told the truth. Then he said, "Okay, I don't have time to check this out just now so you two are gonna be guests of the United States Army for a while." Lance turned, opened the door and said to the guard standing outside, "Take Agents Hickman and Andrews to the back and make them as comfortable as you can. They can use my cubicle."

"Yes, sir," replied the guard.

"You boys have dinner yet?"

"No, sir, we didn't have time."

"Okay," said Lance. He turned again to the guard and said, "Get them something to eat while they're back there."

After the guards took the agents, Lance said to the two officers, "Now that those two guys are off of my mind, I can think better."

John asked, "Do you believe these guys had anything to do with the assassinations?"

"No, I don't think so," said Lance. "If that were the case, they would have done something long ago." Lance thought a moment then turned to Mike and said, "Mike, shuttle the men into town in the government vehicle and get rooms at the Motel 8. It's just across from McDonald's on Highway 26 and the Route 20 beltline. We came by it on the way out here."

"Yes, sir, I remember seein' it."

"Civilian clothes and sidearms only. I don't want anyone to know we're Army. Not yet anyway. No bars and no booze. They know the drill. God knows we've trained enough for it."

"What if they don't have room there?"

"If you have to spread out, I want some tight coordination."

"You got it, General."

"And Mike, better keep four of your men on the plane to watch our guests. John's people will have enough to do without having to babysit those two."

"Why we keepin' them with us?"

"They may come in handy later on."

"Yes, sir."

"John, I want you to take both planes to Truax Field in Madison and park them in the Air National Guard sector for a while."

"How long you want me to stay up there?"

"I don't know yet, but it might be for a while. If you're up there, it'll be harder for anyone to notice because you'll be among other military aircraft. Here, you'd stick out like a sore thumb."

Mike said, "What better place to hide a tree than in the woods, right?"

"Yes, sir," replied the chief pilot. "I'll use the excuse that I'm on a training mission and shoot some landings. After I do a few, I'll develop some kind of mechanical problem. That'll keep anybody from asking too many questions."

"Good idea, John. One other important point," said Lance. "If either of you need to reach me, don't use your transponders with the existing codes. If somebody is on to us then it's a safe bet they already know our codes. We'll use landline or the small radios for the time being. For you, John, the transponder is our only link. If you need to reach me in a hurry, just transmit in hard copy one word

… Help. Then come here. Also, if someone tries to get to you while you're in Madison, just fly outta there and get here as fast as you can. My signal for you to come will be one word … come. Any questions?"

Both men shook their heads. Then he added, "It's a live mission guys so keep on your toes and be ready for anything. Hard telling what we're up against here."

The three men got up from the table, left the command module and shut the door. Lance walked around inside the plane for a few moments speaking with the men in the group. After fifteen minutes, he left the plane and drove back to his daughter's house.

On the way, Lance thought about what had just happened and knew that he ran a risk by keeping the two agents as prisoners. *I have no other choice until I find out what's going on. Besides, they'll probably check out all right.* Lance had many contacts in the intelligence community and he knew he could probably find out tomorrow what he needed to know. *Right now, I just want to get back to Lynn's and get some sleep.*

When Lance arrived at the house his daughter and Gordon had already gone to bed. He pulled into the driveway and parked the Wagoneer inside the garage, turned out the lights and for a moment everything went pitch-black. As he got out of the Jeep, a strange feeling came over him, a nagging sensation like he had missed something and once inside the house the feeling still bothered him.

He just couldn't shake it.

Chapter 13

Lance didn't sleep well that night. He kept waking up with the nagging feeling he'd forgotten something. With the two Secret Service agents in custody, he had time to think about it more. He realized something bothered him all day, ever since he left Chicago, but he couldn't quite figure it out.

That's the way Lance's nearly photographic mind worked. The eyes and ears would see and hear things then the subconscious would haunt his conscious mind until he remembered, often keeping him awake until he did. However, in spite of his nagging thoughts, toward morning he did manage a few hours of sound sleep.

When Lance awoke, he could hear his daughter in the kitchen with the baby and smell the aroma of frying bacon. He got up from the bed, put on a robe and went to the kitchen.

Meredith sat in her high chair, jabbering baby talk, waving a spoon around her head and from the looks of it; she decorated the immediate area around her chair with various bits of baby food and eating utensils. When Lance came in the room, the baby went silent, stared at him for an instant then lowered her arms, then her eyes and finally her head.

Lynn stood at the sink washing a few dishes and when the baby became quiet she turned around, saw her father and said, "Good morning. Did you sleep well?"

"Not the best I'm afraid," replied Lance.

"I know what you mean. I usually have trouble sleeping in a strange bed too."

Lance couldn't tell his daughter that the bed wasn't the problem because then he would have to explain, so he just acknowledged her comment with an, "Oh, is that so?"

"Sit down, I'll fix you something. What would you like?"

"It doesn't matter, but I would like a cup of tea."

"I've got it right here," said Lynn as she came to the table with a teapot in one hand and a ceramic mug in the other.

She poured the tea as Lance sat down. Then she bent over him, kissed the top of his head and hurried to the stove to cook his breakfast of bacon and eggs. Startled by the kiss, he felt somewhat embarrassed, but soon felt a flash of goodness and warmth he had never felt before. *God, it's great to have a family,* he thought as he sipped on the hot tea and looked at his granddaughter who stared back at him from a few feet away. He winked at her. She grinned at him and turned her face away, but like most babies, she soon lost her shyness and started to jabber again, decorating the floor with more food and utensils.

After Lance finished breakfast, he and Lynn talked for a few minutes and made tentative plans for dinner on the following Saturday. He promised to take her and Gordon to one of the area's finest restaurants, noted for its steaks and a specialty dish of Greek style pork chops. When through talking, Lance left the kitchen and went to the bathroom, shaved, took a long shower and put on some comfortable clothes.

Lance expected to see Gordon and when he asked about him, his daughter replied, "He usually works half days on Saturdays. He'll be home about noon or so. Did you wanna use his office?"

"Yes … I'd like to make a few phone calls, if it's all right?"

"No problem. You go ahead. Meredith and I are going to exercise class so we'll see you in a little while."

After Lynn and the baby left, Lance went to Gordon's office. First, he called his mother and said he'd be out sometime in the afternoon around three or three thirty. Next, he called Washington, D.C. to some old friends in the intelligence community to see if they knew what was going on. In the past, someone usually knew something, but this time Lance drew a complete blank. Not one of his contacts could tell him anything that he didn't already know.

He tried to call Hawkins, but no answer. He tried the transponder, but the message did not go through.

Now that's strange, thought Lance. *I wonder if he's dead too?*

Lance got up from the desk and went upstairs to the living room. He turned on the TV, tuned it to the CNN news channel and sat on the couch, and for the next hour, listened for any developments in the assassination investigation. He heard nothing new reported, except the country now had a black President, sworn in while at his farm less than two hours after young President Walker died. A local federal judge, a personal friend of new President, administered the oath of office.

The TV reporter said, "President Earl L. Williams, the first black man to ever hold the nation's highest elective office, announced earlier today that he would soon choose his Vice President, but stated that he would wait until he returned to Washington before he would make his selection known. An aide to the new President said that President Williams and his wife are not expected to arrive back in the nation's capital until the middle of next week, the day of the murdered President's funeral. In the meanwhile, he will remain on his farm in northern Illinois."

The film continued showing President Walker with the narrator, discussing some of the national programs he instituted, making him a very popular U.S. President during his one term in office. Other films depicted his earlier career as a United States Senator, along with obscure home movies of his family life.

When Lynn and the baby came home about an hour and a half later, the baby smiled and held out her arms to Lance. He took the child from her mother then glanced through the open door and noticed a blue van parked up the street about half a block away.

The realization struck him like a jolt of electricity, startling him so badly he almost dropped his granddaughter. He quickly whirled around, turning away from Lynn and started to rush toward the steps, still carrying Meredith.

"Dad, what's wrong?"

His daughter's question stopped him before he reached the stairs so he turned to her saying, "Honey, I have to make a very important phone call."

"Here, let me take the baby then."

He looked at the child grinning at him and making funny baby cooing noises, obviously pleased by the sudden wildness and movements of the moment. He gave the baby a quick kiss on the cheek, handed her to her mother and hurried down the steps. He grabbed the telephone book, looked up the Motel 8 number and called then asked for Mike's room. A few seconds later Mike came on the line.

"Mike, there's more of 'em. They're here about a block away, but I'll bet anything these guys aren't government people."

"Who do you think they could be?"

"I don't know," said Lance.

"Did you get a good look at 'em?"

"No, but I know it's the same ones I saw in Chicago," said Lance. Then he went on to tell Mike about the blond man inside the terminal at O'Hare Airport. "He's here, just up the street from my daughter's house, but I only saw the vehicle he's in, a blue van."

"You sure it's the same guy?"

"I'm positive. When I was at O'Hare, one of the Secret Service guys crossed the street and I recall now this blue van driving by. I remember the blond guy in the front seat on the passenger's side, the same guy that was inside the terminal. I was so absorbed in the Secret Service people at the time, I completely forgot about it."

"You sure it's the same van?"

"I know it's the same one because of the missing front hub cap."

"Okay, General. You want we should come and get 'em?"

"No, Mike, not here. Hard telling who they are and what they may do. I think it's better to try and find out what they're up to and see if we can catch them without any people around. I'm afraid if we try in a residential area during daylight, someone might get hurt, and God forbid it should be a civilian."

"Yes, sir, I see what you mean," said Mike.

"Across the street from the motel there's an Eagle's grocery store. There's a bank at the northwest end of the parking lot. I need some cash so I'm going there to use the money machine on the east side of the building."

"You want us to try and get these guys then?"

"No, but see if you can spot 'em. If they're following me, they'll be there. Put about eight or nine men in the lot, just in case these jokers get any ideas about trying to take me out. If they see people standing around, maybe they won't try anything."

"You got it, General. How soon you gonna be there?"

"I'm leaving the house now so plan on about ten minutes."

"All right, sir… and be careful. Better take your sidearm."

"Don't worry, Mike, I am."

Lance hung up the receiver and went up the stairs then told Lynn, "I've gotta run an errand and I'll be gone for a while. I'll be back around noon."

As Lance got in the rental car, he looked up the street at the blue van. He saw two men in the front seat, but couldn't make any positive identification and wondered, *What are these guys up to?*

Lance backed the car out of the drive and slowly drove up the street in the opposite direction from the parked van. When Lance traveled about two blocks away from the house, the van followed, but stayed at a discreet distance.

At the grocery store parking lot, Lance drove through it and parked his car near the bank's cash machine. When he got out of the car he noticed several unit men standing close by, looking as inconspicuous as they could, but he couldn't see the blue van.

He went to the cash machine, took out his bank card and punched in the code and the amount of money he wanted. When the money came out, he put it in his pocket and walked back toward the car. Before he reached it, he noticed a woman getting out of her car next to his. She looked disgusted because her car wouldn't start.

It's probably flooded, Lance thought.

As he started to walk across the driving lane, the woman went to the front of her car and opened the hood. She bent over and looked inside at the engine. Out of the corner of his right eye, Lance noticed the blue van coming fast up the same driving lane heading at him.

With her back to Lance, the woman didn't see the fast moving vehicle bearing down on them. She stepped backward exactly in the path of the oncoming van. Lance stood in front of the rental car and to one side. The van made a sudden turn toward Lance, but he jumped away and landed face down on the blacktop between the parked cars. He had no time to warn the lady except to yell, "LOOK OUT," as he dove for his life.

Behind him Lance heard a loud crashing noise then saw the rental car jump sideways a couple of inches; at the same moment he heard a scream and a loud thump. He heard the van rev up, spin its tires then change gears and speed off. Before Lance could get off the ground, the van left the lot and headed north on Highway 26.

Within seconds Mike and eight men surrounded Lance.

Helping Lance up, Mike asked, "You all right?"

Lance asked, "The woman. What happened to the woman?"

"The van hit her," replied Mike. "It looked to me like it tried to run you down and hit the woman instead. She got knocked down between the cars on the other side."

"See if she's all right."

"Yes, sir," said one of the soldiers, a trained medic. He turned and hurried to the woman lying unconscious on the ground. A few moments later, he returned and said, "Sir, I think she should go to a hospital. She's unconscious and it looks like she's got a bad bump on the head. Her pulse is irregular, but it's strong so maybe she's not hurt too bad, but with a head injury, sir, you never know."

As the young soldier attended the woman, Lance asked Mike, "Did you see what happened?"

"Yes, sir. The van came up the lane along here and it looked to me like the driver deliberately swerved to hit you, but it hit the front of the rental car then bounced off and hit the woman. Lucky it hit the car first or she'd be dead for sure."

"Okay, Mike, get the guys together and get them outta here, but I want you to hang around close just in case I may need you. I don't want anyone involved with the police, except me. I think the less they know at this point, the better. Here, take my weapon too."

"Yes, sir," said Mike as he took the pistol, turned to the others and said, "You heard the man, go shopping or somethin', but stay around close. Make yourself scarce for awhile."

"Mike, I want you to come back when the police leave."

"Yes, sir."

As the men wandered off, Lance went to the woman still lying unconscious on the ground. He opened her car door, took a blanket off the back seat and put it over her. He found a small pillow in the front seat of her car and put it under her head. He knelt down beside the woman and looked at her face.

Very attractive, nice complexion, looks to be in her late thirties or early forties and seems to have a nice figure, he thought. *There's something about her that's familiar. I think I should know this—*

"Did you see what happened?" asked a voice behind him breaking off his thoughts.

Lance turned, looked up and saw a policeman standing behind him. "Yes, officer, I did. The same van that hit her, almost hit me."

"How bad you think she's hurt?"

"She should go to a hospital. She may have a concussion," said Lance as he stood and faced the police officer.

"You a doctor?"

"No, sir. I'm military on leave."

"May I see some ID please?"

Lance handed his military identification card to the police officer and asked, "Is there help on the way for this woman? She may be hurt worse than we know."

"There's an ambulance coming. It should be here in a minute or two. Meanwhile, you up to a few questions?"

"No problem, officer."

Lance gave the policeman very little about what happened. He said, "This blue van came out of nowhere, hit my rental car and the woman. I didn't see much because I was down behind the cars."

As the officer took his statement, another police officer kept the few gawkers from getting too close to the unconscious woman. Within five minutes after the police arrived on scene, the ambulance pulled up, loaded the patient and took her to the hospital.

The policeman asked, "Have you got a phone number where we can reach you if we need you?"

Lance gave him both telephone numbers of his daughter and mother then said, "I'll sign a complaint if you ever catch the guy who did this."

The police officer replied, "Thank you, General. If we do catch this joker, we'll be in touch."

After filling out an accident report and getting a few more bits of information about the rental car the police officers got in their squad car and left.

Lance had doubts the men in the van would be arrested on a simple hit and run accident charge by this or any other police department. *These people are professional killers and they probably stole the van from somewhere around Chicago. I suspect the police will find it abandoned somewhere in a few days.*

Lance saw Mike standing by the bank and signaled him to come to him then told Mike, "I've got a gut feeling somebody is trying to do me in."

"I think you're right, sir, but I'd call it a little more than a gut feeling. Look at the front end of that car. That coulda been you."

"Let's see what damage there is under the hood," said Lance as he walked to the driver's side of the car and pulled the hood latch. The hood opened and Lance checked for damage to the engine. "From the looks of it the damage is all on the outside."

Closing the car's hood, Lance noticed something underneath the injured woman's car, still parked next to him.

"Mike, see what that is under her car."

Bending down, Mike reached under and picked up the object, a key ring with several keys then handing them to Lance said, "I'll bet they're her keys."

"See if they'll start her car," said Lance.

Getting in the driver's seat, Mike put a key in the ignition and started the engine on the first try. At first, heavy black smoke came out of the exhaust then cleared up after a few moments.

"Just as I thought, it was flooded," said Lance.

After the car started, one of the soldiers walked up to them, stooped down and picked up a billfold from under the rental car.

Handing it to Lance, he said, "I saw this fly out of the woman's hand when she was hit."

Lance took the billfold, opened it up and began looking for some identification. He found a driver's license and read from it.

"Marilyn Alberts, age forty-six, weight one twenty-eight, eyes green and height, five-six."

Pausing for a moment, Lance thought about what he had just read then turned to the enlisted man who gave him the wallet and said, "Sergeant, I want you to drive the rental car and follow me to the hospital. We're gonna take the lady's car to her. Mike, come over here for a second."

Lance walked a few paces out of hearing distance from the sergeant getting into the rental car.

"Whatcha need, sir?"

"I didn't get anything out of DC this morning. Seems as if whoever's behind all of this is really keeping it hush-hush. It's just as if nothing's happened and it's business as usual there. I tried to get Hawkins again, but he didn't answer the transponder. I don't like the looks of this, Mike. I think we're into something really deep and I wish I knew who and what we're up against."

"Whoever it is, I'll bet they don't know the unit is with you."

"That may be true, but they'll eventually figure it out. Whoever it is, I think they know about the unit and they want me dead. We'll let them think I'm alone. Maybe they'll screw up somehow and we'll get a handle on these bastards. Figure out some dummy traffic on the transponder to let them think you're still trying to contact me. If you stop trying all together, they'll know for sure we've made contact. Meanwhile, I'll just keep my transponder quiet."

"How you wanna communicate?"

"We do it either by small radio or the telephone, preferably on a pay phone. Don't call my mother's or daughter's number unless it's extremely important. They might have the lines tapped. Also, have somebody stick close to the phone at all times. I'll contact you twice a day, once in the morning and once in the afternoon."

"All right, sir."

"Everybody in the Motel 8?"

"Yes, sir, we're all on the same floor."

"Make sure you have somebody stand guard on each end. You know the motel routine."

"Yes, sir, it's already done."

"Good. Now get five or six rental cars, mini vans preferably, just in case we need transportation in a hurry, and get me a car to replace this one. I'll pick it up later."

"I'll have Diehl call Hertz and see what we can do," said Mike. "They should have a dealer rep around here somewhere." Mike turned to the sergeant and said, "Get me the rental contract out of the glove compartment."

"Also, Mike, I want a twenty-four hour watch on my daughter and her family, starting tonight. It's hard to tell what these bastards will do so I want to be on the safe side."

"What about your mom?"

"I think it might be wise to put a team in Cedarville too. I don't think they'll try anything there, but we don't know who we're up against so let's not take any unnecessary chances."

"Yes, sir, I agree."

"You got your government credit cards?"

"You betcha," replied Mike.

"Good. Go on back to the motel now, have your meeting and if anybody goes out, they go in groups of three or more and nobody stays out for more than an hour, except on detail. Make sure the guards are armed."

"Got it," said Mike.

"I'll call you around five, give or take a few minutes."

Lance turned to the soldier sitting in the rental car and signaled he was leaving. He got into the woman's car and drove to the Freeport Memorial Hospital, the only hospital in town. It took about ten minutes and when they arrived in the parking lot, Lance told the soldier to wait in the car.

He went to the emergency room and asked the first person he saw, a young nurse, "Was there a woman brought in here within the last half hour? A Mrs. Alberts?"

The young girl replied, "Yes, she's in the emergency room."

"How is she?"

"She seems to be okay now. Just a bruised shoulder and a bump on the head. The doctor said she'll be fine, but she should go home and take it easy for a while. Are you her husband?"

"No, just a friend. I have her car."

"Oh good. She was asking about it. She was wondering how she was going to get home. She's awake now if you'd like to go in and talk to her."

"Thank you," said Lance.

He left the nurse and went into the emergency room. He stood for a moment looking around, but couldn't find the woman. He thought, *She's probably behind one of the drawn curtains*. A slight sound came from behind one of the curtains and a second later, Lance saw the curtain slide back, exposing the examination table.

The woman stood next to the table with her dark hair a little disheveled, looking down while buttoning her jacket.

Lance thought, *She's certainly one attractive lady*, then asked, "Mrs. Alberts?"

Startled by his voice, the woman looked up and said, "Yes, I'm Marilyn Alberts."

As she looked into his eyes, he felt a sensation of recognition for the second time, but he still couldn't place her. *I know this woman, but from where?*

Lance said, "I have your car. I brought it from the grocery store parking lot and parked it just outside the emergency room door."

"Thank you so much. Is it all right? Did it get damaged?"

"No, it's okay. Only my car got hit," said Lance then added as an afterthought, "and of course you too. The nurse tells me you were lucky to only have a shoulder bruise and a slight concussion. It could've been worse."

"I guess I am pretty lucky. I heard someone shout and I started to jump away, but I wasn't quite fast enough." Then her facial expression changed and she asked, "Do I know you? You seem awfully familiar. I think I should know you."

Lance smiled as he remembered who she was and said, "Don't you recognize old high school boyfriends?"

She looked puzzled for a moment then smiled as if a light had gone on and asked, "Lance? Lance Stalwardt, it's you, isn't it?"

Smiling, Lance said, "How are you, Marilyn?"

Marilyn rushed to him, threw her arms around his neck and squeezed him to her body and kissed him on the cheek then let him go and stepped back. "My God ... it's been years and you don't look a day older than you did in high school."

"You look pretty good yourself."

"That may be true, but right now I don't feel very good. Every bone and muscle in my body aches."

"You're lucky it isn't more."

"I know. If it were, I probably wouldn't be able to go across the street to the clinic. I need to see if one of my friends will take me home. I sure don't feel much like going back to work."

"No need to bother anyone, I'll drive you home."

"Would you? It won't be any trouble for you will it?"

"No, no trouble at all."

After Marilyn signed insurance papers and took some pills the doctor gave her to help relieve the pain, they left the hospital. During the drive to her home, they reminisced about high school and told each other about their lives as best they could in the few minutes it took to get to the house.

Lance said, "You mentioned you were going to the clinic to get a friend to drive you home ... do you work at the clinic?"

"Yes ... I'm the supervisor of their accounting department. I've been there for about three years now."

"Where does your husband work?"

She paused for a moment then said, "He's dead. He died about four years ago from an aneurism."

"I'm sorry to hear that. How'd it happen?"

"We were on vacation in Vermont, looking at the fall colors and he just collapsed and died. Shortly after the funeral I left the east coast and came home to my folks. When I got the job at the clinic I moved into my own place. You know how parents can be."

"I know what you mean. Sometimes my mother still treats me like a twelve-year-old."

"How is your mom? I haven't seen her in a while."

"She's good. She's the only one of my parents living. My father passed away about three years ago."

"I know. I remember reading about it in the paper, and I talk to your mom sometimes when she comes to the clinic."

"Did you say your parents are back in town?"

"Yes, after Dad retired a few years ago, they came back to the same house. They never sold it. They only rented it out because they always wanted to come back to Freeport."

"I know how they feel. I enjoy coming back myself when I can, especially now that I have a new granddaughter."

"Yes, I know. Your daughter and Meredith are patients at the clinic, and I see them quite often. Your daughter is really a very pretty girl."

"Do you have any children?"

He could tell the question bothered her because she suddenly looked out the window and didn't respond right away then quietly she said, "No, my husband didn't want any children."

They arrived on the street where Marilyn lived and as she pointed out the house, she said, "Please, just park in the driveway. I'll put the car away later when I feel a little better. Right now I just want to go in and lie down."

Lance got out of the car, walked around and opened her door, helped her out of the car and walked her to the front door.

When they got to the door he said, "If you don't mind, I'd like to drop by later this evening to see how you're doing."

Smiling, she said, "Please do. I'd like that."

"Is seven thirty okay?"

"Yes, that'll be fine."

She went into the house and as she closed the door the rental car pulled up at the curb.

Getting in the car, Lance said to the driver, "Take me to the motel. I'll drop you there."

"Yes, sir."

Chapter 14

Lance dropped the sergeant at the motel, went to his daughter's house and packed his bags. He left Lynn and the baby around three o'clock and drove to his mother's. When Lance arrived, most of his immediate relatives had gathered there, waiting for him, including his sisters from Wisconsin and their families. After he went through a noisy and whirlwind greeting by everyone outside, they all went into the house. Lance's nephew, who spent four years in the Marine Corps, helped him with his bags and took them into the room where Lance's father stayed just before he passed away.

He remained with his family for the rest of the afternoon until five o'clock then left for a few minutes to call Mike from his sister's house just a couple doors away. Mike had nothing to report except he had the rental vehicles and got a replacement for the damaged car that Lance drove.

"I'll pick it up this evening around seven," said Lance.

Mike asked, "You coming in?"

"Yeah," replied Lance. "Thought I'd go see the woman who was injured. Maybe there's something she can remember."

"Yes, sir, I understand perfectly."

"Mike … it's not what you're thinking. I just thought maybe she might've seen the men in the van. Maybe she can give us some idea of who these guys are."

"Like I said before, General, I understand perfectly. Hell, if I were you, I'd interrogate her too, especially since she's so damn good lookin'."

"Well, she certainly is that. I found out we know each other and dated in high school, but seriously though, she might remember something that could help us. After all, she did get a good look at those guys.

"All right, sir, I'll see you later when you get here."

After Lance hung up the receiver he returned to his mother's house. He fixed a plate of food from the buffet his sisters set up especially for his homecoming, trying to sample everything being served. As he finished filling his plate the phone rang and his sister Joanne answered it.

A moment later she said, "Lance, it's for you."

Lance wondered, *Who the hell could it be?* Then asked, "Did they say who it is?"

"No, they just asked for General Stalwardt."

Lance put down his plate, took the receiver from his sister and said, "General Stalwardt speaking."

"General, this is President Williams."

"Yes, sir, Mr. President," said Lance, momentarily surprised by the call.

"I truly apologize for interrupting your leave, but because of the current events over the past few days I feel it is important that we talk sometime between now and the time before I leave to go back to Washington on Wednesday. I feel the sooner the better."

"Yes, sir, Mr. President, I agree," said Lance, now somewhat bewildered because the new President had contacted him.

"Good, I'm glad. Now, General, would it inconvenience you to meet with me on Monday evening at my farm?"

"No problem, sir."

"Shall we make it for eight o'clock?"

"Eight o'clock Monday evening it is."

"I'll expect you then, General."

"I'll be there, sir."

"Goodbye, General Stalwardt."

"Goodbye, Mr. President."

When Lance put the receiver down, he looked up and saw the rest of his family staring at him.

His oldest sister said, "The President. You had the President of the United States call you? Here?"

Lance answered, "Sure, why not?"

For a few minutes the call seemed to strike the whole family dumb then everyone started talking at once and asking questions about the new President. "What's he like? How many kids he got? Is his wife nice? Is he really as nice a guy as the papers say he is?"

Finally Lance said in a loud voice, "Please, I don't know the man that well and I don't know much about his family, so please stop the questions. Besides Mom, you met him when you and Dad went to Washington. He was a senator then."

What Lance had said about not knowing the new President was not quite true, but he needed to stop the bothersome questioning. He had to think. *What does the President want? Why did he call me at Mom's house? How did he know I was here? I'll have to talk it over with Mike when I see him later on.*

After the meal, everyone sat around and talked for the rest of the evening. At six thirty Lance told his family he had to leave and would see them all the next day. By six forty-five he arrived at the motel and knocked on Mike's door.

"It's me, Mike, open up."

The door opened and Mike asked, "You think anybody saw you come in?"

Lance hurried inside the room and said. "No, I don't think so. I took plenty of time and used some evasive measures so I'm sure no one followed me. At least I didn't see anyone, but that doesn't mean they're not around."

"Sir, here's the keys to your replacement rental," said one of the other men in the room. "We have to return the one you've got. Do you have the keys?"

"Here, Sergeant," said Lance as he handed the keys to the man beside him and took the other set. "Will you men please excuse us? The colonel and I have something to discuss in private."

The four men with Mike left without a word then Lance turned to Mike and said, "I just received a call from President Williams and he's invited me over to his farm in Galena on Monday. I want you to run a recon on the place and see what the layout is like. I don't want any surprises when I get there."

"My god, General ... do you think this guy's involved with the DC killings?"

"I honestly don't know, but I do know that whoever pulled off this operation has got to be high enough in the structure to know where everybody was at the time the assassinations took place and a Vice President might be informed about where everyone was."

"Are you sure, sir? Doesn't seem to me that he would know about your movements," replied Mike.

"No, I'm not sure, but I want to cover all the possibilities."

Mike responded by asking more questions, "How about the Attorney General? How'd they know where he was? The paper said he was killed in a health club parking lot just as he was going to his daily workout session, and what about the President's personal secretary? They say he was shot in his car while he sat at a red light. I don't really know what the hell's going on here, General, but it seems to me we better get some answers damn fast or we all could end up being dead meat. We already know they're after you, whoever they are."

"I'm sure you're right, Mike, but what we don't know is why?"

"What the hell do they think they're gonna gain if you're dead?"

"If we knew that then maybe we'd know who was causing all the trouble. Anyway, let's think on it some more and we'll talk about it when I come back tomorrow afternoon. In the meantime, if you have any contacts in DC, try to see if they know anything. Maybe we'll get lucky."

"All right, sir. I'll let you know later what I find out."

"Be damn careful. Don't let anyone know where you are, and if they ask, chances are they might be in on this."

"Right, I'll be careful."

"Good, I'll see you tomorrow."

"What time?"

"About three or so."

"Good, I'll be right here."

"All right, I'll see you tomorrow."

"You said that already," said Mike with a grin on his face. "Have fun tonight."

Lance looked at Mike and saw the grin, but didn't say anything. He just shook his head and went out the door, closing it behind him.

Before Lance went to Marilyn's, he stopped at a flower shop in the nearby mall and bought a bouquet of red roses. He arrived at the house a little before seven thirty and parked the car in the drive, got out and walked to the door. He could smell wood smoke in the air and looked up at the bright stars in the night sky. A wisp of smoke drifted across the almost full moon. As he pushed the doorbell he felt a little nervous, not sure of what to expect.

Marilyn opened the door and said, "Hello. Please come in."

Lance stood for a moment, looking at the woman in front of him. Her shoulder length hair framed her face perfectly and her radiant smile lit up her green eyes. They almost seemed to sparkle. She wore a black, one-piece jumpsuit with a string of single strand pearls around her neck; in her slim delicate hand she held a half glass of white wine. He noticed a subtle scent of expensive perfume, a fragrance he had never encountered before. *Probably French*, he thought. *She's absolutely beautiful.*

As he stepped into the foyer, Marilyn said, "The flowers are positively gorgeous, thank you."

Preoccupied by the woman's beauty for a moment, Lance forgot about the flowers in his hand then said, "Here, these are for you," and held the flowers toward her.

She took the bouquet as he stood feeling awkward and not quite knowing what to do or say.

"I love red roses, they're my favorite flower," she said. She sniffed the roses then turned and motioned toward another room. "Please, come in and make yourself comfortable in the living room while I put these in some water. There's white wine and hors d'oeuvres on the table."

She turned toward the kitchen at the far end of the house.

While viewing her backside, Lance thought, *Now there's a woman who's both comfortable and confident with herself. Nobody would ever guess that she'd been hit by a truck this afternoon.*

While Marilyn left to go to the kitchen, he realized he couldn't help himself staring at her, absolutely spellbound by her graceful movement and perfectly proportioned figure. When she turned out of sight the spell disappeared.

At the moment, Lance felt somewhat embarrassed and mumbled, "Don't be such a putz, Stalwardt, do as she told you."

He went into the living room, looked around and saw her home perfectly coordinated, just as she was. A fire burned in the fireplace and lights turned low, but not too low. Just low enough to seem comfortable. He moved to the couch and sat in front of the empty glass on the table, poured the wine and sipped a taste.

"Hmm. This is pretty good stuff," he said.

He looked at the label and as he suspected—European wine.

Marilyn returned from the kitchen carrying a vase with the flowers in one hand and an empty wine glass in the other. She set the vase on the end table close by Lance, and he could smell the delicate fragrance coming off the roses. Marilyn sat next to him, not too close, but close enough that Lance could detect her perfume.

For two hours they sat and talked of things in their past, drinking the wine in the process and becoming more comfortable with each other as the evening wore on. Around nine thirty, Marilyn excused herself and went to the kitchen to open another bottle of wine. Lance heard her say something, but he didn't understand her.

He got up from the couch, went to the kitchen and stood in the doorway then said, "I'm sorry, I didn't hear what you said."

As he stood there watching her, she began putting the cork screw into the bottle. Before pulling the cork, she turned and looked at him for a moment, not saying anything.

She put the bottle on the counter, and then without a word, she came into his arms in a rush. He kissed her, feeling her warm mouth on his and her soft body pressing tightly against him. She responded to his touch, moaning a low soft sound in her throat, wrapping her arms tightly around his neck.

"Damn," said Lance. "It's been a long time since I've felt this way about anyone."

"Oh Lance, I've never forgotten you and I wished we could have made a life together. My feelings for you are just as genuine now as they were when we were in high school."

Lance leaned down and kissed her neck as she laid her head on his chest. She responded with a kiss that made his head spin and sent a shiver through his body. He stooped down, lifted her in his arms and as she pointed the way, he took her into the bedroom. As they passed through the hallway Marilyn turned off the lights and the house went completely dark.

In the bedroom they both stripped naked and fell onto the bed embraced in each other's arms. They made love for what seemed like an eternity then fell asleep around midnight.

Something woke Lance. He opened his eyes in the darkness and lay still, listening to the silence and Marilyn's soft steady breathing.

Somewhere in the house he heard a motor turn off and thought, *Probably the refrigerator or maybe the furnace*.

More silence.

Again, Lance heard something and thought, *There ... a noise*.

He became more alert and reached down to his pants on the floor, taking his pistol from its holster. As quietly as he could, he screwed a silencer onto the weapon then slipped the safety to off. Rolling over on the bed, he placed his hand over Marilyn's mouth.

When she awoke with a start, he whispered in her ear, "Don't make a sound there's someone in the house. Crawl over me and get on the floor. Move toward the head of the bed as far as you can."

Lance followed her to the floor and crawled to the foot of the bed then chambered a live round into the pistol and waited. He crouched down behind the bed with his pistol pointed over the bed toward the door.

Another noise.

Sounded like someone bumping into a piece of furniture.

Then a man's whispered voice came from the darkened hallway, saying in a harsh tone, "Quiet you fool, you'll wake 'em up."

A few moments later a man's shadowy figure filled the bedroom doorway. Enough light came from a window behind Lance that he could see a man's arm raise a handgun and fire the weapon, bullets hitting the bed where he had been.

The man's gun had a silencer, but the slight noise it made when fired startled Marilyn and she let out a soft muffled scream. Lance reacted immediately by firing three well placed shots into the shadow's center. The intruder let out a guttural moan, sounding like a deep grunt as three 9mm bullets slammed into the man's chest area and through his heart killing him instantly. His body jerked backward, hitting the hallway wall opposite the bedroom door then collapsed to the floor.

After the lifeless body fell, Lance could hear someone running through the house. He hurried to the hallway, stepping over the corpse, looking out through the window across the living room just in time to see a figure run to a van parked in the street, get in and drive off.

"Odds are it's the same van as in the parking lot," said Lance as he turned and stooped down to check the body for life.

"No pulse … he's dead."

Lance picked up the dead man's weapon and went back to the bedroom, walked around to the side of the bed where Marilyn still lay crouched on the floor. He knelt down and took her in his arms and felt her begin to sob quietly against him.

"It's okay, sweetheart. It's over."

"Oh Lance. What's happening?"

"I wish I knew. I'm just as in the dark as you are," he lied.

Lance figured, *There's no sense in scaring her anymore than what she already is.*

He helped her off the floor and onto the bed.

As she sat waiting, he put on his pants and said, "Stay here and get dressed. I'm gonna check the rest of the house. Lock the bedroom door behind me and don't open it up to anyone except me."

"Shall I call the police?"

"Not just yet. Let's wait a while."

Lance went out the door and as he closed it behind him, he heard Marilyn lock it. He heard nothing out of the ordinary from the rest of house. He moved through the entire structure then went back to the bedroom hallway and turned on the light. He recognized the dead man as the one who drove the blue van, trying to hit him that afternoon. The man lay on the floor with his eyes partly open and his face slightly twisted in a painful expression, almost as if frozen.

Lance went to the bathroom and got a large bath towel, wrapped it around the dead man's chest and lifted him onto his shoulder. He took the body to the garage and laid it on the floor, covering it with an old blanket from a shelf. On the way back through the house he noticed a trail of blood spots leading out the front door. He went to the kitchen telephone and called Mike.

Chapter 15

Within twenty minutes Mike arrived in the government sedan with a team of three enlisted men, parking the car inside the garage. Lance met Mike and the team leader as they came through the door from the garage into the dark kitchen.

Mike asked, "You guys all right?"

"Yeah, I'm okay," replied Lance, "but she's pretty shook up."

"Do you know how they got in?"

"They must have used a lock pick on one of the doors. I haven't found any evidence of forced entry anywhere."

"Where's the dead guy?"

Lance replied, "In the garage along the back wall."

"How about the one that got away?"

"He's carrying a bullet. I found a blood trail going out the front door. He was probably standing behind the shooter and caught one of the rounds."

"How bad you think he's hit?"

"I don't know. It's not too bad otherwise he wouldn't have been able to move as fast as he did when he left the house."

"Where'd he go?"

"He ran across the street and got into a van, and I'll lay even money that it's the same van that hit my car this afternoon." Lance paused then asked, "How'd you get here?"

"I used the government car because it's less conspicuous than one of the vans ... and it probably wouldn't arouse suspicion if a neighbor sees it at the house."

"I think the first thing is to recon the neighborhood for a block or so to see if anybody's still hanging around."

"That's already being done," said Mike.

"Good. Stay here in the kitchen and when the guys get back, have them wrap the dead guy in a blanket."

The sergeant standing behind Mike asked, "Whadda ya want us ta do with the body, sir?"

"Let's keep him in the garage for now."

Two team members with Mike checked around the house outside then expanded their search to the neighborhood for a few blocks.

When they returned to the house the ranking NCO told Mike, "Sir, it's all clear outside."

With lights turned off inside the house, Mike placed the three men in different rooms to guard outside entryways in case the intruders came back. Marilyn had gotten dressed and sat on the edge of the bed in the dark bedroom when Lance came in and finished dressing.

As he put on his shirt, he asked, "Is there somewhere you can stay for the rest of the night so I know you'll be safe?"

"I could probably go to my folks, but they'll ask why I'm there. I couldn't possibly tell them that you were spending the night here," she said as she reached over and took Lance's hand. "Well, not just yet anyway. And, I really don't want them to know that someone tried to shoot us."

"Okay, I'll have Mike take you to the motel."

Fifteen minutes later Mike and Marilyn arrived at the motel. After she took one of the rooms, Mike returned to stay with Lance and the three other men in the darkened house, waiting to see if the intruders would return.

At 7 a.m., just a little after dawn, Lance told Mike, "It looks like they won't be back for now so I'm going to my mother's for a while, but I'll be back later on. If the phone rings while I'm gone, don't answer it. Let the answering machine do it. If it's me, I'll let you know where you can call me back."

"Got it."

"And, Mike, I think you better keep the car in the garage so nobody will see it."

"It's already there."

"Good."

"Also, have somebody take Marilyn's car over to the motel."

Mike nodded as he sat at the table sipping his coffee then said in a somewhat quizzical tone, "General, I don't know what the hell we've got here, but I can tell you these bastards are playin' for keeps. You better watch yourself. These guys wanna kill your ass and it's hard tellin' where they'll show up."

"I don't think they're around now. I think I probably scared them off last night."

"Hell, you don't know that for sure. They may be watchin' your every move, just waitin' to get you in the open."

"I don't think so, at least not now anyway," said Lance. "But, I sure wish I knew who and what the hell we're up against here. Were you able to find out anything from your contacts?"

"Not a damn thing," answered Mike. "It's like the intelligence people have quit all together. They're just as stumped as we are. If they do know somethin' they ain't tellin' me. Anyway, none of them asked why I was curious so I think they're all in the dark too, same as us."

"Probably are. Anyway, I'll see you later on this afternoon."

Lance left Marilyn's and drove to Cedarville, arriving at his mother's house as the sun began peeking over the horizon through a partly cloudy sky. He parked the car and as he got out, he noticed birds singing, something he missed while living in the city.

He unlocked the garage side door and walked through, noticing his old bicycle hanging on the hook where he left it after his last medical leave. He used it back then to help get into shape after being badly wounded during his last Vietnam combat tour. The bike appeared to be in good condition so he decided to change and go for a short ride. While taking it down from the wall, he thought, *Maybe the ride will help me put this together. At least it'll help me to think.*

After changing into a sweat suit, he jumped on the bike and headed toward Dakota, a village about six miles east of Cedarville on the Townline Road, a route he often traveled when recuperating.

A few miles out, Lance realized he hadn't eaten yet and thought, *Perhaps I'll stop and see some old friends. I'll surprise them and maybe they'll feed me breakfast.*

He put his thoughts aside and concentrated on pedaling.

Once Lance got into a comfortable rhythm he looked down at the odometer—4.2 miles. He continued to pedal and soon became aware of a growing sound all too familiar to him, the telltale thumping of a helicopter rotary wing, beating the still morning air.

Within seconds a UH-1 Huey helicopter came from over the trees on the south side of the road at about a hundred feet off the ground and passed overhead. Lance saw the side doors open and a man on each side of the aircraft step out onto the landing skids. They wore attached safety straps and each of them held what looked like an automatic weapon. As soon as the Huey passed over him, it went into a hard steep bank to the right and made a one hundred and eighty degree turn then started to run back toward him at about fifty feet off the ground, an altitude just high enough to clear the wires running parallel along the road.

As the helicopter began turning, Lance realized what was about to happen and went for the ditch. He jumped off the bicycle and dove over the fence into a standing cornfield, rolling once and came up on his feet running. He no more than cleared the fence when he heard the automatic weapons firing and the bullet sprays hitting the ground and the dried corn stalks behind him. He dove toward his right as far as he could, landing on a spot perpendicular to and about eight feet away from where he had just been. He lay perfectly still, face down and did not move until the helicopter passed overhead for the second time. He knew he couldn't stay there because they would eventually spot him.

As soon as the helicopter passed overhead, he got up and ran in the direction perpendicular to the helicopter's attack line. He ran up the corn row for about a hundred feet then doubled back toward a small culvert that went into another standing cornfield on the other side of the road. He made it into the culvert before the helicopter made another pass over the area.

Reaching the other side, Lance thanked God with a quick prayer for the concealment. He ran parallel to the rows about fifty meters inside the field, back toward Cedarville, away from the helicopter and toward a small airport he passed just moments before. The helicopter circled the area where he first entered into the cornfield, indicating they hadn't spotted him as he made his escape.

Lance went about a quarter of a mile and came out of the corn at the edge of the small grass landing strip. A man stood next to a metal Quonset hangar, watching the circling helicopter.

He saw Lance and asked, "What's all the excitement about?"

Lance showed his military identification card and told the man, "I don't have time to explain now, but is there someone here that I can talk to about using a plane? I wanna see where those bastards go after they're done shooting up that cornfield."

"Better than that, I'll fly you myself."

"Sir, you don't have to do that. This could be dangerous."

"I wouldn't miss this for the world."

Lance didn't have time to discuss the matter with the other man so he just said, "Okay then, let's go."

The man pointed to a Cessna 172 behind them. "It's unlocked and warmed up enough. I just had her up about an hour ago."

Both men climbed in and they took off from the grassy runway, heading north. At 500 feet the pilot leveled the plane and turned toward the east to find the helicopter. A few minutes later, the pilot turned the Cessna into a climbing 180 degree turn and headed back west. At 1000 feet he leveled off and turned north for a few seconds then brought the plane into a slow easy turn toward the east. Both men could clearly see the helicopter again, but now it headed in a southwesterly direction, flying the nap of the earth.

The pilot took up the same heading and followed, knowing the helicopter pilot wouldn't suspect the small plane following above them. Within minutes the helicopter reached a farm and landed in the yard behind the barn.

The pilot said, "It's the old Gregory place. It's been abandoned for years."

"How far do you make it outside of Freeport?"

"Not far, about two miles or so," replied the pilot.

Lance sat looking down at the farm buildings and surveying the layout of the terrain. He saw two cars parked between the barn and the house then spotted a van, a blue van. Lance saw five men walk from the helicopter and meet two men coming from the house.

"Seven for sure," he said, "but the odds are there's more."

Before the plane reached the farm, Lance told the pilot to go back to the airport. He didn't want to alert the men on the ground and so far he felt they had not been discovered. As the small plane banked away, he could see the men standing where they first met.

During the flight back, the pilot introduced himself, "The name's Jack Dorn. I own the airstrip and the farm across the road."

"It's nice to meet you, Jack. Thanks for helping me keep an eye on those bastards," said Lance.

"No problem, General. Why are you so interested in these guys, aside from the fact they tried to kill ya?"

"I have reason to believe these men are involved with the assassination of the President and some other people."

"Holy shit! You sure about that?"

"Not really, but almost."

"Do the cops know this?"

"Not yet and I would appreciate it if you wouldn't say anything about this incident to anyone, especially the local police. You never know who's involved in something like this."

"You got it. You know, General, you're somewhat of a celebrity around here ... workin' in the White House and all. What's the President really like? The new one I mean ... the black guy?"

"I really don't know, I've never met the man," Lance lied.

"General, you're damn lucky I didn't pick my corn in those two fields. I didn't have space to store the crop so I felt it was better to leave it in the field for awhile."

"Well, it sure as hell saved my ass."

The Cessna touched down and the pilot taxied to the Quonset building that acted as an office as well as a hangar. Lance called Mike and told him how to get to the airport. Fifteen minutes later he arrived in one of the rental mini vans along with three armed men.

"Mr. Dorn, I'd like you to take Mike up and fly over the farm area where that helicopter landed, but not too close. I don't want them getting suspicious." Lance turned to Mike and said, "Look the area over real good, you know what I want. Meanwhile, one of you come with me to get my bicycle. You other two stay and secure the strip just in case we were spotted and those bastards come here."

When Lance returned from getting the bicycle, the Cessna had come back from the farmhouse reconnaissance. Lance and Mike talked in the hangar while Jack Dorn went into the office and made a telephone call to his wife. He had to explain to her that he would be home late because of being hired for a job.

"Mike, we're gonna hit that place tonight, but first I want those bastards in Cedarville that are watching my family. They gotta be there. It's the only way they knew I was on this road."

"Whatcha got in mind?"

"We all go back to Cedarville and take a good look around and see if we can spot these guys. I want one of them alive. Maybe we can get some information about who we're up against."

"Shouldn't be too hard," said Mike. He turned to the men posted outside, "Okay guys ... let's go."

Lance thanked Jack Dorn for his help and again cautioned him, "Please, sir, do not tell anyone about the events that have happened here today, especially the local police and the press. I'm depending on you. If news gets out about any of this, it may cost some more lives and that's what I wanna try to avoid. Have I got your word?"

"Hell, General, I won't even tell the ole lady. I won't say a word until you say it's okay. You can depend on it."

"Thanks, Jack. What do we owe you for the plane rides?"

"Forget it, glad to be of service. You can buy me a beer the next time you see me."

Lance shook hands with the man, said goodbye then got into the front seat of the van with Mike while the others rode in back.

Arriving at the Cedarville limits, Lance said, "Let me off and you go on in. If anyone is here, they'll probably be within a block of my mother's place. Start there and work back. If you spot them just ignore them and get back to me. I'll wait here for awhile then I'll start riding down the main drag to Red Oak. Any questions?"

Nobody answered. "Good, I'll see you in a few minutes then."

After Lance took the bicycle out of the back of the van, Mike drove off. Lance sat on the curb with his water bottle in his hand and the bicycle parked nearby. He strapped on his riding helmet then stood up and began to adjust the front chain derailleur. As he finished, the van came back and stopped beside him.

Mike rolled down the window and said, "We found 'em."

"Where are they?"

"Just behind your mom's house parked at the end of an alley that goes down by the fire station."

"Okay, I'll ride down the alley and go by them on the bike, but before I do, I want you and the men to pull up in a driveway behind them. Then two of you walk toward the alley as if you're going to the house in back. As I go by, take them. They're attention will be on me so they won't be expecting you. I want these guys alive."

Mike then added, "Don't do anything stupid guys. Just because we want them alive doesn't mean you should get careless. If they become a threat, don't hesitate to kill 'em. No need for any of us to get hurt here."

Someone asked, "What're we gonna do after we get 'em?"

"Take them to the cemetery just west of town," replied Lance. "It's quiet, out of the way and I don't think anyone will disturb us out there. Maybe we can get something from them. If we can't make them talk by interrogation then we'll use chemical. Now, if everybody's ready, let's go. And remember, like Colonel Polaski said, if they get funny or cause any problems ... don't hesitate to take 'em out."

"You got it," said Mike as he rolled up the window and drove away. He turned the van around and headed in the same direction as Lance. The van caught up, passed Lance and went on ahead to set up the assault and seizure of the two watchdogs.

The plan worked perfectly. Within a second of Lance riding by the car, Mike had the two men in custody and transferred to the minivan. Mike headed for the cemetery about a quarter mile out of the village limits where Lance waited for them.

Questioned separately for about twenty minutes, neither prisoner said a word.

Lance said, "Take them back to Freeport and we'll continue this at Marilyn's place. I'm going to my mother's to change clothes and I'll be in as soon as I can."

Arriving at his mother's, Lance's sister invited him to join in for breakfast as he came through the door so he had something to eat and a nice chat. After he finished eating he shaved, took a shower and dressed into his green uniform with all his awards and ribbons.

Lance had a plan in mind. Picking up the transponder, he typed in one word and sent the message.

COME.

Chapter 16

When Lance came out of the bedroom he found a note on the refrigerator door, telling him his mother and sister had left the house to go shopping in Freeport for the rest of the day. The note also told him to be home by six o'clock that evening if he wanted to eat dinner with the family. He read it then wrote a brief note of his own underneath it.

MOM:
I won't be able to make it for dinner tonight.
LOVE, Lance

While leaving the house, the response signal came back on the transponder.

Message received: on our way.

I wonder why the response was late. Probably too busy to respond right away.

Ten minutes after Lance left the house he came to the first set of stop lights on the highway between Cedarville and Freeport. Off to the east, he noticed the two Starlifters flying at about 500 feet, heading for the Albertus Airport.

That was sure quick, thought Lance.

Five minutes later, Lance arrived at Marilyn's house, and as he came through the door, Mike asked, "Why the greens?"

"I've got something special in mind. We'll talk about it later. Right now, how's our company doing?"

"Good news. One of the cutie pies talked."

"What'd he have to say?"

"Seems like we've got us a real hornet's nest here. These two guys belong to the mob with connections to the Chicago and New York families."

"I kinda had a gut feeling that organized crime was involved somehow. Ever since Kennedy was shot, those bastards have had their fingers in the government till in some way or another. Did you find out what they're doing here?"

"They're after Williams."

Lance asked, "How many of them are there?"

"Fourteen. Originally there were only twelve, but you showed up and two more of their guys followed you in from Chicago."

"The blue van, right?"

"You got it," said Mike.

"Anything about the dead guy in the garage?"

"We didn't ask."

"Okay, I guess it really doesn't matter. Anyway, to change the subject, the Starlifters are at Albertus."

"I saw the message go out ... but they're here already?"

"I saw them fly by just as I came into town."

Mike said, "That was quick. I'll have a detail pick up the things we'll need for tonight."

"Good, and have them bring in the Secret Service agents. I've got something in mind for them."

"What about the men at the motel? Shall we bring them here or should we get ready over there?"

"Bring them here. I think it's better that we get ready in the basement and use this as our command center rather than set up at the motel. It would look strange as hell if our guys had to run around over there in their combat gear. Here they can load up into the vans in the garage and no one will see them."

"You want everyone here or should we leave somebody back for security?"

"Good point," said Lance. After a moment's thought he said, "Better leave somebody, just in case. Since Delta section has already got one of their three-man teams with the planes, leave one of their other teams at the motel and one here at the house. Tell the two officers to man the command center. And Mike, tell whoever goes to the airport to have John call me at this number from the pay phone out there."

"Anything else, General?"

Lance paused for a moment then continued, "Not for now. Get your people started then come on back and we'll work on the ops plan for tonight's raid. I want this done without any screwups."

After Mike gave the two men their instructions and sent them on their way, he came back to the kitchen and sat at the table where Lance had already drawn up a strip map of their objective.

Lance said, "The first thing we need is a legal reason for hitting this place. That's where the Secret Service comes in. I'm taking the two agents to a judge to get a federal warrant issued."

"Do you think a judge will sign warrants without an indictment from a grand jury?"

"I hope so. Once he hears they're suspects in the President's assassination, I'm sure he'll sign one."

"That's why the greens?"

"I hope the judge is impressed enough to sign without too much of a hassle."

"Who's the judge?"

"Dexter Knowles … he's an old family friend, but the fact that he's a friend doesn't mean a hell of a lot as far as the law goes."

Although Lance felt confident that his boyhood friend would sign the arrest warrant, he knew there were no guarantees.

Lance looked up from the map and saw Mike staring at him and asked, "What's the matter?"

"You know these people ain't gonna surrender just because you have a piece of paper signed by a judge."

"I know," said Lance. "We'll probably have to kill some of them to get them out of that farmhouse."

"It's too bad if it goes down that way. I was hoping maybe we could get more information about how all this is connected and who all is involved."

"Anything more from the two in the basement?"

"Nah," replied Mike. "They don't know anything. They're just imported muscle."

"How did you get them to talk?"

"I had Mendez and Garcia work on 'em. Those guys can make a rock talk." Then Mike looked at Lance with a grin on his face and said, "By the way, I wonder what methods of interrogation *you* used last night. Would you call that the naked warrior torture?"

"Never mind that now, Mike, we've got a lot of work to do and we haven't much time to do it in."

"Seriously, sir, did you get anything from her that we can use?"

"The only thing of any importance was that she remembered seeing a blond guy in the van."

"She recognized him?"

"No, but she said she'll never forget his face."

"How about the dead guy? Did she recognize him?"

"She didn't see him, and I don't think that one's important now."

"What should we do with the body?"

"We take it with us tonight. We'll dump it at the farmhouse so it appears like he's a casualty of the raid."

Lance and Mike continued to discuss and plan the events of the upcoming raid on the suspected assassins at the abandoned Gregory farm. The group would strategically position themselves around the farm buildings so every fire fan would cover the farmhouse. The men in the house would be given a chance to surrender peacefully. Failing that, the group would demonstrate their potential firepower for a few seconds, firing over the building, then cease fire. Again someone would ask the men inside to surrender. If they did not, the group would take the objective in their normal efficient manner and kill everyone inside. If the men inside the farmhouse started firing immediately after the warning, Lance would automatically give the command to assault the building.

Just after Lance and Mike wrapped up their plans, a car pulled into the driveway. Both men rose from the kitchen table and went to the foyer to see who it was. Lance saw Marilyn get out of the car so he opened the door and waited for her to come through it.

As she stepped inside where Lance waited, she smiled at him, slowly wrapped her arms around his neck and kissed him then slowly moved backward a little, whispering, "Morning lover."

"Good morning," said Lance as he wrapped his arms around her waist and pulled her back to him. "What are you doing here?"

"I heard one of the men tell the rest of the guys at the motel to come over here and get ready for some kind of operation. I thought maybe I could help by fixing them something to eat." She paused then said in a more seductive tone, "Besides, I missed you."

She pressed herself closer to him and kissed him again. Lance responded and felt the warm softness of her lips and the pressure of her body against his. He heard someone clear their throat in a manner that could not be mistaken for anything else but an intended interruption.

Standing in the doorway, Mike said, "You two shouldn't do that in front of the children."

Lance quickly released Marilyn then stepped back and said, "Good, I'm glad you're here, maybe you can make some fresh coffee when the men get here. Do you know how soon they were going to leave the motel?"

She replied, "One of the officers said they'd be here shortly." Then Marilyn took Lance's hand and led him to the kitchen. As she passed by Mike in the doorway she gave him a wink and said to him, "This one's mine, and I'm gonna keep him."

Within fifteen minutes the group from the motel arrived at the house. Mike told them to go to the family room in the basement and wait there for further instructions. He detailed two men to help in the kitchen.

A moment later the phone rang and Marilyn answered, "Hello." After a second of silence she said, "Just a moment please, I'll get him." She turned to Lance and said, "It's for you."

Lance took the receiver from Marilyn and said, "Stalwardt."

John Slaughter said, "Whatcha need, General?"

"John, Mike's got a couple of vans coming out to the planes to get the gear. We need it for a little exercise we're going on tonight."

"They're here now."

"Good. Send our two guests back along with the equipment. I'll explain later, but right now I'm going to need their services for a little while. How're they holding up?"

"Not too bad, sir. The older guy's one helluva poker player. I think he's got everybody's money by now."

"Good. That means he'll be in a good mood."

"Anything else, General?"

"Yeah, how the hell did you get here so fast?"

"I had to take off from Truax because I told their operations people I was making a test flight after repairing our so-called malfunction. We were almost to Illinois when I got your message."

"Any problems with Truax?"

"I don't think they believed me when I told them we were having trouble. Anyway, I thought it best to get the hell outta there. I had a gut feeling they were trying to hold us there, but what for, I don't know."

"Okay, John, I'm glad you're here. This way we can keep in closer contact."

"What're we gonna do about the planes? From some of the conversation I had with the Truax people in Air Ops, I got the feeling there's somebody looking for us."

"There's a small landing field north of Freeport about five miles. It might be tight, but I think you can make it. I'll make the arrangements this afternoon and we'll move the planes first thing after dark."

"Okay, General, anything else?"

"Not for the moment, John, but have somebody stay close to the phone. I'll have Mike call you around seventeen hundred. What's the number of the pay phone out there?"

"Five five five nine nine one one."

"Okay, John, I'll talk to you later," said Lance, jotting down the number on a piece of paper.

Lance hung up the phone and went to the kitchen where Mike and Marilyn finished making sandwiches and coffee for the men.

As Lance came through the door, he heard Mike say, "When I dug him out of the bunker he was barely alive. They were gonna burn his body with four other guys that were—" Mike saw Lance and stopped talking. He turned and asked, "How's John?"

"Okay for now. John thinks somebody was trying to hold him at Truax so he took off. That's why he got here so quick. He was already airborne and almost here when he got my message."

"What're we gonna do with the planes? They're like sittin' ducks out at that airport."

"This afternoon I want you personally to go the airfield where you picked me up this morning and ask Jack Dorn if he'll let us use his airfield. I know the field is short, but I think it'll handle the Starlifters. Anyway, check it out and let me know as soon as you can. Then call John and let him know when he can go."

"You got it, General."

"By the way, Mike. What about the recon I asked for on the Williams farm?"

"They left early this mornin'. Should be back anytime now."

"How many men?"

"Three. A team from Delta section."

"Good. Let me know the minute they get back."

A half hour later, the men returned from the airport with the combat gear and the two Secret Service agents. The men took the gear to the basement while Lance and Mike took the two agents into one of the two guest bedrooms.

Lance asked, "You guys okay?"

The older one spoke first, "Other than needing a shower and a shave, I guess you'd say everything's okay."

Lance looked at the man and asked, "You the one that won all the money?"

The older agent looked surprised then grinned as he said, "Yeah. Like shooting fish in a barrel."

Mike chuckled and said, "Okay, now that you've had some fun and games, it's time to start earning your pay. The General's got something to say to you guys so listen up."

Lance began, "First, let me say that I believe you two had nothing to do with the assassinations, but I also believe that someone in your organization set up the President for the shooting. We have some hard evidence that points in that direction with elements of organized crime involved."

Agent Hickman, the older man, responded, "General Stalwardt, you can be assured that neither one of us had anything to do with this. Hell, we've been out of the mainstream of the agency for almost six years guarding former President Carter. Then when he was hospitalized, we got reassigned to Walker, but only in a standby role so we don't have a clue about what's going on."

"I know that. I checked you two out somewhat and I'm sure you're telling the truth. That is up to now anyway. But, let's get down to the business at hand. Tonight we're going after a small group of men that we now know were sent here to assassinate President Williams, and I think they're going try before he leaves for Washington next Wednesday. We know where they're at and we're setting up a raid to take them out. However, we'll need your cooperation."

Agent Hickman said, "You got it, General. Whatcha need?"

"Good. First, you two will come with me when I pay a personal visit to a federal judge here in town. He's a friend of mine and hopefully he'll sign arrest warrants for us so our operation will be legal. That's where you two come in. Your presence will make it an official government operation and once we explain that we're arresting the assassins, I don't think we'll have a problem."

Agent Andrews, the younger of the two agents asked, "What about this being Sunday?"

"Like I said, the judge is an old friend and we'll pay him a visit at his home. After he hears what we already know, I'm sure he'll cooperate."

Agent Hickman asked, "When do we go?"

"Just as soon as you two get ready."

"Can we shower and change clothes first? Our stuff's in the trunk of the car in our suitcases."

"No problem," said Mike. "Here're the keys. Your weapons and ID's are in the glove compartment. You better get those too."

"Whose gonna get the warrant typed?"

"I'll ask Marilyn," said Lance. "Maybe she can do it. Do you have any federal warrant forms with you?"

"Yeah," answered Agent Hickman, "in the trunk of the car in a black briefcase. I think we'll only need one form. Joe here'll help the woman fill it out so there'll be no administrative foulups."

While the agents began preparing for the visit to the judge, the three-man reconnaissance team arrived back from President Williams's farm. Mike answered the door and sent the team into the kitchen where Lance and Marilyn sat at the kitchen table having a conversation over a cup of freshly brewed tea and proofreading the typed warrant.

Lance looked up when the three men and Mike came into the room and he asked, "These the recon people?"

"Yes, sir," replied the sergeant in charge.

"Good, have a seat. You boys hungry?"

"Yes, sir," replied all three men.

"There's sandwiches, tea and coffee on the counter."

While the men began preparing their plates, the team leader started his briefing. "We arrived at the farm before first light and found out the compound was being protected with radar and night surveillance devices so we took the necessary evasion precautions. We were able to get within a hundred meters of the house, but because of the equipment there, I figured if we got any closer we could've been detected. There doesn't seem to be too many people in the compound, but you can never tell. They might be stashed away someplace else."

"How many men did you count?"

"No more than a dozen. They were all in or around the house."

"Was there any activity that looked out of the ordinary?"

"Not that we could see. It looked to me like everyone just kinda stayed in place and did the normal surveillance stuff. I don't think there's gonna be a problem goin' in there, sir."

"Good job, Sergeant. Thank you. After you boys have eaten, go on downstairs and report to your boss. Tell him that you've already talked to me and that I want you and your men as the security team for the house during tonight's raid. Besides, it'll give you a chance to get some rest."

"Yes, sir."

"Also, Sergeant, I would like you to draw up a strip map of the President's farm and a layout of the buildings as soon as you can."

"Yes, sir."

After the briefing, Lance called Judge Dexter Knowles from Marilyn's bedroom and when the judge answered the telephone on the second ring, Lance said, "Dexter, this is Lance Stalwardt."

"My God, Lance. How the hell are you?"

"Fine, Dexter, just fine."

"Where are you?"

"Here in town. I'm home on leave visiting my family and I'd like to see you right away if it's convenient."

"Sure thing, Lance. How soon?"

"How about now? Any problem with that?"

"Hell no. You know where I live, don't you?"

"Are you still in the same house I visited a few years ago?"

"Yes, but it's been more than just a few years, Lance. It's been almost eight years since you've been here."

"Dexter … before I hang up, I have to tell you that I'm coming over to see you on some official business. I can't tell you what it is over the phone, but it's important that we talk."

"No problem, Lance. I'll still be glad to see you."

"Good, I'll be there in a few minutes then."

Lance hung up the receiver, left the room and as he passed the bedroom with the two Secret Service agents, he knocked on the door. "You boys about ready?"

"We'll be right there, General."

The door opened and both agents came out looking better than they had before. After their showers, shaves and change of clothes, they both looked every bit like professional federal agents. They followed Lance to the kitchen where he put on his blouse and service cap then gave Marilyn a quick kiss on the cheek.

Marilyn whispered into his ear, "Good luck, honey."

Lance turned to Mike and said, "While I'm gone, I want you to check with Dorn about the airport. I'll see you when I get back from the judge's place."

"Yes, sir," replied Mike.

Fifteen minutes later Lance and the two agents arrived at the judge's home. The judge met them at the door and after a few minutes of greetings and introductions in the hallway, the judge ushered the men into a well furnished den. It looked more like a law library then a den, with rows of law books on shelves and stacks of legal papers on the desk.

After the men sat down the judge asked, "Would you men like a drink? I'm having a beer myself."

"That'll be fine," said Lance.

The judge produced three cans of beer from a small refrigerator from behind his desk and gave them out to his guests. Next, Lance and the judge began reminiscing for a few minutes.

Then abruptly the judge asked, "Lance, I suspect very strongly that your business has to do with the assassinations. Am I right?"

A bit surprised at the blunt inquiry, Lance replied, "Yes, Dexter, it does. But tell me, how'd you come to that conclusion? We gave no indication of our business before you brought up the subject."

"Easy. First you told me on the phone that you wanted to see me in an official capacity, then you show up at my door all decked out in every medal the army has. Very impressive I might add."

"You came to that conclusion because I've got my uniform on?"

"No. You see, I know you work in the White House on the President's personal staff then when you introduced me to these two Secret Service agents, I just assumed it had something to do with the assassinations. So tell me, what is it you want?"

Lance said, "I need a warrant issued for the arrest of about a dozen men. We believe they're planning to assassinate President Williams very soon and we also believe they may be involved with or have knowledge of, the killing of at least ten other people in Washington, DC."

"On what grounds?"

"Our evidence is very strong and has been verified by two witnesses." Lance continued to relate the events of the last two days to the judge and the testimony of the captured mobsters, explaining he stumbled onto the plot quite by accident. After finishing, Lance asked, "Dexter, will you sign the warrants?"

"You betcha, and by God, I hope this one doesn't turn into a cover up fiasco like the Kennedy killing. If there's anything I can do to help, I'll do it. Where's the warrant?"

Agent Hickman produced the warrant from an inside breast pocket and said, "It's right here, Judge, ready for your signature."

Judge Knowles took the document, read it for a few moments then said, "It looks good to me." As he signed it he asked, "Is there anything else you need?"

"Not right now, Your Honor, but it's good to know there's somebody handy in our legal corner," said Agent Hickman as he took the signed document from the judge.

Lance said, "Dexter, before we go I'd like to ask you not to give any of this information to the local police agencies until after we've attempted the arrest. I'm afraid the locals are ill-equipped to handle this sort of thing, and God knows we don't want any needless killings. Besides, I believe these guys will try to shoot it out and if they do, we have the firepower to take them out. If it comes to that, by God we will. We're not gonna screw around with these guys."

"Who is making the arrest if it isn't the sheriff?"

"We have our own force of government agents in the field, ready to act as soon as we return."

"All right, gentlemen. I'll give you until late tomorrow morning then I'll have to make the warrant signing a matter of public record. Of course, it may not be available to the media for a couple of days or so, depending on where the warrant log is kept. Hell, sometimes we can't find the damn thing for a whole week."

"Thanks, Dexter. We have no problem with that, do we fellas?"

Both agents shook their heads.

Lance and the two agents left the judge's house with Lance promising to have lunch with his old friend sometime before returning to Washington.

On the way back to Marilyn's house, Agent Andrews asked, "General, you want us in on this raid or are we gonna miss the fun?"

"I'd rather you not participate in the actual raid itself because of the way my men operate. However, I do want you along to observe, but don't bother anyone or get in anybody's way. You'll have to stick close to me. By the way, have either of you got any clothing that identifies you as government agents?"

"Yeah, we've got our windbreakers with Secret Service in large yellow letters on the back."

"Good. Make sure you wear them tonight so my men don't make a mistake and shoot you."

Agent Andrews drove the car with Agent Hickman in the front passenger seat while Lance rode in the back, seated behind the younger agent.

Agent Hickman turned around and leaned on the back of the front seat and said, "General, I've been around the government a helluva long time, and I'll be damned if I've ever seen anything like your bunch. Just what kinda group you got here, anyway?"

"Obviously it's a highly secret organization," said Lance, "or at least it used to be, but I guess it's not so secret anymore, is it?"

"Yeah, and you know, it looks like we're not the only ones who knows about your little troop. At least that's what I gather from the talk I've been hearing from Colonel Polaski and Colonel Slaughter. Do you have any idea who's causing the trouble?"

"Not yet, but you can bet your last dollar I'm gonna find out, and when I do, I'll bring the bastard down so fast he won't know what hit him. I know one thing. Whoever it is, he's in the government."

"Think it might be the new guy, Williams?"

"Right now I don't know, but I've not ruled the man out just yet. Which reminds me, I'm supposed to go see the new President tomorrow night. I want you two along."

"Sure, be glad to."

"Maybe then we can find out some things and get you guys back to where you belong."

The younger agent said, "No need to hurry on my account. This is more action than I've ever seen in the six years since I've been with the service."

Lance chuckled and thought, *Maybe I'll keep these guys around for awhile. They may have some contacts that might come in handy. Besides, the Secret Service Agency itself may be involved in this thing and if I'm going to find out the truth, I'll need someone who knows how the agency works.*

Chapter 17

Arriving at Marilyn's house with the two agents, Lance looked at his watch and said, "It's sixteen thirty. That leaves only an hour and a half until the raid. Is there anything you two need to take care of between now and eighteen hundred?"

Both men said no, but a moment after Agent Hickman got out of the car, he said, "General, it's been a while since we've contacted our office. Not that we really wanna do it, but if by some chance there is a connection with the agency and all of this, shouldn't we try to maintain contact? They might suspect something's wrong if we don't call in."

"I think they would already suspect something since you haven't reported in for a while, and especially now since you haven't said anything about the attempted shootings. If the agency is involved, they'll already know there have been three attempts to get me, and they'll also know those attempts failed. I would think that after tonight's raid there'll be no doubt in their minds. They'll know for sure that you two have joined our little group." Lance paused then asked, "What kind of a story were you planning to give them?"

Agent Hickman replied, "Our last contact was after you got to your daughter's house on Friday night, about an hour before you ducked out on us. Of course we didn't know that, so they don't know that either. We'll just tell them we felt nothing was happening and got a room at a local motel, then waited until Monday to resume the surveillance. Besides, the only thing they told us was that you were on two weeks leave at your mother's place, so there was no reason for us to believe you were anywhere else. They didn't tell us to stay on you every minute of the day, just to let them know where you were. We've already done that and besides, we gotta have some time off too."

"You think they'll swallow that?"

"Probably not for very long, but since we're not part of the inside operation, I think we can get away with it for the time being. At least until the judge goes public about the warrant. Right now the only thing they can do is chew my ass out for not being more attentive to duty, but like I said, we're not privy to their plans so we're not supposed to know how important it is to maintain your whereabouts. Besides, what else they gonna do?"

"Okay, I suppose you're right, but I don't think you can get away with this charade for very long. Anyway, after we see the President tomorrow night, maybe we won't have to."

"What have you got in mind, General?"

"I'm not sure yet. Let's just play it by ear until after you've had the conversation with your people in the morning and I talk with the President tomorrow night."

"All right, sir. That makes sense."

Lance and the two men entered the house to prepare for the upcoming raid on the farmhouse. The two agents went downstairs to attend the group's briefing while Lance went to the kitchen where Mike sat at the table.

Mike said, "There's no problem with Dorn. Said he'd be glad to help. Hell, he's even puttin' up some temporary runway lights so it'll be easier for the planes to land in the dark."

"Thanks, Mike. Call John at 1700 and give him the information, but for now, go on down and start the briefing while I change and get ready."

"Yes, sir."

Lance went into Marilyn's bedroom where she had gone earlier in the afternoon to take a nap. As Lance came into the dark room Marilyn opened her eyes, but didn't move or say anything letting Lance think she still slept. She watched as Lance changed into a black non-descript combat uniform. When through dressing, he sat on the edge of the bed, leaned over and kissed her on the cheek then hurried from the room, heading to the basement.

Mike finished the briefing then asked, "Questions anybody?"

"Yes, sir. Who gives the signal to go in and when?"

"General Stalwardt will give it to me and I'll give it to you. It'll be my voice you hear on the radio not the general's." After a slight pause Mike asked, "Anything else?" No one responded so Mike said, "Good. Finish gettin' ready. You've got ten minutes before we load up and move out."

Mike met Lance and said, "Sir, I talked to John personally and gave him the information. He said he's gonna fly the planes to the Dorn airstrip around eighteen hundred."

"Okay … you better get going. It's about time."

At precisely six o'clock that evening, the group assembled in place, ready to assault the Gregory farmhouse located at the end of a long lane off a gravel road. The group arrived without being detected. At the intersection of the road and the lane a three-man team stood guard to keep anyone from coming down the lane during the raid.

As the group moved into place, Agent Andrews said, "Damn, General, these guys are really good. Hell, I never heard half of them and they went right by me. They sure are quiet."

The older agent whispered in Joe's ear. "You better be too, Joe, or somebody might shoot you for being too noisy."

The younger agent realized his intrusion and said, "Oh shit, I'm really sorry, General."

Lance looked at his watch. Time to start. He raised a bullhorn up, pressed a button and said, "YOU IN THE FARMHOUSE! THIS IS THE UNITED STATES SECRET SERVICE. YOU ARE ALL UNDER ARREST! THROW OUT YOUR WEAPONS AND COME OUT WITH YOUR HANDS UP!"

Lance had barely finished when a dozen or more shots rang out, fired toward him from various windows and doors of the house.

Lance said to Mike, "Give the order. They've had their chance."

Almost simultaneously twenty-four foreign made automatic assault rifles, equipped with silencers, opened up at rapid-fire rate, splintering wood around the windowsills, shattering glass panes and ripping holes through the house siding as the bullets tore through the building. Within seconds the gunfire from the farmhouse had been suppressed. A six man team moved quickly to the front wall of the house and commenced to assault the front porch and the side windows of the building. Six concussion grenades went in through windows at various points on the first floor, exploding simultaneously. After they blew, the soldiers entered the building.

Lance could tell the location of the two teams inside the house as they systematically worked their way through the rooms. Besides reporting their exact location by radio, Lance knew by the flash and low muffled sounds of the automatic gunfire. In a little over five minutes the words came over the radio, "All clear."

Mike keyed the radio and asked, "Any survivors?"

The reply came back, "No, sir. They're all dead."

"How many bodies?"

"Ten, sir."

"Okay, Major, hang loose. The general and I'll be right in." Mike paused then said into the radio, "Alpha One."

"Alpha One," came the reply.

"Bring up the single."

This meant for the three men guarding the lane to bring up the body of the man Lance had shot in Marilyn's house the night before then Mike turned to the older Secret Service agent and said, "Okay Hickman, you're on next, but wait till we get back from lookin' over the damage inside the house."

While Mike and Lance toured through the house surveying the damage and the dead men, Mike said, "The poor bastards should've given up. They never really had a chance."

"Hell, Mike, these guys had no idea who they were up against. They thought it was the Secret Service out there, not us." Lance stood in the middle of what appeared to be the living room. He looked around then said, "I've seen enough, let's go."

Agent Hickman saw Lance and Mike leave the house so he went to the government vehicle and set the radio on the local sheriff department's frequency and waited for Mike's signal.

When Mike waved, he keyed the hand-held microphone and said very casually, "Stephenson County Sheriff's Department, this is Agent Calvin W. Hickman with the United States Secret Service."

"This is Stephenson County, go ahead."

"Stephenson County, we've got a situation here at a place called Gregory's farm just north of Freeport on Highway twenty-six and about two miles east on a gravel road. Do you know the place?"

After a pause the dispatcher's voice came back, "Yes, sir. We know where the place is."

"There has been a shootout between Secret Service agents and a band of people in the Gregory house that were highly suspected in an assassination plot to kill the President of the United States. They refused to surrender to a federal arrest warrant and are now all dead. There are ten bodies inside the ... correction ... there are eleven bodies inside the house. There are no Secret Service personnel casualties. Please send the county coroner and some assistance to remove the bodies."

As the county dispatcher answered, "This is Stephenson County, please stand by Agent Hickman," Lance and Mike heard someone in the background of the sheriff's department say in an excited tone, "Jesus Christ, man, what the hell's happening out there?"

A moment later another voice came over the radio that sounded a little strained. "Agent Hickman, this is Chief Deputy Sheriff Hager. What's the situation there?"

"Nothing now, Deputy Hager. It's all over. I request assistance from the county coroner to come pick up the bodies of eleven males killed in an attempt to serve a federal warrant. Will you cooperate or must I call my supervisor in Washington, DC."

The chief deputy asked, "Who signed the warrant?"

"A federal judge by the name of Knowles, here in Freeport. You know him?"

"Yes. I know him. Stand by for a moment."

Mike, who had been listening to the conversation, turned to Lance behind him and said, "They're stalling. They don't know what to make of it and they wanna check it out with the judge."

Lance said, "Go ahead and send the men back to Marilyn's place. Better hurry before someone sees them leave. I want you and a couple of the men to fly that helicopter out by the barn to Dorn's place. I'll meet you over there in a few minutes."

"What are we gonna do with a helicopter?"

"I'll probably fly it over to see President Williams tomorrow, instead of driving."

"All right, sir, I'll see you later out at Dorn's."

It took less than two minutes for the vans to load and leave. It took the helicopter only a few moments longer, but soon it too left. Only Lance, two soldiers and the two federal agents remained.

As he stood next to the black government car, Lance said to Agent Hickman, "Somehow Blondie must have gotten away because

I didn't see the bastard's body in with the rest of 'em. He probably left before we got here. I sure wish we could have gotten the son of a bitch."

Before the agent could reply, the sheriff's dispatcher called on the radio. "Agent Hickman, this is Stephenson County."

"Go ahead Stephenson County."

"The chief deputy and the coroner are on their way."

"Thanks Stephenson County, Hickman out."

"County out."

As Agent Hickman put down the hand mike, Lance said, "It's your show now fellas. Good luck."

When Lance and the two men riding with him left the farm lane, they could see three emergency vehicles traveling at a high rate of speed coming north out of Freeport on highway 26. Lance told his driver to head in the opposite direction and go to Dorn's airport.

At Dorn's, Mike met the car and Lance saw the huge shadowy outlines of the two Starlifters sitting behind the north end of the small hangar buildings. Only a single bulb burned inside one of the empty hangars with one door slightly opened. Lance saw Dorn standing inside talking to John Slaughter.

"How's it going here, Mike?"

"Everything's fine, sir."

"How's Dorn taking this?"

"He's about as excited as a kid with a new toy. The guy is really bending over backwards to be accommodating."

"We'll have to do something for him. He may be putting himself at risk here."

"I think the least we can do is pay the guy something."

Lance said, "Tell him to charge us a landing fee ... the same fee we'd pay if we put down at some of the other civilian airports."

"That oughta make him happy enough, especially if he charges the same as some of those big airports. The guy could retire on just this fee alone."

"Ask him to take a government charge card."

"How long we gonna be around here?"

"I don't know yet, but at least until after my visit with the President tomorrow. By the way, make sure someone checks out that helicopter before tomorrow night. I don't wanna go down somewhere between here and Galena."

"Hey, I can do that for you," a voice said behind Lance.

Lance turned and saw Dorn and John Slaughter coming from the hangar and asked, "You know something about helicopters?"

"Hell, yes ... I used to work on these babies in Nam."

"Good enough, then have at it. Just make sure it's shipshape by six o'clock tomorrow."

"Should be no problem, General. You got anybody that can give me a hand?"

"John, will you see to it?"

"Yes, sir."

After a few more moments of conversation, Dorn left the three military men and went to his office inside the hangar then Lance said, "John, tonight I want you to take your people into the motel where the others are billeted and grab yourselves a shower and a good night's sleep. We'll send some of the guys out here as soon as they clean up."

"Thanks, General. Some of my people are about to go stir crazy, especially the four enlisted female crew members. This should boost their spirits some."

"They causing any problems?"

"Not really. It's just because they don't know what's goin' on or how long this is gonna last. How long we gonna be here?"

"I don't know, John. It all depends on my meeting with the new President tomorrow."

Throughout the rest of the evening the group carried out Lance's instructions and prepared for the meeting with the President on the next evening. Lance spent the night at Marilyn's, with a three-man security team on watch.

All during the next day Lance made telephone calls to some of his military friends, trying to find out the mood back in Washington, but only learned that none of them had any ideas about the present situation. He felt as if the city had completely shut down, and no one could communicate anything.

That afternoon Lance called his mother and said he wouldn't be home until the next day because of some important business he had to take care of out of town.

His mother said, "All right, son, be careful. And call Lynn at work. She called last night and wanted to talk to you."

"Okay, Mom, I'll give her a call as soon as I can."

After saying his goodbyes, Lance turned to Marilyn sitting on the edge of the bed, reached out his hand and took hers, saying, "My daughter wants me to call her. I would like for you to meet her."

Marilyn smiled, squeezed his hand and leaned toward him to kiss his cheek. However, Lance turned abruptly and wrapped his other arm around her, forcing her down on the bed while kissing her.

She responded.

After the hour long romantic interlude, Lance and Marilyn got up from the bed, showered and dressed. Lance put on his greens in preparation for his meeting with the President later that evening. When he finished dressing he called Mike at the motel.

"Mike, how soon you coming over?"

"In about ten minutes."

"Good, I'll see you then."

Next, Lance called his daughter and she asked him to come to dinner that night, but he had to beg off. "I'm sorry, honey. I can't make it tonight, but how about tomorrow night?"

"Okay, Dad, that'll be fine."

"Lynn. Do you mind if I bring a friend? I want you to meet someone ... someone rather special."

"Do I know her?"

"I didn't say it was a her."

"Dad, this is your daughter, remember? I know it's a woman. I can tell it in your voice."

"You didn't answer my question. Besides, she's an old friend from high school."

"Sure ... no problem. It's about time you found somebody. I gotta go now. I'll see you tomorrow night. We'll eat at six."

"All right, honey. We'll see you then."

When Mike arrived, they sat at the kitchen table.

Mike said, "I've been on the phone most of the day to see if I could scare up any more information from some of my contacts, but they haven't got a clue about what's goin' on. It's like everything is shut down. I hate to say this, but I think we're at a dead end here."

"I know," said Lance. "I've been doing the same thing and with the same results. Anyway, is everything ready for tonight?"

"Anytime you're ready to go, just say the word."

"Let's go at nineteen hundred," said Lance. "That way we'll be able to leave Dorn's at nineteen thirty and be at the President's compound by twenty hundred hours."

"Anything else?"

"Yeah, is Hickman around? I wanna find out what happened when he called his boss this morning."

"I know he called, but right afterward he and Joe went to the sheriff's office. Something about giving the sheriff a briefing about what happened at the Gregory place."

"Okay, when he gets back have him come see me."

"Sure thing."

Around six the same evening, Agent Hickman and his partner returned from the sheriff's office.

Lance said to the two men, "Please join me in the kitchen."

Taking off their coats, the men sat at the table as Lance poured each a cup of coffee.

Agent Hickman said, "Thanks, General. I surely need this."

Mike asked, "What's the problem?"

"No problem, Colonel. It's just been a long two days."

"How'd it go down at the sheriff's office?"

"Pretty good except the chief deputy kept wonderin' why there were four barrels of aviation fuel in the barn and no aircraft around. I kept tellin' him that the aircraft probably hadn't arrived yet, but he didn't buy that because he found two of the barrels empty."

"Anything else that's important?"

"Not really. The rest of the stuff was pretty routine. It just took awhile to get everything documented."

Lance asked, "Documented? What do you mean documented?"

The younger agent replied, "Don't worry, General. It's cool."

"Yeah … it's okay," said Agent Hickman. "We only gave the essential facts and not enough for them to know that your unit conducted the assault. They think a special Secret Service detail from the President's compound at Galena came and pulled the raid."

"You tell them that?"

"Nah, they come up with that one by themselves. I didn't lie about anything. I just didn't tell all of the truth."

"Is that the story they're gonna give the press?"

"I really don't know. Anyway, we've got a little time before they release anything to the news media. I asked the sheriff if he'd hold off on any press releases until tomorrow. He said no problem."

"Okay, sounds good," said Lance. "What about your call to DC this morning?"

"I did what I said I was gonna do yesterday, I played dumb. I got my ass chewed, and I mean royally. Bradley told me to find you and report immediately where you are, no matter what time of the day or night. I told him I'd get right on it."

"When are you supposed to call back?"

"I guess not until I find you, whenever that is."

"Anything else?"

"Yeah. Somethin' happened when we were at the sheriff's office. They notified the local FBI office in Rockford and told them about the raid. An hour later I get this call from an old friend that's an agent in the Chicago office and he tells me that he heard through the grapevine that the bunch we nailed were members of the Mafia. He told me to watch my back. The news is out now, and the mob thinks I was responsible for knocking off their people."

"Was there anything mentioned about us?"

"Not a word. I really think they don't know the group is here."

"The mob's not stupid," said Lance. "Sooner or later they're gonna figure it out. Especially since Blondie got away. Dammit, I wish we could've gotten our hands on that bastard."

Mike asked, "Is that it?"

"Yeah," said Agent Hickman, "at least for now anyway."

Lance said, "Okay, fellas, let's get ready for the Galena trip."

Chapter 18

At seven o'clock that evening, Lance, Mike and the two Secret Service agents, along with a three-man team from Delta section, left Marilyn's house and drove to Dorn's airfield. By 7:30 p.m. they were airborne in the confiscated helicopter on their way to Galena to where the President of the United States waited for them.

Passing over the countryside, they saw farm lights dotting the landscape below, along with lights of the smaller towns like Lena, Stockton and Warren. Further out on the horizon they could see the lights from the nearby larger towns, Rockford in the east, Freeport in the south, Monroe, Wisconsin in the north and Dubuque, Iowa in the west. Mike headed the aircraft on 270 degrees, due west.

Within minutes they arrived at the President's farm, and at Mike's command, the acting copilot set the radio on the presidential compound frequency given to him by Agent Hickman, a frequency assigned to the President's security force. After a brief conversation and recognition code, the ground contact instructed the helicopter to land on a lighted landing pad at the south end of the complex about fifty meters from the house. While Mike settled the aircraft on the ground, a security detail of four men came out to meet them.

One of the agents asked, "General Stalwardt?"

"Yes, I'm General Stalwardt."

"Please come with me, General. The rest of you will stay here with the aircraft."

Lance followed two of the agents toward the farmhouse while the other two agents stayed with the helicopter. At the front door, an agent gave Lance a quick pat down search for a weapon.

The three-man party entered the house then into a large room off the entryway where Lance saw the President of the United States standing beside a large ornate wooden desk. The three men stopped. Lance came to attention and saluted his new commander in chief.

President Williams didn't return the salute, but instead extended his hand to Lance and smiled as he said, "Please, General Stalwardt, do come in. Gentlemen, you may leave us. And close the door."

After shaking hands, the President motioned to a couch, a coffee table and three chairs. "I believe we'll be more comfortable over here. Please, have a seat, General." The President went to his desk and picked up a glass saying, "I'm having a scotch on the rocks, will you join me?"

"Yes, sir, I believe I will," said Lance as he sat on the couch.

Turning to an open doorway a few feet behind him, the President said in a raised voice, "Ben, make that another of the same for our guest," then turned back to Lance. "My cousin will join us in a few moments. I believe you already know each other."

The statement puzzled Lance and he said, "I don't think so, Mr. President ... or at least I don't recall meeting anyone that claimed to be your cousin."

A man came through the door behind the President carrying a glass in each hand, and while in the shadows, Lance felt something familiar about him.

When the man approached the light, Lance suddenly recognized him and exclaimed, "Oh my GOD ... it's Ben Hawkins!"

Hawkins only smiled.

Taken by surprise, Lance rose from the couch and said, "I've been trying to reach you on the transponder. When you didn't answer, I thought someone might have killed you too."

Handing Lance a glass, Hawkins said, "It was thought better that I not answer any calls until my cousin had a chance to talk to you. You'll understand why in a moment. Anyway, General, it's good to see you again ... especially under these circumstances."

For a moment, Lance couldn't recall when Hawkins ever spoke to him, but then he remembered the voice on the telephone that had summoned him to the President's office over the past three years and realized it was Hawkins's voice.

The President said, "Gentlemen, shall we get started with the business at hand?"

All three men took their seats, sipped their drinks in silence for a moment then the President spoke. "General, it *is* a terrible thing to have the President of the United States assassinated. It's not good for the country to have a leader shot down, murdered if you will, in cold blood. There are too many emotional ramifications from such an act of violence, and it confuses the governing system to a point where it ceases to function properly. The aftermath of emotional issues, like revenge and guilt, far outweigh the normal day to day business in the government and people tend to forget their true purpose for a while. When that happens, anarchy prevails. No, General Stalwardt, this is not a good time for our country."

The President leaned forward and put his glass on the table in front of him. He sat back in the chair again and continued, "I believe we've come up against some very tough-minded people here. They've killed one President and have attempted to kill another. There are nine or ten others dead because of these bastards, whoever they are, and I believe it's up to us to find out who's responsible for this travesty and end it. That's why I've asked you here today. I would like you and your special unit to find these culprits and eliminate them. That is, of course, if you will agree to the mission."

"Before I do, Mr. President, may I ask you something?"

"Go ahead."

"How long have you known about the group?"

"This may surprise you, General, but I had no knowledge of your unit until after the President's death. Although Ben here is my cousin, he did not compromise his duty, and he did keep the secret until after I was sworn into office. However, as soon as he told me about the group, I called you. I only hope that you will serve me as well as you did your former commander."

"Yes, Mr. President. The group and I are at your disposal."

"Excellent," said the President as he took his glass from the table and raised it toward Lance. "Gentlemen, to our success."

After the men finished their drinks and set their glasses on the table, Lance said, "Mr. President, I have some news I think you should know about. During the past few days I have been involved in some events that I believe are connected to the assassinations."

Lance continued to brief the other two men from the time he got off the airplane at O'Hare in Chicago up until the present time. He told them about the abduction of the two federal agents, Hickman and Andrews, about the three attempts on his life and about the

Gregory farm raid. He also told them about the warning Hickman received from the Chicago FBI agent.

Lance concluded his briefing by saying, "Although I don't know for sure, I think there's a strong possibility that we may have eliminated some of the people who were involved in the President's murder and some of the other killings. Anyway, there are eleven men dead in Stephenson County that we know for sure are members of organized crime."

"Well now," said the President, "it appears there's more to all of this than what Ben and I had originally thought."

Lance asked, "What are your orders on how we should proceed, Mr. President?"

"One thing is for certain, gentlemen. If organized crime is involved here, we must be cautious. Very cautious indeed. It's going to be extremely difficult to know who to trust. These people could be deeply imbedded into the very core of our government and at this point, we could be very vulnerable. When underworld power is connected to leaders within our government ... no one is safe."

The President paused then continued, "General, I am going to give you a free hand in doing what you need to do to get these culprits who are behind this conspiracy, and by God, I want you to make certain that you get them all no matter who or what they are. Is that clear?"

"Yes, sir, very clear," replied Lance.

"For the time being, I think it best if I keep your operation at arm's length and not become personally involved. Ben will be your contact until you get this matter cleared up. Anything I'm involved with in the next six months or so is bound to be under a public microscope, and there won't be much of a chance for me to assist you. You two will have to handle it as best you can."

"What about intelligence information from the other agencies? Will we be able to trust their information or should we just gather our own intelligence?"

Hawkins answered, "I don't think we should depend on anyone else. It'll be too risky. One slip up and these bastards could get us."

"I agree," said Lance. "The two agents with me can maybe help us work the inside and see what's what. I trust their loyalty."

The President spoke again, "As I said a moment ago, I want this problem cleared up as quickly as possible, and I don't want any lengthy trials where they can forever drag this thing through the courts. I want it over and done with, and I want nothing left to chance. I want you and your group to do what you do best. Do you understand, General?"

"Yes, sir, I do." Lance knew full well what the President told him—dispense justice swiftly and to do it with a bullet.

The moment had come that Lance dreaded and one he had vowed against a long time ago—the group being ordered to do business for internal politics. However, under the circumstances, Lance had no choice except to obey his commander in chief. The controversial moment had arrived just as Mike had predicted.

"Good. I'll let you and Ben figure out the operation when we return to Washington. I'm leaving early Wednesday morning and I'll be there to attend the President's funeral service at noon. I want you and your group in Washington too, but only you are to come to the funeral."

"Yes, sir."

"Ben and I were discussing something before you arrived and decided that if you agreed to this mission, you and your group should return to Washington and take charge of the White House while everyone, who is anyone, is at the funeral. I want everyone removed from the White House complex and replaced by your own personnel. I want to ensure that the building and grounds of the White House are absolutely secure so that I'm not a target when I arrive there. Besides, from what Ben has told me about your group, they have the ability to take over and conduct White House operations, at least temporarily until we can get everyone else checked out."

"Sir, do you believe someone in the White House is responsible for the killings?"

"Responsible? No. However, both Ben and I believe that the information about the President's jogging route and the whereabouts of the others on that particular day came from inside the White House. It had to be … there is no other way they could have been that lucky to kill that many people by coincidence."

"I agree, sir. I think you're wise to use the group for White House security, and as far as any other temporary operations, that shouldn't be a problem. As you may know, the group was originally established to beef up the civilian security force at Camp David and had an additional mission to provide security for the President whenever it was needed. Moving them to the White House under the present circumstances shouldn't cause any undue suspicions and I personally think the public will accept the move. They'll probably even be politically sympathetic."

"Excellent, General," said the President with a smile on his face. "How does that sound to you, Ben?"

"He's right, Mr. President. I was there when the unit was first conceived and one of the main reasons for forming the group was to protect the President in time of need. And now, there is a need."

"Mr. President, I have a three-man team with me. They are armed with automatic rifles and have enough firepower to ward off any civilian type attack on your farm if they should try to assassinate you here. I would feel much better knowing they're here protecting you and your family."

"He's right," said Hawkins, "The agents here have only pistols and if somebody really wanted to kill you bad enough, handguns wouldn't stop them."

"All right, General, I see your point. Please leave your three-man team. I'll return them to you on Wednesday afternoon. Now then, gentlemen, that brings us to another matter," said the President as he rose from his chair, walked the short distance to his desk, picked up a sheet of paper and returned to his seat.

As the President sat down he handed the paper to Lance and said, "General, if you will accept the appointment, you are now my National Security Adviser. I will be presenting this document to the appropriate congressional leaders when I arrive in Washington Wednesday morning. And, in view of what has happened, I don't think there'll be any problems. I believe they'll dispense with your appointment as quickly as possible."

Taken by surprise, Lance read the short document and said, "Mr. President, I am deeply honored. I hardly know what to say."

Hawkins said, "Say yes. It'll simplify things."

All three men laughed at the proposed humor by Hawkins then the President asked, "Gentlemen, shall we have another Scotch? Ben, will you please do the honors again?"

While Hawkins went into the other room to replenish the drinks, Lance asked, "Mr. President, may I suggest my replacement for group commander?"

"By all means, General ... please do."

"I'd like to have Colonel Polaski take command."

"Ben said you'd probably recommend him for the job and based on what I've heard, I'll accept your recommendation."

"He's a fine soldier, Mr. President. You'll find none better."

"So I've heard. Since you are both being promoted in job status, you both should be promoted in rank. I'm going to recommend you for your third star and brigadier general for Colonel Polaski."

"Thank you, sir. I really appreciate this, and I know Colonel Polaski will too."

"Is he with you this evening?"

"Yes, sir. He flew the helicopter over from Freeport."

"Is he an aviator?"

"No, sir. He learned to fly in Vietnam. He had three helicopters go down on him because the pilots were shot and he didn't know how to fly the aircraft, so he just learned on his own."

"Sometimes necessity requires diversity."

"That's right, Mr. President. Sometimes it does." Lance paused for a moment then said, "I really don't mean to change the subject sir, but I've heard on the news that you were going to announce your choice of Vice President when you returned to Washington. I'm curious to know if you have decided on someone yet."

"Yes, as a matter of fact I have. But let me tell you, before I made my final decision, I toyed with the idea of presenting the name of someone whom I believe might be adversarial to my presidency. Someone like Senator Baynes from South Carolina."

"Senator Baynes, sir?"

"Yes, Cyrus Baynes. I thought if I could get him out of the Senate, I could better deal with Congress, but then I came to the realization that I would have to share our inside information with a political foe. I finally decided it wasn't worth the risk, even if we are in the same party."

Hawkins returned with the drinks and for another half hour the three men sat and discussed operational strategy for implementing a plan of action over the next few days, with the main topic being the takeover of the White House.

Lance left the President's farm at nine o'clock. He and his party flew back to Dorn's airfield, minus the three-man Delta team.

After Mike reached flying altitude on level flight, Lance keyed the intercom, "Mike, we've got a mission. When we get back to Dorn's, I want a meeting."

At 9:20 p.m. the helicopter touched down in front of the Quonset hangar at Dorn's small airfield. Lance, Mike, Agent Hickman and John Slaughter went into the Starlifter command module while the others waited in the airport office with Jack Dorn. Lance took his usual end seat in the soundproof room while the three other men sat in the booth seats.

"Gentlemen, we've been assigned a mission and it's probably going to be a tough one. It won't be so much physically tough as it will be mentally. We've been asked to secure the White House prior to the arrival of President Williams on Wednesday afternoon."

John asked, "Does that mean we have to leave right away?"

"No. We'll leave tomorrow night before midnight. I want to arrive on the east coast sometime in the early morning. Less chance of detection that way."

"But, General," continued the chief pilot, "is it gonna be safe to go back to Andrews? Remember what happened when we left?"

"We're not going to Andrews. We're going into Dover."

Agent Hickman asked, "How we gonna get back to DC?"

Mike interrupted and said, "Wait a minute guys, let the general finish. I think we'll have our answers if we just show a little patience, OK?" The other men nodded their heads and looked to Lance as Mike said, "All right, General … what've ya got?"

"At twenty-three hundred hours on Tuesday, we leave here and land at Dover Air Force Base in Dover, Delaware, sometime after two o'clock eastern time. Arrangements are already being made to bus us from Dover to Washington. When we get to DC, we'll be dropped off at the White House where we'll proceed to secure the building and the grounds before the arrival of President Williams, which is sometime around fourteen hundred on Wednesday. That means we clear everybody out no matter who they are.

"We're also tasked to act as a temporary operations force within the White House until the regular personnel have been checked out and returned to duty. That means the phones, meals and whatever else comes up. However, we must remember at all times that our first priority is the security of the President."

The chief pilot asked, "What about us, sir?"

"After the group is dropped off in a secure part of the airfield, you and the Starlifters will be parked in the hazardous parking area back by Little Creek. I'm gonna leave the rest of the Delta section with you as a security force, but I'm taking most of your personnel. In fact, I'm taking all the enlisted people you've got except those you'll need as a bare minimum to fly out of there if you have to. Additional security for the aircraft will be provided by Dover security. However, they will not be allowed to come within a 500 meter radius of the aircraft. That's why I've left you the rest of the Delta section. Their mission will to be to provide security within the 500 meter perimeter."

John asked, "Are you expecting any trouble there?"

"Not really," said Lance. "It's mostly precautionary."

"How long do you think we'll have to stay there?"

"I don't think it'll be for very long. Probably no more than a couple of days. One of the first things we'll do after we secure the White House is to bring in the Air Force Chief of Staff and restate in no uncertain terms that there is a hands-off policy of the presidential aircraft by outside military personnel. By the way, find out the name of the two-star general that wanted in the aircraft at Andrews."

"I already have it. Here, I wrote it down before we took off."

John tore a page of paper out of the small notebook he had in front of him and handed it to Lance. The name written on it, Major General Cross.

Agent Hickman asked, "General, how do we fit into all of this?"

"Since you've been in the White House before, I want you to take charge of all security and to start background checks on all of the domestic service personnel. I want the rechecks done quickly and as thoroughly as possible. These people will have priority before anyone else. After all, they're the ones who make the White House run. Next, I want you to start on the career civilians. You can have extra support if you need it from any of John's people. As you compile a daily list, submit it to me and we'll go over it the next day. Hopefully we can start returning people back to work within a few days.

"What about the Secret Service guys assigned to the President?"

"No other agents, except the group he has with him, will be permitted onto the grounds and back into service until the President is satisfied they are loyal and not part of the conspiracy."

Mike asked, "Does that mean someone within the White House fingered the President and his people?"

"We don't know, but we have to proceed on that assumption."

"That's gonna make some people real mad," said Hickman.

"I know, but it can't be helped."

"What about the White House press people?"

"They especially go out. And remember, no one talks to the media. We let the President and his personal advisors handle the press. If anybody talks and I find out about it, they'll wish to God they were dead, because I'll make their life a living hell."

John asked, "What are we gonna do with the Huey?"

Lance said, "Tell Dorn he can have it."

"That'll make his day," said Mike. "He's been itchin' to fly the damn thing ever since we got it."

"Oh yeah?"

"Hell yeah. He volunteered to fly us over to Galena tonight, but because it was official business, I told him he better not."

"Good," said Lance. "It should have a good home then. And Mike, make sure he gets the proper documentation so somebody doesn't confiscate it from him."

Lance paused as he looked around at the men before him then said, "There's one more item before we go. After we get through with securing the White House, I'll no longer be commanding the group. I've been replaced."

The news took the men by surprise, but Lance soon eased their fears after he told them of his new job assignment and that the President had appointed Mike to replace him.

Mike said, "Outstanding."

Lance stood up and said, "Congratulations, General Polaski."

"General? You mean I've been promoted to brigadier?"

"That's right, Mike, and no one deserves it any better than you."

"Damn. I never thought I'd live to see the day."

Lance shook hands with his old friend as did the rest of the men in the room.

"Gentlemen," said Lance, "we've got a lot of work ahead of us, but we've got some time before we have to give it hell again. Therefore, I suggest we all get a good night's rest and start out fresh tomorrow, because tomorrow is gonna be a very long day."

The meeting broke up and the four men went outside.

Standing outside the Starlifter with the others, Lance looked up into the night sky full of bright stars, drew in a deep breath of the crisp autumn air and said, "God, what a weekend." He felt a sudden urge to be with Marilyn and the sooner the better. Turning to Mike, he said, "Let's go."

Lance and Mike got in the car and drove into Freeport.

Chapter 19

On the way back to Freeport, Lance began putting together a mental list of things he had to do then told Mike, "Tomorrow I'll have to tell people I'm leaving, and the hardest one is going to be Marilyn. At the sound of her name and the thought of his leaving, Lance began to feel a bit of remorse then a touch of fear. He blurted out, "Mike, I can't leave her alone. That blond bastard knows she saw his face, and he can't afford to have her alive. He'll kill her."

Mike said, "If he had anything to do with the assassinations he won't hesitate to kill somebody again, especially to protect his own ass. Maybe we oughta leave some of the guys behind to watch out for her and your family until we get this bastard."

"I want her protected every minute of the day, Mike."

"I'll make arrangements for three of the guys to stay and watch her, at least for the time being until we can get things settled. What about your family?"

"I don't think we need to keep protection around my mother and daughter, but I suppose I should tell them about what's going on."

"I agree they don't need protection, but why tell them anything? Hell, if they don't know, they won't worry about it, and if the mob wanted them bad enough, they'd get 'em anyway. If you tell them, you're gonna scare 'em, and maybe it could all be for nothing."

"That's true."

"But you know something, I don't think they're gonna bother your family because none of them are involved like Marilyn is. She actually saw one of them and can identify him. Your family can't because they don't even know what's goin' on."

"You're probably right. Anyway, I can appreciate why Admiral Emerson wanted people in the group without any family ties."

"It's a good policy."

"Another thing we've got to think about, Mike, is what are we gonna do with the two guys tied up in the basement? They know what Marilyn looks like, so we've got to do something about them."

Mike smiled as he said, "Maybe we should just shoot 'em."

"It's a solution, but it's one I don't believe we should be thinking about."

"Why? Don't you think they'd kill her?"

"No, I don't. I don't think these guys were involved with the Washington killings like I think Blondie was. They were just going after Williams. Remember, Blondie was in Chicago with a suitcase. It means he traveled from somewhere and I'll bet it was DC."

"Hell, in my book that makes 'em just as dangerous as Blondie."

"Yeah, but Blondie's on the loose, these characters aren't."

"You think that makes them any less dangerous?"

"No, but since they not only failed their mission, they also got caught. Their mob bosses know they failed and will probably kill them, figuring they'll talk to try and save their own skins. Let's offer them a choice. It'll be interesting to see what they do."

"What are the choices?"

"Freedom or jail."

"I'll bet they'll run like hell."

"I don't think so. Two bits says they'll choose jail."

"What are you gonna arrest them for?"

"Maybe Hickman can include them on that federal warrant."

"I don't think there's any evidence that will justify their arrest."

"True. But, let's just say they go to jail for maybe a month or two. It should take the legal boys that long to bail them out, and if we set up the judge by letting him know the situation, it could even take a little longer. It's not denying the bastards their right to bail, just delaying the process for a while. Anyway, I think it's worth a try, and I think they'll take the opportunity for having the jail time to keep themselves from getting killed."

"What makes you think they'll go for it?"

"It gives them time to set up their own protection on the outside. Anyway, I think they'll probably skip the country."

"Sounds good to me. Why don't you go see your judge friend with Hickman in the morning?"

When they arrived at Marilyn's house, Lance got out of the car and said, "I don't think you'll need to keep anybody around tonight. We'll be all right."

"Okay, sir, I'll see you in the morning, say around ten?"

"That'll be fine," said Lance.

"Send the guys out with the Bobbsey twins and I'll take 'em back to the motel."

After the three-man Delta team and the two prisoners left, Lance and Marilyn had the house to themselves. They sat on the living room sofa, Marilyn curled up and cradled against Lance, his arm around her shoulders, sipping white wine and listening to easy music on the stereo.

Quite abruptly, Marilyn asked, "When are you leaving?"

The question didn't surprise Lance, so he told her the plans about going to Washington. As he explained, he noticed Marilyn starting to sniffle. At first, tears welled up in her eyes then as they began to spill down her cheeks, she let out an involuntary sob.

"I can't help it," she said. "I love you, Lance, and I don't want you to leave me."

As she lay cradled in his arms, he hugged her and said, "I think it's mutual. I love you too."

Marilyn turned in his arms and kissed him with more passion than he remembered. The next morning while Lance slept, Marilyn got up, went to work and left a note on the table reminding Lance about having dinner at his daughter's at six that evening. When he read the note, Lance thought, *Tonight, I also have to leave*.

At 8:00 a.m., Lance went to his mother's house, had breakfast with her and explained, "I have to return to Washington to attend the President's funeral."

He did not lie, but he did not tell his mother the other reasons for leaving. "I'll be in town for the rest of the day on business, and I'll be going back to DC after dinner with Lynn tonight so this is goodbye, Mom. After the new President gets settled in, I promise to come back and spend more time with you."

An hour later, he packed his things and returned to Marilyn's. While pulling into the driveway, he saw Mike and three men in a minivan coming down the street. A black government car with Agents Andrews and Hickman followed—the time, ten o'clock.

Entering the house, the three-man security team headed to the guest bedrooms. The senior NCO took the room with the single bed while the other two shared a room with twin beds.

Lance, Mike and Agent Hickman sat at the kitchen table and Lance asked, "Mike, are the men checked out of the motel?"

"Yes, sir, they're on their way to Dorn's. Diehl's gonna take 'em on a road march this afternoon. They're getting wimpy from just sitting around."

"Good. I want you with me this afternoon anyway. Now, what about the prisoners?"

"They took the jail offer. They actually wanna go to jail now. I can't believe it, they know there's no case against them, yet they want the protection of being in jail for a while. Like you said, I think they're making plans for gettin' outta the country."

"Too bad they won't make it," said Agent Hickman.

Mike asked, "Oh yeah, why's that?"

"They'll both be dead inside a month, I guarantee it."

"Why do you say that?"

"The mob will contract both of 'em and somebody will nail their ass. Besides, it saves us from having to kill 'em ourselves. This way the mob does it for us and we don't have to worry about these two doing anything against the general's family. That's why the general set up the deal, right, General?"

When Mike looked at his boss, the expression on Lance's face gave him the answer.

Lance replied, "We've given the mob something else to worry about besides us. But, enough about them. It's time to get our show on the road. Hickman, we need to talk about what you and Andrews should be doing until you get to DC."

"General, do me a favor and quit calling me by my last name. Call me Cal."

"Okay, Cal," said Lance, "Cal, it is."

"Well, the first thing Joe and I should do is go back to Chicago and turn in the car. Then I think we should go back to DC sometime tonight and meet you guys at the White House in the morning."

"Sounds good to me. Plan to leave right after we see the judge."

"All right," said Agent Hickman.

Lance turned to Mike. "One other thing, Mike. I'd like for one of the men to return my rental car."

"No problem," replied Mike.

"I'll use one of the minivans for tonight. By the way, make sure you arrange to keep one of the vans for the guys while they're staying at Marilyn's?"

"Already taken care of, sir. Besides, we'll need it to shuttle the last group out to the airport. The security team can do that."

"Good, now that we've got that settled, let's get to it."

The three men spent the day visiting the judge, the coroner's office and taking the two would-be assassins to jail. At five o'clock the two agents left for Chicago and Mike went out to Dorn's airport. Lance would join them later that night after having dinner with his daughter and her family. At 5:30 p.m. Lance arrived at Marilyn's house where she stood waiting in the living room.

"I'll be ready in just a few minutes," said Lance as he hurried into the bedroom. "I'll shower and change clothes then we'll go."

At five minutes after six, Lance and Marilyn arrived at his daughter's, and Lynn seemed pleased to meet the new woman in her father's life. Even Meredith, normally shy, came to Marilyn without any fuss and seemed to enjoy the older woman's attention, much to Lance's surprise.

"She didn't take to me like that," said Lance.

"Don't be jealous," Marilyn said. "Anyway, you're the older woman type."

By 9:30 Lance felt it time to go. He told his daughter the same thing he told his mother, that he had to go back to Washington to attend the President's funeral. And, like he said to his mother, he promised to come back after the new President settled into the job.

When Lance and Marilyn arrived at her place, the three men of the security team sat at the kitchen table playing cards. Lance went to the ranking NCO, Sergeant Garcia and took him to one of the bedrooms for a private conversation.

"Sergeant Garcia, you three are responsible for the safety of a woman who is as dear to me as my mother. You see to it that nothing happens to her, understand?"

"Yes, sir, I understand perfectly."

"Good," said Lance. "I'm glad you understand the gravity of this mission."

Later, Sergeant Garcia briefed the other two members of his team, "If anything happens to this woman, and any of us are still alive afterwards, chances are we won't be for long. I feel this general would definitely take us out in a heartbeat if we fail to protect his lady."

Never one for long goodbyes, Lance went to Marilyn, hugged her briefly then quickly kissed her, picked up his bags and left. One of the security team members drove him to Dorn's airport.

Lance went aboard the number one aircraft and headed for the cockpit and as he stuck his head in the door the chief pilot asked, "You ready, General?"

"Let's go, John. Take us to Dover."

Chapter 20

The two C141 Starlifters touched down at the Dover Air Force Base just after 2:00 a.m., and as promised, two busses waited to transport Lance and the group to Washington, D.C., about two hours away. Once they arrived at the White House, Lance knew there would be no trouble with the Park Police and the service staff; however, he suspected there might be a problem with the on duty supervisor of the Secret Service agents still inside the complex.

The agents still performed certain security tasks, even with no one in the White House to guard. The slain President's widow had moved out on Monday afternoon and the new President was not due to arrive until after 2:00 p.m. on Wednesday. The Secret Service Director issued an order to make a complete security check over the entire White House complex by an electronics sweep inside the building at least twice every hour on a random schedule along with roving two man patrols in and around the complex.

Lance knew the assistant agent in charge of the White House Secret Service staff, a man named Harold Bonner, and assumed he also supervised the crew doing the security check.

Lance never liked the man since meeting him over three and a half years ago, saying to Mike one day, "I tell you, Mike, the man's a cold fish. He's like a robot with no sense of humor."

"Yeah, he's an asshole," replied Mike. "I've never seen him yet but what he wasn't complaining or bitchin' about something."

The busses had arrived at the White House shortly after 4:00 a.m. and the unit entered the complex then cleared everyone out and sent them home.

Afterward, Mike said, "The civilian staff was no problem, but a few of the Secret Service and some of the press people raised a lot of hell. They finally left when they saw their bullshit wasn't gonna do 'em any good."

"Everyone gone?"

"Everyone except that damn Bonner. He's still out at the front gate rantin' and ravin' wantin' back in. He told Major Hodges, that as long as he's assigned to the White House he demands to know what's goin' on, along with a bunch of other crap. Hodges told him to cool it or he'd cuff and gag him."

"Call the gate and have Bonner brought in here," said Lance. "I'll straighten his ass out."

Lance looked at his watch, 6:00 a.m. then thought, *Where'd the night go?*

He heard Agent Bonner before he saw him, verbally lashing out at the two men escorting him through the hall to Lance's office. "Gestapo ... thugs ... morons." When the trio arrived, Bonner leaned on the conference table with both hands and glared at Lance as he said, "Listen to me you tinhorn Boy Scout, I want Walt Bradley here, and I want him here now. And, I want you to call him personally, you got that, Stalwardt?"

Lance sat behind his desk, leaning back in his chair with his hands clasped in front of him across his chest, calmly staring at the irate redhead in front of him. He remained silent and appeared calm as the agent spouted off.

Then in a quiet voice, Lance said to the NCO's on either side of the man, "Hold him."

The two sergeants obeyed and grabbed the agent by the upper arms, lifting him off the floor. Lance rose from his chair and walked slowly around the desk until he stood directly in front of Agent Bonner, the agent's face a mask of pent-up rage and as red as a man's face could get.

As Lance approached him, Bonner spat out, "Whadda ya think you're gonna do, ya son of a bitch?"

Lance looked into the other man's eyes and saw small red blood lines mapping the whites and the black pupils starting to enlarge, shrinking out the green irises. As Lance got closer, the man's eyelids started to squint; causing crow's-feet lines to appear at the edges of the eyes and the eyebrows tighten as if a slight frown.

"It looks like you're under a lot of strain," said Lance.

"Go to hell, you Gestapo bastard."

Lance grabbed the front of the man's shirt with his left hand at the same time he reached down with his right hand and took a 9mm pistol from the closest sergeant's holster, raised it up to Agent

Bonner's face then stuck the weapon's barrel into the agent's mouth. Lance saw the expression quickly change in the eyes. A wide-open look with arched eyebrows and creased forehead replaced the squint and frown.

"Good," said Lance, "now that I have your attention."

Lance pulled the weapon's hammer back and applied a little forward pressure, pushing the barrel further into the man's mouth. The agent stiffened and began to lose color from his face. Lance moved closer to the other man and saw perspiration breaking out on the agent's upper lip and forehead.

"You ready to die right now for the President?"

The terrified agent shook his head slightly. Lance eased some pressure off the pistol and said, "Somebody killed the President of the United States and a few other good people recently. They were friends of mine and I'm pissed off. And, when I'm pissed off, I break things and sometimes I shoot people."

The agent didn't move or utter a sound, but kept looking at Lance in wide-eyed terror. Lance removed the pistol from the agent's mouth, un-cocked it and returned it to the soldier's holster.

He let go of the man's shirt, turned around and walked back to his chair and sat down then said, "Let him go." The two soldiers released the frightened man as Lance said, "You two can leave. Mike, stay here in case I need a witness against this piece of shit."

"Sit down, Bonner," said Mike who grabbed the agent by the shoulder and literally pushed him into one of the chairs at the conference table butted against Lance's desk. Mike sat in the chair next to him, leaned over to the frightened agent and said, "The next time you talk to the general, you call him sir ... you got that? He gets real bitchy when people don't call him sir."

The agent looked around at Mike and nodded then meekly said, "Yes, sir. No problem."

The agent calmed down somewhat, but still fearful of what Lance would do if he said the wrong thing so he remained quiet and waited. Lance sat leaning back in his chair, staring at the agent, just as he had done when the man first came into the room.

After a moment, Lance said, "I want you to get on the phone and call your boss. You tell him I want his ass over here immediately, and I want him to bring me every record of every agent under his supervision. You got that, Agent Bonner?"

"Yes, sir, General."

"You go with Mike and make the call. When you're done, you go home and stay there until you're called. Then I want your ass in here pronto. Is that clear, Agent Bonner?"

"Yes, sir, General."

"Good. Now get outta my office."

An hour later the front gate called and said that Walter Bradley had checked in. Lance told the guards to have him escorted into his office. When the agent in charge arrived, he looked haggard and drawn as if he didn't have enough sleep.

While coming through the door, Agent Bradley said, "General, it's good to see you again. Too bad it's under these circumstances."

"Good morning, Walt. You want a cup of coffee or something?"

"Coffee's fine. Make it black. I need it to stay awake."

"Having a rough time of it?"

"I haven't had a moment's rest since the killings," said Agent Bradley as he sat down in a chair at the conference table, laying a stack of folders in front of him. "Everybody's been demanding this and demanding that. Christ, Lance, it's a wonder any of us are functioning at all the way things are going."

"Are those the records I asked for?"

The agent in charge looked down at the stack and said, "Yes, Bonner said you wanted everybody. I even threw in the records of the last four years just in case somebody in that time frame might've had a score to settle. I assume you wanted to go through these records and see if maybe you could find a connection to the shootings, right?"

"Yeah, Walt, that's about it. Do you have any ideas about who might've done this?"

"No. I've been too busy dealing with the panic to even begin to do any investigating. Besides, the damn Justice Department has taken complete control of the investigation and won't let anything out about the assassination or the other murders. Hell, I don't even know how many people were killed. Do you know?"

"So far as we can tell, there are ten people dead."

"Lance, how the hell do you think something like this could have happened?"

"It's gotta be an inside job."

"That's what I figure too. You got any ideas or suspects yet?"

"Not even a clue."

"Well, here're the files. You want me to stay and help?"

"No, I'll take care of it. You go on home and get some rest."

Agent Bradley rose from the table and without taking a drink of his coffee, he left Lance's office. He arrived a half hour later at his two bedroom apartment in Silver Springs and as he unlocked the door, he didn't notice the man standing behind it. When he came through the doorway, the man behind the door raised a pistol to head level and fired.

The shot, barely audible because of a silencer on the weapon, killed Agent Walter Bradley instantly. As he left the apartment, the killer closed the door behind him and hurried from the building.

At 7:30 a.m., outside the White House gate, reporters, protestors, service workers and just plain people clamored for information about the assassinations, wanting to know what was going on.

Mike entered Lance's office and said, "Some of those people are gettin' downright nasty. When we gonna say something to them?"

"We're not. Let the President do that when he gets here this afternoon. I'm sure he's already got some political excuse for all this, other than we're trying to find the insider."

The telephone rang before Mike could speak again.

Lance answered, "Stalwardt."

"General, this is the front gate. Agent Hickman and Andrews are out here. You want me to send them in?"

"Yes. Right away." Lance turned to Mike and said, "Hickman and Andrews are here."

"Good, now we can get started on the personnel files."

"Let them use Admiral Emerson's office so we can keep in close contact. And Mike, have them come see me."

When the two agents came into the office, Lance got up from behind the desk and extended his hand to the senior agent saying, "Hickman, how ... ah, excuse me ... Cal, how was the trip?"

Agent Hickman took Lance's hand and gave it a firm shake as he said, "No problems, sir. And you?"

"Just like clockwork." Lance turned to the other agent, extended his hand and asked, "Joe, how're you doing?"

"Fine, sir," replied the younger agent shaking Lance's hand. "Kinda looks like you gotta rebellion on your hands out front, General. Are those the people we're gonna screen?"

Mike said, "Some of them, but mostly that mob is made up of full time protesters and bums. Come on guys. I'll show you where you're gonna work. It's just next door. There's files already there waiting for you to get started."

Forty-five minutes later Agent Hickman returned to Lance's office and said, "General, everybody's folder is here except two."

"Who's missing?"

"Walt Bradley and Hal Bonner. He didn't include those files. Don't you think that's kinda strange?"

"I don't know. What do you think?"

"Can't really say, General, but it does seem odd and I thought you oughta know about it."

"Okay. You think we should start by checking out the bosses?"

"Might not be a bad idea. Besides, that Bonner's an asshole and it wouldn't surprise me none if he were the snitch."

"Give Bradley a call and see if he's got the files. If not, find out who has them and have them brought here."

"All right, General."

"By the way, Cal, do you have any friends in the Bureau?"

"You mean the FBI? Yeah, I got a few. Whatcha need?"

"See if you can get anything on President Williams. Do it on the sly and for God's sake don't get caught."

"I'll try, but I can't promise anything."

"That's all I ask."

"You thinkin' he's involved some way or another?"

"I don't know, but sometimes it's easier to start with those you do know and eliminate them. That way there's no surprises later."

"Good thinking, sir. I'll have to remember that."

At eight o'clock Lance's telephone rang. "Stalwardt."

The front gate guard called. "General, Agent Bonner's back here and he says it's real important that he see ya right away, sir."

"Okay, send somebody in with him."

When Agent Bonner came through the door, Lance could tell something was terribly wrong as he asked, "What's the problem?"

"General, I'm sorry to bother you, but I went over to Walt Bradley's place about an hour ago and found him dead. He'd been shot in the head."

Mike exclaimed, "Jesus! We were just talkin' to the guy a few hours ago."

Lance asked, "Did you notify the police?"

"No, sir. I came here first."

"All right. Give the Silver Spring's PD a call and tell them what you found."

"What if they want me to go there?"

"Go, but tell them you can't stay very long. Tell them you have to be back for the President's funeral escort. If you get any static, have them call Mike. He'll vouch for you."

After Agent Bonner left, Mike said, "You think that shithead had anything to do with the murders?"

"I really don't know, Mike, but if he is involved, he's hiding it pretty good."

"You know, sir, it might be a good idea to let the police hold the guy, if nothin' more than as a material witness. Hell, who's to say he didn't kill Bradley? It could've been him just as well as anyone."

"No, Mike, I don't think he did it. But, he may know something without even knowing he knows it, and that could be the danger. Maybe you're right about him being safer in jail."

Mike said, I'll call the Silver Springs PD and have them hold him for awhile. At least until Hickman and Andrews can get him checked out. How's that sound?"

"All right, but only for a short while. Maybe he'll turn out to be just an asshole trying to do a good job. Anyway, let's give him the benefit of the doubt for now."

"Okay … I'll call in a few minutes," said Mike. Then he asked, "How soon do you have to get ready for the funeral?"

"First, I need to go to my place and get my dress blues. Get me a team. I want some protection and help with moving my things."

"Where you gonna go?"

"Right here. I'll stay in the residential wing for a while. At least until this thing blows over."

"You sure the President's gonna let you?"

"No, but at this point he's got no choice. By the way, I want you and the unit personnel in the Blair House. Also, call Ft. Meyer and get some vehicles. We'll need some transportation around here."

"I'll get Sergeant Diehl on it right away. He shouldn't have any trouble with that."

"Mike, call Marilyn's after a while and see how things are going out there. I'm still worried about not getting Blondie, and I'm afraid he'll try something."

"I'll check it out at least twice a day."

"Thanks, Mike. I appreciate it."

After leaving Lance's office, Mike returned in a few minutes with three armed men, ready to protect Lance while he went to gather his personal things. When Lance and his bodyguards arrived at his apartment, he could tell someone had been in it. He figured the intruders must have looked around as if searching for something. As far as he could tell, nothing was missing.

Lance got his dress-blue uniform with a few other belongings and returned to the White House. He took his things to the furthest guest room from the presidential suite, not wanting to cause the President and his wife any undue stress when they arrived. He showered, shaved and put on his uniform, but not wearing the three stars of lieutenant general. He would wait for the return of the new President before he did that. Displaying his newly appointed rank now, although not yet confirmed by congress, might be considered as ostentatious and could have a negative political effect on the new President. Lance wanted no trouble from the politicians just yet.

The body of President Walker lay in the Capitol rotunda waiting for the start of the funeral services. The funeral had been scheduled for a church at one time, but the fallen man's widow decided to bring the clergy to the Capitol and have a private religious service with the immediate family just prior to the government ceremony.

After both services, the funeral procession would pass down Constitution Avenue by the White House, proceed on by the Lincoln Monument, cross over the Potomac River to Arlington Cemetery and finally stop at a grave site near the John F. Kennedy memorial.

When Lance arrived at the Capitol, the guard in the western entrance booth gave him a message that the President's family wanted him in the rotunda.

When he arrived, the young widow approached him and with tears in her eyes took his hand, squeezed it tightly and said, "Oh, General Stalwardt, I'm so glad you came. The President spoke of you often and considered you one of his closest friends."

Surprised by the comment, Lance had no idea the fallen young President thought of him as a close friend and always thought their relationship only a working one. As the young widow spoke to him, Lance glanced over her shoulder at the small group of people gathered behind her, waiting for the religious services to begin. He recognized most of the people as family then noticed the only other non-member besides himself, standing at the back of the small group, trying to appear inconspicuous, but being black, Hawkins stood out in the all white group.

Lance nodded and Hawkins barely nodded back, almost as if *not* to acknowledge Lance's greeting. He saw Hawkins look around toward two Secret Service agents stationed at the door, agents that Lance had never seen before and then he realized what Hawkins silently tried to convey to him. *Don't let on to these two that we know each other.*

Again, Lance nodded, letting Hawkins know he understood then looked down at the woman in front of him as she continued to speak to him, but for the last few minutes, he hadn't heard what she said. "And please, General, I'd feel so much better if you would walk with me during the procession."

"Certainly, I'd be honored."

After the small religious service, President Williams and his family, along with a few privileged political party members joined the family entourage. Throughout the rest of the morning and into the afternoon, the widow made certain that Lance always stayed by her side. She constantly checked to see if he was there and if they became separated, even by a few feet, she would seek him out and retrieve him. As an acknowledged member of the slain President's inner circle of friends, apparent to the others because of the widow's amiable display of affection toward him, all the heads of state and various dignitaries attending the funeral introduced themselves after conveying condolences to the widow.

After the last prayer at the cemetery, the young widow turned to Lance and said, "General, I apologize if I have monopolized your time today, but it was a great comfort to me knowing you were here. Your presence gave me strength and I appreciate your indulgence."

At a loss for words, Lance didn't know what to say so he just replied, "It was an honor to escort you in your time of need."

The woman lifted her black veil, came close to Lance and gave him a soft hug, placing her cheek against his and said, "The honor was all mine, General."

The woman turned and hurried to a waiting limousine, got in and it sped away.

As Lance stood watching the car leave, he heard someone behind him ask, "You need a ride back to the White House?"

Lance turned around, saw Hawkins standing a few feet behind him and said, "Sure thing, my ride just left me."

"I saw her go without you so I thought I'd better ask. Come on, my car's just over here a ways."

"How'd you get a car in here?"

"I was one of the lucky ones and got a special pass to bring a vehicle into the cemetery."

Lance and Hawkins walked through a crowd of people that Lance estimated to be in the thousands. When they came to the car, they got in, left Arlington Cemetery and drove to the White House.

While on the way, Lance said, "I never knew the President thought of me as a friend."

"Well, he did."

"He never once indicated that to me."

"He couldn't."

"What do you mean, he couldn't?"

"He didn't wanna jeopardize your position."

"I don't understand."

"You were always kinda hidden away from everyone and that was exactly the way he wanted it. He couldn't openly acknowledge any friendship for fear of compromising you."

"Was he afraid his enemies would find out about the unit?"

"Hell, he never cared about that or himself. It was you he was protecting, and his wife and I were the only people that knew just how he really felt about you. In fact, he asked me one day if you'd be a good Vice President."

"When was that?"

"Just before he asked my cousin."

"What'd you tell him?"

"I said it wasn't a good idea, politically that is. He agreed."

"Well," said Lance, "it's rather funny to find out your a friend of the President of the United States and not even know it until after the guy is dead."

"Sometimes, General, that's the way things have to be."

At the White House gate, Lance got word from the guards the new President and his wife had already arrived. As Lance came in the front door with Hawkins, they saw Agent Hickman and another agent engaged in what appeared to be a heated conversation.

The younger agent said to Agent Hickman, "I'm the agent in charge, and I'll give out the work assignments as I see fit, you got that, Hickman?"

"Morgan, you're not involved in this investigation and your only duty is to guard the President. You have no jurisdiction over the rest of the staff or the operation of the complex."

"We'll see about—"

Hawkins asked, "What seems to be the trouble here?"

Agent Morgan turned to Hawkins and said, "This jerk thinks he's runnin' things around here, and I'm here to tell him different."

"Then you'd be lyin' to him," said Hawkins, staring intently at the shorter man.

"Whadda ya mean?"

"I mean Agent Hickman is in charge of all security in and around the White House, and that means he's agent in charge and your boss. Do you understand, Agent Morgan?"

The younger agent glared at Hawkins then at Cal Hickman. Without a word he turned and walked off, leaving the three men standing in the front foyer.

Agent Hickman turned to Hawkins and said, "He's not such a bad guy, but he is kinda headstrong. He thought he automatically got the top dog slot cause he was with the President in Illinois."

Lance asked, "He gonna be a problem?"

"I don't think so. I'll talk to him later when he cools down. He'll be all right."

"How's the screening going? Any progress yet?"

"Yeah. Joe and I gotta list of about twenty names that we can probably clear without too much difficulty. We should be able to bring them on board tomorrow morning if you okay the list today."

"What about the missing files on Bonner and Bradley?"

"Still haven't got 'em, sir."

Hawkins asked, "You think Bonner or Bradley are involved?"

Lance replied, "We don't know for sure, but somebody killed Bradley this morning."

"What?"

"Somebody shot him in the head in his apartment."

"How come we haven't heard anything about this yet?"

"I wanted to brief the President myself. Will you see how soon we can meet with him so I can inform him of what's happened?"

Hawkins didn't hesitate. "I think I'd better. I'll arrange for it as soon as I can."

Chapter 21

After his conversation with Hawkins, Lance received a call to report to the Oval Office where he briefed President Williams about the events from the time he left Illinois the night before, up until the present when he and Hawkins returned from Arlington Cemetery. Walter Bradley's murder surprised the President and he expressed concern over his death.

"If they can get to an Agent in Charge of the White House Secret Service, we could all be in danger," said the President.

Lance reassured him by saying, "Sir, they'll never get to us inside the White House grounds. My men have the compound secured, and by next week we should be back to some semblance of normal operations."

"I hope so, General, I surely hope so."

At this meeting, Lance learned the Vice President nominee's name—Howard C. Wainwright, a twenty-five year member of the House of Representatives from South Carolina and Minority Leader.

Lance asked, "How did you happen to decide on Congressman Wainwright, Mr. President?"

"Two reasons," replied the President. "One, he's an experienced politician and knows Washington. And second, the party chairman highly recommended him. In fact, he almost insisted that he be the choice and said no other candidate would get a fast confirmation."

"Is a quick confirmation needed?"

"I guess they want somebody in the office in case I don't make it for some reason or other, namely being shot and killed within the next few weeks. If I go, the Speaker of the House is the next successor and he's in the opposite party, so you can see why they want to hurry this nomination. Anyway, Representative Wainwright is the Vice President nominee."

Lance thought about the one and only time he met the selected vice presidential candidate, a few years ago when he came to visit the White House by the invitation of the slain President. Except for that meeting, Lance knew nothing about the representative from

South Carolina, except what he read in the newspapers and what he had seen on television. Since Lance wasn't allowed the privilege to associate with politicians, he never knew legislators on a working or personal basis.

The President spoke, interrupting Lance's thoughts, "I have scheduled a public appearance at the John F. Kennedy Center on Friday to officially announce the appointment of Mr. Wainwright as Vice President. We'll pick him up at the Capitol shortly before noon and then proceed to the center by motorcade to make the announcement at a luncheon for a few invited guests and the press."

"Mr. President," said Lance, "as your National Security Adviser I strongly urge you to reconsider meeting in a public place. I don't think it's safe for you to go into that environment just yet, sir."

"I know, General, but we can't let criminals push us to the point where we'll always be afraid to move. I don't think they'll try anything when I'm that close to a crowd. It appears this bunch likes to get their victims where there's a certain amount of solitude."

Before Lance left the meeting, he mentioned to the President he had temporarily moved into one of the guest rooms and would spend the night in the residential wing of the White House. "I'll move my things to the Blair House, first thing in the morning."

The President said, "No hurry, General, you may stay in the guest room if you so choose, at least for a few days until things begin to calm down a little."

After the meeting with the President, Lance went to his office and as he sat down, Mike rushed in. "Blondie tried to get Marilyn."

"What?"

"Blondie and another guy tried to kill Marilyn."

"Is she all right?"

"She's okay."

"When'd this happen?"

"Just a few minutes ago. I still have Garcia on the line."

Lance grabbed the telephone, punched the lighted button and said, "Garcia, this is Stalwardt. What happened?"

"General, the blond guy, the one who tried to kill you before. He's been here and tried to shoot your lady."

"She all right?"

"Yes, sir, she's okay. Just shaken up a bit."

"Where's she at now?"

"She's in the bedroom."

"Give me some details."

"It happened just a few minutes ago, sir. Your lady came home from work, drove up in the driveway and started to get out of her car when this other car drives by and starts blastin' away. Lucky thing I saw the gun barrel stickin' outta the window as it was comin' down the street. Before he got a bead on her and started shootin', I hollered at her to get back into the car and get down on the floor. She jumped back in and did as I told her so she wasn't hit."

"Did they get away?"

"Yes, sir, but they're carryin' lead."

"How do you know?"

"I put about twenty rounds into their car and saw it swerve. I think I hit the driver, but evidently it wasn't enough to kill him. At least not outright anyways."

"The police there yet?"

"No, sir. I don't think anyone heard the shots because both weapons had silencers."

"Okay, Sergeant. Now, here's what I want you to do. Get everybody packed up and outta there as soon as you can. I don't want you there if the police come."

"Yes, sir, I understand."

Lance continued, "I want all four of you at the Albertus Airport in two hours ready to leave and come to DC. I'm sending a command jet to pick you up."

"Yes, sir, two hours at Albertus."

"You got it. Now go get ready and get the hell outta there before the police come. And, put Marilyn on the phone."

A brief moment later, Marilyn said, "Hello?"

"Honey, I want you to pack some things and get ready to come to DC. I told Sergeant Garcia that a plane will pick you up at the Albertus Airport in a few hours and don't worry, you're gonna be all right. We'll bring you here where it's safer."

"Oh Lance, I'm so scared."

"I know, honey, but just be patient for a few more hours. Now hurry. I want you outta there before any police get to your place."

"All right, Lance. I love you."

"I love you too."

The line went dead as Marilyn hung up the receiver then Lance turned and shouted, "MIKE!"

Mike had gone to the outer office as Lance started talking to Garcia. When Lance yelled for him, he returned immediately.

Lance said, "I want the small jet in Freeport in two hours."

"It's already taken care of. While you were talking to Garcia, I used the phone in the other office and called operations in Andrews. I told them it was an immediate presidential order and to send any command jet on alert. They're already gone."

"Thanks, Mike. I don't know what I'd do without you."

"Glad you appreciate my talents," said Mike with a grin. "I was gonna suggest you get her outta there anyway. She'll be safer here, and you won't be so damn worried about her."

"I'll have to find a place for her to stay."

"She can stay at the Blair House with the rest of us. She'll be plenty safe there."

"Okay. I guess that'll be all right for the time being. Have somebody take my stuff over and put her up in the same suite."

"Don't trust us, eh Chief?"

"You gotta remember, Mike, I know this bunch."

Lance knew the men of the unit wouldn't harm her and knew each man would do everything within their power to keep her safe.

For the next six hours Lance worried over the attempt on Marilyn's life and how to protect her from the blond man trying to kill her. He read reports, looked at files and tried to take on some work to keep occupied, but nothing registered and he gave up.

Lance called Agent Hickman into his office and briefed him about the events at Marilyn's place and said, "Cal, we've got to think of something to keep Marilyn safe. Right now she's a target for Blondie, and it looks like he'll stop at nothing to get to her."

"I would think she'd be safe in the Blair House, especially with all your guys around."

"That's true, Cal, but she can't stay cooped up like a prisoner all the time. We've gotta get these bastards and do it quick. We can't afford to let this thing drag on."

"You want I should bring in some outside help?"

"You know some people we can trust?"

"A few. I've got my FBI friend in Chicago, a guy over in ATF (Alcohol Tobacco & Firearms) that owes me one for savin' his life, and then of course there's Joe."

"Anybody else?"

"I can think of a dozen other guys who'd probably be okay."

"They work in different agencies?"

"Yeah. I've got friends in most of them."

"Good. Make me a list of names. I've got an idea I wanna check out with the President."

Agent Hickman left the office just as Hawkins walked through the office door. "What's going on? I heard from General Polaski that somebody tried to kill your lady friend back in Illinois."

"Yeah, thank God the bastards missed. I'm having her brought here where she'll be safer."

"Good idea."

"Hawkins, I think—"

"Call me Ben,"

"Ben it is. Ben, I think we better start doing some serious looking into who's responsible for these killings and shut 'em down. It's getting out of hand."

"I agree. What've you got in mind?"

"A task force. I want it made up from lower ranking agents from different agencies. People who know their way around in the operations of their respective departments, especially in the area of information files. Maybe if we put them all together into one effort, we might come up with something."

"Sounds good. When you wanna start?"

"Just as soon as I can get the President to okay the plan." Lance paused then said, "Not to change the subject, Ben, but I think this is the first time you've ever been in my office."

"That's right," said Hawkins as he looked around, "Come to think of it, I've never been in this office before."

"In fact, I don't ever remember you speaking to me before the other day."

"I was the one that always called you on the phone whenever the President asked to see you."

"That may be, but I didn't know it was you until that night back in Illinois on the President's farm."

"Which reminds me ... he wants to see us. I think he wants to ask our advice on something."

"Any idea what it's about?"

"No, not really."

The two men went upstairs to the Oval Office, passing two men in uniform who stood guard in the hallway, each armed with an automatic weapon and a sidearm. Inside the hallway near the Oval Office door sat two Secret Service agents. Lance knocked softly on the door.

"Come in."

The two men went inside and approached the desk where the President sat looking over a list of names.

He looked up and said, "I hear there's trouble in Illinois."

"Yes, sir. The man that tried to kill me on at least three separate occasions has tried to kill a friend of mine."

"From what I'm told, she's a very close friend."

"Yes, sir, extremely so."

"Everything okay now?"

"Yes, sir. She's being brought to DC."

"Good. That means you'll have less to worry about."

The President motioned to the two men to be seated at the small oval table with the four wingback chairs then he rose from his chair at the desk, walked to the table and sat in one of the wingbacks. Lance and Hawkins followed.

"Gentlemen," said the President, "I'm planning to make some changes in the cabinet. Basically I'll keep the majority of cabinet members, but I do want a few of my own choices in some of the key positions. For instance, I want to keep Secretary of State Alexander, but I want to appoint my own Secretary of the Treasury. I want both of you to look over the list of candidates I've chosen for various positions and give me your opinions on or before Friday morning."

As both men took their copy of the list, the President asked, "General, how is the investigation progressing?"

"We're just getting started, sir. Mr. President, I would like to establish a task force, made up of trained investigators from various agencies throughout the government, but I'll need your help in getting some of the people together."

"Can't you do this with your own people?"

"Sir, we need to get information from the CIA, the FBI, ATF, DEA, Customs and the Attorney General's office, just to name a few. We don't have the availability to the tons of information on file within all of the various agencies, plus we'll need people who can quickly access these files. We'll probably need to access some state files too, but I don't think they'll be a problem."

"What is it you're trying to do?"

"For one thing, sir, I want to cut across agency lines and remove the red tape on getting important information, especially classified and personal stuff on some of the VIPs in this town."

"Do you know what you're looking for?"

"Not really, sir, but if we look in enough files we might be able to come up with something. Hopefully, it'll lead us to the people responsible for the killings."

"What is it you want me to do?"

"All I need, sir, is your okay to transfer a few people to the White House staff for special assignment. There's no reason their bosses should even have to know why they're really here."

"Perhaps we can smokescreen the reason," said Hawkins, "by telling the department heads that the agents are being asked to present you with a briefing on the fundamental operations of their respective departments and to work as a committee to come up with some recommendations for agency streamlining and reforms. That's always politically popular."

The President asked, "Will the people you need be handpicked?"

"Yes, Mr. President, they will. Agent Hickman is preparing a list of about a dozen or so people that he knows he can trust."

"Okay, gentlemen. You have my blessing."

Next, Lance brought up the subject of his chief pilot John Slaughter and asked, "Sir, would you call the Air Force Chief of

Staff and arrange for him to meet with us here at the White House? I want to reiterate the policy of this office concerning the aircraft in the presidential pool at Andrews Air Force Base."

The President asked, "What's the problem?"

Lance then described the events when General Cross tried to enter the Starlifters and threatened Colonel Slaughter with a court-martial. "Besides, we may learn who pushed General Cross into doing what he did, and it might lead us to somebody."

"Ben, make the call and set up the meeting for later today."

After a few minutes of other conversation, Lance left the two men and headed back to his office. Arriving at the office where Agent Hickman had set up his operation, he knocked on the door.

"Come on in."

Lance went in and as he closed the door he said, "Cal, I just saw the President and he's approved a plan I've been thinking about."

"Have a seat, General, and tell me whatcha got."

"Is your list of names ready yet?"

"Yes, sir, right here," said the agent as he handed a sheet of paper to Lance.

"You keep it. I trust your judgment."

"Thanks for the vote of confidence."

Lance took a chair in front of the desk then said, "I'd like you to set up a secret task force to investigate the assassinations."

"You want me in charge?"

"Since you're now head of all White House security, I want you to oversee the operation. Maybe you could assign Joe to supervise the task force and pick a good man to assist him."

"What're these people supposed to do?"

Lance briefed Agent Hickman about what he had described to the President just a few moments before, and then after outlining a few more details to the agent, Lance said, "I want these guys to be a solid team. I don't want any problems of jurisdiction like they have at the director's level. I want total cooperation from everyone or they don't stay."

"How soon you want this task force?"

"I'd like to start as soon as possible. Contact your list of friends and ask them to be here tomorrow afternoon by thirteen hundred.

There's no need to tell their bosses anything just yet, and don't tell the agents why they're coming, except that the President has asked for them. We'll work out something with the agency heads later."

"Okay, I'll get right on it."

"Good. I'll check with you in the morning."

Lance left the agent to his work and returned to his office. After about an hour, Lance looked at his watch and thought, *It's about time for Marilyn to be here.*

Mike stuck his head in the office doorway and said, "There's a four star Air Force heading for the Oval Office."

"Thanks, I'd better go. Call John at Dover and tell him to bring the planes to Andrews."

"All right, sir. I'll take care of it."

Twenty minutes later Lance returned to his office after his meeting with the President where he briefed the Air Force Chief of Staff on the presidential aircraft policy. The President told the general in no uncertain terms that presidential aircraft were off limits to all officers and men not directly assigned to a specific plane and its support. The President then ordered the general to look into the matter of General Cross and to report within two days why the general wanted in the planes.

As Lance sat at his desk, the telephone rang. "Stalwardt."

"General, this is Major Hodges. Your people just arrived at the Blair House. Thought you'd like to know."

"Thanks, Major, I appreciate the call."

Lance hung up the receiver, left the office and rushed across the street to the Blair House. He ran up the stairs two at a time and hurried into his assigned room. They threw their arms around each other and in the emotion of the moment Marilyn began to cry. Lance kept kissing her on her lips, her cheeks, her neck and anywhere else on her face that he could.

Overcome by a sudden impulse, Lance stepped back from her, held her at arm's length and said, "Marry me."

She lunged herself back into his arms and started kissing his face all over and in between kisses she said, "YES … yes … yes … a thousand times yes!"

That night, with Marilyn safely beside him, Lance stayed awake, thinking over the events of the day. Within twenty-four hours he had taken over total control of the White House grounds by force, attended a slain President's funeral, formed an investigative task force to look into the lives of some of the nation's most influential people and proposed marriage to the woman he loved.

He thought, *God, what a day*. Within a few moments after his mind stopped working, he fell asleep.

Early the next morning, Lance awoke and with Marilyn still asleep, he dressed and went across the street to the White House. Only armed guards from his group occupied the entrances and exits to the executive office wing.

Lance asked the senior NCO on duty. "Is everything all right?"

The sergeant replied, "Nothin's goin' on, General. It's been quiet all night."

Today would be the first day that civilian workers came back to work, but only those essential to running the daily business of the White House, such as the household servants and a few clerical workers. The others would follow later.

Lance kept busy preparing notes for the upcoming meeting at one o'clock with the members of the newly formed task force. At ten o'clock, Agent Hickman stopped in and briefed him on the list of twelve people, everyone from a different agency and all highly trained agents in their own field. One agent could not come because of another important assignment, but that agency had another friend of Agent Hickman's to replace the first choice. Also, two others would miss the meeting because they lived out of town, but would join the investigative group later in the day.

At eleven o'clock, Marilyn called and said, "Sweetheart, I'd like to celebrate our engagement tonight."

"Okay," said Lance. "Pick a restaurant and make reservations."

"Honey, since this is going to be a special occasion, I'd like to do some shopping this afternoon. Do you know of someone that can show me around?"

"I'll check it out and let you know when I see you for lunch."

They ended their conversation just as Agent Hickman came into the office and asked, "General, you gotta minute?"

"Sure, have a seat," said Lance as he hung up the receiver.

Agent Hickman sat down and asked, "How tight we gonna control this task force?"

"I'm not sure what you mean?"

"Well, General, your own men are totally dedicated for twenty-four hours a day, seven days a week, but these guys are civilians. They have families and will probably wanna go home at night."

"What are your thoughts?"

"I see no reason to dedicate them to twenty-four hours since they'll mostly be lookin' through information files."

"You're right. It's gonna be one hellava boring job."

"You got that right."

"Okay. How about eight hours a day during the week, with a half day on Saturday?"

"Sounds good."

"By the way, Cal, would you happen to know someone who can show Marilyn around town? She wants to do some shopping."

"Sure. I'll send Charlotte with her. My wife will be glad to go. Only thing is, I'll hafta give her some money or she'll scream like a kicked mule if I don't."

Lance smiled at the other man's comment and said, "Good. I'll tell Marilyn when I see her at lunch. Tell your wife we'll arrange for someone to pick her up."

"What time?"

"How about one thirty?"

"Let me check and I'll get back to ya. What about security?"

"I'll have Mike send a couple of the men along in civvies."

"You think anybody's gonna try to get to Marilyn here in DC?"

"They killed a President here, didn't they?"

"You're right, General, they sure as hell did."

Chapter 22

During the month of November, heavy storms sometimes blow in from the northeast off the Atlantic Ocean and are often so big they hit the entire east coast of the United States.   When this happens, the storms are usually carried inland as far as Washington, D.C., and although they don't cause much damage that far in, they do bring a lot of rain or snow, depending upon the temperature. The storm that had been blowing up all day began to threaten when Lance and Marilyn left the Blair House that evening. The rain had not begun by the time they reached the fashionable restaurant where Marilyn made reservations for dinner.

The maitre d' greeted them just inside the door, checked their reservation, took them to their table and proceeded to seat them. Before they sat down, Lance noticed people seated around them smoking so he asked the headwaiter, "Could we have a table in a non-smoking section, please?"

The man replied, "Certainly, sir. Please follow me."

They crossed the room and went up two steps to a raised mezzanine dining area, surrounded by a solid half-wall about three feet high, decorated with a few plants and an occasional piece of pottery along the entire length of the top rail. They chose a table along the half-wall that overlooked the main dining room so Marilyn would be able to see any legislative dignitaries in the restaurant or if any came through the front door.

After being seated, they gave the waiter their drink orders, which had not yet arrived when Lance noticed a couple being escorted and seated at the same table they had just left. He watched as the couple sat down, talking to their waiter, presumably ordering drinks, and after the waiter left, they turned to each other and started conversing. When he returned his attention back to Marilyn he saw a sudden look of terror in Marilyn's eyes as she stared over his shoulder and into the other dining room. Her hand came to her mouth to stifle a gasp of fright and her facial color drained away.

Lance turned quickly to look in the direction she stared in. Two men wearing hats and long coats, followed by a third man without a hat approached their previous table.

Lance recognized the third man immediately. "Blondie," he said at the same instant the three men opened fire with handguns, instantly killing the couple seated at the table they had left just a few moments before.

Before Lance could stand up, someone from behind him pulled him down onto the floor. He looked over to Marilyn also on the floor beneath a crouched man with a gun in his hand, looking out over the wall.

The man above him held his finger to his mouth and said, "General, stay down. There's too many of 'em. They've got at least five others in here somewhere and we're no match for these people right now. Quick, follow us out the back."

The two men helped Lance and Marilyn up from the floor, and in the confusion of the standing crowd around them, they quickly left out the back of the non-smoking dining room and into a short hallway. The lead man started to open a side door into the kitchen, but stopped and motioned for them to be quiet and stay still.

The man pointed through the small window in the door to another door coming from the dining room just as the blond killer came through it, looking around the kitchen. A waiter approached the killer and appeared as if accepting something from his hand.

A split second later the waiter lay sprawled on the kitchen floor, dead from two bullets in his brain. After he killed the waiter, the blond man ran back through the other door and into the main dining room then joined by the other two men, they all left the restaurant.

Lance, Marilyn and the two men leading them, hurried through the kitchen, walking around the dead waiter on the floor, leaving the restaurant through the back door. The kitchen help stood frozen and remained motionless as the four passed by.

After leaving the restaurant's rear door the two men took Lance and Marilyn to a car parked in a small lot across the alley, used mostly by the restaurant's employees.

They got into the car just as the rain started to come down and once inside, Lance asked, "Who are you guys?"

"We're assigned to a special task force under Agent Andrews," said the man in the passenger's seat as the other man started the car and drove out of the parking lot.

"What? What the hell are you doing here?"

The driver said, "We were told to keep an eye on you, General. Seems like somebody's worried about you two."

"Not that I'm ungrateful, but I'd like to know who authorized this surveillance."

"We don't know, sir. All we know is that Joe Andrews told us to make sure nothin' happened to you while you're out and about."

Lance said, "I don't remember seeing you two at the briefing."

"Neither one of us could make it, but I understand you gave a wonderful speech."

"Yeah, I heard it was great too," said the other man.

Sitting behind the front passenger, Lance detected a little ribbing by the two men about the speech. "It wasn't that great ... and it was very short and to the point."

With a grin on his face the driver said, "We heard that's what made it so great."

Lance looked closely at the man in the driver's seat and something told him he should know this man. He could only see the man's right profile, but something stirred in his memory.

He asked, "Driver, where're you from?"

"The task force, sir."

"You already told me that. I mean what agency?"

"I'm Jerry Martin, Army CID (Criminal Investigation Division), sir. And this here is Jack Cooper, FBI, Chicago office."

"Martin ... Martin. Do I know you?"

"It's been a long time since we've seen each other, sir."

"And, where was that?"

"Vietnam. I was with Special Forces in that A camp when we got overrun."

"You're the sharpshooter."

"That's right, sir. I'm surprised you remembered."

"Very little, I'm afraid."

"Me too, sir."

Lance asked the other man, "And what about you?"

"What about me?"

"Are you the one that called Agent Hickman and warned him to be careful?"

"Yes, sir."

"I'm curious, Agent Cooper, as to how you knew about the mob being involved with all this?"

"One of the guys you arrested was one of our informants at one time … until we found out he was just using us to get information for the mob."

"I don't think he'll be a problem after this," said Lance. "He'll get his own justice soon, and there won't be any cost to the taxpayer through a lengthy trial."

"Yeah, I heard."

It started to rain harder with occasional flashes of lightning as the car sped its way through the city.

As he drove, Agent Martin said, "Sir, if you two are still hungry we know of a place that'll be safe."

Lance asked, "Where is it?"

"It's a small Italian joint over near Chevy Chase owned by Cooper's brother-in-law. I've been there a few times and I highly recommend the food."

Marilyn nodded and mouthed the words, "I'm starving."

"Okay, fellas, we're game, but let's just order takeout and get back to the White House. I need to talk with Agent Hickman."

After arriving at the small restaurant, Agent Cooper went in with Marilyn while Lance stayed in the car with Agent Martin.

He asked the CID agent, "How'd you guys know we were in that particular restaurant?"

"Same way those other guys knew … a snitch. The reservations were made in your name, General, and their man, who was probably the dead waiter, recognized it and called his people. It so happened that one of the other workers in the kitchen overheard their guy on the phone and called the FBI. The guy who took the call was a friend of Coop's so he called Coop, and Coop told Andrews. Because you had already left the Blair House when Andrews got the call, he sent us to the restaurant to warn you to leave."

"You almost didn't make it."

"You changed tables before we could get to you. Then all the shootin' started."

"Why do you think the blond guy killed the waiter?"

Martin said, "When the blond guy found out they shot the wrong couple, he was either pissed off or he was just tying up a loose end."

Lance paused then asked, "If there were other people in the room that belonged to them, how come they didn't try to kill us or at least try to stop us?"

"I don't think the others knew who you were. From what I saw, it looks like the blond guy was the only one who could identify you and your lady friend."

"You can bet your bottom dollar they won't let that happen again. Next time, they'll all know who they're after and they won't make the same mistake twice."

"To tell you the truth, General, we didn't expect anything to happen tonight. We just weren't sure if these guys were serious."

"You can believe they're serious. They've killed a President and at least a dozen other people are dead because of these bastards. They've tried to kill both Marilyn and me on different occasions."

"Yes, sir, I heard," said Agent Martin, "Andrews told us."

"How'd you two get this assignment?"

"We volunteered."

"You volunteered?"

"Yes, sir. The whole task force volunteered when Andrews asked if anybody wanted to do some extra field work."

"Why's that?"

"Most of us are admin types. Any chance to do some field work, we all went for it. Besides, General, you're almost a famous man."

"How's that?"

"Everybody in DC knows that you practically rule most of the third world countries because of your secret unit."

Lance didn't reply, but stared at the CID agent for a moment.

"I wouldn't worry, General," continued Agent Martin, "Just off hand, I'd say yours is the best kept known secret in DC."

"What does that mean?"

"It means that everyone in the government suspects you have a highly secret covert action unit at your command, but no one knows for sure. They only think so because no one has been able to prove it, and besides, they're afraid of what might happen to them if they do find out for sure."

"What do you think?"

"I think, sir, that right now it seems strange that a military group is occupying the White House with weapons that don't seem to match our own inventory. Only reason I can think of is that these weapons are used so the United States can't be implicated in any foreign operations."

"Martin," said Lance, "if I were you, I wouldn't worry about it."

"No problem, sir."

Lance saw Agent Cooper and Marilyn approaching the car and said, "Now let's get back to the White House. We'll eat there."

"Wouldn't you rather go to the Blair House?"

"No. I'm afraid the press is gonna be around asking about the shooting, and I'll need to brief Hickman before they get to him."

The foursome arrived at the White House and went immediately to Lance's office.

While the others ate, Lance called Agent Hickman at his home and said, "Cal, this is Stalwardt. Can you come to the office right away? It's important."

"Sure thing, General. I'll be there inside an hour."

Less than thirty minutes later, Agent Hickman entered Lance's office and took a seat at the conference table. Marilyn and the two agents had already finished eating and left for the Blair House.

"Whatcha got, General?"

Lance briefed Agent Hickman about the attempt on his life in the restaurant and the couple being killed by mistake because they were seated at the table reserved for him and Marilyn. "It was Blondie and two other men."

"Jesus Christ, General, this guy doesn't quit ... does he?"

"It looks that way. He probably won't quit until he's dead."

"It doesn't make any sense to me. Why would anybody want you dead?"

"I wish I knew the answer to that question, Cal. Perhaps then we might know who's behind all this."

"Is this gonna change anything for tomorrow?"

"No. I think we'll proceed with the President's plan, but we'll make a few changes in the security coverage, now that we know that Blondie's around."

"You want closer coverage?"

"Not really. What I was thinking of is a second and third cordon around the JFK Center. If somebody does get in close enough to the President to attempt an assassination, we must be able to seal off the area so they can't possibly get away. If we could've had a team outside the restaurant tonight we might've had the bastards."

"Okay, General, I'll coordinate this with Mike in the morning and set it up with his people to provide coverage in the second ring. Also, I'll let the director in on our plans and ask him to provide the third ring. Maybe he'll give us a roving patrol to provide coverage along the motorcade route from the Capitol to the Kennedy Center."

"Sounds good. Anything else we should cover?"

"I don't think so … at least not for now anyway."

"Before you go, thanks for having those two agents look out for Marilyn and me tonight. They probably saved our lives."

"It was no problem, sir. The boys were glad to do it. I'll have them permanently assigned to you until this thing is taken care of. I'll pass on to Joe what you said."

"Thanks, Cal. Tell him I really appreciate his concerns."

"It's all in a day's work, General. All in a day's work."

Chapter 23

On Friday morning, the President and his entourage left the White House to meet House Minority Leader Wainwright, his wife Ellen and a small group of political well wishers at the Capitol. Five limousines made up the motorcade, two for transporting dignitaries and three for Secret Service agents. Lance, Ben Hawkins and Cal Hickman rode with the President in the second vehicle while the vice presidential nominee rode in the fourth car with his wife, the Minority Leader of the Senate and the political party chairman. The first, middle and last cars carried the Secret Service. Vehicles carrying the press and other interested parties followed behind.

At precisely 11:20 a.m., the President's five car motorcade arrived at the north gate of the Capitol and passed the guardhouse, stopping at the steps of the main entrance on the east side of the building—the Wainwright party already there and waiting.

The President got out of his limousine, walked the short distance to the small group and exchanged pleasantries. He talked with each member of the party individually for a few moments then gave the media an opportunity to ask a few questions and take photographs.

While the President met with the dignitaries and the press, the limousines began turning around and parking, ready to leave for the JFK Center. However, because of the limited turnaround space set up by traffic horses, the sequence of vehicles became reversed and the President's car became the fourth in line. The limo carrying the Vice President nominee and his party then took the second slot in the motorcade, and because of the tight schedule, drivers didn't have enough time to correct the sequence.

The President said, "It's not important who is where just as long as we all get there."

At 11:45 a.m., the motorcade left the Capitol and turned west on Constitution Avenue. As they neared the JFK Center, the motorcade had to slow down to turn off Constitution onto an intersecting street, Virginia Avenue Northwest. Also, they had to travel slower because of heavier traffic and narrower streets through Edward J. Kelly Park.

As the last car of the motorcade entered the park area, a tremendous explosion erupted ahead of the President's car.

Hawkins exclaimed, "My God! What the hell was that!"

Lance yelled, "DRIVER ... U-TURN THIS CAR AND GET US THE HELL OUTTA HERE, NOW!"

Lance began looking around and trying to see what happened through the cloud of thick black smoke and flying debris. At same time, Agent Hickman pulled the President down from the seat and onto the floor, covering him with his own body.

At the exact moment of the explosion, the President's driver saw a blinding flash, a lot of smoke and heard a tremendous blast. Glass, metal and human body parts flew everywhere, some hitting the front of the President's car. The vehicle in front of him disintegrated and a large piece of the back half started to spin out of control toward the center of the street.

The President's limousine driver, trained to take evasive action, reacted instantly at Lance's command. He spun the steering wheel to the left and mashed the accelerator to the floor. The powerful engine surged as the big car skidded around, slamming sideways into parts of the vehicle in front, bouncing off the car's wreckage then crossed over the median strip and sped from the scene.

Lance ordered, "Driver, take us to the White House. GO!"

At the intersection they came through only moments before, the driver turned back onto Constitution Avenue and headed toward the White House as fast as the limousine would go. The last limousine followed close behind.

Arriving at the White House, Lance and Agent Hickman ushered the President, his driver and Ben Hawkins into the conference room next to Lance's office while the Secret Service agents waited outside the door along with two armed guards of the unit.

Lance called Mike into the room and briefed him then said, "I want this place tightened up. Make damn sure it's secure and from now on don't let anyone in here that doesn't have my personal approval. Also, have somebody contact the capital police and find out what the casualties are. Go!"

"Yes, sir," said Mike, and then hurried from the room to alert the unit members and to telephone the police.

Lance turned to the President's driver seated at the table and asked, "What's your name?"

Still visibly shaken by the ordeal he had just gone through, he answered, "John ... John Washington."

Lance said, "You did one hellava good job out there today, John. You may well have saved our lives."

"I don't know about that, sir. All I could think of was to get the hell outta there."

"Did you see what happened?"

"Not really, but I heard this loud bang and saw a lotta smoke."

"Could you see or tell where it came from?"

"I don't know, sir. I just saw this big flash of light from over the top of the car in front of me then all this stuff flyin' around."

"Was it in front of the car?"

The driver paused then said, "No, I don't think it was directly in front of the car. No, sir, I'd say it was more to the passenger's side." Then as if he suddenly remembered, the driver added, "Yeah, that's right. It did come from the right side."

"Anything else?"

"Just that the car went sideways in the street and I was tryin' my best to get the hell outta there. I kept thinkin' that I didn't wanna be blown up. It sure scared the hell outta me."

"You okay now?"

"Yeah, I'm fine."

"Good," said Lance as he stood up and looked around at the others in the room. "Has anybody else got any questions to ask?"

No one answered.

Lance continued, "All right, John, I guess that's it for now. You may go, but if you remember anything, anything at all, please tell me, no matter how trivial you think it might be." Lance walked to the door, opened it and said, "John, please don't go anywhere outside the complex unless you tell us or until we release you. I may want you to come back after while."

"Yes, sir. I'll be in the rest area if you need me."

Lance called in the Secret Service agent who basically said the same thing as John. The explosion seemed to come from the right side, along the row of parked cars.

After the agent left the room, Lance turned to the President and said, "Mr. President, that blast was meant for you. I definitely believe you were the target. If it weren't for that foul up at the Capitol, you would have been in the second vehicle. And, I must tell you, sir, for your own protection and safety, you should not schedule anymore outside activities until we resolve this situation."

Up until now, the President had not uttered a word. He stayed silent all through the bombing, the frantic ride back to the White House and during the debriefings.

Speaking for the first time, President Williams said, "General, while you were at my farm in Illinois I gave you a mission to undertake. If you have any questions about my meaning, let me repeat it so there is no mistake of what I expect you to do. I want the people responsible for this terror caught and eliminated."

Startled by the President's comment, Agent Hickman looked at Lance to see his reaction to the statement.

Lance only looked at the President and said, "Mr. President, I understand perfectly. There will be no lengthy trials."

Agent Hickman couldn't quite believe what he had just heard. The President of the United States gave an order to his new National Security Adviser to execute the people responsible for and involved with the assassinations without the benefit of the law, and saying it in front of witnesses. Then hearing Lance tell the President that he not only understood the order, but that he would comply with it, equally astounded him.

After making the statement, the President said, "Ben, let's go up to the Oval Office and let these two do their job. I believe they'll do it much better and faster with us out of the way."

With the President gone, Agent Hickman said, "General, I can't believe what I just heard."

"You have a problem with it?"

"No, sir, but I never expected the President to come right out and order you to kill those who are responsible."

"Do you have another alternative on the matter?"

"No, sir. I guess not."

Before Lance could continue, a knock on the door interrupted him. "Come in," said Lance.

Mike entered the office and Lance asked, "What's the news?"

"Sixteen dead and two seriously injured. The driver and the front seat passenger of the first car somehow managed to survive. All the others in the car were killed outright as was everybody else in cars two and three."

"What the hell caused it?"

"A car bomb, in a parked car. It must have been detonated by remote control just as the second vehicle of the motorcade came abreast of it. The first three vehicles were completely destroyed."

"Did you get a list of the dead?"

"Yes, sir," said Mike as he referred to a small note pad. "Those tentatively identified dead at the scene were the vice presidential nominee Harold Wainwright, his wife Ellen—"

Agent Hickman interrupted. "His name was Howard."

Looking up from his notes, Mike asked, "What?"

"His name ... it was Howard not Harold."

"Hmm ... the police gave me Harold."

"Then they gave you the wrong first name."

"Okay, Mike," said Lance, "make the change and continue on."

"Also dead at the scene were the Senate Minority Leader, Senator James Hosler, the party chairman William Baker, ten Secret Service agents and two drivers. The two injured survivors were taken to Walter Reed and are listed in critical condition. They didn't give me the names of the agents."

Lance asked, "Have we got a roster on that assignment?"

"Yes, sir," said Agent Hickman. "The list is in my office."

"Cal, were any of these men with the President in Illinois?"

"Yes, most of them were ... and they were all in the motorcade."

"Damn! That has to mean that all of them were killed. We've gotta have reliable Secret Service protection and we need it now. My men won't be able to take care of the agency work along with their own. Cal, you'll need to get started right away on getting some of your men cleared and get them assigned to the White House as soon as you can."

"Yes, sir."

"Mike, contact the capital police and set up a liaison to find out as much information about the explosion as we can. And, I mean everything. Also, see if the police still have Bonner."

"Yes, sir," said Mike as he left the room and went into an outer office to use the phone.

"Cal, I want you to make an all-out effort to find the missing files on Bonner and Bradley. Like I said the other day, if we can't get the files from the agency, try another one. Start with the FBI."

"Yes, sir," said Agent Hickman. "I think Cooper should be able to help us out there."

"Get the task force up to speed and start getting information in here from their respective agencies. I want things to start moving."

"I'll get Joe on it right away."

"By the way, Cal, how was your talk with Agent Morgan? Is he still upset?"

Agent Hickman replied in a quiet voice, "You needn't worry about Morgan, General."

"Why's that?"

"He was in the second car."

"I'm sorry to hear that. Did you know him very well?"

"Not really, but it's still tough when they die."

"I know," said Lance. After a moment's pause he continued, "You gonna be all right?"

"Yeah, I'm okay."

"You sure? We can continue this later if you want?"

"No ... I'm all right. Go ahead."

A knock at the door interrupted Lance just as he was about to say something.

Agent Joe Andrews opened the door, noticed Agent Hickman and asked, "Jesus, Cal, are you all right?"

"Yeah, Joe, I'm fine."

"When I heard the news about the explosion killing all those agents, I prayed you weren't one of them."

"Thanks, Joe," said Agent Hickman. Then he turned from his former partner and said, "General, if you don't mind, I gotta call the wife before she hears this from somebody else. She'll go crazy if she does."

"Sure, you and Joe go ahead. See me later when you're ready."

Alone after the two agents left, Lance went to his own office. He sat at his desk and started thinking about what had transpired that morning, going over the sequence of events in the hope of maybe remembering something that might shed some light on why and how the car bombing could have happened. He kept mentally coming back to the same question. *How did the assassins find out which car the President was going to be in?*

A sudden thought struck him so he stood up and yelled, "Mike! Come in here!"

When Mike came through the door, Lance began. "Somebody had to give the President's itinerary to those bastards that bombed the motorcade, and that somebody had to have been inside the White House when the plans were being made or sometime before we left for the Capitol. Whoever it was, evidently didn't know about the switch at the Capitol or the bomb would have blown up at the fourth car instead of the second one."

Mike said, "It seems like we've screwed up somewhere."

"I don't know how the hell we could have. We went by the book on everything."

"Well then, the only way I see it, we either missed a guy in the background checks or somebody got in from the outside we don't know about and found out which car the President was gonna be in."

Lance knew what Mike meant because he also thought of the same two possibilities a few moments ago.

"Or," continued Mike, "it's one of the people who was briefed about the motorcade plan."

"The only ones that were told which car the President was going to be in were Ben Hawkins, Cal Hickman, the President's driver John, the agent in the front seat and myself. And, of course the President."

"When was this decision made?"

"Yesterday afternoon. Cal came to me with the suggestion of putting the President in the second car."

"Well that removes one of the possibilities."

"What do you mean?"

"If it was one of the passengers in the car they surely would not have risked getting killed in the explosion. No, I think the choice is one of the other two."

"Which do you think is the most likely?"

"Somebody got in that we don't know about."

"Yeah, I agree. That's what I come up with too."

"How do you suppose they got in?"

"I don't know, but we better find out."

The telephone rang, interrupting the conversation so Lance answered, "General Stalwardt speaking."

"General, I'm Detective Sergeant Fred Carson, Silver Springs PD, homicide division. I'm returning a call from somebody in your office looking for a guy named Bonner."

"Yes, we were asking about him."

"I've looked in our records and we don't show a Bonner ever being held. Ain't he one of the agents at the White House?"

"That's right. His name is Harold Edward Bonner."

"Yes, sir," said the detective. "I have his full name … it's just that we don't have him. The guy who called a few minutes ago said this Bonner found a dead man in his apartment. That correct?"

"Not his apartment, but the dead man's own apartment. Agent Bonner told me he found another Secret Service agent in his own apartment, a Walter Bradley, shortly after Bradley left my office. Said the man was shot in the head."

"Nobody has reported any shooting involving a Bradley to this office and I can't find anywhere when this Bonner came in. What's the address of this Bradley fella?"

"Just a minute, I'll let one of my associates give you that information." Lance handed Mike the receiver and said, "Here Mike, a detective from Silver Springs PD wants Bradley's address. It seems that Bonner never called 'em nor did he go to their station."

Mike took the telephone from Lance then gave the detective on the other end of the line the information he needed and hung up the receiver as he said, "Looks to me like Bonner might be a real good suspect for a murder and an attempted assassination."

"Yeah, it appears that way. Somehow he must have found out about the President's itinerary and gave it to someone. Question is, how'd he get it and who'd he give it to?"

"What next?"

"Get the driver back in here. Maybe he can tell us something."

When the driver entered Lance's office, Lance offered him a seat and asked, "John, do you know Harold Bonner?"

"Yes, sir ... he's the Assistant Agent in Charge of the Secret Service detachment in the White House."

Mike asked, "When did you see Bonner last?"

"Yesterday afternoon."

"Did you talk to him?"

"No, sir. He was in the kitchen havin' coffee with an agent."

"What time yesterday?"

"About five thirty."

"Who was the other agent?"

"Dennis Jones."

"Jones?"

"Yeah, the agent that rode up front with me today."

"Thanks, John, you can go now."

"Is that all you wanted?"

"That's all."

"Can I go home now?"

Lance answered, "Yes, John, that's a good idea. Go on home, relax and be back here on Monday morning."

"Thank you, General."

After the driver left, Lance asked, "Where's Jones at now?"

"I think he's upstairs with the President," Mike replied.

Lance called the President's office and Ben Hawkins answered the call, "Hawkins."

"Ben, this is Stalwardt. Is there an agent Dennis Jones up there with you?"

"Yes, he's outside."

"Bring him down to my office, please. I believe we've got something that he might be able to help us with."

"We'll be right there."

A few moments later Ben Hawkins and Agent Jones entered Lance's office and sat at the table at Lance's invitation.

Lance asked, "Agent Jones, you know Harold Bonner?"

"Yes, sir."

"Have you seen him lately?"

"Yeah. I had coffee with him yesterday afternoon."

"What time yesterday?"

"Wait a minute. What the hell's goin' on here?"

"Don't worry," said Mike, "it's just routine."

The agent looked at Mike and said, "That's my line."

"Seriously, Dennis … may I call you Dennis?"

"Sure."

Mike continued, "Dennis, we have reason to believe that Bonner is mixed up with today's assassination attempt and we're trying to find out if he knew about the President's itinerary."

"Jesus, man, you serious?"

"Like a heart attack," said Mike.

Lance leaned toward the agent and said. "Did he know which car the President was going to be in?"

The agent replied quietly, "Yeah, he knew."

"You say he knew?"

"Yes, sir, he knew all right."

"How'd he know?"

"'Cause I told him."

"You told him?"

Agent Jones responded, "If I'da known he was involved in tryin' to kill me, I sure as hell wouldn't have said anything to him."

Mike asked in an even louder tone, "Why did you tell him?"

"Okay," said Lance, "Calm down. We just want to know why you gave Bonner information about the President's travel route."

"He told me he was asked to put some of the night guys on the duty roster and wanted to know which car they'd be assigned to."

"You believed him?"

"Yeah, why wouldn't I?"

Lance asked, "Did you know that people had to be cleared by me or Cal Hickman to be in here?"

"Hell, I thought he was okay. He was just sittin' there drinkin' coffee. I didn't know the guy wasn't cleared. Shit … and I gave him the whole damn layout."

"Don't worry about that now," said Lance. "I want you to stick around and if you can remember anything else, let me know."

"Yes, sir."

"Good, you can go now."

After the agent left, the three men sat discussing the possibilities of where Bonner could be and who else may be involved.

Ben Hawkins said, "I think we're just spinning our wheels here. Why don't we let it rest for a bit then give it a try later? Meanwhile, I think we should give this to the police and let them try to find Bonner. If and when they do, maybe we can learn something then."

The telephone rang and Mike picked it up saying, "General Stalwardt's office, this is Polaski."

Lance looked up at Mike when he heard his friend say, "Jesus Christ, Hodges, don't do anything till we get there." Mike hung up the receiver and said with a smile on his face, "That was Hodges. The Delta section has got Blondie and two other guys under surveillance in a rat hole off of 16th."

Lance quickly stood up and said, "Get me the off-duty section and call Cal. Tell them to meet in the conference room … NOW! Ben, go tell the President we've got three of the bastards spotted and I'm going to take them alive, especially that blond son of a bitch."

Lance changed from his dress blues into a BDU (Battle Dress Uniform) then put on his pistol belt and weapon while Hawkins went back upstairs to the President's office. Mike in the meantime called the Blair House and arranged for the Alpha section to report immediately to the downstairs conference room.

When Lance finished dressing, he joined Mike, Cal Hickman, Joe Andrews and eleven Alpha section men in the conference room. As he came through the door, those seated all rose to attention.

Lance said, "Be seated everyone, please."

Moving to the end of the table, Lance outlined the pending operation. "First of all, I want one of you Secret Service agents to get me a federal warrant." Lance paused then continued, "Joe, you'll have to be the one because I want Cal with me."

"Any judge in particular?"

"No, just as long as we get it signed."

Agent Hickman asked, "General, you sure you wanna do that?"

"I know what you mean, Cal, but we have to be ready if something goes wrong. CYA." Lance knew that Agent Hickman referred to an earlier conversation about eliminating the assassins, but didn't feel a need for that particular type of clandestine action yet. "Mike, get some transportation out front as soon as possible."

"Already done."

Lance looked at his long-time friend, smiled and thought, *I should've known he'd be ready.*

He began to feel the excitement in the room as everyone began to prepare for the attempted apprehension of the blond killer and the two others with him—weapons checked, ammunition counted and the Alpha section placed silencers on their assault rifles. Within minutes the room became silent.

Lance said, "Before we leave, I want everyone to know that I want that blond bastard alive. I don't care if he's got a hundred holes in his ass, but I want him alive ... any questions?"

No one spoke.

"Good. Now here's how we're gonna do this. Cal, you and one team stay outside and keep any strays away from the building. You never know when a cop or somebody else will show up. Mike, you and the two remaining teams will have the job of clearing the building and getting into the room where these guys are holed up. I'll be right behind you. Remember, I want them alive. Last time, are there any questions?"

The A section commander asked, "What about Delta section?"

"They'll maintain a cordon around the area just in case these characters try to escape. They'll also act as a backup."

Another man asked, "If they try shootin' it out, do we kill 'em?"

"Yes," answered Mike.

Someone else asked, "If they try runnin' ... do we shoot then?"

"Damn right you shoot," Mike replied. "If we can't take the bastards alive ... kill 'em. No one escapes."

Lance looked around at each person in the room as he asked, "Any other questions?" No one answered. "Okay then, let's go."

Chapter 24

Arriving at a location a block away from the suspected killers' hideout, Lance and the others parked the vehicles then approached the building on foot from two different directions. As the unit closed in on the building, Lance noticed Delta section men dressed in civilian clothes, dispersed along the street behind the building.

Lance spotted the assistant section leader, Major Hodges, and immediately went to him asking, "What's the story here, Major?"

"Sir, we believe the ones we're after are on the third floor of that building," said the major, pointing to a building toward the middle of the block. "Both Coleman and Garcia said they saw one of the guys up there on the back porch looking around. Then later saw him at one of the windows."

"How'd you spot these guys?"

"When the bomb went off in the motorcade, we were in the second security cordon parked on a side street. Right after the explosion, Sergeant Coleman saw this car tearin' out of a nearby parking lot. He said he recognized one of the men in the car."

"Which one was it?"

"He said he thought it was the same guy he saw in Illinois that tried to shoot your lady friend. Garcia was ridin' with Coleman and he said the same thing, so they radioed to me they were gonna follow the suspects and check 'em out. When they saw 'em go into the building here, they were sure. That's when I called in."

"Good job," said Lance. "Tell Coleman I wanna see him."

"Yes, sir."

The major reached down in his belt, pulled out a handheld radio and spoke into it. Within seconds Sergeant Coleman appeared.

Lance asked the sergeant, "Are you positive that one of those men upstairs is the same man you saw in Illinois?"

"Yes, sir, absolutely."

"Did Garcia see him?"

"Yes, sir. He said it was the same guy too."

"What's he look like?"

"He's blond ... the one that tried to shoot your lady friend."

"All right, Sergeant," said Lance. "That's good enough for me. Major, I want you and your men to keep the area cordoned off because if these guys try to slip outta here before we get upstairs, your people are the only ones who can recognize them."

"Who's goin' in?"

"Alpha section. Anything else?"

"No, sir."

"Okay, everyone, you all know what to do. Let's go."

Lance and Mike followed the other men into the building and up the stairs toward the third floor with four doors opening into the hallway, two on either side of the stairway.

"The apartment we want is gonna be on the left side," said Mike.

When the group reached the third floor, Lance and Mike waited at the top of the steps while the rest of the men went quietly to the door of the suspected apartment. After reaching it without being detected, the men prepared for a surprise entry.

Two men knelt by the door with one man on either side, ready to cross fire their weapons into the room. Two other men stood above them. A fifth man took a prone position in front of the door so his field of fire would be straight in.

Once ready, two men charged the door straight on, tearing it from its hinges and brought it crashing to the floor inside the room. When the door hit the floor the two men quickly rolled to either side and positioned themselves to fire their weapons. Instantly, seven automatic weapons trained on the three surprised men.

At the moment the door came crashing down all three suspects sat at a small kitchen table. Two men jumped to their feet, drew their weapons and started to aim them toward the door, but there was no door. However, they fired anyway, their shots hitting into the opposite wall across the hallway.

The third man, although surprised and shocked, stayed seated and raised his hands over his head just as seven automatic weapons opened fire. The two standing men died instantly.

From where he stood in the stairway, Lance heard the loud crash as the door hit the floor followed by pistol shots, then the muffled sounds of silenced automatic weapons fire. As he and Mike hurried into the room after the all clear signal, Lance hoped that the man he called Blondie would still be alive. When he stepped around the table he saw the two bodies on the floor—one the blond killer, the other Agent Bonner. A third man sat at the table with raised hands.

Lance asked, "They dead?"

"Yes, sir," replied one of the officers. "We had no choice."

Lance and Mike looked over the two dead men then Mike turned to the man seated at the table and asked, "What's your name, pal?"

The man didn't answer so Mike approached him, drawing his weapon, placed it on the man's forehead and said in a quiet voice, "I asked you a question … what's your name?"

The man mumbled in a foreign language then hung his head.

Lance asked, "What'd he say? Anybody get what he said?"

One of the enlisted men stepped forward and said, "He spoke in Italian, sir. Says he's Mafia and cannot answer."

Mike grabbed the man's shirt collar from behind and jerked him up to his feet at the same time bringing the man's right arm down behind his back. Another soldier took the other arm and brought it down, locking the man's wrists in a pair of handcuffs.

With the man's hands secure, Mike bent him over onto the table, searched him and found an automatic pistol in his belt, a silencer in his back pocket and a remote control device used for setting off blasting charges in a jacket pocket.

Lance could hear the restrained man's labored breathing and see wide-eyed fear in his facial expression as his head lay on the table with Mikes hand on the back of his neck.

Speaking in English the man asked, "What you guys gonna do?"

New York City, thought Lance, and then said, "Mike, take this piece of garbage to the Blair House."

Mike pointed to the two bodies on the floor. "What should we do with these two?"

"We'll let Cal handle it," said Lance. Then turning to one of the men near the doorway, he ordered, "Go get Agent Hickman and have him come up here. I wanna see him right away."

Mike growled at the prisoner, "All right, asshole, move it," at the same time he pulled the prisoner upright onto his feet, turned him toward the door and pushed him through it so hard the prisoner stumbled, falling headlong into the wall on the other side of the hall. He fell helpless to the floor, half unconscious from bashing his head into the wall. Mike casually walked over to his prisoner, grabbed the man's shirt and brought him to his feet again then shoved him down the hall toward the stairs. "I said move, shithead, or I'll kick your ass all the way down the steps."

After Mike and the others left with the prisoner, only Lance and the two dead men remained in the room. A few moments later, Agent Hickman came through the door.

Lance asked, "Cal, how should we handle this?"

"No problem, General," replied Agent Hickman as he bent down and looked at the two dead bodies. "I'll take care of it."

"You sure?"

"Yeah, I gotta friend in homicide that owes me a favor. I'll tell them it's a government investigation and classified."

"That sometimes doesn't work."

"We got a federal warrant. So, there's really no problem."

"What're you gonna do about the bodies?"

"Nothin'. I'll tell the capital boys to take care of the mess."

"You think they'll wonder about Bonner?"

"Nah. I've got an idea that'll take care of that. I figure that even though Bonner didn't kill Bradley, he knew who did. As far as I'm concerned he's just as guilty as if he pulled the trigger himself."

"Are you gonna tell the police that Bonner killed Bradley?"

"Yeah, but I won't come right out and say it. I'll just sortta imply it. Let them come to their own conclusion."

"How you gonna do that if you don't have the murder weapon?"

"I'll bet even money the gun that killed Bradley is the same caliber as one of these three."

Agent Hickman pointed to the three handguns lying on the table and said, "If Bonner's prints are on all three of these guns then all we have to do is to find out which type killed Bradley and wipe the other two clean."

He walked over to the corpse of the former Secret Service agent, put each weapon in the dead man's right hand and pressed the hand firmly to ensure that a good print was on each pistol butt. "There, that oughta do it."

"Are you sure about one of these being the right weapon?"

"It doesn't really matter. It's the caliber that counts. As you can see, all three of these weapons are a different caliber. There's a three fifty-seven (.357), a thirty-eight (.38) special and a nine (9)mm automatic. One of these should be the one that killed Bradley."

"What about the ballistics?"

"Doesn't matter. I know how to make the ballistics match."

"What about a motive?"

"That's a problem, but I'll find something," said Hickman as he labeled each pistol and put them in separate plastic bags.

"All right, go with it, but if this thing blows up, I'll deny any knowledge of it and you'll have to hang by yourself."

"Don't worry, General. We're the only two who'll ever know the truth. And, I sure as hell won't tell."

"Have the police been notified?"

"Yes, sir, so you'd better hurry, you don't have much time. I'll see you later and let you know how things are goin'."

Lance said goodbye, left the room and hurried down the stairs as he heard sirens approaching. As he turned the corner, two police squad cars stopped in front of the building he just left. When he reached his car, he got in and drove away.

Arriving at the White House, he went immediately to the Oval Office where President Williams and Ben Hawkins waited for him. Lance briefed the two men on the events of the raid that captured one man and killed two others, but he didn't reveal the plan that Agent Hickman began setting in motion.

Both men listened without interruption until Lance finished then the President asked, "The captured man, does he know anything?"

"We don't know yet, Mr. President. General Polaski has two interrogators working on him as we speak."

"Where is he?"

"Across the street at the Blair House."

"I want to know everything that man has to say."

"Yes, sir. I'm going over when I finish here to see if they've made any progress. Ben, you wanna come along?"

"Yes, I'd like to."

For a moment, no one in the room spoke then the President rose from his chair behind the desk and came around to Lance. "General, before you go, there's something I would like to discuss with you. Please, let's go sit over there."

The President motioned to the oval table and the four wingback chairs. As they sat the President continued. "General Stalwardt, I have just completed three very important telephone calls with you being the main topic of discussion."

"Me, sir?"

"Yes, General. They were calls to various party members that have now inherited certain decision making powers because of the tragic events this morning. Also, there was a call to the opposition party leadership to solicit their opinion on a proposal that I will be presenting to them very shortly. A proposal that concerns you."

"May I ask what that proposal is, sir?"

"Yes. I've asked for the immediate and unanimous confirmation for you to be my Vice President … if you accept the appointment."

Lance sat for a moment, dumbstruck by the President's news. He looked at Hawkins who smiled at him then looked back at the President, also smiling.

The President asked, "Is anything wrong, General?"

"Mr. President. I'm completely flabbergasted by your offer."

"Will you accept?"

Without hesitation Lance answered, "Yes, sir, I accept."

"Good. Since this nation appears to be in a turmoil there should be no problem in getting you confirmed within a week. They know there's a need for a strong candidate and you're the strongest one I can think of."

"Yes, sir, that may be true, but what if they don't go along with your thinking and don't confirm my nomination?"

"If they don't go for the idea, I'll threaten martial law, that'll scare the hell out of them. In any case that's my worry. Now then, since we've settled the matter, why don't you two go on over to the Blair House, and I'll work on your confirmation."

Lance and Hawkins left the President's office and went to the room in the Blair House where Mike, Sgt. Garcia and several other group members continued to interrogate the prisoner, frightened about his chances of staying alive, and with good cause.

"Sir," said Mike, "this character says he doesn't know anything. Says all he did was supply the explosives and the detonator."

"What's his name?"

"Antonio Gasparini, a capo in a New York mafia family."

"Capo?"

"Yes, sir. That's a high-level boss. Like a captain of a select group of soldiers. Only in this case it's thugs."

"Who hired him?"

"Blondie and some guy. Says he never knew their real names."

"Did he say how he became involved with all of this?"

"He claims his boss in New York told him to bring a few other guys to DC and do a hit. He was told to contact Blondie, except he called him Jones. Said all he was given was a telephone number."

"This other man wasn't Bonner?"

"No, sir. He claims the other guy was older and wore expensive clothes, like the kind a politician would wear."

"Did he say he could identify him?"

"Yes, sir, he thinks so, but who we gonna show him?"

"I don't know. Right now I wouldn't know where to begin."

"You wanna keep this guy around for a while?"

"Yes. Maybe something might turn up. Also, see if you can get the names of those who were involved in the actual shootings."

"This guy claims he didn't shoot anybody. Said all he did was finger the targets for the others."

"Did he say who did Bradley?"

"Yes, sir, he said it was one of the guys who shot the Emersons."

At the name of his ex-boss and old friend, Lance felt a certain rage towards the unknown assailant and said with an outburst of anger, "I want that bastard's name and I want his ass alive."

With a little agitation in his voice, Mike responded, "You'll get him alive if we can take him that way, otherwise I'll bring you his corpse. I can't guarantee the guy will cooperate. Hell, General, you saw what happened today. These guys might not wanna be taken alive and will probably try shootin' their way out."

Lance calmed down and said, "Yeah, I guess you're right."

"Anyway, you shouldn't be worrying about this ... and you shouldn't be jeopardizing your position with these pissy little matters. That's my job now."

"Okay, Mike, I'm sorry. You handle it the best way you can."

"Thanks," said Mike with a smile on his face. "I knew you'd see it my way."

After Lance and Ben Hawkins left the Blair House, they returned to the White House where a message waited for them to return immediately to the Oval Office.

"General, the opposition leadership has agreed to go along with a quick confirmation on one condition," said the President.

Lance asked, "What's that, sir?"

"It has to do with your lady friend."

"What about her, sir?"

"They brought up the matter of you living with your lady friend. I told them that it was none of their business. But, you must admit, General, they have a strong argument about the morality of a Vice President living with a woman without the benefit of matrimony."

"That can be remedied, sir. I've already proposed to her and she's accepted."

"Good, perhaps then we could have the ceremony here in the White House chapel."

"When do we have to decide on a date."

"Will tomorrow be too soon?"

"You want our decision on a date tomorrow, sir?"

"No, General, the wedding."

Surprised, Lance said, "I'll ask Marilyn and see if she'll agree."

Marilyn didn't hesitate for an instant and when Lance told her the news that evening she practically jumped into his arms and said, "The sooner the better."

With the President, the first lady, Hawkins and a few security people attending the ceremony, a local minister married Lance and Marilyn in the White House chapel at 11:00 a.m. the next day. Mike acted as best man and Mrs. Hickman acted as matron of honor.

Later that same afternoon, an envoy of dignitaries made up of members from both houses of congress met with the President to discuss Lance's appointment. After an hour of conversation and persuasion by President Williams, the congressmen reached a consensus. They would accept and support Lance's nomination and would also push for a quick confirmation vote on Monday's agenda. For security reasons, the nomination would not be announced to the media until after the vote.

When Lance returned to his office after the meeting, he had a message to call Agent Hickman at his home.

A woman's voice answered, "Hickman residence."

"This is General Stalwardt. I've a message from Cal to call him. Is he there?"

"Just a moment, please."

After a few seconds Lance heard, "General, this is Cal."

"I got your message."

"Yes, sir. I got a call from the former Vice President's wife and she told me that he wants to see you."

"When?"

"The sooner the better."

"Okay, how about tomorrow?"

"That'll be fine, sir. I'll call and let her know."

"Did she say what the Vice President wants?"

"No, sir, she didn't say."

"All right. And, Cal."

"Yes, sir."

"I'd like you to go with me."

"Sure, no problem. I'll meet you in your office at one o'clock tomorrow afternoon."

"I'll see you then."

Lance hung up the telephone and left for the Blair House to meet his new bride who planned a special wedding dinner just for the two of them.

Chapter 25

At one o'clock Sunday afternoon, Agent Hickman arrived at Lance's office. "Are you ready, sir?"

"Yeah, let's go."

"My car's right outside. Let's take it."

The drive to the hospital didn't take long and the topic of conversation between the two men consisted mainly about what happened after Lance left the scene of the raid on Friday.

Agent Hickman said, "The detectives finally came to the conclusion that Bonner shot Walt Bradley, just like I said they would. I told them that I thought I had the murder weapon and that I'd surrender it as soon as we completed our investigation."

Lance asked, "Did they go for it?"

"Yes, sir. No problem."

"Good. We don't need the police on our ass right now."

"The Silver Springs PD is sending me the ballistics on the slug that killed Bradley. I'll match it to one of the three guns that we've got and that'll close that case. It should also satisfy the media on how Bradley died."

"What about why he died?"

"Yeah, I know. I've been thinking about that one, but I haven't come up with anything yet."

"Well, maybe we'll find out something when we round up some of those people on Gasparini's list. How many names did he finally come up with?"

"Thirty-five."

"Unbelievable."

"Yeah. It surprised me too."

"Any leads on any of them?"

"Not yet. The only thing we've come up with is they're all from one mafia family. My guess is we'll find most of them dead ... that is if we find any of them at all."

Lance made a mental note to speak with Mike about the list to confirm either dead or alive, including the family head. Also, Lance knew that the mafia had a tendency to police their own ranks if anyone caused any undue problems for the rest of the organizations.

Lance said, "Maybe the key to getting this whole thing resolved is to put pressure on the other families and let them dispose of their own mavericks."

"That works. Those people don't like notoriety and they usually eliminate anybody that causes any, especially higher ups. There's probably gonna be a rash of killings in the next few days."

When they arrived at Walter Reed Hospital, Agent Hickman dropped Lance off at the front door and said, "He wants to see you alone. I'll park the car and wait for you in the front lobby."

Lance got out of the car, went in through the front entrance and took the elevator up to the ailing former Vice President's room. Two Secret Service agents sat at a desk stationed outside the door.

One of the agents asked, "May I help you, sir?"

"I'm General Lance Stalwardt. The Vice President has asked to see me."

"May I see your ID, sir?"

Lance produced his military identification card and handed it to the agent, who in turn wrote down his name, card number and time on a log sheet.

When he finished writing, the agent looked up at Lance and said, "Please check in with us as you leave, sir. You may go in now."

Lance entered the room and saw the man on the bed looked nothing like what Lance remembered. The former Vice President appeared emaciated and pallid, looking to weigh no more than a hundred pounds. His sunken eyes made his face appear skull-like and his arm veins protruded through pale skin. With wide-open eyes and pure white hair, he looked as if he had been frightened by something, but Lance knew the man's illness, and being near death, made him appear that way.

The strange looking eyes followed Lance as he came to the bed's side and said, "Mr. Vice President. It's good to see you again."

What sounded like a half cough and an asthmatic wheeze the ailing man said, "Bullshit."

Lance smiled and then sat down when the man gestured toward the chair next to the bed.

Lance thought, *He may be sick, but he hasn't lost his directness.* Then he said, "You wanted to see me, sir?"

Between wheezes the former Vice President responded, "I understand ... you are being ... appointed ... to Vice President."

"Yes, sir," said Lance, surprised he knew of the appointment.

"Don't look so ... surprised. I know ... just about everything ... that goes on ... in the White House." The Vice President slowly reached over and turned a control knob near the head of his bed. "I need more ... oxygen ... when I talk."

"Sir, if I may ask ... how did you find out so soon? It was only agreed to yesterday."

"You forget ... that I came ... out of the Senate."

"I see. So one of the senators on the panel that came to see the President gave you the word ... right?"

"That's right."

"What is it you wanted to see me about?"

With his breathing still labored the Vice President answered, "I wanted to ... warn you ... about things ... that I think ... you should know. First ... watch out for anyone who offers ... a compromise on the ... defense package. As President of ... the Senate ... you have the controlling vote ... in case of a tie and ... your vote is very ... important to them. There are people ... that don't want ... this budget cut ... especially in the New England states."

"New England states, sir ... why not?"

"Yes, New England ... especially Maine. I believe ... the President was killed ... by a highly organized group ... that wanted to maintain ... the federal money flow ... into certain New England companies ... that are controlled by ... people who don't ... have our nation's ... interest at heart."

"Do you know who these people are?"

"No, but they'll ... expose themselves ... soon."

"How do you know this?"

"There are factions ... within this city that want ... to bring down ... this party ... and President Williams. However, they are willing ... to do it properly ... by electing a new President. This group has ... been approached and ... asked to join forces ... and form ... a coalition with some ... New England politicians."

Lance asked, "Do you know who's pushing the group?"

"No, but any … one of several … legislators could be … the man you're looking for."

"That means you believe that President Walker's assassination and the attempt on President Williams was ordered by someone inside the government?"

The Vice President said, "I do."

"I have the same theory. I believe someone who is in a position to know what's going on was the one who ordered the killings. Now all we have to do is find the right guy."

"It won't be easy."

"I know," said Lance. "We already ran up against the mafia."

"They probably … did the shootings."

"Yes, they did. We have one in custody and he's already ratted on thirty-five of his friends. It'll now be just a matter of time before we get them all." Lance then told the Vice President about the explosion killing the designated Vice President and how they raided the building where Bonner and the blond killer were hiding. Lance finished by saying, "I just can't figure how Bonner and Bradley are related in this."

"They were lovers."

Surprised by the news Lance exclaimed, "WHAT!"

"They were lovers. They had … a homosexual relationship."

"My God. They were being blackmailed."

"Probably."

"So that's how Blondie got Bonner to tell him when and where."

The Vice President asked, "What about … the man that met … the blond man … and the mobster?"

"All we know is that he wears expensive suits."

"Start by looking … at legislators. If that doesn't … produce results … try lobbyists. I—"

A sudden coughing fit interrupted the Vice President. A nurse, sitting by the door out of hearing distance for normal conversation, hurried over to the Vice President and started tending to him.

She turned and said, "I'm sorry, sir, you'll have to leave now."

After leaving the room, Lance checked out with the Secret Service agents and went to the lobby where Agent Hickman waited.

They left the hospital and during the ride to the White House, Lance briefed Hickman about his conversation with the Vice President.

Lance said, "I'd like for the task force to start looking into files of all agencies that involve New England area legislators, especially defense type contract investigations."

"I'll get Joe on it first thing in the morning."

During the next two days Lance received reports of twenty-five mob related murders in and around the New York City area, and when he checked, Antonio Gasparini had given him all twenty-five names of the dead men. The remaining ten men seemed to have disappeared and no one ever heard from them again.

Another death that had some significance to Lance appeared in the newspaper the next day.

```
Major General Kenneth E. Cross,
U.S. Air Force, was killed by a
hit and run driver while crossing
the street in front of his home
on Sunday afternoon.
```

Chapter 26

The confirmation of Lance as the new Vice President of the United States came within forty-eight hours of his name being placed in formal nomination and then being sworn in by his boyhood friend, Judge Dexter Knowles, at a private ceremony in the White House. His family stood behind him while Marilyn and Lynn stood at each side, his wife on the left and his daughter on the right.

His long-time friend read the oath of office, and he in turn repeated it, swearing to uphold and support the Constitution of the United States. As he spoke the words of the oath, Lance began to feel the same emotions of humility and pride he felt when he received the Medal of Honor, only this time without the associated feelings of guilt and remorse.

After the ceremony, President Williams held a reception without the press in one of the smaller rooms in the White House. Less than a hundred people attended, mainly family members and a few inner circle power brokers, both elected and appointed, one of them, Cyrus T. Baynes, the senior senator from North Carolina and one of the most powerful men in the U.S. Senate.

"Congratulations, Mr. Vice President," said the senator. "It's quite a jump from being a soldier to being the Vice President of the United States."

Lance could tell the sarcastic tone in the senator's voice and started to respond when Marilyn stopped him. "Why Senator, where is your lovely wife? Didn't she come with you this morning?"

"No, Mrs. Stalwardt, she didn't. It is Mrs. Stalwardt, isn't it?"

"Yes, Senator, it is. Lance and I were married last Saturday in the White House chapel. I'm sorry you didn't receive an invitation, but of course you know how it is when there's limited space and so many friends."

"Yes, ma'am. However, I wouldn't have been able to be here anyway. I had other important business to attend to." The senator turned to Lance and said, "Well now, Mr. Vice President, if you and your new wife will excuse me, I must go and take care of some very pressing business. As you know, next week I'm going to California with President Williams to meet with the Japanese on this trade thing so I've got to clear up a few matters before I go."

"Certainly, Senator," said Lance, "both Marilyn and I are so glad you came. And I hope you have a pleasant trip."

The senator left and went to the President to say his goodbyes. Within five minutes he left.

Marilyn said, "He's certainly a cantankerous bastard. Imagine, insulting the Vice President's wife ... and on purpose too. The unmitigated gall of some people."

Lance said to his wife, "Never mind, love, he's gone."

Looking up at Lance's face, Marilyn smiled at him and squeezed his arm to her body as she said almost in a whisper, "I love you."

Smiling, Lance winked at her and said, "Ditto."

After the reception, Lance and Marilyn spent the rest of the day with the family, his mother, his five sisters with their husbands and children, his daughter and her family, and Marilyn's mother and father. In all, about twenty people. Lance gave them a quick tour of the Capitol, the Lincoln Memorial and the Washington Monument. Early the next morning they all left and flew back to Illinois.

During the next several days, Lance began settling into his new position as Vice President of the United States. A few days later, President Williams left for a good will trip to California, along with a few congressional dignitaries.

As Lance sat in his new office in the White House, Cal Hickman came rushing in without knocking and said with excitement, "By God, sir, I think we've got our man!"

Lance, somewhat excited asked, "What've you got?"

Agent Hickman held a folder with a few papers and photographs inside. "This is what we've been looking for."

"Wait ... let me call Mike in here. I think he should hear this."

"Damn, Gen ... I mean, Mr. Vice President. You ain't gonna believe this."

When Mike came through the door, Lance said, "Have a seat Mike, Cal's got some news." Then Lance returned to his seat and said, "Okay, Cal, fill us in."

"The guy who's behind the assassinations is Cyrus T. Baynes."

Lance responded, "Baynes?"

"None other than the senior senator from North Carolina. He engineered the whole thing through the mafia, the KKK and a small white supremacy group called the White Race for Democracy."

"But how? He certainly never appeared to be involved."

"His aide," Agent Hickman paused and looked in the folder for the name. "Ah ... here it is. A guy by the name of James Callahan did all the legwork. Old Cyrus kept out of the picture pretty much, but when they missed three people on their target list, Baynes took charge and turned Blondie loose."

"That explains why they were so intent on killing you," said Mike. "That old bastard has hated you for years."

Lance said, "I guess he really wanted me dead. It probably started when we snubbed him back when I got the Medal of Honor."

"By the way, sir," said Agent Hickman, "Baynes and Blondie were KKK brothers in the same klan back in South Carolina."

"How long ago?"

"Back before Baynes became a US Senator. That's how we were able to tie this whole thing together."

Mike asked, "How's that?"

"Through cross files of the FBI, the ATF and the South Carolina Bureau of Investigation."

"Well," said Mike, "I guess this task force thing paid off."

"You bet ... big time," said Agent Hickman. "I think we can also tie Baynes in on the Bay of Pigs invasion against Cuba, and we also think he might have had something to do with the Kennedy killing. Some of the files seem to lead us in that direction."

Mike asked, "Where was this information?"

"It was all in the records of various agencies and all we needed to do was search it out. Of course it was piecemeal and some of the stuff is speculation, but I'm pretty sure we've got the right guys."

Lance asked, "Just how sure are you?"

"Damn sure, sir. We know that Baynes was supported by a lot of the industrial types in South Carolina and in New England that had Defense Department contracts. His campaign contributions were in the millions with most of it hidden in offshore accounts."

"What else have you got?"

"We got a copy of the KKK application with his signature on it sponsoring Blondie's membership. It proves he knew the bastard."

"It doesn't mean that he recruited him to do the assassinations," said Lance.

"You're right, sir, but here is a picture of Callahan and Blondie meeting at the Lincoln Memorial a few months ago. They talked for about fifteen minutes then had several meetings after that."

"How'd you get these pictures?"

"The FBI was tailin' Blondie because he was such a radical. The South Carolina state police alerted the FBI and asked if they would keep him under surveillance."

"Because of his Klan activities, right?"

"That and the fact he was involved with this white supremacy group. They professed to have killed a couple of blacks in Georgia and South Carolina and the state police think that Blondie was the triggerman."

"How's he connected to the assassinations?"

"We've got photos of Blondie and Callahan meeting with our old friend Antonio Gasparini," said Agent Hickman, handing Lance half a dozen ten by seven photographs.

Lance said, "Callahan must be the guy Gasparini met and didn't know who he was."

"By the way, sir," said Agent Hickman, "Blondie's real name is Bobby Ray Calhoun. That's how we tied all this together. After we got his real identity, we used him as a reference in all the other files and came up with what I've got here. It took a little while, but I think we've got what we need."

Lance studied the pictures and then said, "It's good enough for me. The former Vice President warned me about some southern connection to all of this, and now I believe we've found it. Baynes is our man. It all fits. He wanted the present administration out of power because they were going to drastically reduce the defense budget and we're talking about revenues in the billions."

"That might have put his friends out of business," said Mike.

"Yeah," said Agent Hickman, "and his friends wouldn't have liked that. Most of the businesses are mob controlled. If he hadn't done somethin' they probably would have killed him too."

"I can understand now why they'd assassinate the opposition," said Mike. "I guess it's one way of doing business."

Lance said, "Remember, they tried to get both the President and the Vice President, hoping to appoint the Speaker of the House to the presidency. Although he's from the opposition party, the House Speaker is from South Carolina and Senator Baynes would have had a tremendous amount of influence with him. He probably could have run the country."

Mike asked, "Isn't Baynes with the President now?"

"Yes, he is," answered Lance. "Who's with the senator?"

"Callahan and a couple of other lesser aides," replied Cal.

Lance said, "Mike, check to see how soon they arrive in LA."

"Before I do that, sir, I have to ask you something."

"What is it?"

"Am I to assume that we're still gonna eliminate the ... the senator, his aides and whoever else is involved?"

"Mike, it came from President Williams."

"My God man, it's the wrong thing to do and you know it."

"Mike, I wish there were another way. I'd give anything if there were, but there's no other choice. We have to take these people out, simply because they're too dangerous to us and the country."

"That may be, but I sure as hell don't like it. It makes us no better than them. I can understand taking out those in the mob, but I can't condone killing government officials. It just ain't right."

No one answered Mike so he called operations at Andrews AFB, saying, "This is General Polaski, military aide to Vice President Stalwardt. Can you please give me the ETA of Air Force One to Los Angeles?"

After a few moments, Lance could see Mike's face turn into a concerned expression as he listened to operations at Andrews AFB.

A moment later, Mike said, "Thanks," and hung up the phone.

"They said the plane is fifteen minutes overdue."

Lance asked, "Anything to worry about?"

"Not normally, but they lost both radar and radio contact. They haven't been able to raise them on the civilian or military channels."

"What about the Air Force cover escorts?"

"They hit bad weather and lost sight of Air Force One."

"What have they done so far?"

"They're sending up search planes to see if they can find them."

"How long ago?"

"Just now. The planes are being scrambled out of Nellis in Vegas and Edwards in California right this minute."

"Jesus, this is almost too hard to believe. I'd better call Marilyn and have her come over. Mike, will you go get her?"

"Sure thing."

"I'll want her with me when I break the news to Mrs. Williams. Cal, better set up a press release for the media right away. Just say they're overdue and everything is being done to find them. And Cal, better get hold of Ben Hawkins. Tell him I wanna see him as soon as he can make it. Thank God he wasn't on that plane."

Both men left the office and hurried to their assigned tasks. Lance stood looking out the window, pondering the news of the missing plane and trying to assess the impact that it would have on the nation and on himself. Only a month ago the nation lost a President, shot down in the streets while on his daily run.

Lance thought, *In that short period of time I've gone from being a major general in the Army, the National Security Adviser to the President, the Vice President of the United States and now—*

The telephone rang. "Stalwardt."

"Lance this is Marilyn."

"Yes, honey, is Mike there?"

"No, he isn't. Lance, I called because I just heard a report on the TV that the President's plane is overdue and they're unable to contact them. Have you heard anything?"

"Yes, we have, that's why Mike's coming over to get you now. I want you with me when I see Mrs. Williams and tell her the news. I think it's better that you go along and maybe stay with her since she's all alone here."

"Oh Lance, that poor woman. I'll be right over just as soon as Mike gets here. I'll see you later, dear. Bye."

After Lance and Marilyn told Mrs. Williams about the missing presidential plane, Marilyn stayed with the first lady while Lance returned to his office. He picked up the telephone and called Mike. When Mike answered, Lance asked, "Any news on Air Force One?"

"I don't know, sir. I'll check with Hickman and let you know. He's handling the verification to Edwards."

"When you're done with that, come on up to my office."

"Yes, sir."

A few moments later Mike came in and had just started to sit down when the telephone rang.

Mike said, "I'll get it, sir. It's probably Hickman. He said he'd call here if there was any news." Mike picked up the receiver and said, "Vice President Stalwardt's office, General Polaski speaking."

"Mike, this is Cal."

"Yeah, Cal."

"Is the Vice President there?"

"Yes, he is. Whatcha got?"

With a bit of excitement in his voice, Agent Hickman said, "Not on the phone. I'll be right up."

After Mike hung up the telephone, Ben Hawkins entered the office and asked, "What happened?"

Lance said, "Los Angeles has lost contact with Air Force One, and it may have gone down."

"When?"

"Just within the last fifteen minutes."

Hawkins exclaimed, "My God!" Then more calmly he asked, "Has anyone told his wife?"

"Yes," said Lance, "Marilyn's with her now."

Hawkins sat in one of the chairs next to Mike and put his face into his hands as if to hide the sudden shock from the others. As Lance looked at his friend in his moment of grief, Agent Hickman came through the door and closed it behind him.

Lance asked, "Did they find the plane?"

"Yes, sir, they did. It went down in Arizona."

Lance asked, "Any survivors?"

"No, sir. Not a one."

Both Ben Hawkins and Mike seated in front of Lance's desk quickly stood then all three men looked at Lance as Mike said, "Mr. President, what are your orders?"

Glossary

The following definitions are military terms and acronyms used in *The Naked Warrior*.

ATF - Alcohol, Tobacco & Firearms Agency.

BDU - Battle Dress Uniform, the camouflage combat uniform worn by US Army personnel in combat situations.

BARRAGE - Preplanned artillery fires used to protect friendly troops in an all-out enemy assault on a defensive position. It usually is spread out over the entire front of friendly positions with a range of 100 to 200 meters in depth from the **FPL**, a line known as the Final Protective Line.

CLAYMORE - An anti-personnel mine that can be detonated by a trip wire or an on call device. It sends hundreds of small steel projectiles toward the targeted area, fanned out on a horizontal plane.

CONCENTRATION - A plotted and preplanned artillery strike on a known enemy point or position.

CONG - Short for Viet Cong, generally Vietnamese guerilla forces fighting in South Viet Nam, sympathetic to the North Vietnamese political doctrine during the period of American involvement with that country.

CYA - Cover Your Ass

DA - Department of the Army, the Pentagon, Washington, DC.

DOD - Department of Defense, the Pentagon, Washington, DC.

DRO - Dining Room Orderly, Enlisted men acting as servers and busboys to the commander's table in a military dining room.

DUSTOFF - Military call sign for a medical airlift evacuation by helicopter.

E GRADES - Enlisted men pay grades, indicated by **E1** through **E9**. Officer pay grades are indicated by the capital letter **W** for warrant officers and the letter **O** for commissioned officers, such as **O1**, second lieutenant, **O4**, major and so on.

ELEVATION - The vertical movement of a weapon measured in degrees.

EXECUTIVE OFFICER - Second in command of a military unit who acts as commander during the assigned commander's absence. The letters are pronounced separately as **X-O**.

FO - Forward Observer, usually a commissioned officer that is attached to front line infantry troops to report enemy targets to artillery support units and to adjust fires on those targets.

FIRE FAN - The area in front of a soldier's position that he is assigned to observe and cover with automatic weapon or rifle fire. Also, the area of effectiveness inside the left and right traverse limits of a mortar or artillery piece.

HE - High Explosive munitions.

HUEY - A type of combat helicopter used in Viet Nam.

LT - A short designation for lieutenant used by enlisted men to address their platoon leader. The letters are pronounced separately as **L-T**.

LZ - Landing Zone.

MACV - Military Assistance Command, Viet Nam.

MILITARY STAFF POSITIONS OF U.S. ARMY UNITS
  S1 - Personnel
  S2 - Intelligence
  S3 - Operations
  S4 - Logistics

NOTE: *The prefix letter **S** usually signifies a battalion or brigade level staff position. The letter **G** replaces the **S** in higher headquarters units, such as division and corps. At army levels and above, the prefix letter becomes a **J**. However, the **G1** and **J1** staff positions still handle Personnel functions in administration and replacement.*

MI-5 - Military Intelligence Five is England's covert worldwide information gathering agency somewhat like the Central Intelligence Agency of the United States.

NCO - A Non-Commissioned Officer that includes the enlisted ranks from corporal through command sergeant major.

OPS - Operations, plans and training staff section of battalion and larger size army units, S3/G3/J3.

PUNJI STICK - A sharpened bamboo stake stuck into the ground and camouflaged so as to impale an unsuspecting enemy.

Q - (**BOQ**) Bachelor Officers' Quarters or (**EMQ**) Enlisted Men's Quarters.

RECON - Reconnaissance, to gather information on enemy strength and positions, usually done by a small unit patrol that avoids all combat contact with the enemy.

RT - A field radioman carrying a portable field radio. The letters are pronounced separately, **R-T**.

SAPPER - A Viet Cong soldier trained to neutralize defensive obstacles, such as breaching a mine field, opening an avenue through protective wire entanglements and to silently kill those in listening posts outside a unit perimeter while the unit is in a defensive posture.

SBS - A top secret paramilitary organization run by the British government, used in covert military operations. Nothing is known about the organization outside the English command.

SOP - Standard Operations Procedures, policy statements that concern routine tasks or functions.

TRAVERSE - The movement of a major caliper weapon on a horizontal plane to adjust fires.

WP - White phosphorous munitions. A highly corrosive chemical shell that is virtually impossible to extinguish once it starts to burn, commonly called *Willie Peter* by military personnel.

Other Books by Nelson O. Ottenhausen
www.booksbynelson.com

Novels

Civil War II - 1ˢᵗ Edition (2004)

The Killing Zone: Evil's Playground (2007)

Jugs & Bottles (2009)

The Sin Slayer (2010)

The Blue Heron - 1ˢᵗ Edition (2005); Second Edition (2012)

Anthologies

Chicken Soup for the Fisherman's Soul (2004)
Emerald Coast Review (1996, 97, 98)

Poetry

Flowers, Love & Other Things (2005)
Mind Mutations (2006)

All books can be purchased on:
www.booksbynelson.com
www.patriotmediainc.com
www.amazon.com
They are also available on Kindle Reader.

To request an inscribed and/or autographed copy of any book above, send an email with your request to: nelson@patriotmediainc.com

Additional Books by Patriot Media, Publishing

All books listed below can be purchased at:
www.amazon.com
www.patriotmediainc.com
Amazon Kindle Readers
Book reviews and descriptions can be seen at Patriot Media, Inc. web site: **www.patriotmediainc.com**.
Check the site often for discounts and special sale items.

D.M. Ulmer, Author:

Silent Battleground
Shadows of Heroes
The Cold War Beneath
Ensure Plausible Deniability
Missing Person
The Roche Harbor Caper
The Long Beach Caper
Count the Ways
Where or When

Brett Kneisley, Author:

DVD-Tour of USS Clamagore,
Featuring Captain Don Ulmer

B.K. Bryans, Author:

Those '67 Blues
Flight to Redemption
The Dog Robbers

Joseph C. Engel, Author:

Flight of the Silver Eagle

Tom Gauthier, Author:

Mead's Trek
Code Name: Orion's Eye

Paul Sherbo, Author:

*Unsinkable Sailors: The fall and rise
of the last crew of the Frank E. Evans*

LTC Peter Clark, Author:

*Staff Monkeys: A Stockbrokers Journey
through the Global War on Terror*

Dari Bradley, Author:

Hickory Nuts in the Driveway

Art Giberson, Author:

The Mighty O

Hannah Ackerman, Author:

I Kept My Chin Up

30424789R00158

Made in the USA
Charleston, SC
16 June 2014